Looking for Trouble

Also by Trice Hickman

Unexpected Interruptions

Keeping Secrets & Telling Lies

Playing the Hand You're Dealt

Breaking All My Rules

Published by Dafina Books

Looking for Trouble

Trice Hickman

Kensington Publishing Corp.
http://www.kensingtonbooks.com

DAFINA BOOKS are published by

Kensington Publishing Corp.
119 West 40th Street
New York, NY 10018

All Kensington Titles, Imprints, and Distributed Lines are available at special quantity discounts for bulk purchases for sales promotions, premiums, fund-raising, and educational or institutional use. Special book excerpts or cus-tomized printings can also be created to fit specific needs. For details, write or phone the office of the Kensington special sales manager: Kensington Publishing Corp., 119 West 40th Street, New York, NY 10018, attn: Special Sales Department, Phone: 1-800-221-2647.

Dafina and the Dafina logo Reg. U.S. Pat. & TM Off.

ISBN-13: 978-0-7582-8723-6
ISBN-10: 0-7582-8723-2
First Kensington Trade Paperback Edition: November 2013

eISBN-13: 978-0-7582-8725-0
eISBN-10: 0-7582-8725-9
First Kensington Electronic Edition: November 2013

10 9 8 7 6 5 4 3 2 1

Printed in the United States of America

In memory of my Grandma Allene. I miss you so much, and I know you're smiling down on me from above.

This book is also dedicated to all the dreamers out there who put their fear aside, stepped up to the mountain's edge, stuck their foot out, leapt forward, and took off soaring!

Acknowledgments

As always, I give honor and thanks to God for blessing me along this journey. He is truly amazing, and I'm humbled by His grace, mercy, and love.

I have to pinch myself when I think about the fact that this work of literature is my fifth book. For someone who suffered from writer's block for nearly twenty years, this is a dream come true. I know this blessing is straight from God, and is made possible by a wonderful circle of friends and family who support me in all that I do.

There are many people to thank, so let the thanking begin!

Thank you; James, Mom & Dad, Melody & Arthur, Marcus & Velma, James E. & Shirley, you've been there from the beginning, and I love you for loving me.

Thank you to all my aunts, uncles, cousins, nieces, and nephews, for your love and support.

Thank you to my girls who are always in my corner; Vickie, Sherraine, Terri, Kimberla, Tiffany, Cerece, Tracy, Kim, Tammi, China, Yolanda, and Downey.

Thank you to my publishing family at Kensington; my editor, Mercedes Fernandez, my publicist, Adeola Saul, and marketing director, Lesleigh Underwood.

Thank you to Janell Walden Agyeman. You are more than a literary agent, you are a valued, trusted, and beloved friend.

Thank you to my Platinum Divas who tirelessly help me promote my books. Your energy and enthusiasm blow me away; Yolanda, Orsayor, Marsha, Jas, Barbara, Demorris, Carmela, Denise, Clarinda, Gail, Tonya, Cheryl, Ernia, Rhea, Kim, Brenda, Debra, Tammi, and Deck-quelyn!

Thank you to all the bookstores, specialty shops, and retailers, who have purchased my books and hosted book signings.

And last but certainly not least. Thank you to every single book club member and reader who has supported me by purchasing my books, reading my work, and helping to spread the word. You all are awesome! Words cannot express how much I appreciate you!

Peace and many blessings

Trice Hickman

Chapter 1

Summertime, several decades in the past
Nedine, South Carolina

Allene Small was glad she'd always been an early riser because on a day like today—which she knew held the promise of danger and deception—she was already up, ready for battle while the enemy was still asleep.

Allene sat on her tiny front porch and breathed in the fresh air around her as she looked out at the pink- and lavender-colored hydrangea bushes lining her neatly manicured yard. Slowly she pivoted back and forth in her ancient rocking chair, straining her eyes toward the east so she could take in the early-morning sun, which had started its climb in the distant sky. She blinked, nodding in agreement with the uncomfortable awareness resting in her heart and mind. She could feel the rumblings vibrating deep in her chest—trouble and strife—and, more specifically, the impending presence of a treacherous woman who was up to no good.

Allene knew that most folks would have been slightly set back or even frightened by such an ominous foreboding, but she wasn't deterred and she wasn't afraid. If there was one thing that ninety years of living and praying had taught her, it was that good and bad were always present, and sometimes the two forces tried to occupy the same space at the same time.

Over the years, Allene had encountered plenty of bad, low-down people, who harbored even worse intentions. And, unfortunately, she'd learned the hard way that evil was all around, and that it often disguised itself under the cloak of good. She knew that evil could laugh and smile in your face while viciously twisting a knife in your back. It could soothe and comfort you while killing you slowly. And it could encourage and uplift you while secretly plotting your very demise.

But Allene also knew how to tell the difference between the two, and she could do that because she'd been blessed with the gift of prophesy, and that precious ability allowed her to see what others couldn't.

"The gift," as it was commonly referred to in the South, allowed Allene to see and predict things accurately before they happened. She could spot liars before they ever opened their mouth to utter a single word. She could discern one's intentions, whether good or bad, simply by looking into the person's eyes. She could forecast events in advance of them coming to pass, and she could foresee blessings, as well as misfortunes, that lay down the road.

Having the gift had been both Allene's blessing and her curse. She'd seen things in her lifetime that she wished she hadn't, and she'd been right when she had wanted to be wrong. But this morning was one of those times that Allene was thankful she'd been blessed with such a unique ability. Because while she sat on her porch, wrapped in the peaceful quiet of a bright new day, she wasn't fooled by its seeming calm. A manipulative woman who was hell-bent on causing trouble was on her way to Allene's small town of Nedine, South Carolina, and Allene knew the chaos that the attractive stranger was bringing was headed straight for her family's doorstep.

"Don't worry, John. I'm ready for the fight, and I'm here to protect and guide you, baby," Allene whispered as she continued to rock back and forth, thinking about her enterprising young grandson. She knew that the danger brewing was directly connected to him, in the form of his girlfriend, and that he didn't have a clue about the mess he'd unknowingly gotten himself into.

Just then, a chill swept against Allene's arm, causing her to pull her thin blue gingham shawl tight around her shoulders. At that moment, she knew that the woman was already in town with her grandson, laying a sneaky trap for him. "It's gonna be all right, John. I'ma guide you, and I know you gonna make the right decision," she whispered into the air.

Allene slowly rose from her chair and walked the short distance to the edge of the porch. She stood impressively tall for a woman of her advanced years—solid and straight. She shielded her eyes with her right hand as she looked out at the beaming sun, which was steadily rising in the cloudless sky. "Life's long, but short," she said aloud as she shook her head. She knew that unlike the slow patience it took to watch a sunrise, people could quickly lose everything they'd worked for in the blink of an eye based on one bad decision. The sudden chill on her arm let her know that mischief was already brewing, because trouble was an early riser, too. "I'm ready for the fight," she whispered.

Allene also knew that a lot was riding on the next forty-eight hours. She lowered her hand to her mouth, stretching her long, wrinkled fingers across her full lips as she continued to think about her grandson. She had to protect John from what he couldn't see—a beguiling woman who could derail his life's dreams if he wasn't careful. Allene's gift had revealed the woman for who she really was. Despite the woman's sweet words, sophistication, and enthusiastic gestures, she was as slick as a serpent and as cunning as a fox. This jezebel was just as determined to destroy John as Allene was to save him.

"I have faith and I know everything's gonna be all right," Allene said with conviction as she continued her talk with the sky. She knew the woman was dangerous in ways that could either ruin a man, get him killed, or both. But again, she wasn't deterred because she knew her family's survival was at stake, and she'd do whatever it took to make sure the Smalls were safe and prospered for future generations to come. As she thought about her family's legacy and the promise it held, her mind shifted to Alexandria.

"I'm gonna help you, too, baby girl," Allene said with a smile.

Alexandria was the hope and the future. She was the vision Allene had seen a month ago when she got her first glimpse of her great-great-granddaughter, who would not be born for several decades to come. Ever since that eye-opening day, Allene had been using all the powers and abilities she'd cultivated over the years to reach across time and bridge the past with the present in order to connect with the young woman who shared her same gift.

Allene could see that Alexandria was standing at a crossroads, and that she was frightened and confused by what was happening to her. She reminded Allene a lot of herself at that age, when she didn't understand her gift, and had been afraid of its repercussions. And just as she'd done, her beautiful great-great-granddaughter was running from who she was. Allene knew it was time for Alexandria to discover the purpose of what she'd been blessed to have, and learn how to use it. It was Allene's new mission to guide Alexandria, just as she intended to guide John now.

"Find what's right for you and open your heart, baby girl. Listen to what I'm sayin' to you, Alexandria," Allene said in a low, sweet whisper. "Listen and learn."

Allene closed her eyes as another vision flashed behind her lids. A warm feeling replaced the chill that had come over her only moments ago, and a sense of peace spread through her body. She saw an image, and it was enough to let her know that she'd just witnessed the answer to Alexandria's quandary. "Look for the diamond, 'cause the one who has that is the one who's gonna help save you." Allene whispered the last part of her appeal with conviction, hoping and praying that Alexandria would hear her plea, pay attention, and recognize the sign when she saw it.

Chapter 2

"Oh no," Alexandria softly whispered, trying to hide her discomfort. Her body tensed, anticipating the annoyance that was about to come. *This can't be happening again. Not now,* she thought.

"What's wrong?" Peter whispered back, still continuing to nibble on the left lobe of Alexandria's ear.

She moved her head to the side, trying to block out the sound that was making its way back into her mind. *Go away! Please go away and leave me alone!* Alexandria shouted to herself as she repositioned her nude body under the weight of Peter's muscular heft. She turned her head back to face him, releasing a low, measured sigh.

"You okay?" Peter asked; this time, there was a bit of concern in between his heavy panting.

"I'm fine," Alexandria lied. She hesitated; then slowly pulled him closer against her bare chest. "Kiss me," she demanded in a not-so-playful tone. She took a deep breath, closed her eyes tightly, and concentrated on her boyfriend's languid tongue as she tried to block out the voice—laced with a deep Southern accent—that was invading her head.

Although she knew that her love life with Peter was woefully lacking, and she couldn't remember the last time she'd had an orgasm, Alexandria had hoped that a quick roll between the sheets would give her mind a break from the recurring loop it had been stuck in. But instead of arresting her anxiety, the physical romp only seemed to kick her senses into overdrive.

As Peter's movements became more urgent, her desire began to quickly wane by the second, sinking into the background of the voice repeating itself inside her head. She tried to concentrate on the moment, but that didn't work, so she willed her mind to take her to another place. But that was no use, either. The harder she fought, the louder the sound of the voice grew. Finally she gave up.

"Peter, I'm sorry, but I have to go." Alexandria gently pushed him away, freeing herself from his hold.

"What?" Peter huffed, looking confused. "You've gotta be kidding me."

"No, I really do need to go," she said as she sat up and kicked her long, slightly thick legs to the side of his king-size bed. She ran her fingers through the mass of long, kinky dark brown curls atop her head as she slumped her shoulders in frustration.

"One minute you want me to kiss you and the next you're pushing me away. What gives?"

"I'm sorry, Peter. I don't mean to send mixed signals."

"Then don't." Peter paused as he moved in close, still trying to nuzzle his body next to hers. He leaned into her, giving her shoulder a light kiss. "C'mon, lay back down with me."

Alexandria ignored his coaxing; instead, she slowly stood to her feet as she spoke. "It's not you. It's me," she told him, knowing how off-putting and clichéd her response, albeit truthful, sounded. She could feel thick tension rise in the air as soon as the words left her mouth, so she tried to speak in a gentle tone. "There's a lot going on in my life right now. Things that have nothing to do with you, Peter."

"I don't believe this." Peter reluctantly reached for his boxers as Alexandria pulled her sundress over her head and then slid it down the length of her curvaceous body. "So where does this leave me?" he asked.

She wanted to tell him, *How the hell do I know? I can't even figure out what's going on in my own life, let alone yours.* But she knew this wasn't the time for such declarations, so she leavened her tone, inserting a measure of compassion in her voice. "I need to be alone tonight so I can think."

"Think? . . . Think about what, Alexandria?"

"Life, and what I'm supposed to do with mine. Like I said, there's so much going on right now. I hope you can understand."

Peter shook his head in dismay. "I've been trying hard to understand you, especially over the last couple weeks. I've been patient when you zone out on me, and I've tried to be understanding when you say you have a lot going on, like now, even though you never give a clue about exactly what the problem is."

Alexandria looked into Peter's dark brown eyes and nodded, knowing he deserved to hear the full truth: She was so scared about what was happening to her that she didn't have time to focus on their relationship. But at the same time, she knew Peter's primary focus was really on himself and his feelings—because not once had he asked her what kinds of things were bothering her.

She'd met Peter two years ago while working as a summer intern at Johnson, Taylor, and Associates, one of the largest law firms in the Atlanta Metro area. She'd been in her last year of law school at UPenn, and somewhat ambivalent about pursuing a career in the legal field. Peter had just graduated from Yale University School of Law, was an ambitious first-year associate at the firm, and was already rumored to be a rising star within the ranks. Although he was a bit uptight and a little too formal in his attitude than what Alexandria liked, Peter's tall, muscular physique, smooth dark chocolate skin, and handsome face had all attracted her to him. They had spotted each other during the first day of new employee orientation and had gone out for drinks during happy hour a week later.

They'd both been seeing other people at the time, but neither had been seriously involved. Their casual lunches and long dinners slowly turned into much more. They kept in touch after she returned to law school for her senior year, and they saw each other whenever time permitted, which wasn't often. Once she graduated the next summer they started dating exclusively, and had been together ever since.

"Who is he?" Peter asked.

"What?"

"Please, Alexandria," Peter said, looking at her with an accusatory glare. "Don't play me for a fool. If you're seeing someone else, I'd appreciate you being up front with me instead of feeding me excuses."

"Oh, like you and Monica?"

Peter let out an exasperated sigh. "I told you, that was nothing."

"Yeah, right."

"I can't help it if the woman showed up on my doorstep out the blue."

"Excuse me, but it makes a difference when *the woman* you're referring to, just happened to be your ex-girlfriend! And for someone who mysteriously showed up unwelcome, you sure did make her feel at home," Alexandria said, returning his accusing stare. "I got here and found you two drinking wine and laughing, acting all cozy."

"Number one, we weren't cozy. We were simply talking," Peter said in a direct tone. "She was depressed because the guy she was seeing had just dumped her. She needed someone to talk to and—"

"And you were the first person she went running to," Alexandria countered. "I think that's very strange, especially given the fact that you dumped her, too. So why on earth would she come to you for a shoulder to cry on? It didn't make sense then, and it still doesn't make sense now."

Until last month when Alexandria had caught Peter and his ex in that precarious situation, he hadn't given her much reason to question his fidelity. He was a pragmatist who preferred diplomacy over drama, and he avoided the latter at all costs. Having extra women on the side only upped the ante for chaos, and Peter wasn't one for the kind of trouble that fooling around could bring. He was the dependable type, almost to the point of being predictably annoying. Because of his anal manner, a small part of Alexandria believed that even if Peter wanted to stray, it would be challenging for him, given the fact that he also spent most of his time at the office.

Peter routinely worked twelve- and fourteen-hour days, sometimes six days a week, all in his self-imposed race to climb the ladder of success, following in his mother's large and looming footsteps. She was a circuit court judge and was currently being courted to run for one of Georgia's congressional seats. She was a demanding overachiever, and Peter wanted to make her proud, which meant working insanely long hours and forfeiting a social life beyond networking functions, where he could make business connections. When he wasn't at the office—which was hardly ever—he was either working from home, working out at the gym, or spending what little time he had left over with Alexandria.

But Alexandria also knew that just because Peter was a busy, regimented man, that didn't mean there weren't opportunities for him to cheat, or that he wasn't capable. Experience had taught her that regardless of one's work schedule and personal demands, a person could make time to do anything they really wanted. The only reason she hadn't followed up on the suspicions lurking in the back of her mind was because of the voice that had been penetrating her thoughts, forcing her to come to grips with a part of her life she'd been trying to avoid since she was five years old.

"I know it doesn't make sense to you," Peter said, "but that's exactly what happened when Monica came over here. Nothing more, nothing less. I'm telling you the truth."

Alexandria shrugged. "Whose truth?"

"If I wanted to sleep with her, I could've done that a long time ago."

"And that's another thing. Why do you still keep in contact with your ex-girlfriend?"

Peter let out another frustrated sigh. "We only talk once in a blue moon, like at the holidays, just to wish each other well."

"And why is that even necessary?"

"It's not. It's just a polite gesture. Besides, if I was trying to hide something, trust me, you'd never know that I'd had any contact with her at all." Peter pulled his T-shirt over his broad chest and taut waist. "But listen, my ex—whom I have absolutely no interest in—isn't the issue. Let's talk about our relationship."

"What I'm going through right now has nothing to do with our relationship. Like I told you, it's about me."

"Cut the shit, Alexandria." Peter smirked. "Call me 'crazy,' but I thought that when you're in a relationship with someone, everything that involves you involves the other person, too."

Although she knew Peter's comment was absolutely right, she didn't like the sarcasm or nasty tone that was planted behind it. Deep down, she knew that he only half-meant what he'd just said. She'd slowly come to realize that he was a bit selfish, hence his "Where does this leave me?" remark. So she knew what he was saying now was clearly meant to draw out a reasonable explanation that would put his mind at ease about the possibility of her cheating on him.

"I hear what you're saying," Alexandria responded, slipping on her turquoise-colored thong-toed sandals, "but this really is about me, and only me."

"Okay, then what's bothering you?"

Her eyes widened with surprise. "This is the first time you've asked me about *me*."

"No, it's not, but I won't waste time arguing that point right now. Tell me what's going on with you?"

She wanted so badly to call him on his lie, but she knew it would be a fruitless cause. "For one, I'm not happy with my career. I feel like I'm settling." This part was true, and she didn't hesitate sharing it.

"You graduated in the top of your law school class and now you're a fast-rising associate at one of the most powerful lobbying firms in the city. You work closely with one of the senior partners, and they even handpicked you to present and testify before Congress last year, which got you that major raise you're enjoying now."

"You act like you're giving me information that I don't already know."

"Okay, since you already know that, you also know how many people would kill—and I mean that literally—to stand in your shoes."

Alexandria looked down at her neatly polished toenails, then up at Peter. "I'm not concerned about other people. I'm talking about me, and what I really want. Being a performing artist is my calling. I've always known that, and now, every day, I feel it more than ever."

"Why did you work so hard in law school if this wasn't what you wanted?"

"That's just it. I didn't work hard in law school at all. It came easy for me, just like high school and undergrad. I went through the motions and I did what I was expected to do. But now, I'm ready to pursue my passion like my mom did."

Peter looked up at the ceiling. "Here we go with that again."

"I'm one of the best spoken-word artists in the city—hell, in this region. Whenever I perform at the Lazy Day, people pack the house to hear me."

"You know that's not a sustainable profession, don't you? What do you make doing that? Fifty dollars a night?"

"You know what . . ." Alexandria drew in a deep breath. "Never mind, I'm leaving."

Feeling tired and frustrated, Alexandria didn't say another word. She gathered her handbag, picked up her leather overnight duffel, and walked toward the door.

"Hold on," Peter said, gently clasping his hand around Alexandria's slender wrist. "I don't want you to leave like this . . . upset with me."

"I'm not upset with you. Like I said, I need to be alone right now so I can clear my head." She leaned into him, planted a small kiss on his right cheek, and told him she'd come by the next day.

Twenty minutes later, Alexandria found herself sitting alone on her couch in her small one-bedroom apartment, devouring a small bowl of Ben & Jerry's chocolate ice cream and three dark chocolate truffles from her Godiva box. Whenever she felt down and out, ice cream and chocolates always seemed to lift her spirits. The cold, chocolaty sweet taste tickled her tongue and almost made her forget about the voice that kept repeating the same words inside her head: *"I'm ready for the fight."* The words were fragmented bits and pieces of a longer sentence that Alexandria couldn't fully understand.

"Stop it!" She hissed into the stillness surrounding her. "I don't care about your fight. All I want is peace and quiet. Leave me alone."

She rose from her couch and went into her bathroom. "This has got to stop," she said as she pulled her long hair back into a ponytail and reached for her facial cleanser. "I can't take this any longer. Why can't I block out this voice, like I can the others?"

After washing and exfoliating her skin, Alexandria looked into the mirror and studied the nude face that stared back at her. She hadn't inherited her mother's chocolate hue, but her light caramel-colored skin— compliments of her white father—was smooth and so even that she looked as though she were wearing foundation. She appraised her sultry brown eyes, perfectly arched brows, and full, bow-shaped lips. She was thankful that despite her stress, she still looked good.

"This is taking a toll," she said, crawling under her soft, cool bed-sheets. She prayed for a restful night's sleep, but she could already tell that wasn't going to happen because of the buzzing that just returned to her ear. Hearing voices and seeing visions—which no one else could—was nothing new for Alexandria.

She'd experienced her first encounter when she was just a toddler, playfully talking with the spirits of children from bygone years. Her imaginary friends were as real as the ones she played with at school. As she grew older, she developed the ability of premonition. When she was five years old, she predicted her father's heart attack before it happened. A few months later, she drew a picture of her younger brother, Christian, before he was conceived. It had startled her teacher so much that she'd called Alexandria's parents. From that point on, she stopped drawing the things she saw happening in her mind.

Growing up the child of a black mother and a white father, Alexandria was taught by her parents that she came from extraordinary people on both sides of her family. But there was another dimension of who she was that she knew her parents would never be able to understand—let alone teach her about—so she made up her mind early on to bury the mysterious haunting that often gripped her in her sleep.

Over the years, she'd developed the ability to tune out voices when they tried to roar inside her mind. For some reason, though, she couldn't do it with the woman who was now drumming words into her ear. When she'd started hearing whispers a few weeks ago, she immediately knew there was something different about this new voice that was contacting her, and the spirit of the person to whom it belonged.

As she sat alone, finishing the last spoonful of chocolate ice cream, Alexandria heard the voice again. This time, the sound came in a little more clearly: *"Look for the diamond, 'cause the one who has that is the one who's gonna help save you."*

"What the hell does that mean?" Alexandria said. She set her empty container of ice cream on the coffee table in front of her. She knew that whether she wanted to or not, she would soon find out.

Chapter 3

Nedine, South Carolina

John squinted and yawned as he slowly opened his eyes, adjusting to his unfamiliar surroundings. He blinked twice, still groggy from the rush of the previous day's activities. He'd traveled from New York City to Nedine, South Carolina, with a pocketful of money and a heart filled with dreams. And as waking consciousness took hold of his strong body, he could tell that something special was going to happen today. He didn't know what wondrous thing was about to unfold, or at what point in the day his good fortune would present itself, but he had no doubt that a great opportunity was coming his way.

John had always trusted his gut instincts—a skill he'd inherited from his wise old grandmother. If something felt right, he went with it. But if he got an uneasy feeling about a situation, he backed away. He was a natural risk taker, with a head for business, and it was a quality that had served him well, helping him to become the only black executive at the privately owned Wall Street investment bank where he worked.

John was lying comfortably in bed, enjoying the peace of the early-morning sun as it flooded through the thin beige curtains in his modest hotel room. He stretched his left leg and felt a warm thigh slide against his skin, followed by the soft caress of smooth, naked flesh pressed against his bare back.

"Good morning," Madeline purred behind him.

"Mornin'," John answered.

"How do you feel this morning?"

"Fine."

Madeline tightened her embrace. "John, I'm hungry. Are you?"

"No."

She let out a long sigh. "I'm ravenous. I worked up an appetite from last night." Madeline grinned seductively, rubbing her foot along John's muscular calf. "I'm surprised you're not hungry, too. Especially after your performance, which, I must say, was so *Mmmm* delicious."

John didn't respond, because although he agreed with Madeline—he, too, had worked up an appetite from their ferocious lovemaking the night before—he didn't want to move a muscle. His only desire at the moment was to lie in bed and enjoy the peaceful Saturday morning as he soaked up the anticipation of good things to come.

"John?" Madeline prodded.

"Yes?"

"Didn't you hear what I said?" she asked, ignoring the fact that his one-word answers meant he obviously wasn't in the mood for early-morning chatter. She gave him a hard nudge, urging him to turn over and face her. "John, I'm hungry, and this piece of a hotel doesn't even offer room service."

Grudgingly John rolled onto his other side to meet Madeline's glaring eyes. "I heard you, but I really don't feel like getting up right now. Let's just lie here and relax for a little while."

Madeline exhaled an exasperated breath. "Oh, I get it. Now that we're down south, in the country, you want to slow things down to a snail's pace."

"You got it."

"John, I'm a city girl."

If you don't like the country, why did you beg me to bring you down here? John thought. But instead of saying what was on his mind, he calmly smiled and told her, "Indeed you are."

"There's only one speed I'm built for, and that's fast."

"Sometimes it's good to slow down, Madeline."

Another exasperated look clouded Madeline's angular face. "The swiftest and the fastest always win the race. You know that."

"Depends on what kind of race you're in, and what kind of prize you're after."

"That's so, so true," Madeline cooed, snuggling even closer to John. "But you see, the thing about me is that I set out to win everything, no matter the prize, and full speed ahead is the only way I know how to run."

John didn't say a word. He simply stared into the intense brown eyes of the attractive woman sharing his bed, hoping he wasn't going to regret his decision to bring her along on this visit. This was Madeline's first trip to his hometown, and he knew it was going to be a learning experience for both of them, and possibly the biggest test of their one-year relationship to date.

John had made the trip because his best friend, Maxx Sanders, was celebrating his thirty-second birthday this weekend. A big party had been planned for Maxx. All their old friends—and practically everyone in town—were going to be in attendance, and John wouldn't have missed the celebration for anything. He knew that bringing Madeline home with him was sure to start tongues wagging with gossip because he'd only ever brought one other woman to Nedine, and that had been five years ago.

John was what people called a "confirmed bachelor" and a "ladies' man." Many of his friends were married, with children, and had been settled into family life since their late teens and early twenties. But John's adventurous nature and ambitious career moves had led him down a single path filled with a multitude of women. His success, polished good looks, and smooth charm all helped him to maintain that status.

But as time was sliding by, John had starting thinking more and more about settling down, getting married, and starting a family of his own. The last few months leading up to final negotiations for the bank he planned to open had been grueling ones, and he'd thought more than once about how nice it would be to come home to the

stable comfort of a loving wife. He and Madeline were both so busy
with their careers that their time was mostly relegated to weekends.
Now, however, he was beginning to want something more—if not
from her, then from someone else.

In the weeks leading up to their trip, Madeline had shown
dogged persistence in her desire to accompany him to Nedine. "John,
we've been dating a whole year," she'd told him. "Once my parents
died, my aunt raised me. After she passed, I didn't have anyone left,
besides my brother, who I barely ever see. But that's not the case with
you. You have a family—yet I've never gotten a chance to meet
them."

John shrugged. "My folks are down south, and—"

"That's no excuse for why you haven't introduced me to them."

"You've met Maxx."

Madeline rolled her eyes. "Friends don't count."

"Maxx counts. He's family to me."

John had tried to dissuade her, but Madeline wouldn't let up,
until she finally got him to agree. He firmly understood the implica-
tions involved with her visit, and he'd made it clear to her that this
wasn't a "you're meeting my friends and family because you're the
one" kind of visit. This was more of a "I'm taking you home to test
the waters" kind of trip.

John knew he needed to settle down soon, and he also knew how
important it was to make the right choice in finding a mate. So he
figured he might as well bring Madeline home and see how things
would work out.

Despite the fact that Madeline was difficult, and at times slightly
abrasive, John had grown to become very fond of her. She was an accountant, and a damn good one. She was smart, accomplished, and
world traveled. Physically she was exactly what he liked in a woman.
Her tall frame, slim figure, pretty face, and milk chocolate brown skin
had drawn him to her when they'd met at a business function spon-
sored by his bank.

She was what Maxx had called a "pistol" when he'd met her six months ago during a weekend trip to the city. John was aware that Madeline was an acquired taste, and that she was what some might even consider obnoxious. But he appreciated that she took charge of situations and was confident and self-assured. She was business savvy and ambitious, just like he was, and he knew that having a woman like Madeline by his side would help him reach his professional goals even quicker than he'd already projected. An added bonus, which sweetened the pot, was that she always met his sexual needs. So he was able to tolerate what he saw as small annoyances because he felt her pluses outweighed her minuses.

"Well . . . ," Madeline said, seductively whispering into John's ear, "if we're not going to venture out for breakfast, we need to find something productive to do with our time, don't you think?"

The look in Madeline's sultry eyes told John all he needed to know. He kissed her slowly, falling back into the same rhythm that had fueled their passionate lovemaking the night before.

It was noontime and the blazing sun was bearing down from the cloudless blue sky as John and Madeline made their way outside the four walls of their hotel room. Although the temperature was soaring above ninety degrees, the unrelenting heat was made bearable by a gentle breeze, which had begun to blow just as they stepped outside their door.

"Mother Nature must've known we were coming. You feel that breeze?" John said, smiling as he looked at Madeline.

"Um, yes, I do," she replied. "But you know the heat doesn't bother me."

"It will, once you've been out in it for a while. Trust me, the humidity of the South is a lot different from the North."

Madeline raised her brow and scoffed. "Please tell me we're not going to be outside all day, rocking in a chair on someone's front porch?"

John laughed and shook his head as they walked toward his car. "No, but this is gonna be a busy day. We've got a lot of people to visit, and with all that running around, you're bound to get hot."

"I thought we were only going to have lunch with your parents and grandmother."

Now it was John's turn to raise his brow as he opened the passenger door for Madeline. "You've been saying for weeks that you wanted to meet everyone I grew up with, and that you can't wait to go to Maxx's party. Now you only want to meet my folks? Are you serious?"

Madeline smiled, fingering her stylishly coiffed bouffant. "Of course not. I guess I can't think straight because I'm so famished. I can't wait to meet everyone."

"That's more like it." John smiled and took his time as he walked around to his driver's side, admiring the beauty of the wide, open space around him. He had traveled to cities across the United States, and in several foreign countries, and he was convinced that summertime in Nedine was the most beautiful place on earth.

Nedine held a special place in John's heart, and he made sure he visited several times a year. All his family and most of his friends were still there because Nedine was the kind of town where people remained firmly rooted. John was one of the few people in his close-knit community who had moved away, and it had almost been mandatory that he'd taken that leap because his father had pushed for it.

"Son, I want you to get outta Nedine and get you a good education," Isaiah Small had told him from the time John was a little boy. Isaiah had invested all his hopes and dreams into his youngest child.

John hadn't lived in Nedine since he'd entered the University of Pennsylvania fourteen years ago. His upscale, sparsely furnished apartment in a highly sought-after luxury building in Manhattan's Upper East Side was where he laid his head; but to John, Nedine was home. Nonetheless, he had to admit that he liked the adrenaline rush of living and working in the Big Apple. It stretched him and the competition had made him sharper.

As John and Madeline drove from the Holiday Inn on the north side, to his parents' house on the south side of town, he pointed out local and historical landmarks while Madeline sat quietly in the passenger seat, looking bored out of her mind.

"Where's the downtown?" Madeline asked, straining her neck as she stared out the window of the rental car.

"You're looking at it." John smiled. "This is our downtown."

"You mean it's *Nedine's* downtown," she corrected.

John shook his head. "I know what I meant, Madeline. Like I've told you before, Nedine will always be my home."

Madeline rode in silence as they passed tiny shops and small buildings. John could see that she wasn't impressed, evidenced by the detached expression on her face. "You all right over there?" he asked.

"How much longer until we get to your parents' house?"

John let out a deep breath. "We've only been driving ten minutes. Relax, baby. We'll be there soon."

"Thank God," Madeline huffed. "I'm starving. Why couldn't we have stopped and picked up something quick from one of those little restaurants we passed back there? At least, that would tide us over until we get there."

"Trust me, my mama's cooking is better than anything you'll find on the menu of those restaurants in town. Plus, the best places to eat are on the south side, anyway."

A few minutes later, John turned off the main road and drove in the direction of open fields and flat land. Shotgun houses dotted the dusty road that branched off into heavily populated, rural subcommunities. The area looked economically distressed, harkening to a history of turbulence and hard times.

"We're not in Kansas anymore." Madeline smirked as she looked out her window. "I can't believe you grew up here. This place is just . . . I don't know . . . so . . ."

"What?"

"Well . . . it's not at all what I expected, let alone pictured myself visiting."

John glanced at her out of the corner of his eye. "Are you forgetting that you're the one who wanted to come home with me? Now you act like being here is a huge inconvenience."

"I didn't mean it in a bad way, sweetie," Madeline said, trying to make nice. "Actually, this whole Southern experience has a certain appeal . . . in a rustic sort of way."

John knew she didn't think much of a town like Nedine, and he hadn't expected her to. She'd been born and bred in New York City, and the home where her aunt had raised her—an elegant brownstone situated on a tree-box–lined street in Harlem's Strivers' Row—was so lavish it had once been featured in a local style magazine. Her world-view had been jaded by fancy homes, tall buildings, bright lights, and fast-moving people. Even though John loved the excitement of the city and was as sophisticated as any Manhattan urbanite could be, he was still a country boy at heart, and that's where he and Madeline would always differ.

As they continued to drive down the hot, dusty road, John thought about how much his life was going to change once he moved back to Nedine in another month or two before opening the bank. Although the bold venture was going to make his life busier than it had ever been, John was looking forward to being home again, sur-rounded by family and friends. Nedine was going to provide a much-needed balance in his life that the hustle and bustle of city living couldn't. It was also going to allow him the opportunity to take things slow, settle down, and perhaps start a family, which was something he'd been thinking about while traveling on the road yesterday.

John glanced over at Madeline's attractive profile, and he won-dered if she was really marriage material. He also wondered what kind of wife she would make and what kind of mother she would be. He wasn't even sure if she wanted children, because they'd never had those kinds of discussions. Most of their conversations centered around business, which jazz spots they'd go to, which restaurants they'd try, and what new sexual positions they'd explore.

He knew that after a year of being with this woman he should know the answers to what she wanted in life beyond a successful ca-reer and a good time out on the town, and the fact he didn't made him pause.

"I thought you said we'd be there soon," Madeline said, breaking

John's thoughts. "This town is small, but it's taking us forever to go from one end to the other."

John pointed in the direction of tall, luscious trees in the distance. "Well, you're in luck. My parents' house is coming up right around this bend."

Chapter 4

John could see that Madeline was impressed as they turned onto the private road that led to the grand estate his parents owned. THE SMALL PROPERTY was written in black calligraphy on a large white placard that hung from a tall pole, announcing entry to all guests coming to visit.

John eyed Madeline closely as they approached the majestic brick colonial-style structure, where he'd been raised. He took inventory of her facial expression, which was one of awe. He chuckled when he saw her eyebrows nearly rise to her forehead. He studied her as she admired what was old hat to him—an expansive, professionally landscaped yard, which complemented the abundant rose and azalea bushes and magnolia shrubs his mother had cultivated over the years—all flanked by a massive wrap-around porch, which greeted them as they walked up to the front door.

John had told Madeline that he'd grown up in comfort and that his parents had money, but he could see that she hadn't expected the type of wealth she saw in front of her, especially after taking in a good portion of Nedine during their drive across town.

"Here we go," John said as he rang the bell. The grand door slowly opened and an imposing figure consumed the entire space.

"He's here, Henny!" Isaiah Small smiled as he called out behind him. "And he's got company with him, so set another place at the table."

The phrase "like father, like son" was coined especially for men like Isaiah and John. They were both tall, with broad shoulders and hands the size of baseball mitts. They shared the same intense brown eyes, which could bore holes through their targets. Their deep baritones sounded as though their voices boomed from the heavens above, and their striking, coal black skin resembled polished iron. The only difference between the two men was the visible signs of aging, which had sneaked up quietly on Isaiah's face and body. His hair was snow white, his skin had begun to wrinkle, and his back was not as straight as it had been a year ago.

Isaiah welcomed his son into the house as Madeline glared at John. It was obvious by the look on Isaiah's face, and by the way he'd announced her presence, that John hadn't told his parents he was bringing his girlfriend home for a visit.

John avoided Madeline's stare as they entered the beautifully furnished living room.

"Your mother'll be out directly," Isaiah said to John. He looked at his son and waited.

"Excuse my manners," John said, clearing his throat. He smiled as he reached for Madeline's hand and held it in his, knowing that gesture would defrost her chill. "Pop, this is Madeline King."

Aside from John's good looks, one of the things about him that women couldn't resist was his dazzling charm, and Madeline was no exception. John knew the simple show of holding her hand and saying her name in a way that made her tingle would erase the full-on annoyance she'd shown just seconds ago.

"It's mighty nice to meet you," Isaiah said with a smile.

"Likewise." Madeline nodded in return.

Just then, Henrietta Small walked into the room. She was proof positive that the Smalls were a family of giants. At five feet eleven inches in stocking feet, she towered above most men. And like her husband and son, her broad shoulders and commanding presence dominated any space she entered. Her thick body was erect, and her skin was the same chocolate brown complexion as Madeline's, and just as smooth despite being twice the younger woman's age. Henrietta walked up to John and wrapped her strong arms around her youngest child. "It's so good to see you, baby!"

"Good to see you, too, Mama," John said, rocking back and forth in his mother's tight embrace.

"Well, who do we have here?" Henrietta asked as she slowly released her son.

"Mama, this is Madeline King." John smiled and motioned to his side. "Madeline, this is my mother."

The two women greeted each other with a cordial handshake and friendly smiles. Their exchange was nothing short of the Southern hospitality that John was accustomed to seeing his mother extend to strangers; but even so, he could tell that something wasn't quite right.

Mama doesn't like Madeline, John thought. He watched his mother closely as she nodded and grinned, engaging Madeline in polite conversation as they headed toward the kitchen. John stood to the side and observed the two women even more. Sure enough, no matter how hard Henrietta tried to be pleasant, tried to appear mannerly, and tried to put forth valiant efforts of courtesy, her eyes confirmed what John's gut had already told him. And his gut was never wrong. *Not only does Mama not like Madeline, she can't stand her. Damn!*

Chapter 5

Alexandria sat cross-legged on her couch as she sipped from her cup of lukewarm lemongrass tea. It was a bright and sunny Saturday afternoon, but she had yet to venture outside the confines of her apartment to enjoy it. Normally, she would have been out and about hours ago, running weekend errands, which included shopping for much-needed groceries, browsing a few of her favorite flea markets, and then finally dropping by her parents' house for a quick visit before heading over to Peter's for the evening. But today she was off to a slow start because she hadn't been able to sleep the night before, partly because of the way she'd left things with Peter, but mostly because of the incessant voice ringing in her ear.

This was the first time a spirit voice had come to her without revealing who it was or exactly what it wanted. She'd been hearing the whispers—from a person who she now knew had to be a Southern woman—for the last four weeks.

It had started as a quiet hum, barely audible enough for Alexandria to register the words as more than a few annoying, disjointed mumbles. But as the days went on, the sound grew, and now it was coming to her louder, with more frequency and greater urgency.

As Alexandria sat in silence, sans the voice still speaking into her ear, she realized two very important things. The first was that she could hear the woman's words so crystal clear that if she closed her eyes, she could swear someone was literally sitting beside her. And the other was that the woman talking to her was someone she knew. The voice, with its calm, warm timber, began to sound as familiar to her ear as her own voice. And although the woman's accent was thickly layered in a rural Southern dialect, there was something about the comfort of it that reminded her of her mother's.

She could tell the voice belonged to that of an old woman, and it carried a mixture of tones and inflections—rugged but kind, sturdy but tender—that resonated with her in a place deep down in her soul. And as Alexandria continued to concentrate, she had no doubt that she was somehow directly connected to whoever was trying to contact her.

"I'm ready for the fight," the voice repeated.

"Please show yourself to me," Alexandria spoke aloud. "Tell me who you are and what you want of me."

"I'm here to protect you, baby," the voice gently whispered.

Alexandria sat perfectly still, closed her eyes, and took a deep breath. "Show me what you want me to know."

Images began to flash in front of her eyes: a long dirt road, tall pine trees, a rocking chair on a tiny front porch, a blue cloudless sky. Then, before she could place the surroundings, Alexandria was staring into the eyes of a woman she'd never seen; yet she felt she knew her. She could tell the woman was old; but because her wrinkles were faint, it was hard to determine her age. Alexandria felt comforted when she saw the old woman smile and nod, as if she could see her, too. Then without warning, her brief vision disappeared.

When Alexandria opened her eyes again, she could feel her heart pounding inside her chest. At that moment, she knew exactly to whom the voice belonged.

Chapter 6

Nedine, South Carolina

They all settled in at the medium-size rectangular-shaped table in the large eat-in kitchen. Isaiah and Henrietta sat on one side, while John and Madeline took their seats on the other. Pristine white linen covered the table, complementing the bone china and sparkling silverware that marked each person's place setting, all arranged in perfect five-star–restaurant fashion.

John took in the freshly cut yellow roses and white daisies, which his mother had carefully arranged in a glass Mason jar in the center of the table. But the artistry of the display paled in comparison to the presentation of each mouthwatering dish she'd prepared from scratch and then placed in handcrafted serving bowls. It was classic Henrietta Victoria Small, through and through. Her trademark style was a delicate combination of understated elegance mixed with a splash of down-home simplicity.

John smiled, noting his mother's distinctive flair. She paid attention to the tiniest of details, making ordinary things seem special. From the signature touches she imparted in decorating the house, to the natural Southern charm and good manners she exercised when dealing with people, Henrietta was the consummate Southern belle, and always spot-on. "It's the little things that add up in big ways," she'd always preached.

John knew his mother took pride in her handiwork, and in being an efficient homemaker. She was a traditional Southern woman, who enjoyed decorating her home, cooking delicious meals, cultivating her garden, and, most of all, entertaining. Not many women in Nedine possessed her skills, nor could their wallets support such endeavors. But Henrietta was married to one of the wealthiest men—and certainly *the* wealthiest black man—in the entire county. Isaiah afforded her any indulgence she so desired.

"I would have set the table in the dining room, instead of here in the kitchen, had I known John was bringing company home," Henrietta said, looking at Madeline.

John felt the uncomfortable glint of Madeline's changing mood as she twisted her mouth, casting her eyes upon him. She clearly wasn't pleased that he'd neglected to tell his parents she was coming for this visit.

"This is just fine, Mama." John smiled. "And everything looks and smells delicious. I've been waiting to eat your food all day. There's nothing like a good home-cooked meal."

"I'm glad you brought your appetite," Henrietta said with a smile. "As you can see, there's plenty to eat. I made fried chicken, collard greens, macaroni and cheese, candied yams, hot-water corn bread, peach cobbler, and sweet ice tea."

John gave his mother a kiss on her cheek. "My mouth's watering already." These Southern delicacies were all his favorites, and Isaiah's as well.

"Should we wait for your grandmother?" Madeline asked, looking at John and then his parents.

"No," Isaiah answered. "She comes over for dinner every Sunday after church. She's restin' at home today."

"We'll go by and visit her later this afternoon," John said.

"I'm looking forward to it. I think it's so nice that your family is close. Having lost my parents at an early age, and then my aunt during my senior year of high school, I understand the importance of what it means to be connected by blood. There's nothing like family."

John was slightly shocked by her words. Never had he heard

Madeline espouse the virtues of family. He wanted to tell her that it wasn't necessary to try to impress his mother and father with what she thought they might want to hear, especially since her words were untrue. But he decided to keep his mouth shut. His parents had only met her five minutes ago, so they didn't need to know the whole truth of the matter: Madeline had an older brother, whom she never saw, never spoke of beyond vague references, or even took the time to contact by phone.

Henrietta nodded. "Yes, there is nothing greater than family and the ties that bind us."

After Isaiah said a short but heartfelt grace to bless the food, they were ready to eat. As head of the house, Isaiah took the lead, lifting one of the large serving platters from the middle of the table. "Let's dig in," he said happily as he passed around the first dish.

John loaded his plate with three pieces of tender, golden fried chicken. But when the platter came around to Madeline, she declined and passed it along to Henrietta. John eagerly piled a generous helping of macaroni and cheese next to his chicken, while Madeline eked out only a tiny dollop from the heaping bowl of savory noodles. When the collards came his way, John licked his lips as he ladled the dark greens and pieces of seasoned pork beside the rest of his food. Madeline, however, scrutinized the dish, picking around the pieces of fatty meat, allowing only a few sparse leaves to make their way onto her plate. After they all had finished serving themselves, Madeline was the only person at the table whose plate was practically bare.

John knew that Madeline was picky about most things, and that she was especially selective when it came to food. She watched her weight closely, priding herself on being fashionably slim, with just the right amount of heftiness in the strategic places he loved.

Although John was well aware of her predilection for fussiness, he'd hoped for diplomacy sake that she would at least make an attempt to appease his mother by sampling the food she'd put obvious time and care into preparing. He knew that every woman wanted to be on the good side of her man's mother, but he'd underestimated Madeline's steely resolve for unconventional boldness.

"You're not hungry, Madeline?" Henrietta asked.

"Well, honestly . . ."

"Madeline's watching her weight, Mama," John spoke up, not sure of what might fly out of his girlfriend's mouth. He wasn't in the habit of feeling uneasy about anything, but right now, he felt more uncomfortable than a sinner in the front pew on Sunday morning.

"For heaven's sake, child," Henrietta said, making a tsking sound with her teeth. "You don't need to watch your weight. You're as thin as a rail."

"Oh, thank you, Mrs. Small!" Madeline brightened, not realizing that Henrietta's statement wasn't exactly a compliment. "I've always been very careful about my weight, and now with so much information available about proper diet and nutrition, I try to make the best choices about what I put into my body. It's my temple," she said, looking at her small portion of macaroni and cheese as if the noodles were going to bite her.

Henrietta tilted her head to the side. "I see. So, Madeline, what kinds of food do you like to eat?"

"Mostly fresh fruits, vegetables, and lean meats. I was starving when we woke up this morning." Madeline smiled, looking at John. "And I really had my heart set on a nice big salad, but—"

John shook his head in disbelief. "You eat takeout nearly every day. The Chinese restaurants know you by voice."

Madeline batted her long lashes. "Yes, but I always order steamed vegetables, and never ever anything fried," she corrected, looking at the platter of chicken.

Henrietta nodded. "I see."

"Mrs. Small, I'm not trying to be rude. I know this is what you call 'Southern comfort food,' but it's really the kind of stuff that can kill you, you know? I can share some delicious low-calorie recipes with you, if you like?"

"You don't even cook," John said, "so how are you gonna share a recipe for anything other than how to mix a cocktail?"

Henrietta and Isaiah looked at each other, then at their son.

"Why are you getting upset?" Madeline asked. "I was simply trying to help your mother so she and your father won't end up with high blood pressure from the food she cooks."

John was so embarrassed that his cheeks became hot. "Madeline! You're way out of line," he said in a low, serious tone. He was going to tell her to apologize to his mother when Henrietta gently stepped in.

"I completely understand," Henrietta said in a soothing voice. She smiled, tossing her eyes from Madeline to John. "Everything isn't for everyone."

John knew exactly what his mother's seemingly innocent double entendre meant. She was talking about Madeline, and she had just told him in so many words that his fancy new girlfriend wasn't the one.

"You're so right, Mrs. Small," Madeline responded, apparently oblivious. "I tell John all the time that taste is a matter of individual choice."

Henrietta eyed her son. "Yes, indeed."

The shift in Henrietta's eyes and the twitch of her lower lip confirmed John's gut feeling. It was official. His mother had no use for his girlfriend; and after the exchange they'd just had, he couldn't blame her. Now all he could do was pray that they would make it through the meal without things turning ugly. He knew his mother would keep her cool—that was just her way. But Madeline was another matter. He'd never realized until now that she was such a loose cannon; and in spite of all her finishing-school education, she lacked common courtesy and manners. He'd never cursed at a woman, but right now he felt tempted.

"So, young lady, whereabouts are you from?" Isaiah asked, tying to lighten the mood. "I can tell by your accent and your clothes that you ain't from anywhere around these parts."

Madeline smiled broadly, holding her regal head high as she ran her slender hand over the silk fabric of her paisley print caftan. "I was born and raised in New York City."

"Oh, my. New York City," Henrietta repeated. "It's a fascinating place. John seems to like it up there."

Madeline leaned into John's shoulder. "Yes, he's grown to become quite fond of the city. You'll have to come up for a visit sometime soon."

John stuffed a forkful of collard greens into his mouth and chewed in silence. Neither he nor Henrietta had the heart to tell her that Henrietta had visited him just two months ago when she'd flown up to attend the wedding of the daughter of her best friend from college.

Madeline moved her plate to the side as she continued to speak. "I'm so glad to finally meet you and visit John's hometown."

Isaiah and Henrietta responded with a quiet and collective nod.

"Although I know you're a very important part of John's life, he rarely talks about his family . . . in detail, I mean. You know how close to the vest he is." Madeline smiled, pausing for emphasis. "That's why I've been dying to find out more about you two."

"Really?" Henrietta said, glancing toward her son. "What would you like to know?"

Madeline drank a small sip of her ice tea, wincing as the sugary sweetness took her by surprise.

"Too sweet for your taste?" Henrietta asked.

"*Quite!* But I'll manage."

John threw Madeline a cautionary stare. He couldn't believe the rude and disrespectful way she was acting, and he was starting to see her in an entirely new light—one that was dim and uninviting.

Madeline set her glass next to her untouched food. "Did you two meet in college?"

Isaiah looked at his wife through loving eyes as he answered. "No, me and Henny been knowin' each other since we was five years old. We grew up in a small town about a hundred miles east of Nedine."

"Did you attend the same college, too?" Madeline prodded.

"Henny went to a fine school." Isaiah smiled proudly. "Spelman College, down in Atlanta. But my schoolin' stopped in the fifth grade."

Madeline looked as if someone had just told her that the Earth was flat. *"Really?"* she blurted out, looking around the beautifully decorated room.

John could see that Madeline's mind was racing with questions. He knew it was inconceivable to her that an uneducated person could possess the apparent wealth that Isaiah laid claim to.

"I come from a family of sharecroppers," Isaiah said.

Madeline swallowed hard, a mortified look overtaking her face. *"Sharecroppers?"*

John aimed his eyes toward the ceiling as he let out a sigh. He'd had enough of Madeline's rudeness, and he wondered what had gotten into her that was making her act so unmannerly toward his parents.

"Yes," Isaiah spoke up, his deep baritone booming with pride. "When I was a little boy, I remember, I would watch my daddy work the fields from sunup to sundown. He picked cotton, tobacco, beans, potatoes—anything that would put food on our table. He was one of the strongest men I ever did know. He died when I was ten, and that's when I had to come outta school so I could work and help support our family. It nearly kilt my mama, but we had to eat."

Isaiah went on to explain that he'd quickly adapted to the demands of the backbreaking work, and that he'd also discovered he had a great fascination with business. He watched how things were done, and he listened and paid close attention to everything around him. He worked longer and harder than the rest of the hands in the field, earning him a reputation as a solid, dependable young man. His efforts caught the attention of the wealthy white man he worked for, who eventually came to treat Isaiah like a son.

When the old man died, he left Isaiah a small portion of land and a little money, to boot. At eighteen years old, Isaiah became the only black landowner in his tiny town. From there, he carefully charted what would become his path to success. He was smart, and he aligned himself with people who could help him as he quietly grew into unprecedented wealth.

"By the time I was in my mid twenties, I had quite a few parcels of property and more than three dozen men workin' for me, but they didn't know I owned the land they lived on or the crops they was pickin', 'cause I worked right alongside of them," Isaiah said.

"Everybody just thought I was a poor field hand, just like them. Back in those days, it was unheard of for a black man in those parts to own anything more than the shirt on his back, so no one gave me a second thought, and that's the way I wanted it."

"But why?" Madeline interrupted.

"I'd seen firsthand how folks acted when they found out you had a lil somethin'. It didn't matter if you was black or white. Green money could stir up red envy, and it could make people plot to stop you dead in your tracks. It's funny how a dollar changes things."

"Well, contrary to what most people think, I believe that money is the root to all good," Madeline said. "It changes things for the better."

John was incredulous; he was at a complete loss for words, as were his parents, whose faces drew a blank stare. They were not sure what to make of the woman their son had brought home.

"How did you do it?" Madeline asked, unfazed by the ire she'd drawn. "I mean, how did you buy land, hire people, and acquire more property without anyone finding out that you owned it all?"

Isaiah regained his composure and leaned forward in his chair. "Mr. Charles Williamson, God rest his soul, was the man I used to work for. He was one of the most honest and fair men, black or white, I've ever known. He left me my first piece of land. He had a cousin who was an attorney, and he told him to look out for me. Attorney Collins was his name. He was a good man, too, just like Mr. Williamson, and he helped me arrange my business affairs so that everything was in my name, without really bein' in my name."

"Hmmm," Madeline pondered. "And how did you manage that?"

Isaiah smiled, resting his large hands on the table. "Let's just say things got taken care of, right and proper. Attorney Collins did all the paperwork, legal and clear. That man helped me more than I can say."

Madeline looked at Isaiah, a mixture of doubt and disbelief covering her face. "So, a generous white landowner and a kindhearted white attorney helped a poor young black man to become wealthy? If that's the case, it's an amazing story."

"I know it's hard to believe," Isaiah responded, "especially in the South. But that's how it happened."

Henrietta nodded her head in agreement. "Yes, it's a pretty amazing story. But it wasn't a bed of roses, either. We went through some things."

"That's right," Isaiah continued. His easy smile became a serious line. "That's why Henny and me moved here to Nedine, right after our oldest son, Billy, was born. People started askin' questions, and the white folks got suspicious when I started buildin' a house. Since we had a baby on the way, I wanted to make sure my family was livin' in a proper place.

"Well, folks started wonderin' how a poor sharecropper like me could afford to build a house on my own. Now, mind you, it was a small two-bedroom home. Nothin' fancy at all, but it was new, just the same. People started diggin' around, askin' questions, and tryin' to figure out where I got the money from. Long story short—the Klan burned down the house that I was buildin' and the lil shack we was livin' in, too."

Henrietta shook her head from side to side. "It was the most awful night of my life. I was seven months pregnant at the time. We were lying in bed when we heard loud voices outside. Then they started screaming and yelling. The next thing we knew, something crashed through our bedroom window and, within seconds, flames were everywhere. We barely got out alive."

Isaiah sat back in his chair. "Yep, they run us outta town. But after all was said and done, that night was a blessin' in disguise 'cause it taught me a valuable lesson."

"Which was?" Madeline asked.

"That I would never live in the shadows again. A man ain't a real man unless he can provide for his family and protect what's his. I knew we couldn't stay because it was too dangerous. We had to leave, but I was determined to start over and stand tall wherever we landed. I was through hidin' and pretendin'.

"At the time, I already owned parcels of land all over the county, so I decided to look farther west, across the state. I did some investigatin' and decided to come here to Nedine."

Madeline frowned, wrinkling her nose. "You had money and real estate, so why on earth would you choose *Nedine,* of all places?"

John cut his eyes at his girlfriend again. He felt bad that as his father was sharing his life's story with her, the only words she could find to say were condescending ones. Even though he was accustomed to Madeline's brusque manner, her tone hit him in an entirely different way when it was directed toward the people whom he loved. He looked at his mother and could see by the expression on her face that she'd had her fill of Madeline.

Henrietta wiped the corners of her mouth with her crisp linen napkin before she spoke. "I know that Nedine might not seem like much of a town in comparison to New York City, but it offered us what we needed when we needed it. That's the way God works."

"That's right," Isaiah agreed. "God blessed me to meet some good people here that I could trust, and Henny and me started over. Been here ever since."

Madeline nodded. "It sounds like you've been a very lucky man, Mr. Small."

"I don't think luck's had anything to do wit' it, young lady," Isaiah said. "It's like my ninety-year-old mama always says, 'Good and evil is all around. You just gotta know which one is which and make the right choices.' "

Madeline's back stiffened as though someone had placed a board behind her.

After Isaiah's statement, the conversation limped painfully into moments of dull chatter, interspersed with quiet pauses. John remained mostly silent throughout the rest of the meal. At one point, he felt both of his parents' eyes on Madeline, and he knew exactly what they were thinking, because he was beginning to think the same thing, too: *What in the hell kind of woman was he dating?*

Chapter 7

Allene sat in front of her large console television, engrossed in *The Guiding Light*. It was her favorite show and she'd been a loyal fan since she'd heard the first radio broadcast in 1937. The soap opera had been the only reason why, against all practicality, she'd decided to let her son buy her a television set. She'd wanted to see her favorite characters visually come to life when the show took to the TV airwaves.

"These folks is somethin' else," Allene mused, shaking her head at the fictitious villains. After the soap opera ended, she rose from her comfortable, worn La-Z-Boy recliner and adjusted the knob to turn off the television.

"Guess I'll fix me a lil somethin' to eat," she spoke out loud as she walked toward her small kitchen in the back. "Think I still got some of that tasty chicken-n-dumplin's Henrietta left in the icebox when she came by the other day."

She was about to open the refrigerator, but something made her freeze dead in her tracks. Her wrinkled fingers released their grip from the steel handle as a tingling sensation spread through her body, causing her to tremble just slightly. It was reminiscent of the foreboding chill that had crept up her arms earlier that morning when she'd been sitting on her front porch, looking out at the peaceful sky, waiting for trouble to make itself known.

Allene nodded her head with absolute knowing. Yes, the trouble cloaked in the form of a beautiful young woman already had begun to rear its ugly head.

Allene had run into all sorts of devious, malicious, coldhearted people who wreaked havoc wherever they went, so she was used to dealing with difficult folks. But this was a little different, because now the danger was directed at John, her precious grandson, whom she loved more than life itself.

She knew instinctively that John's girlfriend was bad news; she was the kind of woman who was seasoned in battle and played for keeps. She was polished and carefully crafted in her delivery. Yet, when you pulled back her layers and took a good look, she was as rough as any back-alley gangster when it came to getting what she wanted. She was the kind of deceptive woman who could wedge her way into the hearts of men who didn't know any better, luring them with sweet talk and good sex. She knew that John was a very smart man, but she also knew he was just *that*—a man, and a man who loved women. His reputation with women was the one thing that always had worried her about his judgment.

"She's over at the house, eatin' at the table right now. Lord help him," Allene said out loud to herself as she thought about John. She shook her head, knowing that even though her son and daughter-in-law had quickly realized John's girlfriend was trouble, they didn't fully understand what kind of woman their baby boy had become em-broiled with.

Allene stood stock-still and said a quick prayer, bowing her head toward her feet. She wished she were twenty years younger so she could set out on foot and walk the five miles down the road to Isaiah and Henrietta's big, fancy house. But she knew her ninety-year-old limbs would only carry her to the end of the road in front of her house before betraying her. "Lord, help me guide my grandson away from that woman before it's too late," she whispered.

Allene suddenly felt another sensation spread through her body, but this one was different from the ominous chill she'd experienced only a few moments ago. A warm comfort flowed through her. At that moment, she knew something else was happening. "She hears me," Allene said with a smile. "Baby girl can hear me, and I think she can see me, too."

She had to take a moment to gather herself, amazed that she'd been able to reach across time, space, and what seemed impossible. She'd made the actual connection, and now she knew the real work would begin. The fact that Alexandria had not only heard her, but had looked into her eyes meant the girl's ability was much more powerful than Allene had thought.

She was glad she was making progress, and that she'd be able to help guide Alexandria through the difficulties that were getting ready to surface in her life. When Allene thought about difficult situations, her mind took her back to the present, straight to the web that John was tangled in and didn't even know it.

She took a deep breath as she opened the refrigerator and looked inside. Slowly, she reached for the plastic container filled with the delicious food Henrietta had made. "Might as well eat," she said, knowing what she had to do next. "Can't fight the devil on an empty stomach."

Chapter 8

The smooth vocals of Gladys Knight & the Pips floated from the car's radio as John and Madeline drove back to their hotel room on the other side of town. Madeline was talking so fast her lips were a virtual blur, but John barely heard a word coming from her mouth. He was lost too deep in his own thoughts to listen to her, or to the soulful music serenading them.

All he could think about was how disappointed and baffled he was by Madeline's behavior.

He'd been confident when he woke up this morning that something great was going to happen today. After having made love to Madeline and watching the beautiful sunrise, he'd been riding on a cloud. Her expert skills had satisfied him yet again, which was a feeling matched only by the excitement of knowing that his plans to open his own bank were finally coming to fruition.

John's day had started off great, filled with high hopes. But after the disastrous lunch at his parents' house, he was left feeling anything but great or hopeful. And worse still, he was dismayed by the fact that Madeline had acted so rude, and without even the slightest show of remorse about the nasty attitude she'd displayed. He didn't understand how he could have misjudged her character, which was now in question.

There were very few times that John had miscalculated a situation or a person. However, as he replayed the afternoon's events in his mind, he knew without a doubt that he had completely missed the mark about parts of Madeline's disposition that he'd obviously overlooked.

John sighed as he thought about the irony of life. His father had talked about how the horrific KKK incident that he and Henrietta had survived had really been a blessing in disguise. And now, as he tossed things around in his mind, John thought the same thing about Madeline. *Maybe bringing her home to meet my folks was for the best. A blessing in disguise,* he reasoned.

Two painfully uncomfortable hours at his parents' kitchen table had opened his eyes to little things he'd glossed over for the last twelve months. He didn't like the way Madeline had turned up her nose at his mother's food. He was appalled by the way she had reacted to his father's attempt to tell her about their family history. And he didn't like the way she had complained constantly about one thing or another from the time they had arrived in town yesterday.

Although the modest Holiday Inn where they were staying was considered the best hotel in Nedine, it wasn't good enough for Princess Madeline. "This is a two-star hotel at best, with outside corridors at that," she'd grumbled, disappointed because it wasn't a five-star property, with a full-service restaurant and cocktail lounge. She was disappointed that there weren't any jazz clubs they could go to for a late-night cocktail and music. She had gone on and on about the fact that there were no "real" stores where she could shop—all this, and they'd only been in town less than twenty-four hours.

"She's a real looker, but . . . uh . . . you sure you know what you're gettin' yourself into, man?" Maxx had asked when he met Madeline several months ago. John wondered how his best friend and his parents had been able to spot right away what he could not.

He momentarily took his eyes off the road as he came to a stoplight. He glanced over at Madeline, briefly scanning her under the microscope of new awareness. On the surface, she was the perfect picture of what he'd always wanted in a woman. She was intelligent, sophisticated, and spoke well. Her ambition complemented his own, and he liked that she knew how to handle business matters. And again, her bedroom skills had capped the bow on her package. But now, none of that seemed to matter.

"The light's green," Madeline said, snapping John out of his thoughts. "You better be glad we're in Podunk, USA." She laughed. "If we were back home, horns would be honking at us right now."

John chose to ignore her acerbic remark as he gave the gas pedal a tap, sending them on their way. He didn't want to talk about how frustrated he was because he knew things would erupt into an argument, which was the last thing he wanted at the moment.

One more day, John repeated in his mind. That was how much time they had left in Nedine. Tomorrow afternoon they would drive to the airport, return the rental car, and then catch their flight back to New York. After that, he planned to have a serious talk with Madeline about their future.

"I thought we were going to visit your grandmother?" Madeline said when she saw the large Holiday Inn marquee in front of them.

John pulled into the hotel parking lot and turned off the engine. "Did you say something?"

"John, you've been acting like you're in a daze since we left your parents' house. Are you all right?"

"I'm fine." He sighed, not able to force a pretend smile. "What were you saying?"

"I was asking about your grandmother. I thought we were going to visit her after we had lunch with your parents, right?"

"We'll visit her tomorrow afternoon on our way out of town. Right now, I think I need to rest before Maxx's party tonight."

Madeline looked disappointed and a bit upset at the news, but John brushed it off. He didn't have the patience to deal with her mood.

After they settled into their room, John removed his clothes in an attempt to make himself comfortable. Wearing only his boxers and T-shirt, he slowly walked away from the bed he and Madeline had made love in just hours ago. He claimed a seat in the chair next to the window.

"I thought you said you were tired and needed to rest," Madeline said. "Why are you sitting in that uncomfortable chair instead of lying in bed, beside me?"

John wanted to tell her that at the moment, the roughly upholstered chair offered more comfort. Instead, he said, "I'm fine right where I am."

Madeline leaned back on her elbows, crossing her long legs at the ankle as she lay across the bed. She stared into John's eyes. "You're in a bad mood, aren't you?"

"No," John responded in a quiet tone. "I just have a lot on my mind."

"Like what?"

He resisted the urge to tell her that he was still shocked and a little hot under the collar about how rude and out of order she'd been. But as unpredictable as she had been acting, he didn't know what she might be capable of saying or doing next. He also didn't want the remainder of their time together to be unpleasant, so he decided to use his head. "It's a discussion for another time," he said honestly, and as gently as he could muster.

"Is it about you and me?"

"Madeline, please . . . let's save it for another time, okay?"

"Fine." She sighed. "Well, anyway, I enjoyed our visit with your parents. They really liked me, don't you think?"

John leaned back in his chair and rubbed his smooth chin, trying to maintain his always-cool composure. "What makes you say that?"

"You saw the way they talked to me, like I was a member of the family."

John shrugged his shoulders. "My parents are very hospitable people. It's almost like a Southern rule to be."

"That may be true," Madeline said, "but I can tell it was more than that. You just don't want to admit that they liked me, because you feel guilty about not letting them know I was coming home with you."

John was baffled. He didn't know if she was delusional or if she was trying to start an argument. Either way, he couldn't hold his tongue any longer. "Madeline, they were trying to be nice. They even tolerated your rude behavior about my mother's cooking and your disrespectful reaction when you found out that my father came from a family of sharecroppers instead of investment bankers. Then the way you suspiciously asked him about his business affairs . . . how could you think either one of them would like you after all that?"

Madeline rolled her eyes. "Give me a break, John." She sat up and crossed her arms at her chest. "Your mother understood my dietary concerns and she was fine with it. And as for your father, he didn't seem to mind at all that I was simply curious about his extraordinary rise from such wretched beginnings."

"Wretched?"

Madeline rolled her eyes again. "How else would you describe life for someone who had to drop out of school in fifth grade, only to go to work in the dirty fields all day? That's a pretty awful beginning, if you ask me."

"Are you purposely trying to piss me off?"

Madeline looked at him as if he was crazy. "What in the world are you talking about?"

"You know what I'm talking about. You're saying things just to push my buttons."

"You have some major problems."

John's eyes widened. "Oh, really? . . . I'm the one with problems?"

Madeline scooted to the edge of the bed. "I didn't stutter, did I?"

"No, I guess you didn't." John took a deep breath, calming himself. "I'm about to say some things to you that a gentleman ought not say in the company of a woman, so I think I'll just take a quick drive to cool off before things get out of hand."

Madeline watched with a blank stare as John rose from his chair. He slid his dark khakis up the length of his muscular legs; then he pulled his white button-down over his broad shoulders. He walked over to the faux mahogany dresser and snatched up his keys.

"I can't believe you, John Small! You're actually going to leave me here in this second-rate hotel all by myself?" Madeline said with surprise.

John was halfway out the door when he said, "I didn't stutter, did I?"

Isaiah and Henrietta Small sat in their reclining chairs. He was watching the Saturday-afternoon Western on their new RCA television; she was knitting an afghan she had been working on for the last week.

"I can't for the life of me understand why John is dating that girl," Henrietta said for what was probably the hundredth time. "Apparently, they've been together for a year, so I guess that means something, especially since he brought her home to meet us. But, Lord in Heaven, I hope he's not thinking about marrying her."

"He's just havin' a lil fun, Henny. Don't you worry. Our boy's got more sense than that."

"I sure hope so. Sometimes a pretty face can blind a man."

Isaiah grunted. "Yeah, but John's not your average man. He knows what he's doin'."

Isaiah and Henrietta were equally protective of John. They always had envisioned big plans for their son and they didn't want him derailed by getting involved with the wrong people or marrying the wrong woman.

Even though their oldest son, Billy, should have been heir apparent to the sizeable wealth that Isaiah had amassed over the years, it was their youngest child, John, whom they had singled out to take over the farms, vast acres of land scattered across the state, numerous rental properties, and a small fortune in private investments, which Isaiah had worked so hard to acquire.

Billy was completely irresponsible. Unlike John, who had always been honest and dependable, Billy was shifty and careless, barely staying out of trouble with the law. And since Isaiah and Henrietta's only daughter, Phyllis, had married a doctor after graduating from college and moved to North Carolina to start her own family, all their hopes and dreams rested on John.

Isaiah's chest puffed with pride every time he thought about the success that his son had already achieved, and he was excited about the bright future that lay ahead for John. He'd always wanted his son to earn his money wearing a suit and tie; and to his satisfaction, John was doing just that, and even had a staff reporting to him.

Isaiah admired the fact that even though John had grown up in the privilege he'd provided, and stood to inherit a great amount of his wealth, his son didn't rest on his laurels. He wanted to create a legacy in his own right. John was going to be the first black man in their town to achieve a goal that no one dared think possible: opening Nedine, South Carolina's first black-owned bank.

It was a plan that Isaiah and John had been orchestrating carefully over the last five years. Now that John was on the cusp of securing all the pieces into place—having gone through the rigors of reporting his financials to state auditors, federal regulators, banking boards, and commissions, and making sure he had several million dollars in cash reserves—he was ready to do business. After a lifetime of hard work, sacrifice, and planning, Isaiah was determined to do whatever it took to help make his son's dream a reality.

Henrietta pursed her lips. "As thin as that girl is, she needs a good helping of fatback and corn bread instead of a tiny salad," she said, with a shake of her head, skillfully working her knitting needles.

"Don't worry 'bout John." Isaiah chuckled. "That girl's fixin' to get a real quick exit. You can bet your last copper penny on that."

"I did my best to be hospitable, but as God is my witness, if she had stayed a minute longer . . . ," Henrietta declared, letting her words trail off into frustration.

"Henny, don't let that gal get you all stirred up. She don't mean nothin' in the grand scheme of things. I told you, John's gonna handle that situation. Trust me. He ain't no fool, and I think after what he saw this afternoon, he knows what he got."

"All right, Isaiah. I'll trust in your word. In all these years, you've never said anything that wasn't so."

"And I'm not gonna start now."

The truth was that Isaiah didn't care much for Madeline, either.

He'd had a bad feeling about her on first sight, but his Southern manners led him to treat her cordially during her brief and unexpected visit. He'd only engaged her in polite conversation to see how she would react to his story of having come up from poverty. And just as he'd suspected, she was shallow and pretentious. He'd also seen calculating greed resting deep in Madeline's eyes as she looked around the house, surveying their belongings, trying to assess a dollar amount to go along with their wealth.

He didn't care what kind of wealth she was used to, or how fancy an upbringing she claimed to have, he could see that Madeline was a gold digger, and she was after his son's money. He recognized her insincerity for what it was, and he'd seen the same cunning manipulation in the eyes of many women over his lifetime. A handsome, powerful man like himself was used to women trying to get what they could, when they saw what they wanted. Women had been throwing themselves at him since he was a teenager. But there was only one woman who would ever own his heart, and that was Henrietta.

She was his soul mate, and the light that gave him strength. Isaiah was grateful that he had a good woman by his side, and he wanted the same blessing for his son.

Isaiah tuned out the Western playing on TV and thought about John's future. He was determined to help his son open the bank, and he would kill with his bare hands before he allowed anything or anyone to sideline all that John had worked so hard to achieve. He knew that he couldn't let John fall prey to the likes of Madeline King.

Just as surely as he could feel the slow-moving cancer working its way through his body, he knew that Madeline had no place in John's life, and she had to go. By any means necessary.

Chapter 9

Alexandria's mind raced in a loop of "what if" circles and "could it be" riddles as she parked her small Toyota hybrid next to her parents' three-car garage. It was only an hour ago that she'd been sitting on her couch when it finally came to her whose voice she'd been hearing inside her head. It was time to figure out what it meant and what she was going to do about it. She had a million and one questions swirling through her mind, and she knew the only person who could help her begin to answer any of them was her mother.

Alexandria was so anxious she could barely grip her slender hand around the knob of the back door leading into her mother's kitchen. As she entered the house, the smell of freshly baked cookies filled the air, causing her to pause her thoughts momentarily. She couldn't help but smile at the sight of her mother—decked out in a monogrammed apron draped over a knee-length bright yellow sundress—as she removed a batch of triple chocolate-chip cookies from the stainless-steel double oven. Victoria Small Thornton was, if nothing else, a one-of-a-kind woman.

Alexandria knew she owed a large debt of her natural beauty to her mother. Victoria had passed along a DNA strand that most people paid good money to manufacture. Her chocolate-colored skin was flawless, and her high cheekbones and smooth, even-tone complexion helped her maintain the look of a woman who appeared much too young to lay claim to having a grown daughter. And even though she ate any and everything she had a taste for, her tall, slim body was still in good shape, thanks to her very active lifestyle. As Alexandria assessed her mother, she knew she had a good future ahead of her, at least in the looks department.

"Hey, sweetie," Victoria said with a warm smile as she scooped the cookies, one by one, off the metal tray and onto a plate to cool. "How is everything?"

Alexandria walked over to her mother and gave her a kiss on her cheek. "Everything just got better, now that I see you made my favorite cookies in the entire world." When she bit into the warm, sweet-tasting treat, she nearly forgot about the life-altering reason she'd rushed out of her apartment at breakneck speed.

"I take full blame for your sweet tooth," her mother said with a small laugh. "I ate Godiva chocolate every day when I was pregnant with you."

"I had some last night, along with some Ben and Jerry's."

Victoria shook her head and laughed even harder. "That's a shame! But I bet it was good."

"Delicious, actually." Alexandria took another bite and then braced herself. "Mom, I need to have a serious talk with you."

Victoria set her spatula and cookie tray to the side and stared at her daughter with concern. "Is it about Peter?"

The tone in which Victoria always said his name, as if she'd just inhaled the aroma of a rotten egg, let Alexandria know her mother didn't care for Peter. She'd never been rude to him—it was against her Southern upbringing and principles—but she'd never embraced him, either.

"We've been dating a year and you still don't like him, do you?" Alexandria said.

"I've never said I don't like Peter."

"You don't have to. It's the way you say his name and look at him."

"And how is that?"

"Like he gets on your nerves or something."

Victoria nodded. "I probably do. But that doesn't mean that I dislike the boy."

"Then what does it mean?"

Victoria placed her hand on the curve of her slender hip. "I've always tried to stay out of your and your brother's business when it comes to your relationships. You know that."

"Yes, I know. And I appreciate it. But why don't you like him, Mom? He's educated, successful, handsome, and hardworking. I thought he's the kind of man you and Dad wanted for me." Alexandria surprised herself by her sudden need to defend Peter, but then she knew that she was really defending herself—and the poor choice she'd made by staying in a dead-end relationship with him for so long.

"I appreciate all those qualities."

"Okay, then why do you treat him with distance?"

"I want you to answer a question for me," Victoria said, looking into eyes that mirrored her own. "Does he encourage your dreams?"

Alexandria returned her mother's stare, but she didn't say anything.

"One of the many things that made me fall in love with your father was that he encouraged me to follow my dreams. When I quit my cushy corporate job to plan events and throw parties, he was one of the first people in my corner cheering me on. Sweetie, I know how much you love performing spoken word and bringing your thoughts to life. You're a brilliant artist."

"Thanks, Mom."

"You need to be with someone who appreciates your talent and supports you in it. And from what I've seen, I just don't think Peter does that."

Alexandria had never told her mother that Peter thought her passion was a ridiculous hobby, and now she was curious as to how her mother knew what had taken her months of dating him to figure out.

"He reminds me a lot of a guy I used to date years ago, in another lifetime," Victoria said, speaking with a flash of emotion that Alexandria couldn't quite place. "He was a lot like Peter. He came from a well-heeled family. He was educated, very handsome, and successful. At the time, I thought he treated me well, but I soon came to realize that he thought my Ivy League education should've been put to use behind a desk in a shiny building, not in a kitchen behind a stove or making out seating charts for events." She paused a moment and the indescribable emotion flashed across her face once again. "Trust me when I tell you, you need to be with someone who supports you and who's going to appreciate every part of you."

Alexandria knew her mother was right. "Yes, I know, and, honestly, I think the expiration date with Peter has passed. But that's not what I wanted to talk to you about."

Victoria nodded. "Okay, good. I really don't want to talk about him, anyway." She leaned against the counter. "Tell me what's wrong."

Alexandria didn't know any other way to begin the conversation, so she blurted out a truth that was long overdue. "I've been hearing voices again." She eyed her mother carefully, waiting for a reaction.

It had been more than sixteen years since Alexandria had uttered a word about the voices she often heard, and now—she wasn't just ready to talk about it—Alexandria was ready to take action. When she saw relief wash over her mother's face, she instantly knew she was going to get answers to her questions.

Her parents had discovered long ago that she had the gift of prophesy. They'd known she was a special child from the day she was born. She had been a small preemie who'd suffered health challenges at birth and had survived despite being very ill. After she recovered as a newborn, she'd never been sick another day in her life. Not even a sniffle or the slightest hint of a cold. But that wasn't the reason why Victoria and Ted Thornton knew their baby girl was special. They knew because of the things she said and did, and because of the voices she often heard.

The first time Alexandria told her parents that she'd heard voices speaking to her, they thought she had dreamed up imaginary friends, as lots of playful children did. But when she recited their conversations, which involved people, places, things, and, most upsetting of all, strange happenings and world events that a five-year-old couldn't have possibly understood, her parents took notice that something wasn't right.

But it wasn't until Alexandria's paternal grandmother died, and then a few months later her father suffered a heart attack—a condition Alexandria had actually predicted one Saturday morning before watching cartoons—did they realize their daughter had abilities that were beyond ordinary clairvoyance. And what they discovered next made them both look upon her with awe and protective carefulness.

After the drama of her grandmother's death and her father's health scare, Alexandria told her parents very matter-of-factly that her late grandmother had spoken to her. She told her to always take pride in the fact that she was born a beautiful little black girl and would grow into a strong woman. The irony of it all was that her father's mother had hidden the fact that she was half-black and had passed for white until the day she was buried six feet under. "Granny Carolyn told me that I'm a pretty little black girl just like she was, only I'm caramel and she was vanilla," Alexandria had giggled to her parents' shock and disbelief. At the time, no one but Ted, Victoria, and one of Carolyn's lifelong best friends knew about that secret.

As the years went on, Alexandria's gift became stronger, and it allowed her to protect herself and her family. She began to take precautions that others might not have, because she could see what was coming.

During an end-of-term celebration at the private day school she'd attended, she didn't pile onto the large merry-go-round at recess with the other second-grade children in her class. She hadn't wanted to end up with a busted lip, gashed chin, or, worse, a broken rib, as several of her classmates experienced when a spoke dislodged in the play equipment's axle, sending all the children spiraling to the ground. Although she was a natural performer, she didn't participate in her fifth-grade class's production of *Cinderella* because one week into rehearsals, the entire cast came down with a terrible case of meningitis. And she was adamant one Friday evening that her mother should not attend a party that her event-planning and catering company, Divine Occasions, had organized. Alexandria even went to the great lengths of hiding Victoria's car keys, making her more than an hour late for the event. When Victoria finally showed up, she was greeted by police cars and yellow tape because two men had gotten into a scuffle that had escalated into gunshots and resulted in the shooting of several innocent bystanders, who caught stray bullets inside the restaurant where her party was taking place.

But the incident that had frightened her parents, as well as Alexandria herself, happened when Alexandria was eleven years old.

Victoria's best friend, Tyler Jacobs, had stopped by one evening to introduce the family to Samantha, his new fiancée, who'd come to visit from out of town. After an hour of chatting and laughter, the two were about to leave. Then Alexandria unknowingly brought the happy time to a screeching halt. She walked up to Samantha, took her by the hand, and said, "Ms. Samantha, I'm sorry about your sister."

When Samantha asked Alexandria what she meant, Alexandria explained that she was sorry that Samantha's younger sister had died. Everyone stood around, looking bewildered by the shocking statement, especially given the fact that Samantha didn't have a sister. Two months later, Tyler delivered news that the woman who'd been carrying Samantha's father's baby had suffered a miscarriage, and that it had been a girl.

"Sweetie," Victoria had said gently, looking into Alexandria's eyes after hearing that news, "how did you know about Samantha's sister?"

Alexandria glanced over at her father, who was sitting on the couch beside her mother. She took a deep breath before returning her mother's stare. "A voice told me."

Victoria and Ted tried not to look disturbed by their daughter's revelation, but Alexandria could see that they were. And, more important, she could look into their eyes and actually read what lay behind them—fear.

Alexandria barely knew what to make of all the mysterious things she frequently saw and heard. Once she knew she'd frightened her parents, she didn't want to have any parts of her special gift. From that day forward, she stopped talking about the voices that spoke to her.

Over the next few weeks her mother tried to engage her in conversation about the premonition she'd had involving Samantha, but all Alexandria would say was "I don't want to talk about it."

When Alexandria reached high school, her mother could sense that she was struggling with something. But whenever Victoria asked what was wrong, Alexandria dodged her questions by changing the subject and pretending things were fine. Now, years later, she could no longer deny or avoid the voices she heard, especially the one that had been whispering words into her ear for the past month.

Victoria looked at her daughter, removed her decorative apron, and laid it on the counter. "So you're hearing voices, huh?"

Alexandria nodded.

"Thank goodness you're finally opening up to me. C'mon, let's talk."

Chapter 10

Alexandria chomped on a triple chocolate-chip cookie as she and her mother sat at the round table near the bay window in her parents' kitchen. She'd always loved having conversations at the kitchen table, and today she knew this talk was going to be life-changing.

She started by telling her mother that she'd never stopped hearing voices or seeing things before they happened. The only reason she'd denied her gift and kept it from her family was because she knew it frightened them, and she didn't want to cause them worry.

"Whenever I saw danger coming," Alexandria said, "I figured out a way to avoid it without saying anything to anyone, and I kept quiet about the things I saw and heard. This mostly happened in the middle of the night."

Victoria shook her head. "You've been carrying that burden for far too long. I wish you would've opened up to me before now. You're my child, my baby. There's nothing that could frighten me so badly it would keep me from being there for you, to help protect you and see you through it."

Alexandria was comforted by her mother's unwavering love, and the fact that she'd been born from one of the strongest, most resilient women she knew. Not only had she inherited her mother's physical beauty, she'd received Victoria's strong constitution and will. Each time she looked into her mother's eyes, Alexandria could see the loss, happiness, pain, and life lessons she'd experienced. And even though her mother had stumbled many times, she always got back up on her feet and never missed a beat in the rhythm of life.

"I know you wanted to help, Mom. But just as you've always wanted to protect me, I wanted to protect you, Dad, and Christian," Alexandria said, referring to her younger brother, who was a senior at Morehouse College.

"You're a good daughter, Alexandria, and I'm so proud of you. But I still wish you would've shared this with me years ago. I remember watching you grow into young womanhood and thinking to myself that you were going through something . . . something much more serious than puppy love crushes and dating dilemmas." Victoria let out a tired sigh. "But I also knew you were determined not to let me in. Keeping all that to yourself had to have taken its toll."

"At times, it did."

The two sat in silence for a moment, absorbing revelations that had been decades in the making. Victoria slowly leaned forward in her upholstered high-back chair. "Tell me about the voices you're hearing."

"Actually, it's a single person who's been talking to me now."

"All right. Do you know who it is?"

Alexandria put her cookie down and wiped her hands on her napkin. "Grandma Allene."

Victoria's back stiffened harder than stone as she blinked, trying to remain calm. This was her father's grandmother, her great-grandmother, and a woman who had been dead for many decades. She steadied her voice as she spoke. "What has she been saying to you?"

"That she's ready for a fight, and that she's going to protect and guide us."

"A fight?" Victoria said, concern lacing her voice. "Who is 'us' and what's she trying to protect you from?"

Alexandria knew she should have started by warning her mother that whenever she heard voices, usually from spirits who had long passed away, they hardly ever came as bearers of good news. "The 'what,' I don't know. But the 'who' is Grandpa John . . . and me."

She watched her mother's brow wrinkle, clearly at a loss for words. Victoria's father, John Small, had passed away five years ago. Alexandria had taken his death hard because he was her last living grandparent. He'd been a tall, strong, and imposing figure, even into his late eighties. But as businesslike as he was, he'd also been loving and kind, always telling her stories about what she called "the olden days."

Alexandria remembered that her grandfather often reminisced about his formative years growing up in his small town of Nedine, South Carolina, and what life had been like for black folks during that time. "We were Negros back then," he'd once said. "Then we became colored, before moving on to black. Now we're African American. But, Alexandria, you can be anything you want to be. Always remember who you are and where you came from. If you do that, you'll have the strength to endure whatever this world throws at you."

Victoria rested her chin in her hand. "I miss Daddy so much. Is he trying to talk to you, too?"

"No, just Grandma Allene."

"Hmmm."

"I've been hearing her voice for the past month. It started off as a very faint whisper, mumbles that I could barely understand. But over the last few days, it's gotten stronger, and now I can hear her as clear as I can hear you. I even saw her this afternoon."

Victoria's eyes widened as big as baseballs. "Oh, sweet Jesus." She looked around the room, as if expecting to see an apparition appear.

"She didn't physically appear," Alexandria said. "No one has ever come to me in physical form. But when I close my eyes, I can see them and what they're doing—that is, if they choose to show me."

"This is so unreal. If I didn't know any better, I'd say you were out of your mind. But I understand this, and I know it's possible."

"You do?" Alexandria asked, sounding surprised.

"Yes, and this is why I said I wish you would've opened up to me about what you've been going through all these years. I remember my mother, your Nana Elizabeth, God rest her soul, used to tell me about Daddy's family. She became very close to them after her own family disowned her for marrying your grandfather."

"I remember you telling me the stories," Alexandria said, with a nod. "It's a shame they didn't like grandpa, just because his skin was dark. That's so crazy."

"Yes, it is, but you know what it's like, even in today's times. We've come a long way, but there are still a lot of ignorant folks out there." Victoria shook her head and adjusted her hips in her seat as she spoke, getting back to the subject at hand. "I remember when you were a little girl, you used to say and do things that made me think about the stories my mother told me about my great-grandmother, whom I called Grandma Allene, and how it was rumored in their small town that she had the gift of prophesy."

" 'The gift of prophesy,' " Alexandria repeated in a low whisper.

"Yes. Mom said everyone loved and respected Grandma Allene dearly because she was such a sweet woman. But they were also afraid of her because her gift was something that people just couldn't understand. The unknown can be scary."

"I thought that was how you and Dad felt, too. I remember seeing the look in your eyes when—"

"You said a voice had told you about your aunt Samantha's stillborn baby sister," Victoria said, finishing her daughter's sentence. She reached out and took hold of Alexandria's hand. "Sweetie, I wasn't afraid. I was *amazed*. Right then and there, I knew you had the gift, just like Grandma Allene. It made me think back to that Saturday morning that I'll never forget."

"When I knew Dad was going to have a heart attack," Alexandria said.

"Yes, you were only five, and you didn't understand what you were saying . . . what it meant. Hell, I didn't, but I knew something about the words you spoke and the vibe around them wasn't right. Over the years, I tried so many times to get you to open up to me, but you wouldn't, so I waited. I knew this day would come, and I've been ready for it. I bet you could see the relief on my face when you told me, couldn't you?"

"Yes, I could." Alexandria smiled, squeezing her mother's hand tightly. "Tell me what you know about Grandma Allene."

Victoria let out a deep breath and shrugged. "I'm afraid not too much. I only saw her a few times when I was a very small girl. She was up there in age, in her late nineties, I believe. Daddy used to take Mom and me back to Nedine, where Grandma Allene still lived independently until the day she died. I remember she was a beautiful old lady and she always wore long skirts and dresses. She had a lead crystal bowl in her living room filled with lemon drop candies. I loved those things," Victoria said with a chuckle. "She'd tell me, 'Baby girl, get as many as you like. You only live once, so you gotta make it count.' Of course, I didn't know what in the world she was talking about, but it made me laugh just the same."

"She was special."

"Yes, she was. I've always regretted that I never got a chance to know her the way you and Christian got to know my parents before they passed away."

"I can tell she's a good person," Alexandria said, smiling, talking about the dead woman in the present. "I was sitting on my couch, listening to her talk. Then I closed my eyes and concentrated, and that's when I saw her. She was sitting in a rocking chair on the porch of a small house with green shutters. And there were all kinds of flower bushes in the front yard."

"Yes!" Victoria said with both excitement and astonishment. "I may have been young, but one of the things I distinctly remember about visiting Grandma Allene was the fragrant magnolia shrubs and hydrangea bushes in her front yard. You could smell them as you walked up to her house. What else did you see?" she asked eagerly.

"Like I said, she was sitting in a rocking chair and she was by herself. Her hair was twisted up into a bun on the top of her head. Even though I could see that she was old, her skin was still pretty smooth and very dark, like Grandpa John's. She had long fingers, too. I could tell, because she put her hand up to her face a few times."

"Yep, that's Grandma Allene."

"And she was wearing a shawl—blue-and-white–checkered, I think—wrapped around her shoulders. She rocked back and forth in her chair while she looked up into the sky as she spoke. I'm not sure who it was that she was speaking to, since she was alone, and I couldn't hear what she was saying."

"This is so unreal," Victoria said, again in awe, as if watching a movie.

"Then I saw her walk to her kitchen and she fixed herself something to eat." Alexandria paused and smiled. "I can't explain how I know this, but I think she could see me looking at her."

"Really?"

"Yes, and it's weird because I've spoken with spirits, either in their time or in mine. But until this afternoon, I've never connected with anyone in a way that merged our worlds into the same moment."

Victoria shook her head, still in awe. "Amazing."

"I saw all this happen in the short blink of an eye, Mom. Oh, and I heard the sound of a car's engine in the background, and that's when the vision faded and my eyes opened with the realization that it was Grandma Allene I was seeing."

"Sweetie, by your detailed description, I know without a doubt it was Grandma Allene you saw. But to my knowledge, you've never seen her, so how did you know who she was?"

"That's a good question, Mom." Alexandria shrugged. "Honestly, I don't know, except to say it was a very strong feeling I got. I don't know how in the world I knew it was her. I just did."

"Wow" was all Victoria could say. "This news makes your breakup with Peter seem as insignificant as dust."

Alexandria blinked her eyes. "Who said we're breaking up?"

"Oh, sweetie, you're not the only one who can see things coming."

"Now I'm in awe."

"Don't be. The way you can sense things, I know you had to have seen this coming."

"That's the funny thing about having this ability . . . this gift. I can hear and see what's going to happen for other people. But when it comes to me, I often draw a blank."

Victoria closed her eyes and shook her head. "Lord, have mercy."

"I know," Alexandria said. "If ever there was a time that I needed to know my own fate, it would be now."

"I'm very worried," Victoria said in a low voice. "If your Grandma Allene is contacting you, and trying to protect and guide you, that means you're in some type of danger."

Alexandria nodded, slowly acknowledging her mother's words.

"And if you're in some sort of danger," Victoria continued, "I can understand why she's reaching out to warn you. But why is she trying to warn Daddy? He's dead."

Alexandria swallowed hard. "I thought about that on my drive over here. I think he's still alive where she is, which is clearly in the past. I can hear her trying to warn Grandpa John about something that's happening in their present time . . . if that makes any sense."

"Lord, I don't know what makes sense anymore," Victoria said.

"Mom, I think . . . No, I *know* that I'm stepping back in time. Usually when someone appears to me, I see them right here in the present day, in my own time. But somehow Grandma Allene has managed to pull me back into her world. And she's doing it because she wants to protect me."

"From what?"

"I don't know. That's why I came over here to talk to you, so you can help me figure it out."

Victoria took a deep breath as she tucked her silky, chin-length bob behind her ear. "If she's trying to protect Daddy and you at the same time, it might mean you're both in danger of the same thing—back in time for Daddy, and in the present for you. What exactly did she say again?"

"She kept saying, 'I'm ready for the fight' and 'I'm here to protect and guide you, baby.' "

"I'm not going to pretend that this isn't disturbing, because it is. But I also have faith that Grandma Allene is going to do whatever she can to help you both."

Alexandria nodded. "She also told me to look for the diamond, because the one who has it will be the one who'll help save me."

" 'The diamond'?" Victoria repeated. "Do you think she's talking about a ring?"

"I don't know, Mom. But whatever it is that I'm supposed to find, I think it's here, in this house. The feeling I had right after I heard Grandma Allene's voice led me straight here to you."

Victoria let go of Alexandria's hand. "There's an old chest down in the basement that I found at your grandparents' house after Daddy died. I brought it here, but I've never been able to bring myself to open it. I think it's time now. Let's go."

Chapter 11

After Allene finished her delicious meal of chicken and dumplings, she walked back out to her front porch and took a seat in her beloved rocking chair. "He should be pullin' up any minute now," she said aloud.

Allene looked out at the clear blue sky and breathed in the fresh air. Just like the magnolias in her front yard, the heat of the day was in full, radiant bloom. She enjoyed the sweet scent of the flowers while she could, knowing the next twenty-four hours were going to be nerve-racking for her, and they were also going to be the most important hours of her young grandson's life. "Lord, I thank you for allowing me to see what's comin'," she whispered into the air.

Allene had come to accept her gift of prophesy. She'd learned never to question what she couldn't explain, because she knew the answers would always make themselves known in due time. When she was a young woman, she had anguished about the powers she possessed, afraid to reveal them to others for fear of being ostracized and labeled a "voodoo woman," as her great-grandmother had been.

But as time moved on, she grew into the awareness of her blessing and quietly cultivated her gift. And now, as she continued to savor the magnolia blossoms' sweet scent, she was finally coming to understand her purpose—the one that Susan Jessup had prophesized to her one cold, dark night, eighty-four years ago.

Allene's great-grandmother, Susan Jessup, died ten years before Allene was born. Susan had been a beautiful Ghanaian woman who arrived on American soil when she was sixteen years old. She was one of three hundred Africans who had survived the harrowing seven-week transatlantic journey on the *Lady Maria,* a pirate slave ship whose destination landed her at the Port of Charleston, in South Carolina. Susan had been kidnapped by European traders, ripping her away from her family and the comfort of the only home she had ever known.

Susan spent less than five minutes on the auction block before she was sold to William Jessup, a fair-looking, middle-aged wealthy plantation owner who had a penchant for expensive liquor and pretty women. Jessup had paid top dollar for Susan, outbidding his competition. He had been amazed by her startling appearance. Her tall, dark body, strong limbs, bright eyes, erect posture, and beautiful face defied the look of someone who had been at sea for nearly two months, cramped in the squalor of unthinkable living conditions aboard the ship. He could see right away that Susan was special, and unlike any other slave he had ever encountered.

He refused to put her to work in the backbreaking fields. He gave the overseer strict instructions not to ever let the lash of a whip near her smooth skin, and he forbade any of the male slaves to bed her. He wanted her to remain pure, supple, and ripe for his own picking.

Jessup remanded Susan to duties in the cook's cabin, where her labor would be lighter than the hardship suffered by slaves in the fields. But as it turned out, Susan was a terrible cook and lasted for only one month before she was given the new duty of washing and mending clothes.

Jessup's leniency and obvious favoritism toward Susan made some of the slaves simmer with jealousy, while provoking mistrust in others. Only the plantation cook, whom she had briefly worked under, even bothered to speak to her directly. Susan's existence on the Jessup plantation was a lonely one. Meanwhile, Jessup coveted young Susan, watching and waiting several months before he made his first trip down to her cabin one hot summer night.

Allene remembered the legendary story, word for word, as it had been told to her by her mother. . . .

When Jessup finally felt the time was right, he gave orders for two male slaves to build a tiny one-room cabin for Susan. He did this so he could make his visits in private. Talk of Jessup's intentions quickly spread throughout the slave quarters. A few of the women who had been victims of their master's lust quietly prayed for Susan, while others who had borne his children became worried about their diminished standing, fearing what would become of them once he took to Susan's bed over their own. Susan was both pitied and reviled in the foreign land she inhabited. But it didn't bother her, nor did she lose one night's sleep over her fate. She wasn't worried, because she knew what the outcome would be before it happened.

Jessup waited until shortly after dusk to walk from the main house down to Susan's cabin. He was determined to have her, taking long strides with intent on his face and heat in his eyes. When he reached her door, he walked through the threshold and found her sitting in a rocking chair, waiting as if she had known he was coming.

Fifteen minutes later, the door to Susan's cabin flew open and a frightened-looking man appeared. In the short span of time that Jessup had been alone with Susan, his thick dark brown hair had turned into a whisper-thin mix of snowy white strands. His large, wide-set eyes became small, sunken slits, outlined by deep, puffy bags. And his clear alabaster skin had morphed into a dull, ashen hue.

From that night onward, Jessup stayed away from Susan, as well as all the other slave women on the plantation. It had been his practice to sell off a few slave children each year to other plantations in neighboring districts. But from that night forward, not a single child born on the Jessup Plantation was ripped from his mother's arms. And from that night forward, everyone feared Susan. She was given the name "voodoo woman."

★ ★ ★

Allene was six years old the first time Susan visited her in one of her dreams.

"You are a very special little girl," Susan told her, speaking in her thick Ghanaian accent. "Only the girl children born of our blood can carry the gift in their veins. Not for three more generations from you will another of us be born this way. When she is old enough, you will go to her, as I have come to you. She will be a princess, born of a queen. When you go to her, she will at first be afraid. But very quickly, she will adapt. She will learn fast, and you will guide her the same way I am going to guide you."

The smooth sound of John's rental car drew Allene from her deep, reminiscing thoughts. A wide smile slid across her face as she caught sight of her grandson walking up to her, crunching gravel under his polished loafers with each step he took.

"It's about time you came by to see me!" Allene grinned as John stepped onto the porch.

"Hey, Grandma!" John said with excitement, bending down to give Allene a kiss on her cheek. He took a seat on the edge of the porch next to her ancient rocking chair.

Allene smiled and her face beamed with pride. "Look at you, just as handsome as you wanna be."

"I get it, honest. Good genes can't be denied. Grandma, you don't look a day over—"

"Twenty-one." Allene smiled and winked.

John nodded. "That's right."

"You want to go inside where it's nice and cool?"

"I'd rather sit out here, if you don't mind the heat."

"I don't mind at all. That's why I'm out here. I love sittin' on this old porch in this old chair. It's somethin' soothin' about it."

"It sure is. And it's a nice change of pace from the city."

"So, where's that girlfriend of yours?"

John sighed. "I guess Mama called and told you about Madeline, huh?"

Allene looked up at the clear sky and smiled. She hadn't spoken with Henrietta since yesterday morning, when she called with news that John had left New York and was headed to Nedine for Maxx Sanders's big birthday party. But Allene didn't need her daughter-in-law or anyone else to tell her what she already knew.

"You left her at the hotel?" Allene asked, sidestepping John's question.

"Yes, ma'am. I know I should've brought her with me because she really wanted to meet you."

"She did?"

"Yes, she did, but I couldn't do it. I needed to get away. I needed some space."

Allene nodded, glad that he was already seeing the light.

She loved her grandson more than she could put into words. Since the day John was born, she knew that he was destined for greatness. He was special, and his offspring would be, too. Allene had seen it as clearly as the bright sky, just as it had been prophesized to her by her great-grandmother.

"You two having troubles?" Allene asked.

John smiled, rubbing his hand across his smooth chin. "Grandma, you're the wisest woman I know."

"It don't take wisdom to know when things ain't right. If a man brings his woman home to meet his family and then leaves her at a hotel by herself, well, that's a sign of trouble."

"Yes, ma'am. It is," John replied.

Allene raised her brow. "She got a name?"

"Madeline . . . Madeline King."

"King? She ain't from around here, is she?"

"No ma'am." John laughed. "She was born and raised in New York, and prides herself on being a serious city girl."

When she asked the question, Allene knew that Madeline wasn't from Nedine, but there was something about the feel of the woman's name on her tongue that made her believe his girlfriend wasn't from New York City, either. "Hmmm" was all Allene could say. "I'll be right back."

She rose from her chair and went into the house. When she emerged a few minutes later, she was carrying two large glasses filled with freshly squeezed, ice-cold lemonade, compliments of Henrietta's trip a few days ago.

"Thanks, Grandma," John said, taking a long gulp of the refreshing drink.

"Tell me what's goin' on with you, John?"

"Grandma, I'm so confused," John admitted. "I don't know what's going on with Madeline."

"How do you mean, baby?"

"I knew that Madeline was spoiled and a bit . . . uh . . . 'fussy,' as you would say. She's headstrong and confident, and she has a forceful personality."

"Oh, does she?"

John nodded. "Yeah, and, trust me, I know she's not for everyone. But she's always treated me well. And when we're together, she's kind and affectionate. She practically caters to my every need." John let out a deep sigh, shaking his head. "I knew she had her share of faults—we all do. But I didn't know how shallow, rude, and downright mean she could be. And talk about moody! She changes from one minute to the next. I've been dating Madeline for a year, but today it was like I saw a whole different side of her . . . like I was seeing her for the very first time."

Allene picked up her glass and took a sip of her drink. "Maybe you was."

"You think she's been pretending this whole time? Or maybe it's just that I've been a big fool?"

"Baby, you ain't no fool. You just human, and a man at that."

"That last part was cold, Grandma."

"But true."

John took another sip of his lemonade and chuckled. "I graduated in the top ten percent of my class at UPenn. I became the youngest member inducted into the Boule's Manhattan chapter. I'm the highest ranking black person at the investment bank where I work, and I'm getting ready to open my very own bank soon, God willing. All that didn't just happen miraculously. I worked hard and I earned it by making smart decisions."

"Yes, you did."

"So how could I be so blind about someone who's right under my nose?"

Allene tilted her head to the side and smiled. "You know I love *The Guiding Light,* don't you?"

"Yeah, I know that's your show."

"Uh-huh, and those folks cut up so bad they make me talk back to the television. But they're just actin'. All that carryin' on they're doin' is made up. It's a careful written script. You know what I mean?"

John nodded.

"Baby, what you said about her pretendin' all this time? Well, sometimes people show us what they want us to see."

"Well, I'm looking with a new pair of eyes now."

"You ain't the first man to be fooled by a woman, and you won't be the last," Allene said. She reached over and patted her grandson's shoulder. "You close to fulfillin' a lot of dreams, John. Dreams that you don't even know about right now, but I do."

John looked into his grandmother's wise, old eyes. "What dreams are you talking about, Grandma?"

Allene wanted to tell John all that she knew was in store for him if he made it safely through this weekend, but she couldn't. The truth—that he would own a bank that would grow to a half-dozen branches in North Carolina's state capital, amass more wealth than even his father had obtained, and be blessed to have a loving wife, a beautiful and successful daughter, loving grandchildren, and would live nine decades in peace and happiness—was too much for his rational mind to absorb in the here and now. She knew that prophesies and spirits didn't exist in his structured world, which was ruled by logic and reason. So instead of telling him what had been prophesized to her by a nineteenth-century ghost and witnessed by her own eyes, she simply told him what he needed to hear at the moment.

"Openin' up that bank ain't just your dream, baby. Your mama and daddy, me, and all your ancestors been dreamin' right along with you. Trust in God and let him lead you in the right direction. He showed you a sign today. That woman over at the hotel ain't the one for you, baby." Allene grunted. "But there's somebody out there who is. Somebody who's real, with a pure heart. She's gonna come to you when you least expect it, but when you need it most. You watch and see."

John looked up into the sky as Allene was doing. "Grandma, you've never told me anything that wasn't true. So, as unlikely as what you said seems, I'll try to be as optimistic as you are."

"Sounds like you done gave up on love."

"Well, kind of. I've had a lot of women, but I've never been in love. I don't even know what that feels like."

"Baby, you just wait. Things are gettin' ready to change."

John laughed and shrugged as he shook his head.

"One more thing," Allene said. "Use your book learnin' for startin' that bank, but use the God-given common sense runnin' through your veins for everything else. Every friend ain't good, and every enemy ain't bad."

"First you tell me I'm going to find true love, and now you're telling me I need to watch my back?"

"That's right. That's exactly what I'm tellin' you."

"Grandma?"

Allene knew what he was going to ask, so she quickly responded to him. "I just get a feelin' about these things. I can't tell you why or how I know. But when God puts somethin' on your heart, you have to pay attention."

John smiled. "I woke up this morning with a feeling that something great was going to happen today. Now I know that I wasn't wrong. Your wisdom and love are the greatest gifts I could have. I love you, Grandma." John leaned over and gave Allene another kiss on her cheek.

"I love you, too, baby."

Allene and John enjoyed another hour of conversation before he headed back across town to the hotel.

"Lord, thank you for givin' my grandson some smarts," Allene said aloud as she watched John's car roll away. "Keep that woman away from him, and let him see her for who she really is before it's too late."

She rocked back and forth in her chair, thinking about what John had told her. *"King,"* she whispered, freeing the word from her mouth. It had curdled like sour milk in the pit of her stomach. A queen and a princess were in John's future, but there was no room for a King.

Allene had done her best to maintain her composure when John had uttered his girlfriend's last name. As soon as she heard the word "king," she had wanted to drop to her knees and pray. But she knew she couldn't alarm her grandson, so instead she rose from her chair, went into her kitchen, and poured two glasses of lemonade. She said a prayer she had been rehearsing all morning—the one that Susan had branded into her memory over the last eight decades. It was a prayer of protection, meant to form a shield against anything that was rooted in bad intentions. Then she parted her lips and took a small sip from the glass meant for her grandson.

When she returned to the porch, she handed John his lemonade and watched him as his lips drank from the exact same spot where she had sipped. It was the first time in days that she had felt any relief. From her lips to John's, she was wrapping him in the protection that only pure and honest love could provide.

"Nothing bad is gonna happen to my grandson. Not on my watch," Allene spoke in a determined voice. "Not on my watch."

Chapter 12

Furious was a mild emotion to describe how Madeline felt. She was out-of-her-mind mad that John had the nerve to leave her all alone at a podunk hotel that she could barely stomach. She went into the bathroom and flipped on the light switch, surveying John's toiletries, which were neatly arranged on the counter. She twisted her mouth into a frown, picked up his toothbrush, walked over to the commode, dunked it down in the water, and swirled it around the bowl several times. "Bastard!" she snarled. "Chew on this!"

She'd wanted to run out behind John and ask him where he was going before he'd practically slammed the door in her face, but she instinctively knew his destination. No doubt, he was headed to his grandmother's house.

Madeline knew he loved his parents, but his grandmother . . . Well, she was John's heart. Although he didn't talk about his family in great detail, whenever he mentioned Grandma Allene, Madeline noticed how his face would light up with the glee of a little boy. And that was all the more reason why she wanted to meet the woman so bad, especially since her meeting with his parents had been a complete disaster.

"A bumpkin and a belle," Madeline said with a smirk, thinking about Isaiah and Henrietta Small. "But I can't blame her for marrying that old bama, because at least he's got money, and lots of it. And if John will just act right, I can get my hands on it all."

Madeline studied her slender face in the mirror and smiled with approval. She knew her beauty was her ace in the hole—that, and the fact that her sexual expertise had reeled John in like a fish on a hook. Since childhood, she'd had a knack for using her beauty and brains to get what she wanted.

Her parents, Samuel and Gloria King, had adopted Madeline when she was six months old. They'd had one son, and had always wanted to round out their small family with a sweet little girl. But their hopes were dashed when the doctor told Gloria she couldn't have any more children. After their son graduated from high school, their empty nest intensified Gloria's desire to have a daughter. Given that Samuel wanted to make her happy, they decided to adopt. They didn't have the money or the patience for the red tape and length of time it would take to go through a New York adoption agency, so they decided to look into orphanages down south, which were much more lenient and overflowing with babies, who all needed a home.

When Samuel and Gloria walked into the Children's Home of Beltsville, Kentucky, they thought Madeline was the most beautiful little brown baby either of them had ever seen. The way she cooed and smiled at them with precious dimples on each side of her chubby cheeks had made them fall instantly in love. It only took a little over a month for the paperwork to be approved before Madeline became their little girl. Samuel and Gloria had been thrilled. They pampered little Madeline with whatever she wanted, spoiling a child who, unbeknownst to them, was already naturally rotten to the core. Her smiles, even as a child, hid the real mischief behind her motives.

After Gloria and Samuel were killed in a tragic house fire, when Madeline was eight years old, she was shipped from their modest two-family flat, where they'd lived in Queens, to a two-room apartment with her aunt Betty, on her mother's side, in Harlem.

Betty was a grocery store clerk from nine to five, and a taxi dispatcher in the evenings. During what little time she could scrounge after working around the clock, she took in laundry in order to piece together a living for her and her only sister's child. She worked tirelessly in her effort to provide a life for her niece—a life that she knew would make Gloria proud.

But despite Betty's hard work and sacrifices, Madeline had no use for the woman. Betty was a strict, Bible-toting disciplinarian whom Madeline couldn't stand. She resented the fact that Betty wouldn't let her listen to the popular tunes on the radio that everyone danced to, or hang on the stoop outside their building after school, like the other kids in the neighborhood. She saw life outside their cramped four walls as much more interesting than the Gospel-laced existence her aunt provided.

But even though she detested her unfortunate lot in life, Madeline quickly learned how to pretend to enjoy going to church, reciting Bible verses, and volunteering with the elderly. These were all things her Aunt Betty required her to do. As long as her aunt was willing to work three jobs to send her to the private school where she was bused—and where she pretended to be just as well-to-do as the privileged kids around her—and buy her all the clothes, shoes, and treats she wanted, she figured faking it was a small price to pay.

As Madeline grew older, she found that not only could she get what she wanted from her aunt and a select few friends she'd made at the ritzy school she attended, she could do the same with men. By the time she was in high school, she'd perfected the art of seduction, and had studied the *Kama Sutra* from cover to cover. She wrapped men in her web, commanding them to do whatever she wanted.

Once she graduated from college and reached adulthood, she had corralled a string of men who gladly followed behind her like puppy dogs, obeying her command. But there was one troubling problem. The great majority of them lacked the ambition, drive, and, most important, the level of financial means she desired. She didn't simply want someone who had money; she wanted someone who was wealthy beyond ordinary standards. She wanted a mogul, and that was why she'd set her sights on John Small and his family's wealth.

★   ★   ★

Madeline knew she'd done a superb job of making up an entire life from whole cloth that John had fully believed, right down to the wayward con artist she'd paid to pretend he was her brother so she could show proof of family who would back up all her lies. But the masterful job she'd pulled off today paled in comparison to any of her past stunts. She let out a hearty laugh when she thought about how surprised she'd managed to act when she saw John's parents' home, as if she didn't already know they lived in a mini-mansion, secluded from the common folks in town.

"I could've won an award for that performance." Madeline chuckled loudly. She wanted to pat herself on the back for the way she'd fooled them all into thinking she had no idea how Isaiah had acquired his wealth. "Those country bumpkins didn't have a clue."

She smiled, carefully inspecting her sparkling eyes in the mirror as she applied another layer of frosted shadow to her lids, which the humidity had swept away. "I didn't scrape and claw my way out of a two-room apartment to settle for just anything," she said as she looked at herself, thinking about how she'd stripped to earn money for college so she could have the opportunity to rub elbows with people of means, who could lead her to riches. "I've gone through a lot to get to this point, and there's no turning back now."

A month after she'd met John, Madeline had spent hours and hours researching him, his family, and his background. She even knew about the town he was from, having read articles about the local goings-on, compliments of the Manhattan downtown library and their microfiche files. She'd grown up poor, but she knew from a very early age that she was destined for a different station in life. She loved money and power, pure and simple, and she spent day and night dreaming about how to get both.

As an accountant by profession, she'd been trained to evaluate numbers, gather information, and investigate for outcomes. As a cunning woman on a mission, she used those same skills to find out what she needed to know in order to squeeze her way into John's world, and ultimately into his wallet. He was the big fish and she wasn't going to let him slip through her fingers.

Her careful due diligence was one of the reasons she knew that Isaiah hadn't told her the complete story about the extent of his wealth. He owned practically every track of land in Nedine, even in some parts of town where the white folks lived. That, combined with his farms—one that grew produce and raised beef, and the other tobacco, supplying grocery stores and cigarette companies up and down the Southeast—yielded millions in net profits each year. Isaiah was sitting on an empire. "I guess he's not as dumb as his poor diction makes him sound," Madeline said, scoffing.

She looked at herself one last time in the mirror, dried John's wet toothbrush with a Kleenex, set it back down, and then walked back out to the bedroom area. "He should be back soon," she said, running her hands across the small beads of sweat that had formed on her forehead. "I have to accomplish my mission so I can get out of this town as soon as possible."

Madeline was thirty years old and she knew her time was running out. Even though she looked like a woman in her twenties, she was all too aware that the aging process would start in a few short years. Soon the elasticity of her smooth skin wouldn't be as resilient. The high rise of her perky breasts would begin to droop. The firm, round behind, which she strutted from side to side, would flatten. After all that, the wrinkles she feared would eventually take up residence at the corners of her eyes and mouth. She had to hook John while she was still young and appealing to his senses. But she also knew that she needed more than good looks and great sex to land him, she needed an airtight insurance policy that would guarantee a ring on her left hand. She needed to get pregnant, and fast!

She'd hoped that John would forgo his usual insistence on using a condom last night, but he hadn't.

"John, I'm on the pill," she'd told him a month after they started dating. "So there's no need to use protection. We're covered."

"Yeah, from pregnancy. But not from anything else," he'd said.

"Now, hold on a minute. What's that supposed to mean?"

John looked her in the eyes. "VD, syphilis, and gonorrhea are all out there. I want to be responsible and I want to protect myself."

"I'm clean and you're the only person I'm sleeping with" had
been Madeline's comeback.

"Good, let's keep it that way while we use protection."

Madeline had been pissed to high heaven. Not because she'd
wanted to get pregnant by him at the time, especially given that she
didn't know if he had any real money or not. The thing that angered
her was the fact that she couldn't get John to do what she wanted. She
knew any other man would've turned cartwheels on one leg to have
sex with her, period, let alone perform the act without a latex barrier.
What the hell is wrong with him? had been her thought.

Even though he wouldn't give in to her, she still managed to seduce him and had gotten him to buy her just about anything she
wanted. They went to the best restaurants, drank the most expensive
wines, and shopped in the finest stores. She laughed at the fact that
John had no idea who he was really dealing with. But neither did any
of the other men who had crossed her greedy path.

But at the same time, Madeline knew that John wasn't the average guy, not just because of his rousing intellect, sophistication, and
gentlemanly manners, but because of what he had the potential to be.
He was ambitious beyond what even she strived for, and she knew
that hitching her horse to his wagon was going to move her forward
on her way to living in supreme luxury.

Neither her adoptive parents nor her aunt Betty had ever managed to scrape together enough money so they didn't have to live
paycheck to paycheck. That was another reason why she'd been so in
awe of what Isaiah had managed to accomplish, especially after meeting him and seeing how terribly country and uneducated he was.

She knew she had to rein John in; and up to this point, she'd done
a pretty good job of it. She'd managed to convince him that her aloof-
ness was just a case of fierce independence, and that her hard heart
was really careful pragmatism. She led him to believe that her reluc-
tance to show compassion was guided by the fact that she had to present a tough exterior in order to be taken seriously in corporate
America; and she made it appear that her unwillingness to get involved in social causes was due to the fact that her plate was full try-

ing to deal with a demanding job, which required so much of her time and concentration.

Madeline sank into the chair where John had sat just an hour ago and let out a frustrated sigh. "After all the work I've put in, and for an entire year at that, I'll be damned if I'm going to let it all go down the drain now. I'm so close."

She'd been pleased with herself when she finally persuaded John to bring her home to meet his family, and she'd hoped she could charm John's parents, which would cement her even closer to the Smalls' fortune. But to her chagrin, that didn't work out as she'd thought it would.

She knew right away by the look in Henrietta's eyes that the woman didn't care for her, and that was one reason why she didn't attempt to go out of her way to be cordial. "Bitch," Madeline hissed as she sucked her teeth, thinking about John's mother. Madeline's one saving grace, as she saw it, was that although Isaiah hadn't been overly welcoming, he didn't seem to dislike her the way his wife did.

But his grandmother was now her primary target. Madeline knew that Allene Small was the golden goose that could solidify her standing in John's eyes. He loved his grandmother and he'd listen to her advice. "If I can meet that old biddy, I'll be able to win her over and calm any reservations John has," Madeline said, plotting her next move. "She's in her nineties, so fooling a scatterbrained, elderly woman will be a piece of cake. Then once I'm pregnant I'll be on easy street."

Madeline reached across the desk in front of her and picked up her copy of *Ebony*. She thumbed through the pages until she reached a particular section of interest. She smiled, admiring the six-page spread of elegant black women draped in some of the day's most fashionable wedding gowns. "This one will look perfect on me," she mused, running her manicured finger along the page that highlighted a woman her same height and weight, smartly outfitted in a traditional white gown with tulle and lace.

She moved from the chair to the bed and stretched her long body across the cool bedspread in an attempt to make herself more comfortable. She had to pull herself together and wipe away the sweat that kept puddling in the middle of her forehead, because she didn't want to show any signs of anger or frustration once John returned. She needed to remain calm and in control so she could prevent an unsightly outburst, which she knew she was prone to do. Besides, she knew she needed to rest up for Maxx's party tonight.

She planned to stay only for an hour or so, just long enough to stomach a few of John's humdrum friends, who she knew would be dazzled by her style and beauty. Then she would convince him to ditch the party and make an impromptu visit to his grandmother's house. He had mentioned that the old woman was a night owl, just like him, so popping in on her wouldn't be out of the question. That's when Madeline would make sure she charmed the old woman into giving them her blessing. After that, they would come back to the room and make love with the faulty condoms she'd pricked holes in, earlier this morning, while John was in the shower.

"I've waited a long time for this," she said, grunting, "and I'll be damned if I let anything stop me."

Chapter 13

After leaving his grandmother's house, John felt renewed. But he also understood that his newfound comfort was only a temporary state because it came wrapped in a sense of uncertainty about what was on the horizon. He sighed deeply as he steadied himself and made a sharp turn into the Holiday Inn parking lot.

So many things were going through his mind, making his head swim with questions he couldn't answer. He parked his car, then sat with the engine running. He took two deep breaths and reflected on the events of the last twenty-four hours.

He was grateful for the advice his Grandma Allene had given him. Her words of wisdom had been like a heaping dose of medicine that lifted his ailing spirit. "Grandma's always right," he whispered to himself. "Madeline might not be the one for me."

"Why didn't I see this side of her before now?" John whispered to himself. But if he was really honest about things, he knew the reason, and it was because he'd chosen to see what he wanted. Given his busy work schedule, which included twelve-hour days, and Madeline's hectic calendar, the only real time they spent together was on weekends, and most of those hours centered around his bed or hers, enjoying each other's bodies as a physical release from their long, power-packed weeks.

He realized that although they'd been seeing each other for a year, their limited contact was almost like being in a long distant relationship. And now, for reasons he couldn't explain, Madeline suddenly wanted more.

After a few more minutes of reflective thought, John finally decided to turn off the engine, head inside, and brace himself for whatever awaited him once he entered his hotel room.

When John walked into the room, he found Madeline stretched out across the bed. The South Carolina heat outside was brutal, but the air in the room was unbelievably frigid, just the way Madeline liked it.

"It's freezing in here," John said, still standing near the door, not moving a muscle.

"You're back." Madeline smiled, purring with seduction. "I adjusted the air conditioner just slightly, but I can turn it off if you like." Madeline rose from the bed and walked over to adjust the air-conditioning unit. Slowly she strutted and swayed her way back across the room, reclaiming her spot on the king-size mattress.

John noticed that Madeline's sultry waltz seemed intentional, meant to get him hot and bothered. But instead of feeling turned on he felt slightly on edge. He looked at her through new eyes, trying to determine what was real and what was an act. He'd let her seduce him more times than he now cared to admit; all because of the physical pleasure she was able to give him.

"I'm so sorry about our little spat," Madeline said. "I didn't want you to leave the room upset with me. What if you had gotten into an accident while you were out? Our last words would have been bitter ones."

John walked over to the bed and sat on the edge, opposite of where Madeline was perched. "You've never worried about things like that when we're back in New York, and the streets and roads there are much more dangerous than here in Nedine."

"Danger lurks everywhere, John."

"Yes, I guess it does."

Madeline lowered her eyes. "Do you forgive me?"

"What's done is done. Let's just try to get through what's left of this weekend."

Madeline scooted over to where John sat. "C'mon, baby," she purred again. "I said I was sorry. I know I shouldn't have overreacted. Now forgive me and don't make me beg."

"Sure, uh, let's just drop it, Madeline."

"I want us to talk about this, honey. You have to understand . . . I really wanted this trip to be perfect. When you said your parents didn't like me, well, I felt absolutely awful. I guess I took it out on you. Forgive me . . . please?"

John looked into Madeline's eyes, noting the brightness they carried. But he knew he had to be careful with her, especially after she'd shown him how she could go from sugar to venom faster than his Mustang could go from zero to sixty. And as he looked even closer, he noticed that it wasn't necessarily brightness he saw. Rather, it was a wild, almost erratic stare. He knew she hadn't been drinking, because her breath didn't smell of alcohol. *Is she doing drugs?* he wondered, quickly glancing around the room. He was going to question her, but then he thought better of it. He didn't want to chance what her answer or reaction might be. So to avoid any further drama, he acquiesced. "Okay, Madeline. I forgive you."

"I missed you while you were gone," she said wantonly, wrapping her long arms around his shoulders. "And regardless of what you think, I was worried about you while you were out."

John felt uncomfortable being so close to her. The feel of her body next to his usually excited him so much that he had a hard time controlling his sexual urges. But now, he had little interest in feeling her flesh pressed next to his. He loosened her grip, releasing himself from her embrace.

He stared at Madeline and could see that although she was pissed, she was trying her hardest to hide it. If it weren't for the vein pulsating on the side of her temple and the deep breaths he could see her taking in an effort to control her anger, he would have sworn she was as happy as a birthday girl. He watched as her eyes suddenly darted across the room, landing on a magazine sitting on the desk. She lingered there for a brief moment before returning her stare to him. When she did, he saw what looked like a hint of sadness rimming her lids.

He didn't doubt that she probably felt a little down because he'd left her in the room by herself, and the "Southern gentleman" side of him hated to see a woman in any type of distress. The thought that he was in any way the cause of Madeline's present state made him feel bad about leaving her all alone in a strange city with no one to turn to. His compassion and guilt took over. "I didn't mean to cause you any worry, Madeline."

"I know. And I didn't mean to upset you."

"I guess we both did a good job of upsetting each other."

Madeline took a deep breath and slowly scooted her body even closer to John's. "Yes, we did. But I'm glad we're back on track, because this is supposed to be a fun weekend for us. I feel terrible about our little lovers' quarrel. I'm glad we can move beyond it."

Although John was remorseful about the way he had treated Madeline, he knew what had happened between them was more than just a simple lovers' quarrel. She'd shown him a side of herself that he was beginning to think only touched the surface of the kind of person she could be.

He again thought about the very real fact that most of their time together had been spent only on the weekends, romping around in a bed. He knew it was foolish to believe he could build a meaningful relationship from that.

From the moment they had arrived in town last night, he had begun to sense that something was different—not only with Madeline, but with himself as well. Outside of their lovemaking earlier that morning, nothing about their relationship felt the same. He knew it was partly her, but it was partly him, too.

"Madeline, when we get back to New York, we need to talk about things."

"I know you're still upset, but we can work out our differences. Every relationship gets tested at some point, and this was ours."

"If today was a test I'm afraid we didn't do well."

"I can't believe you'd give up on us so easily. John, I love you."

You love me? John thought, surprised. *Where the hell did that come from?* John didn't know what to say or do. This was yet another example of why he was becoming leery of the unpredictable, impulsive-acting woman in front of him. Not once had she uttered those words since they'd been dating, but now she was declaring love. The mixed signals and confusion were more than what John cared to deal with. He had far more pressing things on his plate, like executing the lease on the building he had chosen for the bank, finding a temporary apartment to rent in town until he could build a house, meeting with auditors once he returned to New York—and those were just a few of the small mountain of pressure-filled tasks he had to complete. He dropped his head to his hands and took a deep breath.

"I need to start getting ready. I told Maxx I'd pick him up."

Madeline looked puzzled. "You're taking him to his own party?"

"Yeah, Maxx is gonna be drinking and celebrating. He'll need a ride home."

"You mean we're staying at the party all night?"

"Is that going to be a problem?"

Madeline let out a loud and exaggerated huff, as if she were a dragon blowing smoke. "I hadn't anticipated staying all night, so yes, that's going to be a problem."

"We talked about this at least five times, Madeline. You said you were looking forward to the party."

"I just changed my mind."

John stared at her, not knowing what to think. So he did the only thing he knew would work to calm his frustration—pray that the evening would go better than the day had.

Chapter 14

"What's happenin', my man!" Maxx grinned as he walked up to the driver's side of John's car.

The two men smiled as they greeted each other with a firm handshake and a brotherly hug. It always amazed everyone who knew John and Maxx how the two could be best friends, given how different they seemed to be in almost every way. John boasted a refined type of handsomeness, was polished, and always practiced diplomacy and smooth control. Maxx was a pretty boy, slightly rough around the edges, and frequently found himself embroiled in wild drama. But he was also as charming as they came; and just like John, the ladies loved him.

At six feet even, Maxx stood a few inches shorter than John. His fair complexion was smooth and café au lait. His curly black hair framed a good-looking face and a devilish grin, which made women of all ages swoon in his direction when he entered a room.

John and Maxx had been best friends since third grade, when Maxx came to John's rescue. One day during recess, a group of three boys started taunting John. They called him "rich boy," and made fun of his expensive clothes and proper diction. They even threw out the charge that he thought his family was better than everyone else's because they had money and a huge house that sat apart from all the other black folks in town.

The group of bullies surrounded John, but he wouldn't back down, not even after all three boys jumped him at once. Suddenly, from out of nowhere, Maxx appeared. Fists and elbows flew so fast and hard, it was difficult to distinguish who was hitting whom. By the time the teacher came to break up the fight, John and Maxx were a bloody mess. The three bullies they left on the ground had fared a worse fate, sharing cuts, bruises, and a broken bone among them. From that moment onward, John and Maxx declared themselves to be brothers.

By the time they reached high school, the two young men were inseparable. John was voted Most Handsome and Most Likely to Succeed; Maxx was voted Best Dressed and Most Fun to Be Around. After graduation, they each went their separate ways. Maxx landed a good-paying factory job at Reynold's Plastics, Nedine's largest employer, and further cemented his reputation around town as a ladies' man. Meanwhile, John entered the University of Pennsylvania, an Ivy League school, where he earned a reputation as a serious student and was inducted into Phi Beta Kappa, the nation's oldest academic honor society for the liberal arts and sciences.

Though their paths led them in different circles, they remained thick as thieves through the years. They did everything together from partying hard and chasing beautiful women, to consoling each other over their first broken hearts.

John slapped five with Maxx. "Happy birthday, man. Or as Josie would say, *old man.*"

"What? I know Josie's old ass didn't call me *old*?" Maxx laughed. "I'll show her who's old."

"Yeah, I bet you will."

The two friends shared a private laugh about John's comment, while Madeline sat in the passenger seat, peering at them.

"You ready to celebrate your big day?" From the smell of alcohol on Maxx's breath, John knew Maxx already had started his own private party.

"Man, I been ready since last week. As a matter of fact, I took next week off so I can recover from tonight."

"You took the entire week off? See, that's why I can't hire you at the bank," John said, laughing. "I'd have to send a posse out to find your ass."

"Watch it now! I still get my work done. Ain't a cat out there who can touch me."

"Just as long as you get your beauty rest."

"Joke if you want to, but I know how to handle my business."

Despite Maxx's womanizing and partying ways, he cleaned himself up from nine to five, Monday through Friday, and had been promoted several times, making him one of the few black supervisors at the factory, where he'd been employed for over a decade. He took pride in a job well done, never half-stepping when it came to his work.

John reclaimed his place behind the wheel and Maxx slid into the backseat.

"What's happenin', Madeline? How've you been?" Maxx greeted.

Madeline turned around and gave her best attempt at a smile. "I'm fine, thank you. Happy birthday, Maxx."

"You all right?" Maxx asked, taking in the pained look on Madeline's face.

"Yes, I'm absolutely splendid."

John knew what her problem was, but he didn't want another argument so he remained silent. They'd had a discussion on the drive over about how she didn't want to stay long at Maxx's party. But just as he'd told her in the hotel room, he was going to be there long enough to make sure his best friend had a good time and got home safely.

As John backed out of Maxx's driveway and put his car in gear, he couldn't help but notice how Madeline's irritation was growing. He couldn't hold back any longer. "Madeline, do you want me to take you back to the hotel so you can rest? I know you don't want to be out late and this way you'll get a good night's sleep before we fly back tomorrow."

"And miss the party?" Madeline said with determination. She leaned over and said, "Not on your life." Then she smiled slyly before delivering a soft kiss to his lips.

Slowly Madeline pulled away, bringing her hand to her mouth as if she had just experienced an electric shock. "Wow, did you feel that?" she asked.

"Feel what?"

"That tingling sensation . . . when I kissed you."

John didn't know what she was talking about. All he felt was confusion about her behavior. When he looked through his rearview mirror and saw Maxx shaking his head in the backseat, he knew he was in for a few jokes, once the two of them were in private. "I didn't feel anything," John responded flatly.

"Well, I definitely felt it. It was like magic, but I guess that's what happens when you're in love. We might just have to leave the party early, after all."

Maxx coughed loudly in the backseat as John tried to gather a response to Madeline's wild claim of love. He could tell by his friend's reaction that Maxx was also wondering what in the hell had gotten into her.

Madeline reached into her small handbag and reapplied her frosted pink lipstick, while both John and Maxx stared at her in bewilderment. "Sweetheart, don't look so surprised," she said. "You should know by now that I love you. You love me, too, don't you?"

John didn't know what she was trying to pull, especially given the fact that Maxx was in the car with them. Her behavior was starting to unsettle him. He didn't want to anger or embarrass her by telling her the truth, so he simply said, "Love is complicated."

"No, it's not," she quickly shot back in a caustic tone.

"Maybe not for you," he shot right back at her.

"And it shouldn't be for you, either. We're great together. What's so complicated about that?"

John glanced over at Madeline and then looked into his rearview mirror again to see an expression on Maxx's face that matched his own—complete discomfort. John couldn't figure out why Madeline was making such declarations in front of Maxx, but he was tired of her games and was ready to put them to an end.

"Madeline, something's wrong with you. You're talking all crazy, so that must mean you're tired or not feeling good. I'm taking you back to the hotel right now."

"Over my dead body," she said playfully, but with force. "Or on second thought, maybe over yours, if you go to the party without me!"

"Damn," Maxx whispered under his breath.

"What's that supposed to mean?" John asked with surprise.

"I've been in that miserable little room all day, thanks to you. I'm not going back, and especially not by myself. If I go back, you're coming with me."

John looked at Maxx again and saw his friend staring straight at him with caution. Maxx was giving him a signal that said loud and clear: *She's gonna be trouble! Take her ass back to the hotel right now!*

But against his better judgment, John headed to the Blue Room, uneasy about what the rest of the evening might bring.

Chapter 15

Alexandria and her mother stood in a small room that was situated at the back end of her parents' huge basement. It was a room rarely visited and was reserved for items that held deep sentimental value, too precious to throw away. This section of the house was unfamiliar to Alexandria, as she had never had a use or reason to plunder through what she called "Mom and Dad's junk room." Now she was as curious as a detective to find out what clues her grandparents' old trunk would reveal.

She knelt down beside her mother and watched closely as Victoria slid a gold-colored key into the lock of an old, leather bound storage trunk. When it opened, Alexandria felt a warm breeze tickle her face. "Did you feel that?" she asked her mother.

"No, what is it?"

"A warm breeze. I think it's Grandma Allene."

Victoria's eyes widened. "She's trying to communicate with you again?"

"Yes, I think so. And I think she's letting me know that I'll find what I'm looking for in this trunk."

"Thank the Lord. Now I can breathe a little easier."

Alexandria nodded. "Me too, Mom. I feel a sense of comfort, like I'm safe and everything's going to be all right."

"Good, now let's go through this trunk and see what we can find."

Thirty minutes later, Alexandria and Victoria sat side by side on two folding chairs, which Victoria had taken from a small closet down the hall. They were sifting through the contents of the trunk, marveling at each new treasure they found that connected them to the past: trinkets, travel souvenirs, photographs, old jewelry, newspaper clippings, a few old romance novels from Victoria's mother's collection, and important documents, such as birth certificates, a marriage license, and land deeds. All of this had been hidden for decades, and now each item was coming to life, painting a picture of their family's history.

"I never knew Mom and Daddy went to Paris for their honeymoon," Victoria said as she looked at a picture of her parents sitting at a bistro table outside a Parisian café. Her father's youthful grin and her mother's love-struck eyes told the story of a couple enjoying their newfound happiness. The inscription on the back read, *Our honeymoon in Paris.* "They were so young," Victoria said, smiling at the photo. "They had a whirlwind courtship."

"Really? I didn't know that."

"Yes, it was one of those love at first sight stories that you see in movies and read about in romance novels."

"Kind of like what dad says about you the first time he saw you."

Victoria smiled. "Yes, but your father and I didn't date right away and we definitely didn't rush in like your grandparents. They fell in love after only one day and dated for six months before they married."

Alexandria shook her head. "Wow, that's fast and pretty amazing."

"Mom said everyone thought they were crazy, but she and Daddy proved them all wrong."

"Nana and Grandpa John really loved each other," Alexandria said, peering over at the photo in her mother's hand. "I remember how much fun I used to have when I visited them during the summers in North Carolina. Those were the best times."

"And they loved having you. It was the highlight of their year."

"One thing I remember so clearly was that they always held

hands whenever they were out walking. Whether it was at the grocery store, the movies, or church, his hand was always on hers. I didn't appreciate the significance of how special that was when I was a child, but I do now. I hope I can find that kind of love one day. It's the kind you and Dad have."

"You will, sweetie. When the right one comes into your life, you'll know it."

"Is that how it was with you and Dad, you just knew?"

Victoria paused for a moment, as if trying to figure out the right thing to say. Alexandria knew that her parents' marriage had experienced a bump after her father's heart attack when she was a little girl, and she remembered seeing flashes of hurt and sadness in her mother's eyes, which she instinctively knew had something to do with more than just her father's health.

Alexandria had never ventured to talk to her mother about matters of the heart until now, because much of Alexandria's life had been spent trying to keep things to herself. But now that she'd opened up about the voices she'd always heard, she was ready to talk about other things, too.

"Yes," Victoria answered. "I knew there was something special about your father when I first met him. But at the time, we were working together. Plus, I'd just met someone who I thought was a more appropriate choice."

"Why did you think he was a better choice than Dad?"

Victoria hesitated. "Honestly, the main reason was because he was black."

"Oh." Alexandria was surprised. "That made a difference?"

"At the time, it did. I'd never dated outside my race, and, quite frankly, I was afraid of the unknown, and of being judged by others. But things happen, people change, and it makes you view life differently. Your father stayed consistent through it all. He showed me what real love was."

Alexandria could read through the lines. "That guy hurt you."

"Yes," Victoria whispered.

"Mom . . ."

"Yes?"

Alexandria knew she shouldn't probe, because deep down she already knew the answer. However, her newfound openness and a gut-gnawing feeling led her to ask, "Did you ever get over him?"

"He was my first real love. I'm not sure if it's possible to ever stop thinking about your first love in some form or fashion. But what I know without a doubt is that real love doesn't make you question a thing. You won't be in doubt—you'll know—and that's what your father and I have."

"That's beautiful, Mom."

"Indeed it is."

They were quiet for a moment, absorbing the fact that this was a first for them. Victoria smiled and reached for her daughter's hand. "I'm glad we're talking like this. It's something I've always wanted. Even though we've always been close, there was a part of yourself that you kept hidden from me. But now that you've opened up, I want you to know that you can ask me anything, talk to me about anything, and count on me for everything."

Alexandria leaned over and hugged her mother tightly. The two sat holding each other for a few minutes, until Alexandria slowly pulled away. She looked at Victoria and then toward the trunk. "She just spoke to me."

Victoria clasped her hand across her mouth, looking at her daughter with wonderment. "What did she say?"

"She said, 'You doin' real good, baby. Trust in yourself and keep lookin' 'cause what you're searchin' for is right around the corner.' " Alexandria repeated each word in a dialect that mimicked exactly what she'd heard.

"It's amazing how you sounded exactly like I remember Grandma Allene speaking." Victoria shook her head from side to side. "This is so unreal."

"I know, and the strange thing about it is that it feels so normal," Alexandria said, letting out a deep breath of relief. "I've heard voices all my life, but I've never quite gotten used to it, and sometimes the things I would hear really frightened me. But this is different. I feel loved and protected, and unafraid of anything. I know this might sound strange, but it's like I'm truly alive for the first time."

"Maybe it's because you're embracing what's inside you, instead of running from it."

Alexandria sat very still and concentrated. She closed her eyes and then opened them again. When she did, her mother was staring at her.

"Are you okay?" Victoria asked.

"I just saw Grandpa John and Nana."

Victoria's eyes widened. "Did they anything to you?"

"No. They couldn't see me, but I looked back in time and saw them. They were young, Mom, like in this picture," Alexandria said, looking down at the photo her mother was still holding. "They were at a bar, in a club."

Victoria burst into laughter. "Mom and Daddy in a club! Oh, I wish I could see what you're seeing."

"And Uncle Maxx was there, too. They were all so young."

"Wow. Old Uncle Maxx."

Alexandria laughed. "And Mom, he was drunk as all get-out, talking to a woman at the bar. I think he was hitting on her."

Victoria laughed even harder as Alexandria joined in. This was exactly the kind of situation Maxx Sanders would have been in. He was Victoria's mother's older brother and John's best friend. He'd always been full of life and equally as much trouble. It wasn't until Maxx's seventy-fifth birthday that he finally slowed down, swore off alcohol and partying for good, and became a one-woman man. He was now in his nineties, living quietly with his oldest grandson in Dunwoody, a suburb right outside Atlanta.

"Oh, sweetie. I see why you're not afraid. Everything that Grandma Allene is speaking and leading you to is filled with people who love you. She's surrounding you with love."

"Yes, I see that now."

Victoria suddenly became quiet as a puzzling look filled her face.

"What's wrong, Mom?" Alexandria asked.

"I just thought about something. You said that Grandma Allene came to you because you and Daddy needed protection from something, and that she wanted or needed your help."

"Yes, that's right."

"I don't mean to bring a dark cloud over the good time we're having, but do you think you're still in danger? And what kind of help can you give her if she's the one who's supposed to help you?"

"I'm not sure," Alexandria replied. "But the one thing I do know is that something's going on in my life that's drawing me to the past and connecting me with Grandpa John."

"I'm trying to think of things that Daddy shared with me about his past, but nothing dangerous comes to mind. He was a very methodical man, a lot like your father, and he made sure he was careful in all his dealings."

"Hmmm . . ."

"What?" Victoria asked.

Alexandria ran her hand over the top of her thick mass of curls. "Maybe whatever he was in danger of is no longer a problem."

"Sweetie, I don't understand."

"Well, kind of like that movie from the 1980s, *Back to the Future,* when the guy goes back in time and ensures that things work out for his parents. Maybe things have already worked out for Grandpa John."

Victoria shrugged. "I sure hope you're right. All of this is so new and confusing to me that I don't know what to think."

"In a way, it's all new to me, too. A lot of what I'm experiencing is a first. I've seen the present, and I've been able to glimpse into the future. But I've never gone back into the past and watched life as it was unfolding. It's like I'm in the middle of two worlds, because I'm still here in this one while I'm there."

"This is more fascinating by the minute."

"Yes, it is. But one thing I can say with a fair amount of confidence is that I think whatever danger Grandpa John is in, he's *almost* out of it. I also think that Nana and another woman, whom I can't place, have something to do with it."

"Another woman?"

"Yes, I don't know who she is. But she's going to help with what-ever trouble Grandpa John is in."

Alexandria could see the puzzled look that remained glued to her mother's face, so she took the liberty of answering one of Victoria's many questions. "I can't explain how I know this, but I can feel it . . . here," she said softly, holding her hand to her chest.

Victoria shifted in place, adjusting herself on her folding chair. "I'm glad you feel that your Grandpa John is almost out of danger, but what about you? Do you get any feeling about what's going to happen to you?"

"No."

"How about the diamond ring?" Victoria asked, looking down at the trunk again. "I didn't see any diamond jewelry in there, but the reference Grandma Allene made has to mean something, and it's got to be here in this trunk."

"Let's look again."

Alexandria and Victoria started over again, shifting through old pictures and items that John and Elizabeth Small obviously had thought were too precious to throw away. But rechecking with a fresh pair of eyes didn't shed any new light on the answers that Alexandria was looking for.

"I guess we need to call it quits," Victoria said as she handed Alexandria one of her mother's old romance novels to put back in the trunk for safekeeping.

Just as Alexandria was about to lay the book inside, a small pho-tograph fell out. "What's this?" she said, looking at the aged picture. When she studied it closely, a warm rush came over her body that made her tingle. "Look what I found!" she said, turning to her mother.

Victoria looked at the picture in her daughter's hand and shook her head. "Oh, my goodness."

Alexandria and a little boy, who looked like he could be her twin brother, were sitting, side by side, in small chairs in a colorfully deco-rated classroom. Their arms were draped around each other as they grinned for the camera.

"I still remember the day you took this picture of PJ and me," Alexandria said, referring to her childhood friend. "We were in kindergarten, in Mrs. Baldwin's class. Well, she was Ms. Snow back then." She smiled, remembering her kindhearted teacher. "He was my best friend. I used to love that boy."

Victoria shifted in her chair.

"I wonder whatever happened to him. We lost touch after I transferred schools that next year." She held the picture close, studying it in detail. "Mom, do you mind if I keep this?"

Victoria shook her head and smiled. "No, sweetie, go right ahead. Sometimes it's good to hold on to memories."

The distance in her mother's voice made Alexandria pause. "Are you okay?"

"I'm fine, just a little tired from sitting down here on these hard chairs. You ready to go back upstairs?"

A few minutes later, they were back in the kitchen, where their journey had started.

"I thought for sure you would find what you were looking for in that trunk," Victoria told her daughter as she reached into the cabinet for a plastic container.

"On some levels, I did. Coming here forced me to open up to you, and it freed me. Now I feel like something good is going to happen, like the threat of danger is gone, and my life is going to take a new turn."

Victoria smiled. "I'm glad we had this talk, too. And knowing that you feel safe is all I want."

"Me too."

"But I still wonder about the diamond. Lord, I hope it doesn't involve Peter!"

"Well, tell me how you really feel!" Alexandria laughed. "I don't think you have to worry about him. As a matter of fact, I'm going to take care of that situation tonight."

"Good. Now here," Victoria said as she handed her daughter the plastic container. "Take those cookies on the platter over there with you. They're great with ice cream."

All Alexandria could do was smile. She'd come over to her parents' house looking for answers. While she hadn't gotten complete resolution to all her questions, she was leaving with a better frame of mind, a new direction for her life, and a container of triple chocolate-chip cookies, to boot!

"There you two are," Ted said, smiling, as he walked into the kitchen.

Ted Thornton was the picture of handsome sophistication, even now in his older years. His once–jet-black hair had turned into a pleasant salt-and-pepper mix. His olive skin was still supple, but now it showed small lines of age. His ocean blue eyes were still hypnotic and captivating to those who looked into them, and people often commented that he looked like the male models in the Jos. A. Bank ads. Ever since he experienced four life-changing events over twenty years ago, he'd refocused his energies and was happier now than he'd ever been. But the road getting there hadn't been easy.

The first blow came when his mother passed away after battling a long illness. Then, shortly after her funeral, he was hit with the secret she'd kept—that she was half-black, and had passed for white all her life. But the most devastating event, and what had hurt him worse than the heart attack he'd suffered, was when he found out that Victoria had come close to having an affair with Parker Brightwood, her ex-boyfriend. It had taken him a full year to get over his anger, suspicion, and resentment. But slowly the two worked their way back to each other, and the life-changing birth of their son, Christian, had served as a healing symbol.

Ted and Victoria shared a love that could be felt by those who watched them as they went through life together. When Victoria was diagnosed with breast cancer ten years ago, it was Ted who was by her side through her mastectomy, chemo, hair loss, and night sweats. When he decided to expand ViaTech, his privately held, multimillion-dollar telecommunications company, into the international market a few years ago, it was Victoria who encouraged him to take that big leap, opening him up on the world stage.

★   ★   ★

"Hey, Dad." Alexandria walked up to Ted and gave him a hug.

Looking at her father, and then over to her mother, it once again made Alexandria think about how much she wanted a meaningful relationship. Although she always had boyfriends in a plentiful supply, her struggle to deal with her gift had no doubt affected each of her romances. But now that she'd released what had long been inside, she was ready for a true love of her own.

"How's my princess doing?" Ted said with a smile.

"I'm good, Dad. Really good."

Ted looked over at Victoria, his ocean blue eyes scanning hers for clarity. Alexandria could tell her father detected something different in her demeanor, so she answered the question she knew he'd be asking her mother once she left. "Mom and I had a great talk today. She'll tell you all about it."

"I sure will," Victoria spoke up.

Twenty minutes later, Alexandria found herself heading down the street to Peter's house. She knew what needed to be done, so she planned to have a calm discussion and let him know that their relationship had run its course. "I'm not happy and I know he can't be all that happy, either," she said aloud, coaching herself toward their breakup. "This'll be for the best. Besides, maybe now we'll both be able to find the right person."

As Alexandria neared Peter's driveway, a force hit her so hard that it caused her to stop her car in the middle of the street. This time, it wasn't voices that froze her in her tracks. Instead, it was an overwhelming feeling that she needed to be somewhere else. Something was calling her. She could tell that it wasn't Grandma Allene, but she couldn't identify exactly who or what it was. She sat still for a moment, knowing she had to obey her gut. So without a second thought, she made a U-turn and headed downtown to the place where she knew she needed to be.

Chapter 16

"The joint is packed!" Maxx said with excitement.

John surveyed the crowded parking lot of the Blue Room. He'd never seen so many people there on a Saturday night. Nearly every space in the paved lot was full, and it seemed as if new guests were arriving every second. Maxx whistled when he saw two women in tight skirts and high heels heading up to the front door.

"Pace yourself," John told his friend. "The night's still young and there's more of that inside." He cut his eyes at Madeline, fully expecting her to launch a snide remark after his slip-of-the-tongue comment. But to his astonishment, she remained silent and actually smiled at him.

This, combined with her crazy declaration of love for him, and the fact that from the moment Maxx had entered the car she seemed unfazed by the potent smell of liquor on his breath, was further confirmation in his mind that she must be up to something. Her current behavior was uncharacteristic of the hellcat he now knew she could be. Docile, agreeable, and smiling with care were not traits he'd have ever associated with Madeline. Yet, there she was, acting like an ambassador of goodwill.

Madeline's strange moods were beginning to make John question her mental stability. Ironically, her disposition had been one of the things that had drawn him to her when they had first started dating. She'd been consistent in everything she did, whether good or bad. But now, he didn't know what to make of her ever-changing temperament.

Despite his uneasiness and confusion, there was one thing that John was very sure of. After this weekend, he was going to think long and hard about whether to continue a relationship with Madeline.

"Slim knew there would be a big crowd," Maxx said, breaking John from his thoughts, "so he got Mr. Hanks to reserve a space for us around back."

Once John parked in the lone space next to the proprietor's Cadillac, the three headed up the steps and entered through the back door of the building. They stopped in the middle of the hall when they saw a tall, gangly man approach.

"Slim, what's happenin', man!" Maxx yelled out.

"Well, I'll be damned. If it ain't the birthday boy hissself!" Slim howled with laughter. "Man, how you gonna show up late for your own damn party?"

" 'Cause the party don't start till I arrive," Maxx said with a wide smile.

"I hear ya, brothah."

"Thanks for talkin' Mr. Hanks into lettin' me use this place, Slim. Shuttin' down on a Saturday night just to help me celebrate . . . that means a lot to me, and I appreciate it."

"No need to thank me. You my family, you know that." Slim smiled, looking from Maxx to John as he gave each of them a soul brother handshake and hug.

The three men had been friends since high school when John and Maxx welcomed Slim into their fold, dubbing him their "honorary little brother." "Slim," whose real name was Maurice Jones, had moved to Nedine from Los Angeles when he was fourteen years old. His father had been murdered in a drug deal gone wrong. After the funeral, his mother packed up everything they owned and headed back to Nedine, where she had family.

Even though Slim was only one year and one school grade behind John and Maxx, he seemed much younger, and had always been treated as such. His adolescent acne, rail thin body, slightly awkward demeanor, and goofy grin had made his adjustment to Nedine a difficult one. John and Maxx were the popular, nice guys who always befriended the underdog. So when they saw the other kids teasing Slim, calling him "four eyes" because of the thick lenses inside his black horn-rimmed glasses, they immediately came to his rescue. After that, no one ever picked on Slim again.

Slim had literally begged Mr. Hanks to shut down the club on his busiest night—all so Maxx could hold his party there, at no rental charge. He felt proud of himself for being able to talk the notoriously tightfisted owner into obliging him—a mere busboy and kitchen cook—on such a lofty request. But the truth that neither Slim nor anyone else knew was that Mr. Hanks's decision was made easy by the large check that John had so generously paid last month to secure the spot.

Slim grinned. "Mr. Hanks even gave me the night off so I can celebrate with y'all. But first things first. . . . Who do we have here?" he asked, looking at Madeline.

"Madeline King, meet Mr. Maurice Jones, aka Slim." John smiled as he made the introduction. "Slim works at this fine establishment."

Slim stretched out his bony hand and shook Madeline's. "It's always a pleasure to meet a beautiful lady," he said, bowing his head politely before turning his attention to John. "You sure know how to pick 'em." He flashed John his trademark goofy grin and gave him a pat on the back. "I can tell this fine lady is one of a kind," Slim said, looking at Madeline as though he was about to salivate.

John had a response for that; but since it wasn't a kind one, he decided to keep it to himself. He took a deep breath. "Let's get the birthday boy out there to greet his public."

Slim nodded, then leaned in close to John and Maxx, giving both men a serious stare. "Uh, Josie and Thelma . . . they're both here."

John let out another deep breath and shook his head; but again, he kept his comments to himself.

"Ain't nothin' but a thing." Maxx laughed, seemingly unaffected by the potential danger. "Matter of fact—the more, the merrier."

Slim ran his hand over his scarce patch of hair. "I love you like a brother, Maxx, you know I do. But I don't want no shit goin' down in here tonight. I put my hide on the line so you could have your party here. There ain't been one single disturbance at the Blue Room since Mr. Hanks opened the doors ten years ago, so please don't make tonight be the first."

John and Slim exchanged worried glances; both men were aware of the damage that could be done. In John's book of rules, two women who had been known to fight, and one man who'd been involved with them both, always equaled trouble.

Maxx threw up his hands and smiled. "Hey, they just women. I got it under control."

Maxx led the procession as he, John, Madeline, and Slim entered the heart of the Blue Room. The mundane exterior belied the true ambience of the establishment. From the aqua blue walls, to the navy blue suede lounge chairs, to the mirrored bar with top-shelf liquor, to the large chandelier, which sparkled with brilliant faux sapphires and dazzling crystals in the middle of the dance floor, the Blue Room was the place where one came to see and be seen in the small town of Nedine. It was the nicest club for black folks in the entire county, and each weekend the place was packed. Tonight it was filled to capacity for Maxx's birthday celebration.

"The party's in full swing," Slim yelled over the lively voices and pounding music that flooded all sides of the room.

From women wearing everything from Afros, to press n' curls and mini skirts, to men sporting tight fades and tailored pants mixed with raw silk shirts, everyone had come dressed to impress, ready to have a good time. When the latest soul tune boomed through the speakers, the movement on the dance floor magnified. Everyone, including the woman they called "One-legged Amy," who walked with a limp, was shaking to the beat.

John wanted to enjoy the good time, but both Madeline's presence and the threat of a catfight between Maxx's women were preventing it.

"I'll be back," Madeline said in an extra-chipper voice, sounding syrupy sweet. "I need to go to the ladies' room."

John reached out and touched her arm. "You sure you're okay?"

Madeline manufactured another smile and said, "I'm fine, John. Why do you keep asking me if I'm okay, and why do you think something's wrong with me?"

"Because you're being nice, and *nice* isn't what you do." He could see that Madeline wanted to tear into him, but instead she shook her head and laughed.

"Remember how you told me this afternoon that if you didn't know any better, you'd have thought I was trying to piss you off on purpose? Well, I feel that way right now."

"I'm not trying to piss you off. I just want to know what's going on with you."

Madeline drew in a deep breath and blew out irritation. "I'm tired of this whole scene. When I come back from the ladies' room, we need to leave this party."

John looked into Madeline's face, not believing her unreasonable demand. "First you begged me to bring you to Nedine with me so you could meet my family and friends and attend this party. Then once you got here, you disrespected my parents, and now you want to leave the very party you said you wouldn't miss for the world and actually threatened me over during the drive here. I knew bringing you on this trip was a bad idea. I should've trusted my instincts and left you back in New York."

"I told you earlier that I didn't want to stay at this party for too long."

"But you said you changed your mind."

"Well, I've changed it again. I'm entitled to do that, aren't I?"

"Not if it involves the kinds of games you're playing."

"I'm not the one playing games, John. You are."

"What?"

"That's right. You claim to love your family so much, and especially your grandmother. But the truth is that you'd prefer to spend the night partying inside a club rather than go visit her. You know we won't have time to see her tomorrow, because she and your parents will be in church by the time we leave in the afternoon. So we need to go now."

John eyed her with suspicion. "What's the real reason you're itching to meet my grandmother?"

"I don't know what you're talking about."

"Disrespecting my parents wasn't enough, huh? Now I guess you want to show out with my grandmother? Well, not on your life. I wouldn't let you near that sweet old woman if someone offered me a pot of gold."

"Fine!" Madeline said in a slightly raised voice. "You don't have to take me to your grandmother's house. But if you don't leave this club with me when I get back, I guarantee you that you'll be sorry."

John's eyes narrowed on hers. "I've been trying to be a gentleman with you, even though you haven't been acting like a lady. But now, Madeline, I've had enough. Threaten me one more time and I'll show you a side of me that you'll live to regret."

Madeline craned her neck in response. "Watch your step, motherfucker, or I'll show you what real regret looks and feels like!" she hissed, then turned on her heels and charged off to the ladies' room.

John was so livid that he felt as if he were having an out-of-body experience. He wanted to run behind Madeline, snatch her by the arm, and follow through on his words. But he knew he couldn't and shouldn't make that kind of move. Number one, he didn't want to go to jail. Number two, high drama wasn't his style. And number three, his father had taught him to be a gentleman, no matter the situation, and always to use his head. So for those reasons, he let Madeline slide.

John couldn't believe the way she was behaving, almost as if she was another person entirely. He wondered what in the hell had gotten into her. Again, he was tempted to confront her, but her present state was so unpredictable he feared she might cause more trouble than Josie and Thelma combined. He hated to leave Maxx, but he knew he had to do something. Once Madeline came back from the ladies' room, who knew what kind of stunt she'd pull?

After Madeline was out of sight, Slim walked over to him. "Your lady looks like one of them models straight outta *Ebony* magazine." He grinned. "She's beautiful, John, and I'm glad to see you finally gonna settle down."

"What makes you think I'm going to settle down with Madeline?"

"Well, I know it ain't every day that you bring a woman back here to Nedine. Plus, we ain't gettin' no younger, so I just thought maybe this one might be the future missus."

John chuckled. "Think again, partner. Everything isn't what it seems, by a long shot."

"Oh? Damn, I guess everything that glitters ain't gold."

John rubbed his chin and nodded. "Man, you don't know the half of it."

"Trust me, I do. Even here in little ol' Nedine, you'd be surprised how crazy the women be actin' nowadays."

"Speaking of crazy," John said, looking over at Maxx, "I don't think he knows that he's playing with fire."

Maxx was at the bar, flirting with an attractive young woman. Now, instead of two women vying for his attention, he'd upped the ante to three. Josie's and Thelma's scowls grew larger by the second as they both looked on from opposite corners of the room while Maxx flirted shamelessly at the bar.

Josie had been Maxx's on-again, off-again lover for as long as anyone could remember. They couldn't live with each other, but they couldn't go too long without having some type of contact, either, even if it involved cursing and screaming—always on Josie's part. They were a complicated mess. On the other hand, he and Thelma had enjoyed what appeared to be a blissful year-long relationship. But they had recently broken up a few weeks ago . . . in large part due to Josie.

Slim shook his head; his eyes were filled with worry. "I told that fool I didn't want no mess tonight. Now look at him. He ain't gon' stop till some shit hits the fan."

"Looks like it." John sighed, hoping it wouldn't come to that, but knowing it probably would.

Maxx was laughing, holding up his glass, and signaling for the bartender to pour him another drink. He leaned over and whispered something into the young woman's ear; whatever he said made her throw her head back and join him in laughter. Seeing this only made the scowls on both Josie's and Thelma's faces grow harder.

"Go talk to him, John. You're the only one who can reason with him. He'll listen to you," Slim said.

"I wish I could, but I'm gonna have to leave in a few minutes. I need to take Madeline back to the hotel."

"What?" Slim said, panicked. "You can't leave. I need your help!" Slim watched as Josie's and Thelma's stares intensified. "If anything goes down, I'm on the hook for it."

"Sorry, Slim, but I've got to get Madeline back to the room. I might be able to return after I drop her off."

"Why do you have to take her back? Is something wrong with her?"

Yes! She's mean as a snake and crazy as hell, he thought, but he couldn't say that aloud. "We're not getting along too well. I just need to take her on back."

"Women!"

"You can say that again. I had no intention of leaving this early, but she wants to go, so—"

"You stayin' at the Holiday Inn, right?" Slim asked.

"Yeah."

"I'll make you a deal. I'll take her back to the hotel if you go over and talk to Maxx. I can't afford to have a fight breakin' out. The boss man's gonna hold me responsible for whatever damage is done."

John wanted to help his friend, but he knew that Madeline would never leave the club without him, especially after the threat she'd leveled. "I'm sorry, Slim, but I have a responsibility, too. I brought Madeline here, so I need to make sure she gets back to the hotel safely."

Slim looked almost crestfallen as he surveyed the trouble brewing over at the bar and on each side of the room. "John, I'll get your girl back to the hotel, safe and sound. I just need for you to help me out, man."

Both men were startled when they heard Madeline's voice interrupt their conversation as she walked up on them. "Slim, thank you for being such a gentleman and offering to take me back to the hotel. I'm ready to leave whenever you are."

John was stunned. "You've got to be kidding me."

"No, I'm not. You heard me right."

"You were just complaining and demanding that *I* take you back."

"I changed my mind," she said as she gave him a nasty stare.

John was so heated he wanted to hit something. This was the proverbial straw that broke his back. He'd tried to be reasonable beyond measure and had even given in to her unreasonable request, all for the sake of civility. But Madeline's crazy games had pushed him over his limit. "Take her," he said.

John was through with her now. He didn't even look at Madeline as he headed toward the bar to play peacemaker.

Chapter 17

Madeline was slowly losing control, sliding down a steep slope. All her well-laid plans were cresting toward a dramatic and disappointing crescendo. Everything she'd worked so hard for was about to crumble—all because she'd left two tiny bottles of prescription drugs back home in her medicine cabinet.

She'd been taking anti-anxiety and psychotropic medications for seven years now. The drugs had helped her tremendously in her struggle to keep her temper in check and her fury-laced mood swings at bay. When people angered her, she no longer lashed out or became violent at the drop of a dime like she used to. Instead, she calmed herself and calculated her strategy in a rational manner before exacting deadly revenge. Yes, she was so much better!

She'd only had a few outbursts in the years since she'd been taking her meds, and those were minor in comparison to the incidents she'd been involved in during her tumultuous past. These days she was able to maintain a lucrative corporate career and enjoy romantic relationships in a manner that would never lead one to believe she was capable of blackmail, fraud, and murder—all of which she had committed in the past.

She never took her medication daily, as was prescribed by her doctors, because they often made her feel sleepy and not her full, vibrant self. But she made sure she kept just enough in her system to function without slipping back into deviant behavior. However, the excitement of traveling to John's hometown and finally getting close to his family and his money had enticed her so much that she'd completely forgotten to take her pills over the last several days.

She'd been in a rush the night before they left town, busy with last-minute packing, and had only gotten a few hours of sleep before they left for the airport the next afternoon. She'd hurried out the door so fast that she once again forgot to take her medication, let alone pack the bottles in her travel bag.

Madeline didn't realize the mistake she'd made until late yesterday afternoon, when she and John were riding in their rental car, about 30 miles outside Nedine. They had stopped at a gas station to fuel up again and grab a quick snack. When she climbed out of the car, she felt slightly unsettled and more than a little annoyed. John was smiling about the beautiful trees and scenic landscape they would pass on their way to town, but she was less than thrilled.

"You'll enjoy seeing God's gift of nature and the special beauty it holds when you look out and see the trees and wide, open pastures," he'd said.

Little did he know, she didn't give a damn about nature and she had no interest in looking at trees or pastures. But again, she did what she had done all her life and faked it to get what she wanted. Now she was beginning to feel a bad mood coming on and she was close to giving John a piece of her mind.

At first, she thought she was feeling agitated because of the long travel day she'd endured. But when an urge came over her to kick the passenger door while John was pumping gas, she instantly knew what she'd done. *Fuck! I forgot my medicine!* she shouted inside her head.

"What was that?" John asked, peering over the top of the car at Madeline.

"What was what?"

"That bang. It sounded like something hit the side of the car where you're standing. You didn't hear it?" he asked.

Madeline shrugged her shoulders innocently as she put her foot back on the ground. "No, I didn't hear a thing. I think you're just tired. We need to get off the road because you're starting to hear things."

Once they arrived in Nedine, she was in full-on panic mode, but she knew she needed to be calm. She'd thought about taking a cab to one of the local drugstores in town so she could get her prescriptions filled while John was out earlier today. However, she remembered that she'd forgotten to bring the fake ID for the alias under which her medications were written.

She knew her only hope now was to try and maintain her temper as best she could and pray that the slow-minded hillbillies around her wouldn't piss her off. But it was a battle she was losing because John's parents had already managed to work her last nerve. She didn't like the fact that they were standing between her and John's money, which she planned to make her own. She could tell his attitude toward her was already starting to change.

Nothing was going the way she wanted, and she knew she had to quickly reassess the situation so she could turn around her fate and potential fortune. When she excused herself to go to the restroom in the club, she used that time to splash water on her face, gather her thoughts, and craft a new plan. Getting in good with John's family and even his grandmother was out of the question, so now she had to set her sights on ensnaring John in a different way.

"I got it," Madeline whispered to herself with a mischievous grin as she exited the crowded ladies' room. "He'll never know what hit him—and even if he does, it'll be too late."

She walked out and heard John and Slim squabbling about who would drive her back to the hotel. "Perfect," she whispered under her breath. This was going to be easier than she'd thought. "They're feeding right from my hands."

She wanted to laugh at the look that clouded John's face when she thanked Slim for being such a gentleman and agreed to leave the club with him. She couldn't get out of there soon enough so she could carry out her plan. And the best part was that she didn't have to look for some poor, unsuspecting victim because goofy-acting Slim had volunteered himself on a silver platter.

Madeline and Slim headed on their way out, walking side by side toward the back door through which they'd come. Madeline followed Slim to the far right side of the parking lot, and watched him smile sheepishly as he opened the passenger door to his rusty old Chevy truck. She thought it looked like the first motor vehicle ever made. She had deep reservations about getting inside when she cast her eyes on the tattered front seat.

"I know it ain't a fancy Mustang, but it'll get us to where we need to go," Slim said.

Madeline didn't want to stand near Slim's raggedy piece of what she barely considered a truck, let alone have to actually ride in it. However, she knew what was at stake, so she sucked up her disdain. She raised her arched eyebrow and gave Slim a wicked smile.

"You all right?" he asked.

Madeline reached over, took Slim's hand into hers, and held it tightly. "Yes, as a matter of fact, I'm feeling great."

"Uh, well, I reckon that's a good thing, huh?"

"It's a fantastic thing."

Slim nodded. "All righty, I guess we'll be on our way."

Madeline slid into Slim's front seat and watched him closely as he walked around to his driver's door. She almost felt sorry for the unsuspecting fool because she knew he had no idea what he was getting himself into.

Allene's feet slowly shuffled across her immaculate hardwood floors as she walked back to the comfortable La-Z-Boy recliner that Isaiah had bought her a few years ago. Her heart was filled with joy when she thought about what a good son Isaiah had always been.

When she'd carried him in her womb, she never had a day of morning sickness. When he was born, the midwife who delivered him said it was the smoothest birth she'd ever witnessed. When he

was just ten years old, he went to work to help the family after his father died of pneumonia and Allene had been stricken with grief.
During those hard years, Isaiah never complained. Instead, he looked
for ways to make life more comfortable for the family while toiling in
the fields each day. "That boy's always been special," Allene said aloud.
"Just as smart as a whip. He might not have the gift, but he's so wise
he's pretty close to it."

She continued to think about Isaiah as she sank down into the
plush chair, and then her mind fell on John. Although she was fairly
certain that her grandson had begun to see the light and had discovered his girlfriend for who and what she really was, she knew he still
wasn't safe from the clutches of Madeline King.

Allene had wanted to intervene and tell John that Madeline was a
world full of trouble, and that he should break up with her before
they returned to New York. *Let her walk back home if you have to,* she'd
wanted to blurt out when they were sitting on her front porch earlier
today. She knew he would have listened to her, because he trusted
her, and he knew she would never steer him wrong. But she also
knew it was best to keep quiet so he could find out on his own.

Allene had learned long ago that she had to use her gift wisely,
and that sometimes knowing the outcome of something could dis-
rupt the journey of getting there. On more than a few occasions, she'd
seen how intervening at the wrong time could alter situations in unexpected and sometimes disastrous ways.

Allene closed her eyes and tilted her head back as if talking to the
heavens. "Thank you, Lord Jesus, for givin' me the family I have," she
said aloud. "And bless me to help them as best I can."

Allene took a deep, cleansing breath. Having premonitions was
like second nature to her. As she concentrated, with her eyes still
closed, a smile came to her lips. The scene appeared to her as clear and
as bright as this morning's sun had been. There, in her line of vision,
was her great-great-granddaughter, standing before a large crowd.
The young woman was speaking passionately, pouring out the desires
of her heart.

"That's right, baby. Follow your passion just like your mama did,"

Allene whispered. "Speak what's in your heart. Say what it is that you desire, and watch it walk into your life."

Allene smiled again. "Alexandria," she whispered into the air. She could see the young woman: tall, slender in build, but curvy in shape, with the kind of posture girls were taught at finishing school. Allene could see that Alexandria was beautiful, with smooth, light caramel-colored skin and eyes that looked as though they could see right through you. "She looks just like her mama," she said with a nod.

Allene was proud of her great-granddaughter, Victoria. She was grateful she would live long enough to meet her. She smiled wide when she thought about the vision she'd had a few days ago. She'd closed her eyes and saw John bringing little Victoria back to Nedine for visits. Allene's heart leapt with happiness when she saw a pigtailed Victoria happily eating the lemon drops she always kept in her crystal bowl on her living-room coffee table.

She let out a small sigh when she saw the ups and downs Victoria would struggle through. Some of her visions were clear, while others were a bit murky. Allene was glad that she'd contacted Alexandria to set things into motion. Now, not only would Alexandria be able to help herself, she'd be able to help her mother for the trouble that was about to come.

As Allene thought about Victoria's journey, her mind shifted to Alexandria, whom she would never meet in this lifetime, but whom she would come to know through the precious gift they both shared. She reflected on that knowledge in the quiet that surrounded her. She was thankful that Susan Jessup had prepared her for these moments, guiding her with wisdom.

But she had to remember that just as Susan had guided her—and, in turn, Allene had guided Isaiah, and now John—Allene could only show Alexandria the way. The girl would have to walk the path for herself.

"Choose wisely," Allene whispered, knowing that Alexandria could hear her in another time and place. "The love you want is already waiting for you."

Chapter 18

After circling around the crowded block several times, Alexandria finally found a parking spot. She waited for a moment before turning off the engine, debating whether or not she should call Peter and ask him to come join her. She'd been going back and forth about what she should do. Her instincts, along with her mother's good advice, told her that she needed to end her relationship. But the compassionate part of her had a hard time making that decision, because she knew all too well what it felt like to be dumped by someone you cared about.

After several minutes of contemplation, she decided to give things between them one last try. "All right, here goes."

Peter picked up on the second ring. "I thought you'd be here by now," he said, sounding slightly annoyed.

Alexandria ignored the frustration she heard in his voice. "My day got off to a late start, then I went over to my parents' and stayed quite awhile. I just left, and with a container full of my mom's triple chocolate-chip cookies." She hoped that last part would lighten the mood.

"Uh-huh . . . so, are you on your way?"

"Actually, I was hoping we could hang out tonight."

Peter breathed heavily into the phone. "I had hoped we could spend a quiet evening here and finish our discussion from last night."

"What more is there to discuss?" She wanted to move forward, not backward, and now she had a feeling she was going to regret dialing Peter's number.

"Our relationship, Alexandria. How about that for a start?"

"I can tell by your tone that you're pissed, so I'm not sure that's a good idea, given that it's very hard to talk to you when you're like this. That's why I was hoping we could put last night behind us and hang out and have some fun for a change."

"So you don't think we have fun?"

"You interpret everything the wrong way. Why are you being so negative?"

"You're the one who said it, not me."

"I'm trying to give us a chance, Peter. Can't you see that?"

The line was quiet, with neither of them saying a word. Alexandria finally spoke up and said, "I was hoping you could meet me at the Lazy Day so we can—"

"You know I hate that place," Peter interrupted.

Alexandria moved the phone away from her ear and looked at it as if to say, *What the hell?* Now she was becoming upset. "You don't see me getting all geeked up about going to soccer games with you, but I do it because I know it's something you enjoy."

"I thought you liked soccer."

"Peter, when have you ever heard me say that?"

"Well, you've never said you didn't."

"When we first started dating, I told you that soccer wasn't my thing, but I'd go with you if you wanted me to, and I have, without one single complaint. You don't even play the sport, but I go to those long, boring games because you enjoy watching it. I eat and breathe spoken word, yet I've practically had to drag you to the Lazy Day on the few occasions you've bothered to come. And the entire time you're in the audience, you sit there like you're sucking on a lemon."

"I don't remember you saying you didn't like soccer."

She noticed that he completely sidestepped the point she'd just made, and his insensitivity rubbed against her nerves. "Have you even been paying attention to me? Have you been listening to me at all?"

"If I had known you didn't like coming to the games with me, I would've never asked you to. I don't think you should expect people to do things you know they don't like."

Alexandria could only shake her head. The fact that Peter had the nerve to say what had just come out of his mouth let her know he was completely clueless. His comment also spoke volumes about his willingness, or lack thereof, to compromise.

Alexandria knew from watching her parents that husbands and wives often did things they didn't necessarily want to do in order to make their spouse happy. Her father had once told her, "If you love someone, Alexandria, you'll do what you can to make that person happy because the smile he'll wear will end up being your own."

A tidal wave of emotions mixed with reality came crashing down on Alexandria. She'd often wondered why she had stayed in her relationship with Peter for so long. Why had she put up with his regimented lifestyle? Why had she made excuses for and purposely overlooked his lack of consideration? And to top it all off, why had she tolerated his inability to make love to her the way she wanted and needed, always leaving her sexually unfulfilled? Now as she stood at the gateway of truth, she knew the reason she'd accepted those shortcomings—it was because she was scared, and he was safe.

With Peter, she didn't have to dig too deep or go too far because those exercises required effort and sometimes pain, and she'd had no interest in delving into either. He was predictable; and in a world that had been filled with random voices and spirits she couldn't control, she needed something steady to anchor her in normalcy. But what she hadn't known until today, after coming full circle with her mother, was that she had an anchor all along and didn't even know it.

Her small car had become stuffy with her thoughts, along with the absence of a running air conditioner, so she stepped outside into the sticky heat of the night. She took a deep breath, looked up into the black sky, and smiled. It was nothing less than beautiful. Shining stars beamed down from above and made her shiver. A feeling came over her that could only be described as love. It was warm and different from the summer heat saturating the air. It was close to the same feeling she'd experienced while driving down Peter's street.

As she continued to stare into the sky, Alexandria thought about how glad she was that she'd called Peter, after all. Their conversation had proven beyond a doubt that everything tied to the other end of her phone was over.

"I think you're wrong, Peter," Alexandria said. "When you love someone, you do things for that person because you want to see them happy."

"How about my happiness?" Peter retorted.

"It's always about *you*. You're so selfish. Grow up and act like a man!"

"So now you're challenging my manhood? What the hell's wrong with you? I've bent over backward, trying to understand you. It's like a job trying to figure you out."

Alexandria smiled into the phone. "Don't worry. This is one shift you won't have to work anymore."

She pressed the end button on her phone and headed down the street toward the building that held her future.

"It's great to see you, Alexandria!" Kyle greeted her in his thick British accent. "Where've you been hiding, luv?"

Alexandria knew right away that Kyle, the manager of the Lazy Day, had had one too many drinks. Whenever he was loaded, his accent seemed to grow heavier. Tonight it was so pronounced that he sounded as though he'd swallowed the entire cast of *Downton Abbey*. His thick red hair and light smattering of freckles defied his olive-toned skin, which on most redheads would have been pale and burned, thanks to the unrelenting Georgia sun. But in many ways, Alexandria knew that Kyle was the exception to nearly every rule, just as she was.

"I've had a lot going on. But I'm back," Alexandria responded, accepting Kyle's wet, bourbon-drenched kiss to her left cheek.

"And looking as lovely as eva."

Alexandria could see Kyle's blue eyes roaming her body. If she'd known she was coming to the club tonight, she would have worn something other than the denim shorts and hot pink cotton T-shirt she was sporting. She was glad she'd had an extra pair of strappy stiletto sandals in her backseat. She'd doubled back to her car and slipped them on her feet just before walking into the club. The shoe's unique shape and added height accented her thick thighs and shapely legs, giving her a carefree, sexy edge.

"Thanks for the compliment, Kyle," she said with a hint of a smile. "How's it going tonight?" They were standing to the side of the stage, nodding and giving light hugs to familiar artists as they walked by.

"It's poppin' as you'shal," Kyle slurred. "The house is packed and the crowd is hyped."

Alexandria surveyed the large, dimly lit room and could see that it was indeed packed, maybe even more than most Saturday nights she could remember. "Think you can fit me into the lineup?" Alexandria knew that regardless of how many artists were scheduled to appear onstage tonight, Kyle would make sure she was one of them. She was just that good, and she knew that he knew it, too. Still, she wanted to be respectful and never act as though she was full of herself.

"Are you bloody kiddin' me? Hell yeah!" he said with excitement. "It's been a whole month since we've seen your beautiful face or heard you spit some wisdom for us mere mortals fortunate enough to live in your world."

"Kyle, you're too much."

"I'm serious as a fuckin' heart attack, luv. You know I don't bull-shit."

Just then, Cheryl, a tall, blond-haired waitress, with a build befitting a *Muscle & Fitness* model, walked by. She was carrying a tray full of drinks with the ease of a professional.

"Don't mind if I do," Kyle said as he reached for a drink.

Cheryl swatted at Kyle's hand. "Connie has her eye on you, so slow your roll."

Alexandria exchanged a knowing glance with Cheryl as they watched Kyle back down into submission.

Connie Mallet was the owner of the Lazy Day, and also Kyle's longtime girlfriend. In their case, mixing business with pleasure worked very well. Connie was the brains of the operation, and Kyle was the tough brawn.

"You better not misbehave," Alexandria teased. "Connie don't play!"

"So what are you going to perform tonight, anything new?" Kyle clearly wanted to change the subject and get back to her performance.

Alexandria had asked to take the stage, but she hadn't thought about what she would perform. She usually knew exactly what she was going to say and do, but tonight was unplanned. All she knew was that she needed to be there. So she surprised herself when she told him, "Yes, I have a new piece I'd like to try."

Where did that come from? she thought.

"All right!" Kyle said. "I'll introduce you after the Dead Poet."

Alexandria knew that meant she had less than five minutes to take the stage, because the artist known as the Dead Poet was about to finish up. She had an arsenal of pieces she could perform, but she didn't have anything new. In fact, she hadn't written anything in her journal in weeks. Now she had to scramble to come up with something good, especially since she had to follow an artist like the Dead Poet, who always brought down the house with his performances.

Just as she was gathering her thoughts, she heard applause from the crowd and saw the Dead Poet take a bow. He winked at her as he exited the stage in her direction.

"Sister Alexandria, so good to see you again," the Dead Poet said with a genuine smile.

Alexandria had always admired the man's oration and performance skills. Tall, dark, and handsome, he didn't have to say a word to mesmerize a crowd; his good looks did that trick. But when he spoke, it was magic.

"I'm doing well, Poet." Alexandria smiled as she received his full-body hug.

"We've missed you, sister."

"I've missed being here."

Before they could exchange more pleasantries, Alexandria heard Kyle's voice revving up the crowd.

"It's been a while, but this phenomenally gifted lady is back!" Kyle bellowed. "Please give a warm Lazy Day welcome to the beautiful and talented Alexandria."

"Do your thing out there," the Dead Poet said.

Alexandria slowly walked onto the stage, smiling as she heard hands clapping in a vigorous rhythm, which formed applause. She felt good standing before the crowd. The only problem was that she still didn't know what she was going to say. She closed her eyes and suddenly she heard the now-familiar voice of her great-great-grandmother whisper into her ear.

"Speak what's in your heart. Say what it is that you desire, and watch it walk into your life."

Alexandria felt the truth of Grandma Allene's words. She thought about what she wanted, and what she desired. She opened her eyes and looked out upon the packed crowd. The lights were down low; the large room was so quiet, you could hear cotton fall to the floor. She took a deep breath and began to speak.

"How y'all feelin' tonight?" she asked.

There were various responses, including one person who yelled out, "Ready to hear you drop somethin' on us!" The crowd roared and clapped again.

Alexandria smiled and nodded her head. "You know, life is funny," she said. "I had other plans tonight, but something deep within my soul spoke to me and I ended up here, on this stage, and I know this is exactly where I'm supposed to be."

A woman in the crowd belted out a hallelujah, while another raised her hand silently pumping a power fist into the air.

"I asked Kyle if I could perform tonight, not knowing what I was going to get up here and say. I haven't written any new pieces, and I don't want to repeat some of the ones I've already performed. So I'll tell you what I'm going to do. I'm going to take my great-great-grandmother's advice. She's been guiding me lately," Alexandria said with a chuckle. "Grandma Allene, as we call her in my family, whispered into my ear, and she told me to speak what's in my heart. She said to say what it is that I desire, and watch it walk into my life.

"So I'm going to speak what's in my heart, and Lord knows I hope I get what I desire, but, more important, what I need."

Alexandria took another deep, cleansing breath, releasing the last of her fears. "I know exactly what I desire," she said, and then paused. "I want to experience real love. The kind of love I don't have to question. The kind I can believe and trust in. The kind that'll have my back when the chips are down and support me when I need it most. The kind of love that'll catch me if I fall, and then help me stand up tall again. And I want the kind of love that'll make me cry out in sweet ecstasy when he's making love to me. How many of y'all out there want that kind of love?" she asked the audience.

Nearly everyone in the room, men and women alike, threw their hands in the air and waved their arms, too.

Alexandria smiled. "All right, so tonight I'm going to talk about how it's supposed to feel when you experience that kind of love. Here goes." She closed her eyes and held the microphone close to her lips:

"Making love is all five senses at once.

"It's one of the most natural, organic, and intimate ways of showing affection for another person.

"It's powerful.

"It's captivating.

"It's all-consuming.

"Making love is one of the few acts you can enter into with another person that allows you to engage all five senses at once.

"You touch them—the delicate feel of their warm skin as you run your fingers along the length of their soft body, caressing them gently.

"You hear them—their lust-filled cries and moans as they pant their pleasure, beat for beat, into your ear.

"You taste them—their salty-sweet skin on the tip of your tongue as you devour them, inch by inch.

"You see them—the contours of their naked flesh pressed against your own as rhythmic thrusts create ecstasy.

"And you smell them—the undeniably, intoxicatingly hypnotic scent that only raw, uninhibited sex can create.

"When you make love, make it count. Making love is a magnificent and wondrous act.

"It nourishes.

"It awakens.

"It strengthens.

"It lets you know you are alive.

"Making love allows you to embrace all your senses, free your emotions, and touch life with your whole hand.

"Tap into your senses. Embrace your partner. Taste them slowly, touch them gently, look upon them lovingly, hear them fully, and breathe in the sweet fragrance of their scent.

"Make love, and make it count.

"Thank you," Alexandria said in a quiet whisper.

She took a small bow; and when she lifted her head, she heard the dizzying sound of clapping hands and the sight of several people standing to their feet.

She left the stage just as quietly as she'd come out, with the crowd still cheering her on. The Dead Poet bowed to her, and Kyle walked over, arms extended. "See what you've done," he said. "Now I've got to find Connie so I can make it count."

Alexandria laughed. "I'm sure she'll appreciate that."

"I betta make sure she bloody well does," Kyle said with a mischievous grin.

Alexandria felt as though she was floating on a cloud. Performing tonight had been the boost her spirit needed, and she thanked Grandma Allene for guiding her toward what she needed to do.

An hour later, Alexandria was on her way out of the club when she spotted a tall man standing in the distance. He was leaning casually, with one shoulder pressed against the wall, right outside the exit door, which had been propped open to accommodate the in-and-out flow of tonight's unusually large crowd.

Even in the distance, she could see that the man's physique was that of someone who spent time in the gym, as was evidenced by his bulging biceps, which outlined the light blue shirt he wore. Alexandria could also see that his faded jeans hung well on his frame, and that his body language screamed of masculine confidence. Even in the distance, the one thing she knew for sure was that whoever this man was, he was definitely fine!

The closer she got, she could see that his eyes were focused on her; and when she returned his stare, she saw his lips curve to form a smile. Any other time, if she'd seen a shadowy figure—handsome or not—who appeared to be hanging around waiting for her after a performance, she would have been ready to call club security. She'd come to learn that there were a lot of lunatics running around Atlanta's night scene masquerading as sane people. But for some reason, she wasn't the least bit afraid of this man.

As Alexandria drew even closer, her body felt the same type of warmth she'd experienced earlier when she had looked up into the night sky just before entering the club.

She was only a few feet away when the mystery man came into full view under the overhead lighting. He was indeed handsome—beautiful, in fact. Looking at him, Alexandria was so stunned that she was at a temporary loss for words. He was familiar to her in so many ways. She knew this man, but she couldn't put her finger on how or from where.

"Alexandria Thornton," the handsome man said. His voice was deep, rich, and full. The sexy familiarity of his tone made Alexandria smile, despite trying not to do so.

"Yes, that's me," she replied, managing to keep her composure intact.

"Do you remember me?"

Alexandria slowly walked to within an arm's length of the six-three Adonis, looked into his eyes, and smiled as if she'd just won a prize. She could barely believe it, and she blinked twice to make sure he was real.

He was her playmate when they'd been children in Jack and Jill. He was the best friend she tagged along with on the playground during recess. He was the little boy who'd grinned happily beside her in the picture she'd seen this afternoon. And now, over twenty years later, he was standing before her in front of the Lazy Day, looking fine enough to devour.

Alexandria's heart raced a mile a minute. "PJ, is that you?"

"Yes, Ali. It's me."

Chapter 19

John quietly counted to ten, finally slowing his pulse to a manageable rhythm. It was an exercise he rarely had to practice, save for the few occasions when he stood in jeopardy of losing his cool composure—and this time was one of them. Madeline had managed to test his gentlemanly principles, grinding his nerves down to a tiny nub. And now, as he headed toward the crowded bar of the Blue Room, it looked as though Maxx's antics were about to finish the job.

Maxx was downing another glass of potent brown liquid, inviting trouble with each sip of his drink. He leaned forward, making sure his suggestive smile landed squarely between the plunging cleavage of the pretty young woman sitting on the barstool beside him. John could see from their body language that Maxx and his companion were just a few moves shy of full-on body groping and a heated lip-lock.

The sight made John uneasy because he knew that if Josie or Thelma saw Maxx kissing another woman, they would both come out of their corners, swinging.

I have to stop him before things get out of hand, John thought as he walked slowly toward the side of the bar where Maxx was courting danger.

As John maneuvered his way through the tightly packed crowd, women smiled, flirted, and made not-so-accidental body contact with

him. All were offering a hint of something more than genteel Southern hospitality in their gestures. But John wasn't interested in their advances. After having dealt with a neurotic girlfriend all day, meeting
new, untested women was the last thing on his mind. His only focus
was aimed on his best friend and the trouble brewing just a few feet
away.

"How're you holding up?" John asked Maxx when he finally
reached the bar. He looked at his friend; then he gave the scantily
dressed young woman beside him a friendly nod.

"Man, I'm havin' a ball!" Maxx said, slurring his words.

"Yes, I can see that."

"John, I want you to meet the most beautiful woman in this
whole club," Maxx yelled out above the loud, thumping music. He
leaned in toward the pretty woman at his side. "This sexy lady right
here is Ginger. Ain't that right, baby?"

The seductress tossed back her head full of freshly pressed curls
and smiled. "Actually, my name's not Ginger. It's Jennifer. But, honey,
you can call me 'baby' anytime you want, 'cause I like the sound of
that."

A mischievous grin slid across Maxx's face. "Oh, so you like that,
huh?"

"Um-hmm," the woman purred. "I like it a lot."

"Well, baby, I got somethin' else I think you gonna like even
better."

Just as Maxx was about to make his next move, John interrupted.
"Jennifer, please excuse Maxx for just one moment." John didn't wait
for Maxx to object or for Jennifer to react. He took Maxx by the arm
and led him to the back of the bar, near the employee entrance.

"Man, why'd you pull me away?" Maxx asked. "I was just about
to—"

"Start some shit and cause some trouble," John told him in a calm
voice.

"Man, I'm just enjoyin' myself. Hell, it's my birthday. I'm entitled
to have some fun."

John spoke in an even and deliberate tone. "Fun, yes, you're entitled. But to cause a scene and start some shit? Hell no, you're not. Slim
nearly pissed his pants just thinking about what might happen if your
women get out of control in here. His ass is on the line with his boss,
and yours is on the line with those women." John nodded toward
Josie and then to the other side of the room at Thelma. "Just be cool,
you dig?"

"Man, I know what the hell I'm doin', do *you dig?*"

John shook his head, still maintaining a calm, even voice as he
spoke. "You can't possibly understand what you're doing, otherwise
you'd walk away from that woman at the bar."

"Brothah, there ain't a cat in this club who'd walk away from
some good stuff like that."

"You're right. A cat wouldn't, but a grown-ass man would. You're
too old for this shit, my friend."

Maxx opened his mouth, poised with a comeback, but then he
fell silent. Even in his inebriated state, he had enough clarity to see
that John was sincere and that he meant business. His best friend's no-
nonsense glare spoke volumes for what his cool exterior did not.

"There's a right way and a wrong way to do everything," John
cautioned. "And right now, you're headed in the wrong direction.
Don't turn a celebration into a disaster, man. You've got two women
in here who won't think twice about making a scene. They've done it
before, and they'll do it again," he said, referring to the incident last
summer when Josie and Thelma cursed out Maxx and then each
other at the county fair. "Just drink, have some fun, and keep your
hands to yourself until you leave this club."

Just as John was about to drive his final point home, an impossi-
bly soft-spoken voice managed to float above the noise and made him
pause. At first, he could barely make out what the woman was saying;
but as he strained to pay attention, her words became clear.

"You should listen to your friend, Maxx. He's giving you some
good advice."

John turned around to find a woman standing in front of him

whose beauty was so stunning his mind couldn't process the feeling that instantly resonated within him—a feeling that rendered him speechless, which wasn't an easy thing to do.

Her smile was wide and inviting; her eyes were clear and bright. He took in every inch of the petite beauty. Her milky, fawn-colored skin was so smooth that it looked like raw silk. Her rosy pink lips were full and ripe, like succulent fruit, and her high cheekbones and regal nose beckoned that attention must be paid to her prominent features. He could see that his obvious stare had made the beautiful woman blush, as was evidenced by the demure smile she gave him when their eyes met.

John was intrigued by everything about her and by every small movement she made. He watched her closely as she lifted her delicate hand toward her face and pulled her hair back, exposing her high-sweeping forehead. He smiled as she blushed again and tugged on her slim-fitting miniskirt, pulling it against her shapely leg.

Her beauty was unlike any he had ever seen; it was an intriguing combination of traditional meets exotic. The light complexion of her skin, the fine, straight texture of her hair, and the sharpness of her nose and cheeks called out the European blood that obviously flowed through her veins. But her sumptuously full lips, high forehead, thick thighs, and curvaceous hips all led to a trail that went back to the motherland of her African roots.

He didn't know how he knew it, but in that instant, John was sure that the five-two blushing beauty in front of him was the feeling he'd awoken to this morning—the feeling that something great was about to happen. She was what his grandmother had told him would enter his life when he least expected it. And she was a force that continued to hold him speechless until Maxx interrupted his thoughts.

"Lizzy! I can't believe you came!" Maxx said with new excitement.

If Maxx had not called the young woman by "Lizzy," the nickname he'd given his sister when she was five years old, John wouldn't have known that the gorgeous creature in front of him was none other than Elizabeth Sanders, the youngest child of the Sanders clan, and Maxx's baby sister. *This can't be little Lizzy?* John thought.

Elizabeth was ten years younger than John and Maxx, which, for John, had put her out of sight and mind until this very moment. He hadn't seen her in years, and now he marveled at the beautiful woman she had become.

Elizabeth walked up to her brother and gave him a tight hug. "I wasn't about to miss your birthday party, Maxx."

"Thanks, sis." Maxx grinned as he received his sister's affectionate embrace. "I didn't know if you'd make it. The club scene ain't really your thing."

"No, it's not. But you know I wouldn't miss your party," she said with a smile.

After Maxx and Elizabeth's warm greeting, John was still silent, but he realized he had to say something. "Wow, Lizzy, it's good to see you." He immediately wanted to bite his tongue. He couldn't believe he had actually greeted a woman by saying "wow." The only thing cornier would have been "golly." He felt like a tongue-tied, lovesick schoolboy, and he knew he had to pull himself together. "How long has it been?"

Elizabeth smiled, blinking through thick, dark lashes. "About ten years."

"I can see that the last decade has served you well."

"Likewise."

"Damn, time flies," Maxx said, looking at John. "You haven't seen my baby sis since she was in pigtails. And now look at her, tryin' to hang with us grown folks."

"Maxx!" Elizabeth said with embarrassment.

"Lizzy, why you actin' all shy and embarrassed? It's just John."

"Yeah, Lizzy." John smiled, looking into her eyes. "It's just me."

John, Maxx, and Elizabeth returned to Maxx's spot at the bar. John breathed a sigh of relief when he looked over and saw Thelma leaving the club. He knew she was angry because of the scowl she wore on her face when she stormed out the door, but at least she was gone, removing the threat of a catfight. Less than a minute later, Josie sauntered up and gave the "evil eye" to the woman whom Maxx had been talking to; then Josie leaned over and planted a birthday kiss on Maxx's lips that was so salacious it could've made a sinner blush. She'd staked her claim, prompting the scantily dressed woman to look elsewhere for her night's pleasure.

Now Maxx and Josie were holding court at the bar like the king and queen of Nedine, laughing, drinking, and accepting birthday wishes from the room full of partygoers.

"My brother is something else," Elizabeth said to John as they looked on at Maxx.

"That's an understatement."

"Thanks for helping him. I'm glad Maxx can always count on you."

"He's my brother, too," John said. "And please pardon my manners, can I get you a drink?"

"Um, yes, thank you. A Coca-Cola would be real nice." She smiled, straining her soft voice so she could be heard over the sounds of the music thumping in the background.

John smiled back, not surprised that the woman who looked and sounded like an angel wouldn't touch alcohol. He walked down to the other end of the bar and returned with two Coca-Cola bottles in hand, deciding against his preference of vodka and juice.

"Thank you kindly." Elizabeth nodded, taking the soft drink, which John handed her. She raised her bottle and lightly tapped it against his. "Cheers."

Her simple Southern charm felt like the warm sun against his skin. He'd been living up north since his college days and had become accustomed to, and in many ways fond of, the direct nature of northern-bred women. Their sassy boldness and confident air was a turn-on for a powerful young business executive like himself. But as he watched Elizabeth, taking in as much of her as he could without being too obvious, he noticed something that startled him. Her easy way and unassuming sweetness reminded him of his mother. They both possessed the same type of tender gentleness and quiet strength that only Southern women could—the type of women his father referred to as marriage material.

He thought about the fact that he'd been toying with the proposition of getting married someday, but deep down he'd wondered if he would ever find a woman whom he truly loved enough to make his wife. He wanted to be like his father—happily married with children. Isaiah was one of the most blessed men John knew.

Not only was Isaiah a good son, father, and husband, he was loved by many and respected by everyone in his community. He possessed material and personal wealth beyond what most men could ever dream of. And John knew that a large part of his father's considerable success could be attributed to Henrietta Small. "Son, listen to me and listen good," Isaiah had once told him. "There ain't nothin' you can't accomplish if you got a good woman standin' by your side. Your mama is livin' proof of that. I was already doin' good before I married her—but once I made her my wife, she made me a better man."

John had never forgotten his father's words, and he thought about them now as he and Elizabeth stood beside each other, sipping their sodas in silence, surrounded by a room full of noise.

They exchanged a few wordless glances before John finally gathered himself and cleared his throat. "So what have you been up to?" he asked. He had to bend down to talk to Elizabeth. Even though she was wearing high heels, he still towered above her.

Elizabeth moved closer to John, rising up on the tip of her toes so he could hear her. But when the DJ blasted James Brown through the speakers, her soft voice was no competition for the get-down sound.

"You want to step outside where it's a little less noisy?" John asked.

Elizabeth smiled. "Yes, I'd like that."

Chapter 20

Elizabeth was both elated and nervous about being in the company of John Small. His smooth, dark chocolate skin, straight white teeth, and muscular body made her weak in the knees. The smell of his expensive cologne tickled her nose and stirred her senses, causing her to take small breaths in order to maintain her composure. Her delicate hands were shaking slightly, trying not to drop the ice-cold Coca-Cola bottle in her grip. But no matter how hard she tried, she couldn't quiet her excited jitters. She was walking next to the man whom she'd secretly loved for as long as she could remember, and that truth alone made her tremble.

Just as she'd always been taken by John, she knew there were a slew of others who were probably head over heels for him, too. Even as a young girl, Elizabeth had known that John was a magnet for women. She had grown up hearing "ooh" and "aah" whenever her brother's best friend's name was mentioned, followed by "Girl, that John Small is a real catch!" or "He's so handsome, it don't make no sense!" or "Rich and fine!"

The last time she had seen John, face-to-face, she was twelve years old. He had just graduated from college and his parents had thrown a big party in his honor at the local Masonic Lodge temple. Nearly every black person in Nedine had come to the graduation celebration, and even some of the prominent white folks in town had made an appearance.

Her parents had brought her to John's party with them because they didn't want to leave her home alone on a Saturday night. They had stayed less than fifteen minutes, just long enough to place their gift on the table, eat a slice of cake, and drink a glass of punch before leaving. But Elizabeth remembered every detail of the grand affair as if she'd remained there throughout the entire evening. And what had stuck with her most of all was her brief interaction with John.

His smile had been warm and sincere. When he looked at her, his eyes were penetrating, yet gentle. She had been overjoyed when he called her by name and gave her a hug of appreciation for coming. "Thanks, lil Lizzy," he'd said.

But until tonight, that had been the last time she'd had contact with him. There had been several occasions where Elizabeth had seen John over the years, but he'd been completely unaware of her presence. Whenever he was in town for a weekend visit, he would come by her parents' house and pick up Maxx for a boys' night out on the town. Those moments served as her opportunity to see him. She would eagerly rush to the window, like the giddy teenager she was, admiring him as he leaned against the side of his car and waited for her brother in the driveway.

But once Maxx moved across town into a house of his own, Elizabeth's John Small sightings dwindled to once a year, if she was lucky. She found herself looking forward to the holidays, not because of the season's festivities, but because she knew he would be in town. If the stars aligned just right in her favor, she'd be able to spot a glimpse of him at one of the downtown stores when she was out shopping with her mother.

But she knew she wasn't on John's radar because she was too young, a full ten years his junior. Even so, she never gave up hope that one day he would notice her—as a woman.

Now he was thirty-two and she was twenty-two. There was no getting around the fact that he would always be a decade older; but according to the romance novels that filled her bookshelves, love had a way of conquering all things, including age.

As Elizabeth breathed in the humid night air, strolling beside the man who had always given her butterflies at the thought of him, she felt goose bumps creep up on her smooth arms.

"So tell me about yourself, Lizzy?" John asked.

Elizabeth cleared her throat and gave him a smile. She wanted him to know right away that she was no longer the little girl he re- membered, so she gently said, "Well, for starters, I go by 'Elizabeth' now."

"Oh, forgive me, *Miss Elizabeth,*" John said with a chuckle.

His playful teasing made her giggle. "That's okay. I guess folks will always see me as Maxx's little sister, Lizzy."

John slowed a bit and looked into her eyes. "Elizabeth, for what it's worth, you certainly don't look like the little girl I remember."

Elizabeth blushed.

"And I mean that with sincere respect."

"Thank you, John."

They walked a little farther into the parking lot, winding their way through row after row of parked cars. When they came to the edge of the street, they stood still, looking around for what to do next.

"I guess there's really no place to sit and talk out here," John said, wiping away a trace of sweat, which had formed on his brow from the punishing night's heat. "Do you want to go back inside?"

Elizabeth looked up at the sky. "Not really. I know it's hot out here, but it's such a beautiful night. Look at all the brilliant stars in the sky. It's magical."

John looked up. "You ever wished on a star?"

"Plenty of times." She closed her eyes, smiled, and then opened them again. "I just made a wish."

"What was it?"

Elizabeth cut him a glance and smiled, but she didn't answer.

"C'mon, you can tell me," John probed. "It'll be our little secret."

"If I tell you my wish, it might not come true."

"You superstitious?"

Elizabeth shook her head. "Normally, I'm not. But in this case, I don't want to jinx things. Who knows? Finally all my wishing might come true."

"In that case, I hope it does."

They chatted more as they walked up and down the small stretch of gravel at the very edge of the parking lot. They both wanted to continue their conversation, but neither of them wanted to do it standing in front of a nightclub surrounded by cars.

"I'm parked around back," John said. "We can go there and talk, if you like?"

Elizabeth was a little hesitant. As much as she wanted to be in John's company, she knew that women who sat in parked vehicles with men late at night usually did so with a specific mission in mind—like the ones steaming up the car windows that she and John had just walked by. Even though she considered herself a modern, sophisticated young woman, she was still a down-home, old-fashioned Southern girl at heart.

Elizabeth knew that John had had his share of beautiful, worldly women, and she suddenly felt insecure. She quietly wondered how she—a small-town girl—could possibly measure up. She wanted to show him that she was mature and adventurous, the kind of girl who didn't mind steaming up a few windows of her own. But the truth was that she had very little experience with men, or in the ways of the world.

She knew that John was in an entirely different league. Even though she'd gone away to college and had experienced a tiny slice of life, the world in which she lived was a universe away from John's existence. He was a handsome, well-to-do investment banker. Everyone in town knew that he was about to open the city's first black-owned bank. He was in demand, and tonight's display had made that quite evident.

She was deliberating on what to do about John's offer to sit inside his car, when he suddenly spoke up. "We can sit on the hood of my car and look up at the stars. Like you said, the night sky is magical."

Elizabeth gave him a wide smile filled with relief. "I'd like that, John."

Chapter 21

John quietly chuckled to himself as he and Elizabeth walked around to the back parking lot. He had seen the hesitation on her face when he'd asked if she wanted to sit in his car. He knew that many other women would have gladly jumped at the invitation, and some would have even initiated it, but not Elizabeth. She was a "good girl," as he and Maxx would say. He could tell that she was the type of woman who guarded her reputation with care because it meant something to her, and he respected that.

As he and Elizabeth strolled together in the heated darkness, he was glad that Mr. Hanks had allowed him to park in the restricted area around back. The small lot was reserved for the owner and two other employees, making it private from the bustle going on in front of the club and on both sides of the building.

When they reached his car, John extended his hand and helped Elizabeth onto the center of the hood.

"Thank you." She smiled, inspecting the gleaming, freshly waxed auto. "You've always had very nice cars."

John sat beside her at a respectable distance and smiled back. "I can't take credit for this one, it's a rental."

"Well, it's still very nice."

"Thanks, and by the way, what do you know about my cars?"

"You used to pick up my brother in front of our house, remember?"

"That was back in the day. You were—"

"Old enough to remember," she interjected, causing them to break into easy laughter.

John turned toward her, taking in her beauty once again, this time under the shining stars and the glow of the moon. His eyes zeroed in on her petite, yet shapely frame. Her legs were surprisingly long for her size, and her miniskirt highlighted their shapeliness. He wanted to unbutton the front of her fitted, short-sleeved blouse and explore her breasts underneath, then travel up to her inviting lips for a long, passionate kiss. He knew his thoughts were out of the question; so, instead, he breathed deeply, inhaling the whisper sweet fragrance of her rose-scented perfume.

"Tell me about yourself, Elizabeth."

She tilted her head, then looked down at the brown-colored heels that adorned her dainty feet. "What do you want to know?"

"Everything."

"That's a mighty tall order."

"I've got time."

"You sure?"

John gave her a smooth smile. "Of course, I'm sure. Right here is the only place I need and want to be."

Elizabeth looked up at the sky, then back at John. "I thought you might have to leave soon, seeing that Slim left a while ago to take your lady friend back to the hotel so you could help my brother stay out of trouble," she said in her sweet, soft-spoken voice. "Please feel free to correct me, if I'm wrong."

John rubbed his chin, and this time he chuckled out loud. *She's a quiet storm,* he thought. He knew he had been right when he'd sized her up earlier, recognizing the understated strength she possessed, just like his mother.

Elizabeth had just shown him that she was soft enough to be sweet and tough enough to be bold. He was instantly turned on, but he controlled the feeling. He leaned forward and rested his elbows on his knees. He hadn't even thought about Madeline again until Elizabeth mentioned her. "So you saw her?" he asked.

"Yes, I did. I saw you two together, then I saw her leave with Slim."

John straightened his back, wanting to get his point across. "Elizabeth, it's not what it seems."

"You're an eligible bachelor, John."

"My relationship with her isn't what you think."

"Then tell me what it is."

John laughed. "You're really something, you know that?"

"I don't mean to sound abrupt. I'm just curious."

"Curiosity is a good thing. And you're right. Slim took her back to the Holiday Inn, where she and I are staying. But I'm rethinking my relationship with her," he said, pulling no punches. "Once we get back to New York things between us will most likely come to an end."

"Really?"

"Our relationship has run its course, and, unfortunately, it took coming here to Nedine for me to realize it. It's funny how a change of environment can make you see things in a completely new light."

"Sounds like you've had a few revelations."

"You could say that."

They both took in a silent pause, digesting what John had just said before he continued. "When I get back to the hotel, I'm checking into a new room for the night."

Elizabeth nodded her head slowly. "She didn't look like she was too happy when she left with Slim. I'm sure a breakup won't make her feel any better."

"Elizabeth, I know it seems callous. But, like I said, everything isn't as it appears. The revelations you mentioned, well, you don't know the half of it. I realized that she isn't the person I thought she was. As far as a relationship goes, she's not what I want."

"What do you want, John?"

He folded his arms and thought for a moment. "You know, it's funny. We started this conversation with me asking you about yourself, but somehow we've been talking about me this whole time. How did that happen?"

Elizabeth smiled. "I'm sure your life is much more interesting than mine."

"I'll be the judge of that." John winked. "Tell me about yourself. And this time, I'll ask the questions."

They shared another easy laugh. In that moment, John realized that he had laughed and smiled more in the last hour spent with Elizabeth than he had in the last few months.

"Well," Elizabeth began, "I just graduated from Spelman three months ago with my degree in education. I'm staying with my folks for the next two weeks, and then I'm moving to Raleigh, North Carolina. I've been offered a teaching position there this fall."

"Congratulations," John said, clapping his hands in a celebratory applause. "My sister and her husband live in Raleigh."

"I didn't know that. It's a small world."

"Hey, I think I received a graduation invitation from you."

"Yes, I sent you one."

"I'm sorry I couldn't make it. I should have followed up and—"

"That's okay."

"That was a really busy time for me," John said, hoping she knew he was sincere in what he'd just said. He wished he'd sent her a gift or even a simple card. "I'm sorry I missed such a momentous occasion."

"Oh, that's all right. I didn't expect that you'd be able to stop your busy life and come to my graduation. But since you're my brother's best friend and practically family, well, I thought I would invite you, anyway."

"I'm practically family, huh?" John asked.

"Well, um . . . yes. My brother considers you his brother."

"So you see me as what? A big brother, like Maxx?"

Elizabeth shifted in place, pulling her long black hair behind her small ears.

"Is that how you see me?" John asked again.

"No, John. That's not how I see you at all."

"Good, because I certainly don't see you as a sister. And again, I mean that with respect."

"I'm glad." Elizabeth smiled. "Everyone's always seen me as little Lizzy Sanders, Maxx's kid sister. That's who I used to be, but I'm a grown woman now, and I've got dreams and ambitions."

John perked up. "What are they?"

"For one, I want to help shape the lives of young people through education. Children are our most valuable resource and it's important to get them off to the right start at an early age. That's why I'll be teaching second grade. I'm going to make a difference in children's lives, as well as my own."

"Your own?"

Elizabeth nodded. "Yes. I want children."

"How many?"

"As many as God will bless my husband and me, when I get one, to have." She paused and looked at him. "How about you. Do you want children some day?"

John smiled. "As many as God will bless my wife and me to have."

The next hour sped by as if on roller skates. John and Elizabeth talked with a comfort that was both familiar and excitingly new. He discovered that although they appeared to be very different on the surface, he had more in common with her than with any other woman he'd ever dated. He knew it was a good sign that they shared the same social values, outlook on life, work ethic, and love of family. And the clincher was that she was a budding jazz aficionado who loved to cook. *It doesn't get any better than this!* John thought.

"So tell me, Elizabeth, why isn't your man here with you tonight? Is he back in Georgia, at Morehouse?" John asked.

They both let out a nervous laugh behind his question, their first awkward moment since they'd ventured outside the club. John knew why he was uncomfortable, and it was because of the possible answer she might give. But he wondered why Elizabeth seemed to be as well.

"I don't have a man," Elizabeth quietly answered.

"Come again?"

"I said, I don't have a man. A boyfriend, that is."

"Here or back in Georgia?"

Elizabeth shook her head. "Neither."

John didn't want to believe she'd tell a lie. At the same time, though, he found what she'd said nearly impossible to believe. "Why not?"

There was a quiet pause in their conversation; then Elizabeth looked down at her watch. "It's getting late." She hopped down from the hood of the car. "My mother sent a huge cake over from Cora's Bakery and I'm supposed to make sure that Maxx cuts it. I think I better head inside."

John slid from his side of the hood and joined Elizabeth where she was standing, towering over her like a large oak tree. "Yes, I spoke with your mother last week when I was helping with the party plans. I told her that she and your father should come out and celebrate."

"Oh, you know how my folks are. They wouldn't be caught dead in a nightclub."

"Yeah, that's true. My parents are the same way."

Elizabeth nodded and walked toward the steps leading to the back entrance of the club as John followed close behind. But when she reached the second landing, he gently touched her arm, stopping her. "You're good at avoiding questions, you know that?"

His touch made Elizabeth turn around and face him as he stood on the step below. They were now eye level, affording John the opportunity to get a better gauge on her expression. "You never answered my question about why you don't have a man."

Elizabeth fumbled with her hands. "I guess I just haven't met the right one yet."

"Maybe your luck is about to change," John said, repeating the very thing his grandmother had said to him earlier that afternoon.

"It just might."

Even though her actions were subtle, her tone and expression told him that she wanted him just as much as he wanted her. He'd never been as captivated by a woman as he was by Elizabeth, but he knew he had to proceed with caution. She was his best friend's sister, so he had to be mindful in his approach. Still, his overwhelming desire for her led him to do something bold and completely unexpected.

"Elizabeth," John said, taking a small step forward, which planted him so close to her that their bodies touched. "This may sound absolutely crazy, and I actually can't believe I'm saying this, but, hell, it's how I feel. I think you're the woman I've been waiting for all my life."

Elizabeth searched his eyes, as if not believing him.

"I know it sounds a little crazy, especially given the circumstances, but I know when something feels right. I'm thirty-two years old, I've experienced more than most men twice my age, and this is the first time I've felt this way; connected. Connected to you." He paused, taking a deep breath before continuing. "We both want the same things out of life. We both value family and friends. And I believe we'll be good together."

Never had John uttered those words to another woman. He wasn't a man prone to expressing his innermost feelings or falling so hard, so fast. If anyone had told him twenty-four hours ago that he would be on the verge of breaking up with his girlfriend and confessing such emotions for his best friend's sister, he would have thought they were fit for admission to an asylum. But, there he stood, completely enraptured by a woman whom he had known all his life, yet had just discovered tonight.

Elizabeth looked directly into John's eyes, as if searching for something, but she said nothing. So he decided to make an even bolder move. He gently reached out and wrapped her inside his strong arms. He could feel her delicate body tremble against his broad chest. Her sensual heat ignited his manhood, causing it to rise. When he saw her glance down, he knew she could feel his hardness pressing against his pants.

His mouth was mere inches from hers, close enough to smell her warm breath. He was glad she didn't move away or flinch whatsoever. "What do you think about what I just told you?" he softly whispered, his bottom lip lightly grazing hers.

Elizabeth slowly exhaled. "I don't think it sounds crazy at all," she answered in a low, serious voice. "No crazier than the fact that I've wanted to be with you for as long as I can remember."

John's eyes searched her face and saw her truth and sincerity, but he still ventured to ask, "You have?"

Elizabeth nodded. "Yes, John. This might feel new for you, but I've felt this way for a very long time. I always hoped you'd want me the way I want you."

"I do."

"I guess there's something to be said for being patient."

"And fate."

She smiled. "And wishing upon a star."

"Elizabeth?"

"Yes?"

John held her tighter in his embrace, slowly moving his hand up and down the middle of her back. "I want to kiss you," he said, his lips skimming the edge of hers as he spoke. "May I?"

She nodded.

John slowly covered her mouth with his. When their lips met, their bodies hugged even tighter. His arms enveloped her small waist, while hers rested easily on his broad shoulders. Their kiss was long and passionate, and it made him hungry to devour her on the spot. His erection rubbed harder against her inner thigh; this time, when she looked down, she smiled.

"See what you do to me?" John whispered into her ear.

"This feels like a dream, but I know it's not. This is real, right?"

John smiled, nudging her gently so she could feel the full effect of the large bulge resting in his pants.

"Oh, my," Elizabeth purred. "This is definitely real."

Elizabeth closed her eyes and inhaled a deep breath, then let it out. John could feel her heart pounding against his chest. He knew she was either super excited, super nervous, or both. He remembered what she'd said about not having a boyfriend and he wondered how much experience she'd had with men. "I hope I'm not moving too fast."

"Fast?" Elizabeth smiled. "I've been waiting to kiss you all my life, John Small."

They kissed again, this time allowing their mouths to search with more urgency as their tongues mingled and danced. Their hands found new territory to touch above the lightweight fabric of their clothes, causing them to release low moans.

But as good as she felt against his body and in his arms, John knew they needed to stop, because he was on the verge of ripping Elizabeth's clothes off, right there on the back steps of the club. He wanted to make love to her, but he also respected her. And, added to that, he respected his brotherhood with Maxx. He wanted to make sure his best friend was okay with him pursuing Elizabeth before things went any further. So as much as he wanted to check into a new hotel room and bring Elizabeth with him, he eased off, using his iron-tough willpower to tame himself.

They stood in peaceful silence, holding each other. Their bodies swayed back and forth amid the heated night air. "You made me forget all about Maxx's birthday cake," Elizabeth said.

"This is much sweeter than Miss Cora's cake."

"Yes, it is," she whispered into his ear. "John?"

"Yes, baby?"

Elizabeth smiled widely. "What do we do now?"

He kissed her one last time and said, "Let's go inside and have some cake, shall we?"

Elizabeth grinned, looking down at John's pants bulge again. "Okay, but, um . . . let's wait a minute or two."

Chapter 22

After the entire club sang "Happy Birthday" to Maxx, he made a wish, blew out the candles, and then cut the gigantic sheet cake his mother had arranged for his celebration.

John and Elizabeth toasted with another bottle of Coca-Cola, while Maxx settled on water, thanks to Josie. "There's no need in you gettin' so tore down that you won't be able to remember a thing in the mornin'," she had told him.

"This is the best birthday I've ever had," Maxx said with a smile.

Josie fed him cake and they frolicked openly, like love-crazed teenagers. Everyone was having a good time, but in a split second everything changed.

"*Oh no!*" someone yelled out. "*She's got a gun!*"

It was as if the scene was unfolding in slow motion, only it was real time in live action. The loud pop of a bullet sizzled from the gun and sent hot screams careening through the air. Everyone on the dance floor scattered like field mice running for cover.

John's first instinct was to protect Elizabeth. He quickly pulled her behind him, shielding her with his broad body as they ducked to the ground. When he raised his head, he saw a deranged-looking Thelma standing across the room, holding a silver-plated pistol pointed in the direction of the bar.

"You ain't shit, Maxx Sanders! To hell with you!" Thelma screamed. "I'ma kill you, but I'ma get your bitch first." Her face was the definition of rage, and her body was a testament to what unrelenting revenge looked like.

She aimed her gun directly at Josie. Just as she pulled the trigger, letting the deadly bullet fly into the air, Maxx leapt on top of Josie, who was crouched down in fear.

"*Agggghhhh!*" Maxx screamed out in pain as the bullet caught him from behind.

Two men standing by the door rushed Thelma, taking her down to the hard cement floor. "Somebody call the police!" one of the men yelled.

"And an ambulance!" John roared, standing to his feet as he and Elizabeth rushed over to Maxx.

Tears streamed from Elizabeth's eyes and her voice was frantic with fear. "Oh, God! Maxx! Maxx!" she screamed.

Josie lay beneath her longtime love, crying hysterically and screaming just as loudly as Elizabeth. That's when John stepped in and took control. He gently moved Elizabeth to the side and then helped Josie slide from under Maxx's limp body. He knelt over Maxx, who was taking short, labored breaths.

"Just hold on," John told his best friend. "You're gonna be all right. An ambulance is on the way." He looked on as Maxx grimaced in pain. "Damn, where're you hit?"

Maxx grunted and winced in agony. "In the ass."

John blinked twice. "Huh?"

"That crazy bitch shot me in the ass!"

Chapter 23

Madeline was so fed up she wanted to scream, but she knew that measure would only serve to thwart her plans before she could put them into action. So she painted on a fake smile as Slim tinkered with the engine under the hood of his truck. It was bad enough that the radio didn't work, but now the raggedy heap had stalled along the side of the road. It was pitch-black and they were in the middle of nowhere. If it wasn't for the fact that she didn't feel like walking the rest of the ten miles back to the hotel, she would have set out on foot a few minutes ago.

"Can you reach over and give it some juice?" Slim yelled to her from outside.

"What?" Madeline was incredulous.

"Turn the key. Can you turn the key in the ignition?"

Madeline huffed and puffed as she leaned over and turned the key in the ignition. A sputtering sound slowly rolled into a low hum and the engine was purring again.

"Old Betsy's back in business," Slim said as he hopped back into the driver's seat. "Pardon me." He reached over Madeline and opened the glove compartment, removing a tattered old rag, with which he began to wipe his hands.

Madeline looked on in disgust. She was so frustrated that she nearly cursed. At this point, she could feel her anger building again and she knew she needed to get to the hotel quickly, before she lost control with him, like she had with Roger. She silently laughed with satisfaction when the thought of her ex-boyfriend crossed her mind. It had been three full years and his body still hadn't been found.

"You ready?" Slim asked, breaking Madeline from her wicked thoughts.

"I was ready ten minutes ago."

"Oh, well, here we go."

Once they were on their way back down the road, Madeline's temper calmed a bit. She'd never been this long without her medication; but now, the more she thought about it, the better she felt.

For the first time in years, she recognized her old self again, and she liked the old Madeline. No longer did she have to abide by other people's rules or worry about what anyone thought of her actions. She was the one who decided how she was going to act. She was in control. And she could do whatever she damn well pleased.

Yes, she had complete control over the situation at hand, and soon she was going to show John Small that she was not to be trifled with. His money and power were a waste in his hands. Opening a bank in Nedine—of all places—was the most ridiculous, harebrained idea she'd ever heard. But once she convinced him to marry her—and she was able to get her hands on his fortune—she would do away with him, put a halt to the bank before it ever had a chance to open, and live the life of luxury she knew she'd always been meant to enjoy.

"Thank you, Slim," Madeline said with a smile as he helped her out of his truck. "I thought chivalry was dead, but I'm glad to see that you're a true gentleman, and a handsome one at that."

Slim's eyes grew wide. "You think I'm handsome?"

"Of course, I do," Madeline cooed, wiping her sweaty brow. The night was thick with heat, and she knew it was about to get hotter. "In my opinion, you're much better-looking than John."

Slim pushed his thick eyeglasses up the small bridge of his wide nose and looked at Madeline sideways. "You do?"

"Of course, I do. John is okay, but, honestly, he can't hold a candle to you."

Slim gave her a funny look. "I think you about the only person who has that opinion."

"Then I guess you're in luck, because right now I'm the only one who counts." She could tell that Slim was nervous and excited at the same time. She wanted to laugh, but she knew she couldn't blow her cover just yet.

"Come on, I'll walk you to your room," Slim told her with a smile.

When they reached the door, Slim stood at a safe distance as Madeline inserted her key into the tiny hole in the knob.

"Now that I got you here safe, I'ma be on my way." Slim gave Madeline a polite nod and turned to leave.

"Don't go just yet. I was hoping you'd walk me inside."

"Uh, I don't think that's a good idea."

"C'mon, Slim. We're practically friends. Plus, I'll make it worth your while."

"Now I really don't think that's a good idea."

"Of course, it is."

"I told John I'd drop you off and head on back." Slim looked around as if someone was watching him, and Madeline could read in his eyes that he didn't feel comfortable standing in her hotel room's door.

She knew she had to do something before Slim walked out of her clutches and ruined her plan. She quickly feigned dizziness and leaned against the door as she pushed it open. She wiped heavy perspiration from her forehead and breathed in and out, as though taking in air was a laborious task. "I think this Southern heat has gotten the best of me. If you could just help me inside, over to the bed, I'd really appreciate it." She reached out and wrapped her slender arm around Slim's narrow shoulder, giving him no other choice but to help her.

"All right, just hold on to me, real steady-like," Slim said as he helped Madeline into the room.

Once they entered, Madeline quickly closed the door behind them and turned the dead bolt. When Slim heard the heavy lock click into place, he stood in front of her, looking flummoxed. "Hey, what're you doin'?"

As soon as the words escaped his mouth, Madeline smiled widely. She could see that a deep part of Slim knew he'd just made a huge mistake.

Chapter 24

Isaiah and Henrietta had just finished watching the Saturday-night movie and were now settling into bed.

"I wonder how Maxx's party is going?" Henrietta said as she turned out the light on her nightstand.

Isaiah lay on his back, looking up at the ceiling. "I'm sure them youngin's is partyin' and carryin' on like young folks do."

"I guess you're right, dear." Henrietta nodded, letting out a deep sigh.

"What's wrong, Henny?"

"Well, to tell you the truth, I'm still a little worried about John. I know what you said about that girl, but I have a bad feeling in the pit of my stomach that I can't explain. I know that she's the cause of it. Every mother knows when her child is in danger. I have a very uneasy feeling that something bad is about to happen."

Isaiah tilted his head, looking at Henrietta through the small beam of moonlight that shone brightly through their bedroom window. "Henny, you worry too much. I told you that John knows what he's doin'. We raised a smart young man. He can handle himself."

"I don't doubt that, Isaiah. I'm talking about Madeline."

"Oh, shoot. She ain't gon' be around much longer. I already told you that."

"I pray you're right."

Isaiah turned on his side, faced his wife, and smiled. "Have I ever once led you astray since you've known me?"

"No, not even when we used to play in the school yard when we were kids." She smiled and touched the side of her husband's face.

"Henny, I'll do whatever it takes to protect my family, and I'll never sit idly by if I think any of my blood is in danger. So hear me when I say that I know everything's gonna be all right."

"How can you be so sure?"

" 'Cause I have faith in our son. Plus, Mama told me it would be."

Henrietta looked at Isaiah, suddenly filled with a mixture of curiosity and high anxiety. She loved her mother-in-law dearly, and she doted on her more than Isaiah did. Over the years, she and Allene had become very close. When Henrietta's own mother passed away from cancer, nearly thirty years ago, it was Allene who had stepped in and helped with everything from babysitting duties to giving practical, womanly advice. Allene loved Henrietta, and Henrietta loved her right back. But she wasn't blind about her mother-in-law or who the old woman was. In the nearly forty years that she'd been married to Isaiah, it had become impossible for Henrietta to ignore that Allene possessed a special gift—a gift that, at times, frightened her.

Henrietta's mind went back to that fateful night so many years ago when the KKK—Knight Riders, as they were called back then—had burned down the tiny house that she and Isaiah had once shared. She remembered, with an eerie chill, how Allene had predicted the horrific event.

"You and Isaiah need to be careful," Allene said those many years ago. "I been smellin' smoke all day."

"Smoke? Where's it coming from, Mama Allene?"

"A fire."

Henrietta chuckled at her mother-in-law's dry wit. "I figured that much, Mama Allene. But where's the fire coming from?"

"I don't know, chile. But I been smellin' smoke all day long. A fire's on its way, and it's gonna be real bad. You and Isaiah be careful, you hear?"

Later that night, as Henrietta and Isaiah stood in front of the small shack they called home, watching it burn to the ground, Henrietta thought about her mother-in-law's words.

As time went on, there were other instances when Allene had warned them of things that would eventually come to pass, both good and bad. It was her "intuition" that had led the entire family to relocate to Nedine.

"I got a good feelin' 'bout this town, son," Allene had told Isaiah. "Plus, you got some land nearby, so it won't be hard to rebuild. I think Nedine is where you gonna really make it big. Mark my word."

Henrietta marveled at Allene's amazing gift to foretell the future; but unlike her husband, she had never been completely comfortable with it. And now, knowing that Allene had talked to Isaiah about John's safety, she was certain that some sort of trouble was waiting in the wind.

"What did your mother say, and when did she tell you?" Henrietta asked.

Isaiah stared into his wife's worried eyes. "I stopped by to check on her on my way home yesterday afternoon. We talked for a little while and she said she was glad that John was comin' to town 'cause she needed to talk to him. Said there was gonna be some kind of trouble in his path—"

"See, I knew it!" Henrietta cut in. "I told you that Madeline was nothing but trouble. I got a bad vibe from that girl the minute I laid eyes on her."

"Me too. But like I said, she ain't even a issue, Henny. Mama said trouble was comin', but she also said he's gon' be all right. John's got good sense, and he's probably already thinking about how he can get rid of that gal."

"I hope so. Tell me more about what Mama Allene said?"

"Well, you know how Mama is. She don't say a whole lot when she's prophesyin', but you can kinda figure out what she means. She told me she's got to help protect John for the future of this family . . . to secure things for the next generation to come. She's got to be talkin' 'bout the legacy he's fixin' to build with the bank, and that ain't got nothin' to do wit' that gal he's 'bout to be through wit'. Our boy's gon' create a dynasty," Isaiah said, a mixture of pride and sadness hovering in his voice.

Isaiah let out a deep breath as he thought about the cancer that was slowly moving through his body, and the fact that he wouldn't live long enough to see his son fulfill most of his dreams. He had yet to share his condition with Henrietta or anyone else. He'd been praying that the specialist he was scheduled to see in Charleston next week would give him a glimmer of hope for fighting the deadly disease. But after visiting his mother yesterday and hugging her close to him while he swallowed the death sentence she quietly delivered, he knew there was no need to keep his appointment. What was done was done, and he'd have to tell his beloved wife soon. But even though his prognosis was fatal, he was glad he could report that his son was in no danger.

Isaiah reached over and took hold of Henrietta's hand, gently squeezing her soft fingers inside his callused ones. "Henny, Mama made sure to make special mention that John's gon' come through whatever storm is in front of him. We just need to stay prayed up."

Henrietta nestled in close beside her husband's strong body, settling into the comfort of the only man whose bed she'd ever shared. "I have faith in you. And even though it scares me sometimes, I have faith in Mama Allene's words, too. And most of all, I have faith in the mighty God we serve."

Isaiah and Henrietta lay silent and still, syncing their hearts and minds into one unified beat.

Chapter 25

Alexandria still couldn't believe her eyes, or her good fortune. If anyone had told her a few hours ago that she'd be looking into the face of the handsome man whose picture from more than twenty years ago she'd just seen, she wouldn't have believed it. But as she sat across from Dr. Parker Brightwood II—her very first best friend from childhood, whom she'd affectionately known back then as PJ, and whom she hadn't seen since they were six years old—she would have thought it highly improbable.

For someone who had the ability to reach back into the past and glimpse toward the future, this was one thing that she hadn't seen coming.

After standing in front of the Lazy Day trying to talk among the throng of clubgoers, she and PJ decided to continue their game of catch-up in a more private setting. They found a small booth inside the coffee shop around the corner and settled in, talking with ease as if they saw each other every day.

"I still can't believe it's you, and after all these years," Alexandria said.

"As soon as I heard your name and saw you walk out on that stage, I was speechless."

"You remembered me?" she asked, surprised.

PJ nodded and smiled. "Of course, I did. And the funny thing is that when you said you hadn't intended on being there tonight, well, neither had I. I had a long workweek and all I wanted to do was crash tonight. But a couple of my buddies convinced me to hang out with them and blow off some steam. Now I'm glad I did—otherwise, we wouldn't have reconnected." He paused. "At least, not tonight."

"So you think this was fate?" Alexandria asked, searching his eyes.

PJ tapped his long fingers against the ice-cold glass of Coke sitting in front of him. "I don't believe there are any coincidences in life. Things happen the way they're supposed to. I went there with my friends tonight because I was supposed to see you. And get this—it's the first time any of us have ever been to the Lazy Day."

"Really?"

"Yes, and what'll trip you out even more is that I live only a few blocks away."

"Stop playing!"

"I kid you not. Because I'm in the neighborhood, I'd heard about the place—that it's a really cool spot to listen to live performances. But until tonight, I'd never walked through those doors."

Alexandria was quiet, still processing what all this meant. She knew he was right, and that there were no coincidences. The fact that she'd come across his picture from out of nowhere, after all these years, confirmed that she was supposed to meet PJ tonight. In that moment, she knew he'd been the force that had made her turn around in the middle of Peter's street and head toward the Lazy Day. He'd called her to him without even knowing it, and the thought made her shiver.

"You're gonna freak out when I tell you this," Alexandria said. "I was going through an old trunk in my parents' basement today and I found a picture of us when we were kids."

"Get outta here."

Alexandria opened her large handbag and pulled out her wallet, where she'd placed the small photo for safekeeping. "Here, look."

PJ took the picture and studied it, smiling and shaking his head. "I remember this day."

"You do?"

"We were in Ms. Snow's class and your mom came to pick you up after school. She took this picture right before my dad came to get me. I guess he never got a chance to get a copy, because I've never seen it before."

"I can't believe you remember that," Alexandria said, sounding surprised.

"I remember everything about you, Ali."

She put the picture back in her wallet, trying to hide her trembling hands and ignore the warm fuzzies she felt from PJ's presence.

He smiled at her. "When I told my buddies I knew you, they all went crazy. You should've heard them."

"What did they say?"

PJ shook his head and let out a light laugh. "I hang with some pretty wild dudes. Let's just say that they all wanted a personal introduction to the lovely Alexandria."

Alexandria blushed, which was something she didn't normally do. She was beginning to feel the heat of PJ's intense stare; it made her bare thighs tremble against the vinyl-covered seat. He was sexy and direct, and she liked the way he carried himself. His cool confidence and rugged masculinity were tempered by a sweet humility, which she could see in his eyes.

She wasn't prepared for the rush of feelings suddenly bubbling up inside her, all caused by a man with whom she'd been reacquainted for only an hour. She knew she couldn't let on how she felt, so she decided to change the subject from her to him. She looked at him and smiled. "I'm looking at you and I'm thinking how you haven't changed a bit."

"I don't know if that's a good thing." PJ let out another light-hearted laugh. "The last time you saw me, I was wearing a Power Rangers shirt and corduroys."

Alexandria laughed along with him. "Let me clarify that. I was referring to your essence. It hasn't changed."

"Really? And what's my essence?"

She looked into PJ's dark brown eyes and wanted to tell him what she could see. At his core, he was still a sweet, adorable little boy, but he had grown into a handsome man, with a sexy, fine swagger, which was dangerously intoxicating. His golden yellow skin, short, curly black hair, and finely trimmed goatee complemented the rest of his package, elevating him to what she deemed as "fine-as-hell" status.

But she couldn't divulge that, so instead she concentrated on his nonphysical attributes. "You're a kindhearted, all-around–nice person. I remember that when we were kids, you always shared your toys, and whenever we went outside for recess, you held my hand until we reached the playground, to make sure I was safe." Recounting the past made Alexandria think about what she'd told her mother that afternoon—how Grandpa John and Nana used to hold hands.

"You remember that?" he asked.

"You never forget your first best friend."

PJ nodded, looking into Alexandria's eyes. "You were my first, too, Ali."

She smiled. "You're the only person who's ever called me that."

"My kindergarten mastery of language wasn't developed enough to pronounce your name properly, so I improvised. I hope you don't mind that I keep calling you 'Ali.' I mean, you're a woman now, and my vocabulary has improved a bit."

Alexandria shook her head and smiled again. "Actually, I like it."

"Good, so do I. It fits you."

Alexandria found herself enthralled. She loved listening to PJ's deep, robust voice. His tone was powerful, yet gentle at the same time. His crisp diction and command of words let her know right away that he was well read—an attribute she found very appealing, since she was a writer and a spoken-word artist. She remembered that his father had had a deep voice as well, and that he'd always been nice to her when he came to pick up PJ from school.

"Have you been here in Atlanta this whole time?" PJ asked.

"Yes, except for when I went away to UPenn for law school. Then after graduation, I came back here. How about you? Have you been here all along, or did you move away?"

PJ explained that at the end of their kindergarten stint, his father was offered a position to head the cardiac care unit at Johns Hopkins, which landed them in the DC Metro area, home base to most of the Brightwood clan. After high school, he followed a nearly identical path to his father's. He entered Howard University at seventeen, graduating in three years, and then moved on to medical school at Harvard. But when it came to his specialty of practice, he'd chosen a different path. Instead of becoming a cardiothoracic surgeon for adult patients, he chose to work with children and was currently completing his residency in pediatrics at Emory University Hospital.

"You're well accomplished," Alexandria said. "Your dad must be really proud."

"Yeah, he is. He's been my biggest supporter for as long as I can remember. And he never pushed me into medicine, either. He always told me he'd support me in whatever I chose to do with my life—so long as it made me happy." PJ smiled and took a sip of his Coke. "Everyone thought I'd be a heart surgeon like him, but I've always wanted to work with kids, so pediatrics was a natural choice."

"Really? What draws you to children?" Alexandria was curious to know. She knew that most of the men their age viewed children as an annoyance, and they had no interest in having any—let alone, working with them.

"I developed asthma when I was seven years old," PJ told her. "My condition got so bad that I was in and out of the hospital constantly. Being an only child made it tough. I never forgot how scared and lonely I felt during those days. My dad and grandparents were there, but it was still rough on me."

Alexandria tilted her head; a quizzical look settled on her face. "I hope you don't mind me asking, but what about your mom?" She remembered meeting his mother only once, and that was when they'd celebrated PJ's birthday at school. She'd dropped off cupcakes and then left abruptly.

PJ shrugged. "She's never really been a part of my life. Instead of the stereotypical absentee dad, I grew up with an absentee mom."

"Oh, I'm sorry."

"Don't be. It happens. Anyway, because of my experience as a child, when I decided to go into medicine, I knew it would be in a capacity to help kids."

"You must really enjoy what you do."

"I love it."

Alexandria smiled. "That's a beautiful thing. You're very blessed, because not everyone can say that."

"Yes, I am. But you know what it's like. I saw you up there tonight and I can tell you love what you do, too."

"Yes, I do. Writing and performing spoken word is my passion. But it's not what I do full-time."

"Oh, what's your day job?"

Alexandria took a small sip of her iced mocha latte and let out a sigh. "I'm an associate at a lobbying firm downtown. I spend my days writing briefs, proposals, and doing litigation research for one of the senior partners at the firm. I've been told some people would kill to be in my shoes."

"I'm sure some would, but you sound like you're ready to put on a different pair."

She nodded. "How'd you guess?"

"It doesn't take a genius to figure that out. Besides, I can't see the woman who was up on that stage tonight sitting behind a desk in a cubicle, grinding it out over briefs and proposals."

"I know! Me either. I feel like I'm suffocating every time I walk into work."

"Then why do you do it?"

"I have a master plan," she said with a smile. "Just as you followed in your dad's footsteps, I'm using my mom's blueprint."

"Oh yeah?"

"Yep. My job pays me very well, and because I live in one of the buildings my dad owns, I don't have to worry about rent. I've been saving up over the last two years. When I have enough to float me for a while, I'm going to quit my job and dedicate myself to my craft full-time."

"That's a great plan. I know you're close to your folks, so how do they feel about it?"

"They told me that even if I fall short of money they'll help me with expenses until I can get established. I love them so much for always supporting me, but I'm going to keep working for a while because I want to make it on my own."

"That day is coming sooner than you think."

Alexandria smiled. "Tell me when, where, and how, because I want to be there when it happens."

PJ leaned back against the side of the booth. "I don't know all the details, but what I can tell you without question is that you're a great performer. I loved what you did tonight."

Alexandria blushed again, thinking about the words she'd spoken onstage. "Thanks, I'm glad you enjoyed it. The piece I performed was totally unplanned. I just spoke what was on my heart and let it flow."

"Can I ask you a personal question?"

She shifted a bit in her seat and prepared herself for something she might not want to answer. "Sure, go ahead."

PJ took a sip of his now watered-down Coke as an intense look formed at the edge of his lips. "Are you seeing anyone?"

Alexandria laughed. "Are you sure you listened to my piece?"

"Every single word."

"Then you know the answer to your question."

"Not really. You said you want 'real love,' and I get that, but it still doesn't answer my question. Are you seeing anyone?"

Alexandria's mind flashed back to Peter and the fact that she should be telling him what she was about to explain to PJ. "There's a guy I've been dating for a year. He's a good person, but he and I want and need totally different things. So tonight I finally decided to call it quits."

"A year is a decent clip of time."

"Yeah, but to be honest, we probably should've broken up six months ago. He works so much that we only see each other on the weekends, and lately, that's even been sketchy."

PJ nodded. "What made you decide to break up with him tonight?"

Once again, Alexandria thought about what PJ had said about there being no coincidences. Sitting across from him, and looking into eyes she felt she could get lost in, she knew he was the reason she'd finally made her decision to end things with Peter. She wanted to tell him the truth, but she knew she couldn't. Instead, she settled on a light version, which she thought he could handle.

"Have you ever had a feeling about something you couldn't explain, but you just knew it was right? Well, that's what I felt tonight. I want and need more than he and I can ever have together. I guess that's why when I got onstage, I spoke about what I desire, and what kind of love I want."

PJ nodded. "I raised my hand when you asked the audience if we wanted the kind of love you were describing."

She was taken aback by his very open admission, and she knew it was his way of telling her that he, too, wanted a meaningful relationship. But just as her statements could be interpreted as ambiguous, so could his. She wondered if he was seeing anyone, too. "Are you seeing anyone?" she asked.

"No, I'm not."

"So you're not dating?" she asked again, a little skeptical.

He shrugged. "I go out from time to time, but there's no one serious in my life right now. And, honestly, I'm tired of the dating scene. Every time I meet someone new, I feel like I'm taking my life into my hands."

"Goodness!" Alexandria said, raising her brow.

"I've met some real nut jobs. I think the older you get, the harder it is to find someone who meets what you're looking for. It's rough out there."

"Don't tell me that. I'm about to jump back into the water."

PJ looked at her closely and smiled. "You don't have to jump back out there. *You* have a choice."

"Oh, really? And what might that be?"

As soon as Alexandria asked the question, she knew what PJ's answer was going to be. She could see it in his eyes and read it on his face, so she sat back and waited for him to change her world in one night.

"You can date me," PJ said. He straightened his back and sat more erect, letting her know he meant business. "And I don't mean casual dating either. This would be for real."

Alexandria let out a small laugh and shook her head. "So you want to skip through all the formalities and start dating straight out the gate."

"Yes, an exclusive thing. Just you and me."

"I can't believe you're serious."

PJ's voice was playful but also focused. "It's a no-brainer. I think you're smart, beautiful, talented, and, well, I think you get me, which is important. Look how comfortable it feels being together. We can make this work."

"A relationship takes time to build. We can't just jump there over an iced latte and a Coke. We need to get to know each other again."

"I'm not the type of man who wastes time, Ali. In that respect, I'm a lot like my dad. When I see what I want, I go for it." He smiled and leaned forward. "I'm a good brother, and you don't even have to go through a vetting process because you already know me."

"We knew each other a million years ago when we were kids. We're adults now and we've only been reacquainted for, what, five minutes?"

"Actually, according to my watch, it's four hours and counting," he said as he glanced at the stylish Cartier Tank on his wrist. "But, like you said, we go way back."

Alexandria laughed. "Yes, we do. All the way back to the playground."

PJ moved his glass to the side and cleared his throat. "I used to hold your hand when we walked to the playground because that made you my girlfriend in my six-year-old mind." He slid his hand across the table, palm side up. "Ali, I'd like to hold your hand again."

Alexandria looked down at the smooth lines that crisscrossed PJ's large palms, then into the depths of his deep brown eyes. "This is very sudden. Very fast."

"And very right."

"What makes you so sure?"

"Like you said, it's a feeling that I can't explain, but I know it's right."

Alexandria knew it was time to take Grandma Allene's sage advice again. Slowly she slid her hand into PJ's and watched him smile.

Chapter 26

Alexandria and PJ left the coffee shop, hand in hand, and walked to where she had parked her car. It was midnight, and they didn't want to go to another club or public establishment, but they also didn't want their evening together to end. They sat atop the hood of Alexandria's hybrid, gazing at the brilliant stars shining in the sky. They talked and caught up on one another's lives.

With each minute that passed, they erased the years that had separated them. They revealed more to one another in an hour than they ever had during the duration of any of their past relationships. They savored important details of one another's loves and losses, highs and lows.

Alexandria wasn't surprised to learn that he'd been involved with a lot of women, or that there were a few whom he still saw, here and there, on what he called a "strictly casual" basis. "It's nothing serious," he said.

She was relieved when she looked into his eyes and her gut told her that what he'd said was true. She also respected the fact that unlike Peter, PJ wasn't condescending or so driven by ego that he couldn't see beyond his own shortcomings. She felt she could talk to him all night.

"What's your biggest fear?" PJ asked, looking into Alexandria's eyes.

She took a minute to think about his question. Until today, it had been that something terrible would happen to her as a result of her gift. But that barrier had been removed, and now she felt as if she'd broken free of what had been holding her happiness hostage. "Honestly, I don't have any fears. Right now my life is open for everything."

"Spoken like a true artist."

Alexandria laughed. "Hey, it's true. It took me a very long time to get to this place. I like how it feels and I'm going to enjoy it for as long as I can."

"I respect that."

"How about you? What's your biggest fear?"

PJ looked up at the sky. "That my dad will go through life without ever finding real love."

His words struck a chord deep inside Alexandria. Not just because of what he'd said, but because of the emotion in his voice when he spoke his honesty. "Is he unhappy?" Alexandria asked.

"I wouldn't say he's unhappy, but I do believe his life could be richer if he had someone in it. He's put everything into me and made so many sacrifices to raise me. It's time for him to enjoy himself. I don't want to see him grow old alone."

She could tell he loved his father just as she loved her parents, and that endeared him to her heart.

Even though they were floating on love clouds, they couldn't ignore the muggy heat or the hard fiberglass they were sitting on, which had begun to make comfort a challenge.

"Let's go to my place," PJ said. "I've got a comfortable couch, AC, and wine. Plus, it's only four blocks away."

"I don't make a habit of going to a man's house within hours of meeting him."

"That's a good rule, and I'm glad you don't. But this is different. I'm not just any man, Ali."

Alexandria smiled and nodded. "No, you certainly aren't."

"Remember, we're dating now." PJ gave her a sexy wink.

"Oh, that's right, I forgot." She smiled and stared into his eyes. "I've had a wonderful time tonight, but I think I'm going to head home now."

"I don't want the evening to end, but I understand." PJ slid off the hood and then helped Alexandria down, like a perfect gentleman.

She smiled from ear to ear when she felt his hand reach for hers and then hold on tightly as they stood in front of her driver's-side door. She couldn't believe how natural and effortless it felt being with him. She had to agree—she didn't want the evening to end, either.

PJ reached into his back pocket and pulled out his phone. "All right," he said, still holding her right hand in his left as he handled his smartphone. "Give me the vital information I need so I can start blowin' you up."

Alexandria laughed and gave him her cell and work numbers. After he secured her information in his phone, they stood in front of each other in silence. They were getting ready to part and she knew this meant they were going to seal their evening with some type of physical gesture. When he reached for her slim waist and enveloped her into his arms, she willingly came.

They stood wrapped in each other's embrace, ignoring the sticky heat and the fact that their bodies were creating even more slick wetness.

Alexandria felt aroused when she pressed her soft breasts against his hard chest when he hugged her. She took a deep breath when his left arm tightened around her waist and his right hand slowly massaged the middle of her back through the thin material of her cotton T-shirt. Her body trembled when his soft lips lightly touched the edge of her shoulder, giving it a small kiss.

"Mmmm," Alexandria moaned, letting the low, seductive sound escape her mouth before she could stop it.

She tilted her head back when she felt PJ's lips move from her shoulder to the center of her neck. By now, they were leaning against her car; his body was pressed against hers as she felt the hardness in the front of his jeans begin to grow. When his mouth moved to her lips, their wet softness sent another wave of arousal through her entire body. She tingled when she tasted the saltiness he'd gathered from her skin as his tongue entered her mouth for a slow, deep, passionate kiss.

As their lower bodies began to slowly grind against each other, Alexandria knew she had to put the brakes on the moment before she either had sex with PJ in the middle of the street or walked the short distance it would take to get to his place. Reluctantly, and with willpower she didn't know she had, she pulled away. "I need to go."

"When will I see you again?"

"I haven't left yet."

PJ smiled. "Nor have you answered my question."

"How about tomorrow?"

He glanced at his watch. "You mean later today?"

"Yes, PJ, later today." She wanted to kiss him again, but she knew what was going to happen next if she did, so she turned and opened her door.

"See you in a little while," PJ told her before waving as she watched him fade away in her rearview mirror.

When Alexandria walked inside her apartment, she went straight to her bedroom, feeling exhausted but also excited. She kicked off her stilettos and sat at the edge of her queen-size bed, falling back onto the comfort of her pillow-top mattress. She was startled when she heard her cell phone ring, but then she smiled when she looked at the caller ID.

"Hey," she said in a low whisper.

"Hey, you," PJ piped through the line in his deep baritone. "I was calling to make sure you got home safely."

"Awww, that's so sweet of you. Yes, I'm home, safe and lying on my bed."

"Me too. Wish you were here beside me."

She wanted to say she wished the same thing, too. Instead, she chose a safer response. "I had a great time tonight, and I'll see you soon."

After she took a quick shower, Alexandria lay in bed and smiled. Last night, she'd been frustrated and unsure about her fledgling relationship with Peter and the voices ringing inside her head. And now, as she drifted off to sleep, she smiled with peace and comfort, knowing that things were finally looking up.

Chapter 27

It was early afternoon when Alexandria parked her car on the side of her parents' garage, just as she'd done yesterday. She was excited, but she was also tired and hungry from her late night and early morning with PJ. She knew she could get a good meal from her mother's kitchen, and she couldn't wait to pile her plate and share her good news.

"Something smells good," Alexandria said as she entered the kitchen, inhaling an aroma, which made her mouth water with hunger.

"Hey, sweetie," Victoria called out as she stood at the stove. "I just finished making the gravy for the meat loaf."

Alexandria looked at the food that had been placed in serving trays and bowls on the long granite counter: succulent meat loaf, creamy mashed potatoes with chives, fresh green beans and mushrooms, sautéed spinach, mixed salad greens with vegetables, cinnamon peach pie, and a basket of buttery homemade rolls on the side. For as long as Alexandria could remember, her mother always made a big feast on Sunday, which was a tradition in their family—one that dated back several generations before her. Sunday was the day to toss healthy recipes and careful eating to the side and enjoy the richness of down-home food.

She couldn't wait to eat some and then tell her mother about PJ.

"Sweetie, are you okay?" Victoria asked, looking at her daughter with a curious stare.

"Yes, Mom. I'm a little tired, but I'm feeling great."

"Oh, good," Victoria said, giving her a questioning look. She walked back to the stove and poured the gravy, which she'd just made, into a ceramic boat. "What's going on with you? Something's different. I can tell."

Alexandria smiled and leaned against the counter, glad that her mother knew her so well. "Where's Dad and Christian?"

"You know the drill. They're down in the basement, watching the game with the TV blasting at full capacity. I'm surprised they're not both hard of hearing."

"Good, I want to tell you something."

"By the smile on your face, I know it's something good. Did you find out what Grandma Allene's been trying to protect you from?"

"Even better. I found out what she's been trying to lead me to."

"Really?"

"Yes, Mom."

"Something tells me I'm going to need a seat," Victoria said as she walked to the breakfast table, where she and Alexandria had started their eye-opening conversation yesterday.

After they settled at the table, each with a glass of Victoria's sweet, ice-cold lemonade in front of them, Alexandria began. "You'll never guess in a million years who I saw last night?"

"This has something to do with what Grandma Allene's been leading you to?"

"Kind of. It's about something she told me, so yes," Alexandria answered. "Now guess who I saw?"

"You know I hate guessing. Just tell me."

"Mom, this is gonna totally freak you out, so just guess," Alexandria said as she smiled even harder.

"Okay, male or female?"

"Male."

"Young or old."

She tried not to blush. "He's my age."

"Ooohhh," Victoria let out with an excited smile. "Is it the handsome young man who graduated from Harvard, the one you used to date a few years ago?"

Alexandria had nearly forgotten about Michael, but she could see that her mother clearly hadn't. "No, I haven't seen him since we broke up. But actually, you got the Harvard part right."

"Hmmm, I don't know who it could be. Just tell me, sweetie. I told you, I hate guessing."

Alexandria's smile was really wide. "Okay, I'll tell you. I saw PJ!"

"Who?"

"*Mom!*" Alexandria nearly yelled. "We just looked at the picture of him and me yesterday." She could see that her mother's face was blank. "My best friend from kindergarten, Parker Brightwood Jr. And, actually, it's Dr. Parker Brightwood Jr. now."

Right away, Alexandria could see that not only was her mother shocked into a blank stare, she was visibly uncomfortable. From the stiffness that had seized Victoria's back to the long worry line stamped across her forehead, she clearly wasn't excited about the news.

"Mom, why are you uncomfortable?"

"Who said I'm uncomfortable? Where did you see him?"

"I can tell you're uneasy about something by the way you're acting, and it's making me feel uneasy, too."

Victoria let out a breath of frustration. "Where did you see him? Is he living here?"

Alexandria leaned forward and looked deeply into her mother's eyes. She concentrated . . . and in a split second, she knew. "You mean, is his father living here?" she said. "That's your real question, isn't it?"

"How did you know that?"

Alexandria went silent and averted her eyes.

Victoria shifted in her seat and folded her arms across her delicate cotton blouse. "You just claimed your gift yesterday and now you're a regular soothsayer, huh? Well, I'll not have you reading my mind and playing games with me, young lady."

"I'm sorry, Mom. I couldn't help it."

Victoria shook her head. "I didn't know you could do that."

"Neither did I, until this very moment," Alexandria said, a little shocked herself. "I've never done it before. I looked at you and images started flashing in front of me really fast, kind of like what happened yesterday when I saw Grandpa John, Nana, and Uncle Maxx in that club. Only this time, I was able to look into your eyes and see what you were thinking, and then go back and see what was attached to it. It was like watching a movie in a matter of seconds. I saw you and Mr. Brightwood, and well . . ."

"Lord, have mercy . . ." Victoria's voice trailed off, too. "What did you see?"

"Everything."

"Like?"

Alexandria looked toward the long hallway.

"Don't worry," her mother said. "Your father and Christian will be down there glued to that TV until I call them up to eat. They may even be down there napping. So come on, tell me."

Alexandria fiddled with the glass of lemonade in front of her as she began to speak. "You and Mr. Brightwood used to date. You were in love, and he hurt you."

Victoria nodded.

"You still loved him during the time that PJ and I were in school, didn't you." Alexandria said it in a tone that was more a statement than a question.

"Yes, I did."

Alexandria wanted to know if her mother was still in love with PJ's father. If she looked into Victoria's eyes, she was confident she could get the answer, but she didn't know if she wanted it. She also wasn't comfortable with the newfound power of her gift. She needed to have time to herself to understand the extent of the information she could now access without people's permission. Even without thinking about it too much, she knew that kind of knowledge could be dangerous.

"So," Victoria spoke up, breaking Alexandria's thoughts, "where did you see PJ?"

"At the Lazy Day last night. He was in the audience."

"He lives here now?"

Alexandria told her mother all the information she knew about PJ and his father. "Mr. Brightwood's coming to town this Friday. He's presenting at a medical conference downtown."

"Tell me more about you and PJ," Victoria asked, purposely ignoring the information she'd just gotten about her ex-lover.

"Mom, I can see that you don't approve of my relationship with PJ."

"Relationship? You just met the boy last night. What in the world have you done to make it a 'relationship'! . . . Wait, don't answer that," she said, holding her hand up into the air as she lowered her head and shook it from side to side.

"We only talked," Alexandria said, feeling the need to make it clear that although she'd wanted to do what her mother was suggesting, she'd exercised good judgment. "We connected in a deep, powerful way. And even though we haven't seen each other in over twenty years, it feels like we've known each other all our lives. I know it sounds strange to you, but, trust me, it's real. We know more about each other than some people reveal in a lifetime."

"Sweetie, do you know how ridiculous this sounds?"

"No more ridiculous than Grandpa John's and Nana's story of how they fell in love in just one night."

"This is very different from your grandparents."

"How so?"

Victoria knotted her brow, searching for words. "They were in a small town and it was a much different time back then."

"Mom, I can't believe you're being so negative."

"I love you, and I'm only trying to look out for you," Victoria said. "Last night, you were debating whether to break up with your boyfriend, and now you're talking about being in a relationship with someone whom you barely know."

"I know what's right. And PJ's right for me. As a matter of fact, we're going to see each other later tonight."

Victoria looked completely frustrated and more than a little worried. "Alexandria, as a woman who's been through a few things, I'm telling you to be careful. I know how charming those Brightwood men can be. And if PJ is anything like his father, Lord help you . . ." Victoria took a deep breath and let her words trail off. She pushed back from the table and stood. "The food is getting cold. I'm going to call your father and brother up so we can eat."

Instead of sharing a meal with her family, Alexandria filled one of her mother's plastic containers with food and hurried out the door before her father and brother came upstairs, narrowly missing them.

As she drove home, she thought about the irony that even though she had the ability to see the past and the future, her conversation with her mother proved that life was still unpredictable—one never knew what was waiting around the corner.

Chapter 28

As soon as PJ walked through Alexandria's door, he embraced her in a tight hug, followed by a soft, lingering kiss.

"That's a nice greeting," Alexandria said. "How was your day?"

"Better, now that I'm with you."

She smiled. "Mine too."

Thirty minutes later, Alexandria and PJ were sitting across from each other in a booth inside the Cheesecake Factory. She'd eaten there for what seemed like a thousand times before—but for some reason, tonight felt different. She didn't know if it was the fact that she was falling for the gorgeous man in front of her, whom she'd only reunited with last night, or if it was the fact that what she planned on telling him during their meal could either make or break their newfound relationship. Either way, she knew being there tonight meant something beyond a simple dinner.

They picked up where they'd left off in the wee hours of this morning, falling into conversation so naturally that it seemed as though sharing Sunday-night dinner was part of their routine. Alexandria laughed at a funny joke he made, but her smile broke when she saw a guy walk by whom she thought looked just like Peter. She breathed with relief when, upon closer inspection, she could see it wasn't him.

She'd called Peter on her drive home from her mother's house earlier that afternoon, hoping she could stop by his place and break the news to him in person. But he hadn't answered his phone, so she left a short voice message asking him to call her.

"You have a faraway look," PJ said. "Tell me what you're thinking?"

"You're just like my mom."

"Damn! I've been compared to many things, but never someone's mother."

Alexandria laughed. "I didn't mean it the way it sounded. It's just that you're both very inquisitive, and you say what's on your mind."

"I guess asking questions comes from my natural curiosity and years of training as a medical professional. It's important to get to the root of a patient's problems, and asking questions is one of the best ways to do it. Does that bother you?"

"No, not at all. Actually, I like the fact that you want to know more about me, and that you're so willing to express how you feel about things."

"It's necessary in a relationship."

"Yes, but it's also hard to open yourself up completely to someone."

"Is that hard for you?"

Alexandria took a small sip of her wine, then bit into her chicken enchilada. "Yes," she whispered.

"I'm surprised. You're so open and expressive onstage. Plus, you've shared a lot with me. . . . Wait a minute." PJ raised his brow in a playful gesture. "You're not holding back something crazy from me, are you?"

Everything had been going so well, and Alexandria wanted their good time to continue. However, she also knew that if she was serious about entering into a relationship with PJ, as she'd told her mother she was, she needed to start things off on a good footing. She needed to share things with him that she'd never discussed with another person, not even her own mother, until yesterday.

For once in her life, Alexandria wanted to take a risk. She wanted to feel completely free from burdens and secrets. But she knew that freedom came with a price; if this was what she truly wanted, she had to be willing to pay up.

"I'm going to share something with you," PJ said, pulling Alexandria from her thoughts. "My father taught me a lot of things about being a man, and one of the most important lessons he drilled into my head was to be a person of my word." He reached over and gently stroked her hand. "I know we're moving really fast, but I give you my word, Ali, I'm gonna do everything in my power to make you happy and support you in whatever it is you want to do. I don't want you to feel afraid when you're with me. You can open up and tell me anything, and I won't judge you or walk away. I'll be there for you, and you have my word on that."

Never in her life had Alexandria had this kind of conversation with a man, not to mention so quickly in a relationship. But as they'd both acknowledged, what they were building was very different, and they couldn't put rules or a name to it. With newfound courage, Alexandria decided to finally start living.

"Now I have to be straight up with you."

PJ pushed his plate of half-eaten steak and a baked potato to the side. "This sounds serious."

"It is."

"Okay, then let's go where we can talk in private."

They left the restaurant, hand in hand, and buckled up in PJ's SUV. Twenty minutes later, they were back at Alexandria's apartment, both nervously anticipating what would happen next.

Alexandria led PJ back into her small living room and offered him a seat on her couch.

"I like your place," PJ said. "It's just like you."

"Really? And how am I?"

"Stylish, elegant, and sophisticated, with a little bohemian vibe goin' on. I'm really feelin' that." He looked at her Charles Alston painting hanging prominently on the wall opposite her couch. "Everything is put together nicely. It's beautiful, just like you."

"Are you trying to sweet-talk me?"

PJ laughed. "Yes, but what I said also happens to be true." He leaned back against the soft cushions, making himself more comfortable as he rested his hand on the fabric of Alexandria's flowing, vibrantly colored skirt. "So what's up? What is it that you want to tell me?"

Alexandria sat cross-legged, looking down at PJ's hand on her thigh. She wondered what his touch would feel like if he ventured under her clothes, but she pushed the thought out of her mind. Instead, she concentrated on what was at hand.

She took a deep breath, reached for PJ's hand, and held on to it tightly in hers. "I have baggage and issues."

"We all do."

"Yes, but mine . . . Well, it's not what you think."

"Then tell me. I want to know."

Alexandria looked into his eyes and began what turned into an hour-long conversation about her gift. She was surprised when PJ didn't flinch, not even once, as she told him about situations she'd encountered and voices she'd heard since she was a little girl. She even told him about Grandma Allene, and how for the first time she was able to travel back into the past and see and hear things as they were happening.

When she searched PJ's face for a reaction, it was void of the disbelief, skepticism, or even the fear she'd expected to rest there. Instead, she saw a man who was trying to understand her and, as unbelievable as it seemed, love her. He held on tightly to her hand for a solid hour; now he was cradling her in his arms as they lay on her couch.

It amazed Alexandria how completely comfortable and safe she felt with this man, as if they'd been together for years. She thought about what her Grandma Allene had said to her about not being afraid to open up and let love walk into her life.

"I thank God for Grandma Allene, because if it weren't for her, I wouldn't have opened up to my mom, which gave me the strength to unburden myself and made it easier to confide in you."

"I'm amazed, Ali. You're so strong and fearless."

"Ha!" Alexandria laughed. Her head was resting on PJ's strong chest as she looked up at him. "I'm a lot of things, but *fearless* isn't one of them. I remember so many nights, lying in the dark, scared to death that I'd see a vision or hear a voice that might harm me."

"Most people wouldn't have been able to handle what you've been through on their own for all these years. At least, not without—"

"Going crazy," she said, finishing his sentence.

"No, I was going to say without getting some help, like talking to a professional."

"Do you think I'm crazy?"

"I think you're beautiful."

"Beautiful and crazy?"

PJ laughed. "Will you stop saying that!"

"I wouldn't blame you if you thought I was unstable, or at least a little weird. That's one of the reasons why I don't talk about it." She raised herself up off his chest and looked at PJ closely. "I see how calm you're acting about what I've told you, and I'm wondering if maybe you're placating me until you can break free. Then the minute you're out the door, you'll change your number and I'll never see or hear from you again."

PJ shook his head. "Ali, if I wanted to leave, trust me, I would've been gone five minutes into this conversation. I'm calm because what you've told me doesn't surprise me, not coming from you."

"What do you mean 'not coming from' me?"

"I remember that when we were kids, you used to say and do things that were . . . different."

Alexandria was so surprised, she sat up at full attention. "What did I do?"

PJ continued lying on her couch, resting his arm behind his head as he reached back into his memory. "I remember we had playtime at the end of the day before our parents would come to pick us up from school. And, Ali, somehow you always—*and I mean always*—knew the exact time my dad was about to walk through the door. You'd say, 'PJ, we have to put the toys away 'cause your dad's coming.' Sure enough, he'd walk in the door a few seconds later. It was like you could feel him coming."

Alexandria's hand flew to her mouth. "I did that? I don't remember it at all."

"I didn't know what it meant back then. I just thought it was a neat trick. And actually, something else happened that I didn't realize until last night. I meant to bring it up while we were talking but somehow I got sidetracked."

"What? Tell me!" Alexandria asked with urgency.

"One day, we were sitting in the back of our classroom, drawing in our sketchbooks, and you told me you were going to miss me because we wouldn't be able to see each other for a very long time," PJ said as he readjusted his position on the couch. "Well, this was only a few weeks after your father had that heart attack when he came to pick you up from school. You'd missed a couple days after it happened, so I thought you were going to be out again because of your dad or something. I told you we'd still see each other because I'd get my dad to bring me over to your house for a playdate.

"But then you told me that we'd be too far away to have playdates, but you'd play with me again when we grew up." PJ shook his head. "It's so strange. I've always remembered that. Even last night, when I first saw you at the club, I remembered what you told me. But I never thought about it the way I'm thinking about it now. This is wild."

A quiet calm washed over Alexandria. "I'm no longer going to be afraid of my gift. I can't run or hide from it any longer. I have to embrace it. If I'd done that a long time ago, I probably wouldn't have suffered so much hurt, alienation, and failed relationships. I would've known how to develop and cultivate the ability with which I've been blessed."

Alexandria suddenly closed her eyes and stayed quiet for a long pause; then she opened them to find PJ staring at her with concern.

"Ali, what's wrong?"

"I just heard my Grandma Allene's voice again."

PJ's eyes grew wide, and he sat up beside her. "Really?"

"Yes, I heard her singing 'Amazing Grace,' and then she was talking with a woman. The lady was young, about our age, but she was wearing a very old-fashioned dress. I don't know who she was, but she looked very familiar." She paused for a moment. "They were talking about me. I could see them both, but I could only hear Grandma Allene."

"What did she say?"

"That she's going to be there for me. She's going to guide me with my gift."

PJ shook his head from side to side. "This is incredible. I've read and heard about patients having out-of-body experiences and being able to connect with the deceased. For some people, the very thought defies practicality and logic, but I know it's real. You had this ability when we were kids and you still have it now." He pulled her in close to him. "Let me know how I can help you, baby. I'm here for you."

He'd called her "baby," and it made her feel a jolt of excitement. Alexandria smiled and kissed him softly on his lips. "My Grandma Allene is in my life now, and she's going to help guide me. And together with you, I know everything will be all right."

They kissed and caressed on her couch, holding each other as their bodies pressed against one another. When Alexandria felt PJ's excitement rise once again, she wanted to see and explore what she knew would, without a doubt, give her pleasure. But she also knew that even though her mother had cautioned her—for personal reasons of her own—she'd been partially right about one thing: the fact that Alexandria needed to slow things down—at least on the physical level.

When she thought about her mother, it made her mind flash back to the situation between her and PJ's parents. Alexandria already had brought up one heavy topic tonight, and now she knew she had to bring up another one.

She pulled away, still lying in PJ's arms. "There's something else we need to talk about." She sat up and motioned for him to do the same.

"Ali, if you're trying to kill the mood, you're succeeding."

"I'm sorry, but this is important. I think we need to get all the major stuff out in the open right now."

PJ adjusted the crotch of his pants and sat back into the couch. "Okay, what's up?"

She looked into his eyes and was going to ask him if he knew about their parents' history, but there was no need to inquire. One hard glimpse let her know that he'd spoken to his father earlier that afternoon. She tilted her head to the side. "You know about my mom and your dad, don't you?"

PJ paused for a moment, as if mulling over something. "You're reading my mind, aren't you?"

"I'm sorry, I didn't mean to. It just happened."

"Shit, Ali. You can really read my mind!"

"Like I told my mom this afternoon, I didn't know I had this ability until today. It just happened. I looked at you and, poof, I knew."

PJ leaned forward, resting his elbows on his knees. "I don't have anything to hide. But the fact that you know what I'm thinking and you can read my mind . . . that's kind of unnerving."

Alexandria nodded. "I know. It's intrusive and I'm going to work on controlling it and figure out exactly what I can and can't do with my gift. I'm learning as I go."

PJ nodded. "Okay, but we need to get some ground rules straight."

"I won't go around reading your mind. I promise."

They were silent for a few moments before PJ spoke up. "So, about our parents, it's wild, right?"

"Yes, and problematic."

PJ raised his brow. "Why do you say that? They had a past, but that was over before we were even born."

"Think again."

"Wait a minute. What do you know that I don't?"

Alexandria told him that their parents had been deeply in love, that it was very serious, and their feelings for each other were still high when she and PJ had met in kindergarten. She also told him that her mother had come close to cheating on her dad with his father, which had caused even more tension between the two men who had never cared for each other. But she held off on divulging the fact that she was almost certain her mother secretly harbored feelings for his dad.

PJ shook his head. "This makes sense now. I guess that's why my dad sounded so concerned when I told him about us. He asked me a million questions about you and your mom. Which isn't like him at all."

"He did?"

"Yeah, but in his defense, I guess he was curious because he's never heard me talk about anyone the way I talked about you."

Alexandria knew she shouldn't do it—because she'd just promised she wouldn't—but she couldn't help herself. She wanted to know what he'd said to his father, and if he had indeed talked about her in a special way. She looked into his eyes to see if what he was saying was true. She blinked and saw that not only was it true, he'd told his father that she was "the one." She saw that Mr. Brightwood had told him to slow down, and that he was moving too fast. *"Let's talk about this over drinks when I get in on Friday night,"* she heard him say.

"Ali, you're doing it again, aren't you?"

She lowered her head and nodded. "Yes, I—"

"You just promised you wouldn't."

Alexandria felt awful. "I know, and I'm so, so sorry, PJ. It won't happen again. I'm *really* for real, this time."

"This is gonna be a problem. I can't have you reading my mind and knowing my thoughts. I'm a secure man, and, like I said, I don't have anything to hide. But I don't want you knowing every little thing I say, think, or do."

Alexandria looked into his eyes, but PJ looked away. "Don't do it, Ali."

"I'm not." She reached out and held his hand. "I want you to trust me, and I don't want you to be afraid to look me in the eye. I was wrong for what I did, and it won't happen again." She could see that he was still unconvinced, and she couldn't blame him. She felt terrible. "I'm sorry, honey."

PJ's head turned back to her when he heard her whisper her words with sweetness. He let out a heavy sigh and shook his head. "Damn, see, this is why my dad's concerned for me. You got a brothah sprung, and we haven't even—"

Alexandria raised her brow.

"Hell, you already know what I was gonna say."

Alexandria nodded and looked him in the eye. "I'm serious, PJ. I'm going to work on controlling my abilities."

"I'll help if I can."

"I have a feeling this is something I'm going to have to learn myself, with the help of Grandma Allene, of course."

They paused for a moment. "So," he said, breaking the silence again, "do you think there's something still there between your mom and my dad?"

Alexandria didn't want to lie, but she also didn't want to speak out of turn about her mother's feelings, so she told him what was true. "I'm not one hundred percent sure."

"That means there's a chance there is."

"Yes, it does."

"Does that bother you?"

"Of course. Does it bother you?"

"Hell yeah. That would be too weird and complicated for a number of reasons. But I'll find out what's going on when I have dinner with my dad this Friday night."

Now it was Alexandria's turn to raise her brow. "You're going to ask him?"

"Yep, man-to-man. My dad and I have that kind of relationship, and if there's anything going on, he'll tell me."

Alexandria was filled with contradictory feelings. On one hand, she was happy that she was no longer afraid to claim her gift, and that she'd embraced the fact that it was a blessing that was handed down to her. But there was also a part of her that was already beginning to see what a burden having the gift could be. She didn't have to wait for PJ to confirm what she already knew—that both their parents still had feelings for each other after all these years.

PJ held her hand and rubbed her soft skin with his fingers, pulling her back into the moment. "Are we still going to the Lazy Day tonight?" he asked.

"I didn't think you'd be up for going back again so soon. Don't you have early rounds in the morning?"

"Kyle wants you to perform tonight, right?"

"Yes, but I didn't commit to it. Besides, it's late—"

PJ cut her off. "Then we have to get going. This is your future."

All Alexandria could do was smile. She was going to grab hold of her future, and she knew PJ was going to be a definite part of it.

Chapter 29

It was Thursday night, but Alexandria couldn't tell whether it was Friday or Saturday, because every day had felt like the weekend since reconnecting with PJ.

They talked on the phone every day. His was the first voice she heard when she awoke in the morning, and the last to whisper in her ear before she went to sleep at night. They had even managed to carve out time to meet for a quick cup of coffee in the hospital cafeteria during lunchtime yesterday, in between his rounds. Alexandria had thought he looked good enough to sip through a straw when she saw him in his lab coat, with his stethoscope hanging around his neck, and she had to control herself when he hugged her tightly before they said good-bye.

Now she was meeting him at his place for dinner, and she was slightly nervous. When they were at her house, she felt more in control of what might happen; but she knew that once they were on his turf, all bets were off. She'd quickly learned that although he was one of the sweetest, most compassionate men she'd ever met, he was also a serious alpha male, who was used to getting what he wanted. His bravado was sexy, and it gave him an edge, which she found irresistibly appealing, but also a little dangerous.

When she came up to PJ's building, Alexandria felt a twinge of déjà vu, as if she'd been there before. She tried to shake the feeling as she pushed the intercom button for PJ's unit. Once he buzzed her inside the elegant lobby of his luxe building, the sensation she couldn't quite explain grew even stronger.

Alexandria looked around the opulently decorated space, inhaled the scent of fresh-cut flowers, which sat inside a huge bronze urn on the table in the center of the lobby, and tried to figure out why this place seemed so familiar. She knew she'd never been here before; yet she felt a very real connection to everything around her.

She forced her mind to push away the puzzling feeling as she entered the richly paneled elevator on her way up to PJ's unit. Her stomach fluttered, replacing her nervousness with excitement and anticipation about the evening ahead.

"Your building is really nice," she said when PJ greeted her at the door with a warm hug. She looked around as she walked inside. "I knew you were a high-end brother." She smiled, nudging him with her elbow.

PJ laughed. "I've got to be, if I want a princess like you on my arm."

"Now this is really getting weird."

"What?"

" 'Princess' is the nickname my dad calls me."

"Really?"

"Yes, he's called me that ever since I can remember."

PJ looked at her with seductive eyes. "See, I told you we belong together. This is a soul connection, baby."

Hearing him call her "baby" made her smile. Five minutes later, Alexandria was sitting on PJ's couch as she watched him move about his small gourmet kitchen, gathering a bottle of wine and glasses. He'd already called ahead for their Chinese takeout and told her that their delivery would be there any minute. Just then, his doorbell rang.

"Can you get that?" PJ called out from the kitchen. "It's probably our food."

Alexandria strolled over to the door, accepting the bag of delicious smelling food. Instead of eating at his small dining-room table, they opted to kick their shoes off and enjoy their meal in the living room on the comfort of his soft leather couch. Alexandria used her chopsticks to remove their food from the containers onto their plates, while PJ lit a candle and poured the wine.

"Chinese is my favorite," he said.

"It's my second favorite, next to Italian."

"Italian's my number two, so now we know we can switch up the next time."

They enjoyed laughter and seductive flirting throughout their meal. A subtle smile here, a light touch there, and a hint of suggestive sexual banter was tossed back and forth between them. Alexandria was feeling more and more aroused; she wondered if she could continue to maintain her desires as the evening went on.

After they finished eating, PJ put away their dishes, selected a vintage bottle of after-dinner wine, and settled back on the couch next to Alexandria. She looked at him and wondered if he was feeling the same wanton desires and thoughts that were running through her body and mind.

She'd been seeing him for less than a week; and even though she disagreed with her mother about the quickness of the relationship she and PJ were building, she did agree that sex shouldn't be a part of it so soon. From her experience, sleeping with a man too quickly usually led to disaster. She knew PJ was different from other men she'd been involved with in the past, but she still didn't want to test the law of averages. On the other hand, life had recently taught her that nothing was for certain, and things could change in the blink of an eye.

"To us, and to new beginnings," PJ said as he held up his glass in a toast.

Alexandria tipped her glass against his and took a small sip. The wine, just like PJ, was strong, with subtle notes of sweetness that went down smooth, with a little kick to let you know what you had.

"This is good," she complimented as she took another sip. She sat back and looked around, giving his home a closer inspection. She took in the floor-to-ceiling windows, strategically placed recessed lights, and warm, earth-toned walls, which matched the living room's rich décor in both design and comfort. "I see why you wanted to come home and crash last weekend. Your place is very relaxing."

"Thanks, and, actually, this is my dad's place."

"It is?"

"Yeah, he purchased this condo a few years before I was born and he never sold it. Over the years, he rented it out, but when I decided to do my residency at Emory, he told me I could live here as long as I wanted. So I did a few minor upgrades, slapped some new paint on the walls, and here I am." PJ smiled. "My dad doesn't own the building, like your father does yours, but it's worked out pretty well and saved me a ton of money."

Now she understood the familiar feeling she'd experienced when she first approached the building. She'd been there before, through her mother. When she'd looked into Victoria's eyes last Sunday and saw flashes of her with PJ's dad, this place had been one of the many things that played out in front of her eyes in a matter of seconds. She now realized that her abilities ran much deeper than she'd ever imagined.

The thought of what she could do was too much for Alexandria to process at the moment. So instead of killing the intimate mood with her surreal vision, she tucked her new revelation away and kept the conversation flowing. "Well, I'm impressed. You did a great job decorating."

"Thanks, I'm glad you like it."

"I'm really glad I'm here."

"So am I. Having you here feels good."

His deep voice oozed of raw sensuality and it made Alexandria's heart beat fast. She shifted in place from her right hip to her left and took a deep breath. "What we're building is really special, and I want us to be careful with it, you know?"

PJ swirled the wine in his glass, took a sip, and raised his brow. "What're you trying to say?"

"I want us to develop our relationship the right way."

"Ali, relax. This is the second time you've said that."

"It is?"

PJ nodded his head. "You said it yesterday when we had coffee."

"Oh. I'm sorry. I just want to be clear about certain things."

"Like sex?" he said in a serious tone. "I know you can look into my eyes and tell how much I want you."

His directness turned her on even more, but she knew she had to fight against it and also set the record straight. "Yes, I was talking about rushing to bed too quickly. But, PJ, I want you to know that I haven't used my gift to read your thoughts since the other night. I told you I wouldn't do that again, and I meant it."

"I appreciate that. But it still doesn't change the fact that I want you, and you know that, don't you?"

"Yes, I do."

"And you want me, too."

Alexandria swallowed hard, but she didn't say anything.

"Ali, when it comes to us, there's no right or wrong, fast or slow. The dating rules we applied to others in our past don't count when it comes to what's happening between us. You're different from any woman I've ever known."

"I am?"

"Of course. Our whole vibe is different. *This,*" he said, pointing between the two of them, "is different. Can't you feel it?"

Alexandria nodded. "Yes, I can." She took another sip of wine and uncrossed her long, shapely legs. She could see PJ's eyes glued to her smooth thighs, which peeked out from beneath her pencil skirt. The sexual tension between them had been building all night, and now it had reached a crescendo.

PJ picked up the remote from the coffee table and hit the play button. When Sade's sultry voice crooned through the Bose speakers, Alexandria knew he was setting the mood for what was sure to turn physical.

"Want a refill?" he asked, motioning toward her half-empty glass.

She shook her head and set her wineglass on the coffee table. "Um, no. I'm good."

"Me too." PJ smiled seductively and set his empty glass beside

Alexandria's. "I'm a man of action, and I don't believe in beating around the bush."

In one quick move, he slid closer toward her so they were now sitting side by side, with only a few inches separating their bodies. He took her hand into his and held it, stroking her palm with his thumb. It was a sensual gesture, which made her stomach do small flips. She was sure he could feel her excited jitters as he held her fingers gently in his grip. Things were moving fast, and Alexandria wondered if she could slow them down, or if she even wanted to at this point.

"Ali?"

"Yes?"

PJ looked at her, but he didn't say another word. Slowly he leaned in so close that Alexandria could feel his warm, wine-scented breath on her skin. His nose almost touched hers as he planted himself in her personal space. His breathing became slow and steady, while hers grew short and rapid, matching the pace of her pounding heart. Her body was flush and hot, and she could feel the wetness starting to form on the cotton strip of her silk, hot pink–colored panties.

PJ looked into her eyes, wrapped his arms around her waist, and lifted her onto his lap with such comfort and ease that Alexandria found herself giving in to the very thing she'd tried to fight.

Once she settled on top of him, she pulled her skirt up a little farther and rested her round bottom against his bulging hard-on, causing her to let out a small gasp of excitement. She smiled at his arousal and leaned into him, touching her forehead to his. With delicate care, he pulled from her hair the jewel-toned clip, which had been holding it in place, and released her massive bundle of curls as they fell into a cascade around her slim shoulders. She shook her thick, curly brown mane, threw her head back, and let out a slow moan.

"Damn, you're sexy," PJ said as he pulled her in even closer.

Now they were both breathing heavily, rocking back and forth. Their lower bodies began to roll in a slow, grinding motion as they grew more and more aroused. She placed her hands on his shoulders while he gently caressed her back. All the reservations Alexandria had held were starting to fade, and the only thing she wanted to do was please and be pleased.

"I want you," PJ softly whispered into her ear.

He pulled her in for the kiss she'd been fantasizing about all day. When she felt his soft lips press against hers, tiny bursts of light spread through her body. It was so bright that it outshone the stars in the night's sky. She eagerly opened her mouth and accepted PJ's gentle tongue as he pushed his erection against her slightly dampened crotch, which was growing more wet with desire. His kiss was wanton and warm, giving her just the right amount of lip and tongue to make her body crave more. His strong hands moved slowly as he rubbed her thighs; then he gripped her hips as she gyrated them in a slow, circular motion.

They moved in one spot—touching, kissing, caressing, and feeling their way into uncharted territory. Alexandria watched PJ closely as he removed his shirt, and then his cotton T-shirt, revealing a broad, muscular chest.

She paused when her eyes narrowed in on his right shoulder. Slowly she traced her fingers over the diamond-shaped tattoo on his upper bicep.

"Look for the diamond, 'cause the one who has that is the one who's gonna help save you."

She stared into PJ's deep brown eyes with intensity as feelings and memories from last Saturday night came rushing back to her. The warm sensations she'd felt several times that day were the same tremblings that ignited her skin at PJ's touch. The memory she'd recounted of her grandparents holding hands was the same sweet gesture PJ now made with her. And as her eyes ventured back to the tattoo on his arm, she knew she was right where she needed to be.

Whatever small hesitation lingered in her mind about jumping into bed too soon was now tossed out the proverbial window, and she was ready for everything that was going to happen.

"Let me help you out of that," PJ said, tugging at the base of Alexandria's silk blouse.

She lifted her arms into the air, allowing him to pull her blouse over her head before tossing it to the side. Slowly he unhooked her bra, letting her full breasts fall to their natural position. She leaned forward and moaned as he circled his finger around her sensitive flesh before taking her into his mouth. She moaned again with newfound pleasure when she felt him gently suck her right breast, then roll his tongue around the rim of her hardened nipple.

A soft whimper spilled from Alexandria's lips, and her body begged for more. "Oh, baby," she whispered.

PJ panted hard and scooted his body toward the edge of the couch. He held Alexandria firmly in place so she wouldn't fall as he rose to his feet with her legs wrapped around his waist. He carried her to his bedroom, and there he laid her down with care across the length of his king-size bed. She spread her legs slightly and watched as he quickly pulled off his jeans. Then he slid his gray Calvin Kleins to the floor.

Although the room was unlit, the streetlights outside provided a bright glow through the miniblinds at his window, allowing Alexandria a view of the impressive hardness she'd felt on the couch. She smiled with lust and delight when she saw his large, swollen manhood standing at attention, ready for her.

"Mmmm," PJ said, looking at Alexandria as he reached for her skirt and slid it down her legs. He hooked his finger along the side of her panties and slowly removed them.

"Ali, I'm going to make love to you with all five senses, and I promise you that I'll make it count," he said, whispering the words she'd said onstage during her performance at the Lazy Day.

He gently rubbed his hands along her bikini line, and his touch felt so good that she wanted to scream. "Oh, PJ," she whispered in a heavy breath.

He kissed her slowly as their tongues once again explored each other's mouths. She inhaled with anticipation as he slid his finger from her inner thigh and then dipped it into her moist middle.

"Damn, I love that you're so wet," PJ said.

She squirmed with ecstasy as his finger swirled around inside her while she moved her hips against the gentle pressure of his hand.

Slowly he removed his finger, brought it to his mouth, and licked it like candy. "I want to taste more of you."

Alexandria eagerly spread her legs as he positioned himself between her thighs. When she felt the tip of his tongue at the base of her creamy folds, she dug her heels into the pillow-top mattress, releasing a slow moan, which let him know he was on point.

"I'm gonna lick you from the bottom to the top," PJ whispered seductively, spreading her legs farther apart so his tongue could reach its target. With gentle, concentrated skill, he took his time, trailing her heated flesh in a circular motion, which delivered on his promise. He used attentive care—licking, sucking, and stroking her wetness, devouring her sweet juices as they flowed down into his mouth.

"Yes, baby. That's it. Right there," Alexandria called out as his mouth engulfed her clit.

He nibbled and sucked her gently, using his lips and tongue to take her to a place of new discovery. Her thighs trembled as she bucked against his mouth and released an orgasm so deliciously powerful that all she could do was pant and smile. *"Damn!"* she called out as her chest heaved up and down with pleasure.

PJ dotted kisses along her stomach, across her chest, up to her neck, and then onto the side of her cheek before he reached her mouth, kissing her deeply.

"I want to return the favor." Alexandria purred as she made her way down PJ's body, planting tender kisses on his skin as he'd done to hers. When she reached his hardness, she held him in her hand and gently stroked his thick shaft from the base to the tip of his large head, and then back down again. She twirled her finger around every inch of his throbbing stiffness that she could touch, enjoying the sound of his low moans and the fact that she was pleasing him. Slowly she licked her lips and opened her mouth wide, enveloping him whole, running her tongue up and down his hardness as she sucked with steady and gentle pressure.

"Oh, baby," PJ moaned.

Alexandria loved the feel of him in her mouth and against the palm of her hand as she alternated between gently licking him with her tongue, and applying subtle pressure as she stroked him with her hand. She tickled, and teased, and licked, and sucked, and swallowed, until PJ couldn't take it any longer.

He reached inside his nightstand, pulled out a condom, ripped the package open, and slid it on so fast that Alexandria barely had time to brace herself for the feel of his thick head as he slowly penetrated her.

With gentle, measured force, PJ began to ease his way inside her. He thrusted his hips forward, burying each rock-hard inch into her creamy wetness. Once he filled her with his full erection, he paused for a moment and lay there, resting in a warm, welcoming spot that made both their bodies tremble.

PJ nestled his head in the crook of her neck and inhaled deeply. He smiled and looked into her eyes as he whispered softly. "You smell so sweet, you taste so delicious, you feel incredibly soft, and you look absolutely beautiful. I'm going to make love to you, baby."

If she thought she had felt pleasure before, Alexandria was amazed at how her body could reach such heights now. She held PJ close to her chest as he thrusted deep inside her, hitting her special spot with a hard force that sent a wave of sweet pain through her entire lower body. She enjoyed the feel of their slick, sweat-covered skin dancing in a rhythm that she knew was going to make her explode again.

Just as she was about to reach her tipping point, he slowed his movements and whispered into her ear, "Turn over, baby. I'm gonna get you from behind."

His deep voice and sexy command made Alexandria smile with wicked lust. "Mmmm," she moaned. Slowly, she crawled onto all fours and burrowed her knees and elbows into his soft brown sheets.

She panted heavily as she felt his hands gently grab hold of each side of her hips, and this time she readied herself to receive him. But instead of entering her right away, he teased her, rubbing his hardness against her quivering lips and the sides of her inner thighs. She arched her back and moaned, ready to feel him inside her once again. Then slowly, as he'd done before, he made his way to the place that brought both of them pleasure. She closed her eyes and nearly screamed with ecstasy as he pounded her at a steady pace, which made her body jerk forward. She whimpered softly when she felt him lean onto her back, reach around her waist, and trail his fingers down between her legs until he reached the mound of her throbbing clit, rubbing it as he slid in and out of her wetness.

"You like that, baby?" PJ panted as he continued rubbing her delicate middle, never breaking his deep, unrelenting thrusts into her creamy warmth.

She wanted to respond, but she was too caught up in the hot orgasm bursting at the meeting between her thighs. She turned her head, looked behind her, and found him staring back into her eyes with a determined look on his face, which was etched with tender care and filled with purpose. She let go and gave in to her pleasure as she called out his name, over and over and over again.

He'd satisfied her, and now it was his turn. Within a minute of her explosive release, Alexandria felt PJ's rhythm quicken and his thrusts drive deeper and harder inside her. She knew he was approaching the euphoria she'd already reached, and she could hear his panting grow louder as his movements became more urgent. Knowing he was at the edge, Alexandria eased herself flat onto her stomach while he continued to thrust. "Ooohhh, Ali," he called out as he exploded inside her, slowly releasing a pleasure-filled moan.

They lay, exhausted and satisfied, wrapped in each other's arms, resting for a moment before they began their next ride.

Chapter 30

Allene Small remembered when her Saturday nights were busy and filled with work: getting her children's clothes washed and ironed for church the next morning, going over the Bible verses and the lesson she would teach the young children in her Sunday school class, and cooking Sunday-afternoon dinner so all she had to do was pile food onto plates when her family came home from church. But now, her Saturday evenings were filled with watching *The Lawrence Welk Show*, stargazing at the sky, and sleep, whenever it finally decided to come.

On this particular Saturday night, Allene sat on her front porch and enjoyed the unusual chill that had nipped the air. It had been scorching hot earlier today, but now it felt like early fall instead of late summer, requiring her to wrap her shawl around her shoulders as she'd done this morning. Her rocking chair slowly creaked back and forth, creating a beat in syncopation with the rhythm of her voice as she sang "Amazing Grace," her favorite gospel hymn, which she'd been humming throughout the night. She paused for a moment and looked up at the bright moon hanging in the dark sky. The stars looked like diamonds sprinkled across a never-ending canvas of black space, giving the night an air of beauty and mystery.

She shook her head when she thought about the saying she had heard all her life—that it was good luck to wish upon a star. Contrary to that belief, she knew there was no such truth to the old wives' tale. And furthermore, she knew there was no such thing as luck at all. Luck was good fortune brought about by chance; and if life had taught Allene anything, it was that nothing happened by chance. That's why she was grateful that not only was she guiding John to safety, but she was guiding Alexandria, too.

Her grandson and her great-great granddaughter, who were living in different times, were caught in the same tenuous situation—having to make the right choice in matters of the heart. Allene knew how tricky love could be. It could make you soar high or bring you down low, depending upon the person you chose.

She breathed a sigh of relief, knowing that Alexandria was already in the safety of someone who was going to love her, accept her, and help her along her journey. "Thank you, Lord, for givin' that child courage," she said aloud. Now her biggest worry was making sure John came out of this weekend unscathed.

"Everything is as it needs to be," Susan Jessup had told her decades ago when she'd come to Allene in one of her many restless dreams. *"There is no such thing as coincidence. God makes everything happen."*

Over the years, Allene had come to see the truth in the old woman's wisdom, and she'd witnessed firsthand that coincidence was simply God's way of remaining anonymous through whatever lesson was to be learned. Now, at her ripened age, Allene was comfortable standing in the sunset that had become her life; and more than ever, she was secure in her gift.

There was a time when just like Alexandria, Allene had rejected her gift of prophesy, not wanting the weight or burden that came along with being able to see and hear things that others couldn't. But after the terrifying night when the KKK burned her son and daughter-in-law's house to the ground—and they barely escaped with their lives—her entire world changed. That night demonstrated to Allene how blessed she truly was to have inherited the gift—and that her abilities could be used to help her family not only survive, but flourish. So from that point forward, she set out to hone her abilities, to trust her gut, and to listen and learn from everything that Susan Jessup taught her.

Allene's gift made her aware of many things that others couldn't begin to fathom. All human beings born into this world knew that one day they would die. But Allene could pinpoint the exact year, day, hour, and minute she'd take her last breath. She knew she had eight more years of living left in her body, which was five more than her son had left in his. Her heart ached every time she thought about having to bury her child, but she understood the cycle of life. She knew that this world was just a temporary thing, and what rested on the other side was forever.

Allene rose from her chair and went back inside the house. It was almost midnight and she was beginning to feel every one of her ninety years nipping at her bones.

"Think I'll make me a nice hot cup of tea, with some honey. That'll soothe my insides and help me sleep like a baby," she said as she walked slowly back to her kitchen.

After she made her tea, she returned to her spot on her La-Z-Boy. She took a sip of the hot sweetness in her cup, already feeling too tired to finish the remainder of the drink. She put her hand to her mouth and whispered, "Life sure is somethin'."

"Yes, it is, my child," a strong voice answered back.

Allene turned her head and nearly dropped her teacup when she saw Susan Jessup standing within two feet of her recliner. She was startled and confused, not because it had been several years since Susan had last paid her a visit, but because this was the first time she could remember the woman ever coming to her during her waking hours, in the flesh, no less.

Susan always had appeared to Allene in her dreams; but now as Allene looked at her great-grandmother standing tall in the middle of her living room, breathing the same air and connecting in the same time and space, Susan Jessup appeared as real and as human as any guest walking through Allene's front door.

Susan took a few steps and eased her body down onto the soft couch next to Allene's La-Z-Boy. "We must talk."

Allene was almost in disbelief. Everything about Susan seemed multiplied by ten. When Susan came to Allene in her dreams, she always appeared as a muffled voice inside a murky image. But experiencing her now, in real time, was very different.

The richness and fine tone of Susan's African accent beat against the air like Ashanti drums, and her crisp enunciation spoke to the fact that she'd been educated in some manner, whether formally trained or self-taught. Allene wanted to reach out and touch her, feel her smooth-looking skin, and embrace her for a long, warm hug. But the look on her great-grandmother's face told her that it wouldn't be wise to mix their worlds through physical contact.

Allene studied the woman who had visited her countless times over the past eighty-four years. She admired Susan's onyx-hued skin, deep, penetrating eyes, and noble posture—all reminiscent of her own features. Susan's thick, wiry black hair was pulled back into heavy plaits away from her slim face, giving her the appearance of a young beauty who couldn't have been older than her midtwenties. She took a seat on the couch next to Allene and smiled.

Allene sat back in her recliner, examining Susan's clothes—a plain, tan-colored dress made of densely spun cotton—and watched as the ancient ghost crossed her bare feet at the ankle, revealing long toes that looked exactly like Allene's very own. "You're young" was the first thing that came out of Allene's mouth.

"Yes, I was thirty-seven when I left this world."

"You look in your twenties."

"And you look in your sixties, but you are not. The gift is not the only thing that runs in our blood." Susan smiled. "Youth is in us, too."

The two women studied each other for a long moment before Susan continued. "I would have come a little earlier, but I wanted you to enjoy the night sky in peace."

"You could've joined me," Allene said. "I love gazin' up at the stars, especially when they're shinin' bright, like tonight."

"Yes, it is breathtaking. When I was a small girl back in Ghana, I used to watch the sun smile over the African sky each morning, and the moon kiss the day good-bye each night. There was nothing more magnificent to behold. But once I came to these shores, the sun, moon, and even the sky itself felt different," Susan said with a hint of sadness.

"Do you ever go back? I mean, can't you travel across space and time?"

"No, I have never gone back. This is my home now. This is where I will be until the end of my time."

Allene wanted to question her. When was her time going to end? She was a ghost. Didn't they float around forever? But she knew that everything with Susan was like a slow dance; and over the years, she'd come to learn that the ancient ghost did nothing without a purpose. So she didn't probe, because she knew that once the time was right, Susan would reveal the answers to all the questions she'd wanted to know, but had never asked.

Allene leaned back in her recliner and sipped her lukewarm tea. "Isaiah and Henrietta will be comin' by in the morning to pick me up for church. You wanna come?"

"I'm sorry, but I will have to decline. I cannot stay that long."

Allene took another sip of her tea. "I wish you could share a cup with me," she said with a smile.

"I was never a tea drinker, but I did like coffee."

"Oh, I like it, too. I only drink tea at night before I go to bed 'cause it helps me sleep. But every mornin', I drink a cup of coffee as soon as I get up."

"I remember the taste. Strong and bitter like the earth, but rich like life."

Allene nodded and looked at Susan closely. "What was your life like?"

"Full," she said with a smile. "My life was full the day I was born, because I came into this world with a purpose. I lived my life so that you could live yours, Allene. I watched over you before you were even born. You are my greatest hope and my destiny."

Since she was six years old, Allene had always felt a strained distance between herself and the ghost sitting in front of her. When she was a young girl, she'd been afraid of Susan and her haunting appearance, but as she grew older she'd gotten used to her. Then as she slid into the twilight of her life, she'd come to respect and revere her. And now, as she looked upon the woman who had been a part of her life for longer than anyone on this side of the earth, she felt nothing but love for her. She loved Susan Jessup with all her heart and soul.

"I love you, too, my child." Susan nodded as she read her great-granddaughter's thoughts.

Allene smiled, but then she realized why Susan was there, and that knowledge turned her smile into a flat line. She took a deep breath and sighed. "Thank you for bein' my light," Allene whispered, "and for lovin' me all my life." Allene wasn't one to cry; so when the tear fell from her right eye and traveled down her cheek, she simply let it roll.

"You know why I have come to you on this night, in this form, don't you?"

Allene slowly nodded. "Yes. I believe so."

"Then tell me."

Allene looked at Susan with a measure of sadness. "It's time for you to go. I ain't gonna see you again. Not in this lifetime."

Susan nodded. "Your skills are very good. Yes, my child. I must forever return to where I belong. This is my last visit in your world, in this time."

Allene nodded, affirming what the old African had just said.

"I have been here since yesterday, watching over you, Allene."

"So that *was* you," Allene responded in a whisper. "The warm feelin' on my skin this mornin' and the extra-sweet smell from my magnolias this afternoon . . . that was you."

"Yes, that was me. Just as the cold chill came to warn you about trouble that was headed for John and Alexandria, I brought you warmth and light to let you know that love is all around you. And, in turn, you guided our grandchildren to it through your words and advice."

Allene let out a deep breath. "Thank you, Lord."

Susan smiled again. "Yes, and just as I guided you for all these years, it is now time for you to guide our precious Alexandria. She's on the right path, and if she listens to you, and you teach her all that you've learned, her gift will become more powerful than yours and mine. She will be able to do things that even I cannot fathom."

"Yes, I know. I can feel that child's energy. It's strong, and now that she knows what she's got, it's growin' more powerful each day."

"Yes, you are correct, Allene. And she has an important element that makes her very special."

"A pure heart."

"That she does. Just like yours. And she will need you, Allene, now more than ever."

"Because of her mama and that man," Allene said softly, shaking her head with worry.

Susan sighed deeply. "Yes, exactly. What is brewing is a situation that I did not see coming. I thought it was laid to rest many years ago, but apparently not."

"I guess that sleepin' dog didn't lie."

"What?"

"It's a sayin'." Allene chuckled. "It means the same thing you just said. What happened in the past is back again."

"Yes, it is."

The two women shared another quiet moment, thinking the same thoughts as they reflected on the marvelous gift they shared. Allene looked at her ghost of a great-grandmother who appeared full of life. "Even though I haven't talked to you in a few years, I sure am gonna miss you."

"And I, you." Susan smiled.

"Besides the good Lord above, you're the only one who's been with me in this world through all these years. Now you're gonna leave me, like everybody else who's already passed on."

"Yes, but I'll always be with you. You will feel me, and so will Alexandria."

"You're gonna be that warm breeze?"

"Yes, my child. Whenever you feel the warmth of the sun upon your skin, that will be me."

Allene smiled.

"I must go now," Susan said, her voice slowly becoming the muffled sound that Allene's ears had been trained to recognize. "I am so proud of you, Allene. Continue to watch over John, and take care of our Alexandria. Guide her well and teach her all that you know."

As Susan began to fade into vapors right before Allene's eyes, Allene called out to her, "I love you!"

"I love you, too, my precious Allene."

Then in the snap of a finger, Susan was gone.

But instead of feeling sad, Allene's heart was filled with happiness and hope. The torch had been passed on to her. It had taken her a long time to earn and accept it, but now it was in her hands, and she was grateful that she knew what to do.

She knew that John was going to be all right. He still wasn't out of the woods with his lunatic girlfriend; so although she hadn't wanted to, she knew it was time for her to intervene. She had to call upon someone who could help him. She closed her eyes, calmed her mind, and searched for the person who could come to John's aid.

Allene concentrated, going through space and time, reading the thoughts of anyone she could find who was connected to the energy that could eliminate John's problems. After several minutes, it came to her, and she smiled, knowing exactly who it was that she needed to reach out to. "You can never go wrong doin' right," she whispered, carrying her message to the person who needed to hear it . . . the person who would help John. "You can never go wrong doin' right," she said again. "Go ahead and do the right thing. Help John tonight."

Allene nodded, confident that her words had been heard and received, and now her heart rested a little better. "Whew!" she breathed out. "All this prophesyin' has worn me out," Allene said with a sigh. "Time for me to get my beauty sleep."

Allene drifted off in her comfortable recliner, knowing that when the sun came up tomorrow, both John's and Alexandria's worlds were going to be very different.

Chapter 31

The first-floor waiting room of Nedine Memorial Hospital was packed with more people than the moderate-size space had seen since the flood of 1945. The facility had become desegregated a year ago when changing social times and an ambitious new mayor had imposed the long-overdue move.

The nearly all-white nursing staff looked upon the crowd with a mixture of concern and curiosity. They had never seen so many black folks in the hospital at one time. Tall and short, slender and heavy, light and dark—they were all black—and they were standing vigil, waiting for an update on Maxx Sanders's condition.

From the sketchy report the doctor had given the family, which had soon trickled by word of mouth to everyone in the room, Maxx was listed in critical condition by the time the ambulance had transported him to the emergency room. He'd lost a massive amount of blood, and the single bullet was still lodged in his backside, causing the threat of a very serious complication.

"Judging from the entry wound," Maxx's doctor had said, "it looks like the trajectory of the bullet made it probable for intra-abdominal bleeding. But we can't be sure how much damage has been done until we get him on the operating table."

In laymen's terms, Maxx was in danger of losing his life because of excessive blood loss and the possibility that the bullet had traveled in the body. Maxx had gone from celebrating his birthday to fighting for his life, and now it was just a waiting game.

"This is awful. Just awful!" Grace Sanders cried as she hung her head against her husband's narrow shoulder while he patted her back. She wiped her tears with a tissue as she shook with worry. Her nose had become a rosy pink bulb of sniffles, the result of nearly an hour's worth of sobs. "They should lock up that woman and throw away the key," she cried, referring to Thelma Porter, the scorned, vengeful woman who had shot Maxx.

Grace and Milford Sanders had been lying in bed, resting up for Sunday-morning church service, when their phone rang shortly after midnight. As soon as Grace answered and heard John Small's deep voice pipe through the line, she immediately knew that something terrible had happened to her son. She knew it because John never called their house, not even when Maxx had lived there. With the rare exception of last week when a looming deadline forced him to reach out in order to coordinate Maxx's big birthday celebration, John had never ventured to dial their number.

Grace's disdain for John went way back. From the moment an eight-year-old Maxx had come home from school one afternoon, beaten and bloody from a vicious playground fight that had involved John at its center, Grace had looked upon young John with nothing short of contempt. She didn't want any of her three boys getting mixed up with the wrong crowd, and especially not Maxx, who at the time was her youngest and most favored child. She knew how dangerous consorting with the wrong people could be, even for children, and that was one of the reasons she didn't want John Small anywhere near her son.

It didn't matter to Grace that John hadn't started the rumble, or that Maxx had inserted himself into the fight without provocation. What had mattered to her was that her son had been injured as a direct consequence of being involved with the type of person she'd spent her entire life consciously avoiding—"dark-skinned black folk." In Grace's opinion, they were nothing but trouble. And now, twenty-four years later, her son had been injured again—and just as before, dark-skinned, black-as-tar John Small was on the scene.

At the sound of John's first words, an alarm had sounded through Grace's veins that mimicked thunder. She hadn't bothered to pay attention to the details of what John had said. Once she heard "Maxx" and "been shot," she woke her husband, who'd been sleeping like the dead, and hurried to the hospital at a speed that could have rivaled a freight train's.

When Grace and Milford arrived, the waiting room was already full of people—both family and friends—who had been at the Blue Room partying with Maxx until Thelma's gun ended the celebration.

"What would make someone do such a thing?" Grace lamented between loud sniffles. "This is why respectable people should stay out of nightclubs. Nothing good can come of it. Might as well be in the gutter!"

"Now hold on just one minute, Grace," Sylvester Hanks spoke up. "It won't the Blue Room that got your boy shot in the ass. It was his ways. He drug that trouble he had goin' on wit' them two women right up into my club."

Grace Sanders cut her eye at Mr. Hanks, the wily proprietor of the Blue Room. "It's the kind of crowd that your establishment attracts that caused all of this, not Maxx," she shot back.

"Woman, you can't be serious!"

"I certainly am. Everyone knows that the Blue Room is a sinners' den full of drunken men and loose women with absolutely no morals."

Everyone in the waiting room was silent, holding their breaths and rolling their eyes.

Mr. Hanks raised his brow. "I guess you half-right, 'cause Maxx was sho nuf drunker than ten skunks. Your boy couldn't handle his liquor or his women, and that," he spat back, "is what caused all this!"

Grace put her hand to her chest and drew in a deep breath. "My son is a gentleman and a hero. He's in there on that operating table right now because he took a bullet trying to save a woman's life."

"He took a bullet 'cause his drunk ass was tryin' to pick up one woman while his other two womens was right there in the club."

"You should be ashamed to say such a despicable thing!"

"And you should be embarrassed that it's true!"

Seeing that things were about to escalate out of control, a tired and timid-looking Milford finally spoke up. "Let's all calm down. Placin' blame ain't gonna do nothin' for nobody right now."

Mr. Hanks shook his head. "Henpecked son of a bitch," he said under his breath in Milford's direction. A few heads nodded in agreement.

The tension in the room turned thick and sticky, and that's when John stepped in. He walked over to Mr. Hanks and began speaking to him in a serious tone.

Grace was furious with Sylvester Hanks. Even worse, though, she wanted to scream at John Small for inserting himself into matters that didn't involve him. She held him partly responsible for what had happened to her son. At the moment, she couldn't stand the sight of him.

She had known from the start that celebrating a special occasion like a birthday at a nightclub was a bad idea. She'd tried to warn Maxx against it, but his mind had been set. And once John encouraged it, even offering to help with the affair, Grace felt as if all reason was lost. Now she wished with all her might that John would disappear back to New York City where he belonged. She didn't want him anywhere near her son, and especially not her daughter.

When she and Milford first walked through the waiting-room doors, she noticed that Elizabeth had been standing a little too close to John for Grace's comfort. She didn't like the feeling she'd gotten when she saw the two huddled, side by side. There was something in Elizabeth's face and John's body language that made Grace's antennae rise. But the moment Elizabeth had seen Grace and Milford, she'd run into their embrace and gathered with them so they could console each other as a family.

Grace started sobbing again as she thought about her son lying on the operating table, all because of the company he kept. Then she looked around the room in search of Elizabeth, who was nowhere to be found. She wondered where her daughter had gone to so quickly. She'd been sitting beside them just moments ago and now she was gone. But Grace knew she could only focus on one calamity at a time. So for now, she concentrated her attention and prayers on her son. Once the good Lord brought him out of danger, she would make sure she did everything in her power to keep John Small as far away from her daughter as life would allow.

Chapter 32

John cast a cautionary glare aimed directly at Sylvester Hanks. Anxiety and rising tension had gripped every person assembled in the hospital waiting room. Mr. Hanks's verbal volleying with Grace Sanders had proven to make a bad situation even worse. John felt like telling both of them to shut the hell up, but he knew he had to rise above the urge.

John wasn't a man who worried about things over which he had no control; at the moment he had to steel himself against the emotion. He was on edge because so much had happened in the blink of an eye, and he felt nearly powerless to the events swirling around him: the laughter, the screaming, the shooting; following the ambulance to the hospital; phoning Maxx's parents and then calling his own; trying to get updated information from the doctors and nurses; trying to be a voice of calm for Elizabeth; and finally, trying to keep himself from breaking down.

The weight of John's frustrating day with Madeline, and the trauma of witnessing his best friend get shot right in front of him, had all come crashing down on his shoulders. And now, looking at Sylvester Hanks, who'd foolishly bickered with the mother of a man who was fighting for his life, John had had enough.

John respected Mr. Hanks, but he knew that the man was more

concerned about the reputation of his establishment than Maxx's well-being. The club owner didn't want the Blue Room's pristine reputation tarnished behind a shooting—or, worse, a fatality that might result from it. John knew that was the only reason why the penny-pinching businessman had even bothered to show up at the hospital shortly after giving the police his statement and closing down his club. He'd walked through the waiting-room doors bearing irritation instead of compassion. When he heard Grace Sanders's remark, it was too much for him to hold. He'd blurted out his true thoughts, instead of using diplomatic refrain.

John saw that poor, docile Milford wasn't equipped to handle the situation; and although he'd never cared much for Grace, he felt empathy for what she must be going through. So he attempted to calm the moment by trying to reason with Mr. Hanks. He walked over to the man and looked him in the eye.

"Mr. Hanks, like my wise, old grandma Allene always says, 'Just because something is true, that doesn't mean you have to say it.' We all know how things really went down in the club tonight, so—"

"Listen, John," Mr. Hanks interrupted. "I ain't never had no trouble wit' you. You and your daddy is fine, upstandin' peoples. Respectable Negro bidnessmen, just like myself. I know what you sayin', but I ain't gonna stand by and let that woman talk shit about my establishment on account of her fool-ass son."

"Mr. Hanks, please lower your voice. This is getting out of control."

"I'm not the one outta control. It's y'all young folks that can't control yo'selves. I tried to do a good deed, but, *hmph,* never again!" he balked. "I don't care how much money you paid me or how much Slim begged, I shoulda never shut down my club for some birthday party bullshit!"

John officially had reached his limit. His steely eyes narrowed in on Mr. Hanks's. The older man was his height and nearly twice his size, but just like Mr. Hanks, John didn't take kindly to bullshit, either. "Mr. Hanks, this isn't the time or place. I respect you, but you need to respect this situation, too."

Mr. Hanks continued his rant, ignoring what John had said. "I told Slim that I didn't want no shit goin' down in my club, and now look at what happened! Where is he, anyway?"

"He ran an errand for me, but I'm sure he'll be here shortly," John replied, still holding Mr. Hanks's stare. "But don't worry about Slim. Right now, we're all gathered here to make sure Maxx comes through this safely. So unless you can offer a prayer or some words of encouragement, it might be best for you to leave . . . right now." John's words were bitingly sharp, delivered in a threatening tone.

Mr. Hanks stared back at John and then glanced around the room. The tension-filled eyes, which had boomeranged in his direction, all supported what John just said to him. "This ain't even worth the damn hassle," Mr. Hanks hissed before turning on the heel of his brown loafers and stomping out the door.

John let out a deep breath and walked over to the other side of the waiting room so he could have a moment to himself. He rubbed his hand over his clean-shaven chin, thinking about how he'd just been seconds away from creating a scene of his own. He leaned against the wall and looked up as he saw a voluptuous young woman approach.

"Hey there, stranger." The pretty woman smiled, planting herself by his side. Her name was Mary-Marie Jackson, and she and John had a history.

Mary-Marie and John had enjoyed lustful dalliances over the years whenever he came to town for visits. Even though Mary-Marie had a steady boyfriend, whenever John rolled through town they always rendezvoused in his hotel room, enjoying heated nights of sexual pleasure. But a year and a half ago, she'd told him that she wanted more than the weekend thrills they shared every few months.

"I want to move to New York and make a go of it with you, John," Mary-Marie had told him.

John didn't want to lead Mary-Marie on, so he quickly let her know that what they shared between the sheets was all it could ever be. Since then, he had purposely stayed away from her whenever he came to town. He hadn't seen her again until now.

"Hey, Mary-Marie," John said. "It's been a while."

"A year and a half, to be exact. I see you're still looking as hand-some as ever."

John smiled; and even though she looked good, too, he held off on returning the compliment. His life was complicated enough; he didn't want to add to it by encouraging an ex-lover.

Mary-Marie moved in close. "That was real noble what you just did, handling Mr. Hanks like that."

John nodded, casually taking a small step back to put distance be-tween them. "I just did what needed to be done."

"Yeah, I remember how good you are when it comes to taking care of business." She licked her luscious lips and took a step forward into the space that John had created.

John caught Mary-Marie's hint and recognized the look in her eyes—a look that let him know he could still have her, if he wanted her.

"If I was the sensitive type, my feelings would be hurt right about now," Mary-Marie said. "I saw you at the club tonight and you didn't even speak to me."

"It was so crowded—I didn't even know you were there. I would have spoken if I'd seen you."

"I guess you had your hands full trying to juggle that tall heffa you walked in with, and then Lizzy Sanders on your way out."

John tilted his head and nodded. "Thanks for your observation."

"I'm always watching out where you're concerned."

"I appreciate that, but right now my interest lies with Maxx. That's why we're both here, right?" John knew that like Mr. Hanks, Mary-Marie had her own set of reasons for being there.

"Yes, of course. But if you want to forget about your worries, you know I can help you do that, right?"

"I'll be just fine."

"Ray and I aren't together anymore."

John looked at her as if to say, *And . . . ?*

"I got my own place about six months ago," Mary-Marie said with a smile.

"Good for you."

"It could be good for you, too." She pulled out a scratch piece of paper from her small handbag and placed it inside the front pocket of John's now-slightly-wrinkled oxford shirt. "Here's my new number. Call me."

John didn't want Mary-Marie's number, and he had no intention of taking her up on her hint to come over to her new place. However, he didn't want to appear rude, because, after all, they shared a long and vivid history. So he let her down as gently as he could. "I'm starting a new relationship, Mary-Marie. This woman really means something to me and I'm going to do right by her, so I can't accept this." John reached into his pocket to give her back her number.

Mary-Marie shook her head and held her hand to his pocket, brushing her body against his. "Keep it. You never know—you might want to use it one day."

John looked at her ruby-colored lips and ample DD breasts; but instead of feeling aroused, he longed for something else. He scanned the room and realized that Elizabeth wasn't around. The last time he'd seen her, she'd been sitting in a chair near her parents on the other side of the waiting room, but now she was gone. He hoped she hadn't seen Mary-Marie flirting with him and gotten the wrong impression. "Excuse me, Mary-Marie, I need to find someone."

John walked away, leaving his ex-lover standing in the corner, wearing disappointment and a frown.

John quickly scanned the other side of the waiting room; then he went over toward the nurses' station in search of Elizabeth. When he didn't find her there, he walked in the opposite direction and searched the long hallway, but still no luck. He returned to the waiting room, wondering where she could be.

Until a few moments ago, he and Elizabeth had been together nearly the entire evening. Now her sudden absence felt like a gaping hole. He could still feel her delicate hand trembling inside his when he'd driven behind the ambulance on their way to the hospital. "Maxx is going to be all right, Elizabeth," he'd told her.

A small rush of panic began to beat inside him until he felt a warm touch against his hand.

"She went outside," Josie said. "I think she needed some air."

John noticed the weathered look beaten across Josie's face; his thoughts momentarily shifted to concern about her well-being. "Are you all right, Josie?"

He knew she was in a fragile state, still shook-up from all that had happened. He'd had to coax her from under Maxx's bleeding body after he'd been shot. He knew that had to have been a traumatic experience for her. "You've been through a lot this evening. Is there anything you need? Anything that I can do?"

"Nah, I'm as tough as they come." Josie smiled. "I've got to be, to put up with your crazy friend for all these years."

"I can't argue with you on that."

"Everybody thinks I'm a damn fool for stickin' around so long, 'cause of all the drama, the other women, you name it. We've been through some storms, me and Maxx. Truth is, I just plain love him." She sighed. "But sometimes I wonder if he loves me back."

John didn't want to put words in another man's mouth, but he knew his best friend better than anyone, so he told Josie what he knew to be true. "Maxx stepped in front of a bullet that was meant for you. Men protect what they love."

Josie smiled. "Thanks, John. Now go see about Lizzy. She needs you."

John nodded and gave Josie a small kiss on her cheek. "Come and get me if the doctor gives any updates."

When John walked outside, the first thing he noticed was the chill that had seized the air. Earlier that evening, he and Elizabeth had been sweating in the night heat. Now the temperature had dropped considerably, which was unusual for this time of year. But he ignored the cool nip on his skin when he spotted Elizabeth in the back of the parking lot. She was sitting on the hood of his car, her bare arms gathered around her exposed knees as she shivered.

"What are you doing out here?" John asked as he approached.

Elizabeth looked up and gave him a small smile. "I needed to get out of there. I couldn't think straight after Mr. Hanks and Mama started arguing, so I decided to leave."

John breathed a little easier, knowing that she'd left before Mary-Marie's unsuccessful attempt at seduction. "Yeah, that was pretty bad."

"Mr. Hanks isn't the most agreeable man, but he wasn't entirely wrong about what he said, either," Elizabeth acknowledged. "Believe me, I know how my brother is, and, truth be told, I know how my mama is, too."

John didn't say a word. He knew it was never a good idea to talk about somebody's mama—however true the comment might be.

"I just pray that Maxx will be all right. If anything happens to my brother—"

"He's going to be just fine, Elizabeth. He's a fighter." John was trying to boost her spirits as much as his own. Maxx was more of a brother to him than his own blood brother, Billy, had ever been.

He had to believe that Maxx would pull through. Initially he, as well as most of the partygoers, had secretly snickered when they realized Maxx had been shot in the ass. But when he lost consciousness right before the ambulance arrived, that's when all jocularity stopped and real fear set in. Maxx had always been a popular man-about-town. He was loved by many, which was why the waiting room was packed with people.

"You're shivering," John said, changing his thoughts to focus on something he could control.

"I'm all right."

John went to the back seat and then returned with a navy blue cardigan in hand. He sat beside Elizabeth and draped the garment over her small shoulders with gentle care. "Better?"

"Yes, thank you." She smiled. "You're a good man, John Small."

"I can't let a beautiful woman freeze in the cold."

"I'm not just talking about your chivalry with this sweater. I mean everything. Everything about you." She looked at him closely, scooting her small body next to his large frame. "You're strong, fearless, thoughtful, and kind. You care about people, and you're respectful of others. You're always cool and calm on the outside, and you rarely get emotional. But you're gentle on the inside, because you have a genuinely good heart."

"I'm flattered that you see all of that in me, and after just one night."

"I told you, it's about more than this one night. I've known this all my life."

"How?"

"Maxx not only loves you like a brother, he admires you like a hero. He's always talked about how smart you are and what a good friend you've been to him. He said you're one of the most honest people he knows, and that's why he trusts you so. That says a lot about your character."

John smiled. "Maxx and I go back a long way."

"Yes, I guess we all do in one way or another."

"You're right." He reached for her hand. "We . . . you and me, are connected, and not just by Maxx. I feel something deep with you, Elizabeth."

She nodded and smiled. "Me too."

Maxx has to live, John thought. *He's got to pull through, because I have to tell him that I want to be with his sister.*

John knew he was falling hard and fast for Elizabeth, and there was no denying it. As implausible as it seemed, she'd managed to touch his heart in one night. His grandmother's words came to him again, and he smiled inside, confirming that she'd been right, as usual.

Elizabeth squeezed John's hand. "I appreciate you, John."

"I want to be with you, Elizabeth."

They looked at each other for a long beat, resting in the moment.

"I want to be with you, too," Elizabeth said. Then she leaned into the man she loved and kissed him tenderly.

Grace eyed her daughter closely when Elizabeth walked back into the waiting room holding John's hand. The sight nearly made her hyperventilate. After everything that had happened within the last few hours, it was more than she could take. She stood up and marched over to Elizabeth, ignoring John completely. "I need to speak with you in private."

"Did the doctors give an update about Maxx?" Elizabeth asked with hope and concern. "You can talk in front of John, Mama."

Grace acted as though Elizabeth hadn't said a word. Instead, she looked down at Elizabeth's hand still clutched inside John's and wanted to swat him away like a pesky fly. "Lizzy, follow me, please," she said through gritted teeth. Then she abruptly turned and started walking down the hall.

"Um, excuse me, John." Elizabeth was clearly embarrassed by her mother's openly rude behavior. "Don't go anywhere. I'll be right back."

John nodded. "I'll be here, waiting for you."

He took a seat in one of the chairs and counted to ten. This was the second time tonight he'd had to practice that exercise. Again, he had to temper his emotions. He knew why Grace was so upset, and it made him want to curse.

John wasn't a conceited man in the least, but he knew most mothers would toast to the heavens if their daughters brought him home on their arms. So the fact that Grace couldn't stand him was almost farcical, especially since the reason for her dislike was rooted in pure absurdity. Even though he was accustomed to prejudice and racism, having grown up in the South, and working in the world of high finance, he found it hard to swallow when that behavior was directed at him by other black people.

Grace's skin tone was almost alabaster, as was her mother's, her mother's mother's, and her mother's before her. Her family was filled with mildly-colored people of African descent, whose milky-white complexions had masked their heritage and afforded them certain privileges in the deep South—privileges that separated them from their darker-skinned brethren.

Grace's ancestors had been light-skinned house slaves who worked in the false comfort of their master's home, not the dark-skinned field slaves who toiled under the blazing sun and unrelenting lash of the overseer's whip. But even though the family was full of mulattos, quad-roons, and octoroons, they were equal-opportunity bigots and stood firmly against the notion of interracial marriage with whites.

Beyond the bleaching that Caucasians had afforded their skin from generations ago, Grace's family had very little use for white folks outside of their color. They chose to intermarry with other light-skinned blacks in order to keep their complexions intact. They under-stood that their hue was a valued commodity, and they'd been taught to protect its value.

Maxx was one of the very few in his family who actually had the nerve to consort with and even date people darker than he was. Grace had blamed it on Milford's side of the family. The Sanderses were a light-skinned brew, too, who were just as bad as Grace's people were. But every now and then, they let a darkie slide through the cracks and marry into the family.

John knew that Grace merely tolerated him because of his money and status. But now that it was clear to her that Elizabeth had joined her brother's ranks, John knew that Grace couldn't and wouldn't ac-cept it.

"She better hold on tight," John said aloud to himself with deter-mination. "I'm going to be with Elizabeth, and there's nothing that Grace Sanders can do about it."

Chapter 33

Madeline leaned against the closed door, looked at Slim, and smiled. "What's wrong?" she asked innocently. "You look like you've seen a ghost."

"Why did you close the door and put the lock on?"

"Because I don't want anyone to disturb us."

Slim rapidly blinked his eyes behind his thick glasses. "I shouldn't be in this room with you like this. It don't look right."

"It looks perfectly fine. There's nothing wrong with two friends spending a little time together."

"But we ain't friends. I barely know you," Slim said nervously. "Look, I need to get goin'."

"Awww, Slim, don't leave yet," Madeline pleaded, smiling deviously. She gestured toward the chair at the desk. "Have a seat and stay awhile so we can talk."

"I don't think that's a good idea, Madeline. Please open the door. I'm fixin' to leave."

Slim made a move toward the door where Madeline stood, but she held her hand up and gave him another sly smile. "Don't leave so soon. Once you're gone, I'll be all alone."

"I ain't tryin' to be mean, but that ain't my problem. I need to get back to the club. Besides, John will be here in a lil bit."

Madeline formed her lips into a pout. "I don't care about John. It's you that I want."

Slim shifted in place. "You makin' me real uncomfortable with this kinda talk. Now I already told you, I got to go."

"And I said I don't want you to."

Slim frowned. "I'ma ask you nicely one more time. Please move out of the way so I can get back to the club. I won't mention none of this to John, and we can forget this whole thing ever happened."

"Slim, if you keep talking like this, you're going to make me very angry, and you don't want to see me when I'm angry."

Slim's eyes narrowed, as if he'd had enough. "Woman, don't threaten me. Now move away from that-there door so I can leave."

Madeline wanted to laugh at Slim's weak attempt to be tough. She'd met ruthless people—hell, she was one—and she knew that Slim was anything but. He'd walked into her trap so easily, it almost seemed too good to be true. Little did he know, but the longer he stayed in the room, the more believable her lie would be. "Okay, Slim, calm down. I didn't mean to threaten you. I just really don't want you to go."

"I don't know what kinda game you playin'," he said, frustration starting to creep into his voice, "but I don't want any part of it. John's like a brother to me, and—"

"Oh, shut the hell up about John, you stupid motherfucker!" she screamed in an outburst. Madeline was fed up with hearing him say John's name, and she could feel her anger quickly rising. His whiny mouth had pissed her off, and she didn't want him to say another word, especially not about John. Plus, even though his being there was in her favor, she knew she couldn't run the risk of John coming back early and spoiling her plan before she had a chance to set things into motion. She needed to act fast.

With the speed of a cheetah, Madeline rushed past Slim, picked up the ceramic ashtray, which was sitting on the wooden desk, and banged it against the side of her head.

"What the hell!" Slim said as his eyes bucked wide.

Madeline didn't answer. Instead, she crashed the ashtray against her smooth jaw before tossing it to the floor. She took a deep breath, balled her hand into a tight fist, and punched herself in the eye before delivering a hard blow to her mouth, until her bottom lip began to bleed.

"You crazy bitch!" Slim yelled. "What the hell's wrong with you?" Now he looked as if he'd indeed seen a ghost.

Madeline quickly glanced down at the desk and braced herself. She swung her left leg out to the side and banged her thigh with force against the wood's hard edge. She grimaced, muffling the scream that wanted to leap from her bloody mouth as a sharp pain shot through her lower left side.

Slim looked on, wide-eyed and speechless. He wanted to move, but shock and disbelief held him in place. He watched as Madeline pulled at the fabric of her thin sundress, until she ripped it open, down the front.

Bloody and disheveled, Madeline lunged toward Slim, tackling his thin, gangly body so hard that he fell to the floor. They tussled and rolled around on the stiff carpet, until Slim managed to pin her down. He loomed over her, breathing hard. "I ain't never hit a woman! But as God is my witness, if you don't stop, I'ma whup yo' ass like you a man!"

Madeline laughed. "You weak son of a bitch. Is that all you got?" She spat in his face and started clawing at him like a wildcat.

Slim tried to restrain her, but his clumsy hands were no match for Madeline's stealth ones. She scratched his cheek so hard that blood ran down his face as she bucked and twisted underneath him.

Finally, after a few more scratches, Madeline was satisfied with her results. She dropped her hands in surrender as droplets of Slim's blood trickled onto her dress. She looked into his bewildered eyes and laughed again.

Slim rolled off her, still breathing heavy. He fumbled for his eyeglasses, which had fallen off his face. Once he found them, he slowly rose to his feet.

"You can go now," Madeline said, "and don't forget to tell John to hurry back over here, I'm going to need his help."

"You need help, all right!" Slim shouted. "I don't know what's wrong with you, but I'ma tell John the truth about all this." Slim's chest heaved up and down as he stood in the middle of the room. His shirt was torn, and his face was bloody and scarred. "Look what you did to me, and to yo'self! You crazy as hell!"

Madeline crawled from the floor to the bed and sat down. Her right eye had already begun to swell shut; a knot had formed on the side of her head; her jaw was bruised and her bottom lip was busted. "Slim, you poor, pathetic fool. This all boils down to your word against mine." She stood up, removed her panties, and dabbed them on the blood that had trickled from her bottom lip. She then tossed them on the other side of the bed. She sat back down and smiled.

"Oh, hell no," Slim said in a low, stunned whisper as his eyes filled with panic.

Madeline nodded. She could see that for the first time the simple man understood what was really happening. "I'm going to tell John that you raped me."

"You crazy bitch!"

"Now, now." Madeline waved her finger with caution. "It's not nice to call people names."

"He ain't gonna believe you, and neither is nobody else."

"Don't be so sure. I'm a beautiful, sophisticated woman, who can have any man I want. You're a goofy-looking busboy and cook, who works at a nightclub and couldn't get a prostitute if you paid for one." Madeline leaned forward. "Who're they going to believe, you or me?"

"Everybody who know me know I wouldn't hit a woman, let alone rape one."

"That's not true. You told me you were gonna whup my ass like I was a man."

" 'Cause you crazy as hell!" Slim said loudly, backing closer toward the door.

"Think about it, Slim. You were the one who practically begged John to drive me back here to the hotel. You complimented my looks and gushed over me in front of both John and Maxx. And now you're standing in my room debating with me after you just beat and raped me." Madeline made a tsking sound with her mouth. "It's not looking too good for you, Slim."

"You crazy bitch!"

"If you call me names one more time, I'm going to have to do something drastic."

Slim shook his head in bewilderment. He turned to walk out the door, but then he stopped in his tracks when he heard Madeline pick up the phone.

"I think I'll call the police and report this attack. That way, it'll look more official." Madeline wanted to laugh out loud when she saw a fresh wave of panic streak across Slim's scratched-up, pitiful-looking face. She had no intention of calling the police, because she knew she had more to hide than Slim ever did. There was no way in hell she wanted the authorities digging around or asking her questions.

She knew from experience how tricky and conniving police detectives could be, once they started interrogating you. She'd learned that lesson long ago when they almost uncovered the truth about her burning down her parents' home while they slept in their beds. But she'd acted so innocent, traumatized, and shaken that they stopped asking her questions, feeling sorry for the poor little adopted girl, who had become an orphan all over again.

No, Madeline didn't want officers of the law sticking their noses into her business and possibly ruining her plans. Picking up the phone and making Slim think she was going to call the police was her mischievous way of having a little fun at his expense. "I can even tell them that I scratched you in self-defense," she said, leveling another false threat.

Slim stood motionless, just as he had in what seemed like a lifetime ago before Madeline went berserk. "I can't believe this is happenin'. What's wrong with you?"

"Oh, you better believe it!" Madeline slowly put the phone back on the hook. "But because I'm a good-hearted person, I won't turn you in. I've heard about the bad things that happen to men when they go to jail, especially the ones who're in for rape."

"You a sick woman. John was right about you."

Madeline wanted to know what John had said about her, but then she decided not to even venture down that messy road. "Okay, Slim. Get going before I change my mind."

Slim tried to move his feet, but they stayed planted where he stood.

"I said *go!*" Madeline shouted. "Get the fuck out of here before you make me do something you'll regret."

Within the flash of an eye, Slim unlocked the dead bolt. He raced out the door so fast that he caused a breeze to rush into the room.

A few minutes later, Madeline slowly limped into the bathroom. When she flicked on the light switch, she bristled at the damage she'd done. She hated to see her beautiful face swollen, bloodied, and bruised; but at the same time, she had to smile with pride at her hand-iwork.

She limped out of the bathroom and headed straight for the bed, where she planned to lie until John got there. She knew he would have a hard time believing that Slim was capable of causing the state she was in; but she also knew that he'd seen the way his friend had looked at her tonight, like he wanted her all to himself.

Madeline also knew that John's sense of honor and reputation ran deep, and that he would feel responsible and guilty as sin about what had happened to her. "It'll be hard for him to explain that while he partied his ass off in a nightclub, his helpless girlfriend, whom he brought home to meet his family, was being raped and beaten in a hotel room across town," she said with a sinister laugh.

Because of that ungentlemanly, embarrassing fact, Madeline knew John would keep it quiet and do whatever it took to make things right with her—and for Madeline, that meant his nursing her injuries and giving her the diamond engagement ring, which would put her on the road to gaining his fortune.

Chapter 34

Alexandria was lying in PJ's bed, fully awake, eyes closed, with a satisfied smile on her face. Under any other circumstances, she would've been in disbelief and a little shocked by what she'd done last night—gone to bed with a man she'd only known for a short amount of time, waking up naked in his bed. However, instead of feeling disturbed about her actions, Alexandria felt freer than she could ever remember.

She tingled when she thought about the love she and PJ made, the laughter they enjoyed; telling silly jokes while reminiscing about the past, the secrets they shared; her revealing more about her gift, and him confessing his fear of never receiving love from a woman because of abandonment issues with his mother, and the future they discussed; plans to build their relationship and keep their lines of communication strong; before drifting off to sleep late last night.

Their connection last weekend had been instant and seamless; and now that they'd bonded physically, Alexandria knew that PJ was the one for her.

She exhaled deeply as she felt upon her skin the warm beams of light, which peeked into the room through the slats of wooden mini-blinds at the window. The sun's rays felt almost as good to her as the soft hum of PJ's breath against the back of her neck as he lay next to her, spooning her from behind.

"Are you awake?" she asked softly.

PJ moved a little. When he did, he tightened his hug around her body. "Mmm-hmm. What time is it?" he asked in a sleepy voice.

"Six-thirty."

"What time do you have to go into the office?"

Alexandria smiled. "I'm taking the day off. I got up and texted my assistant to let them know not to expect me."

PJ yawned and squeezed her even tighter. "You've been up for a while, huh?"

"About an hour or so."

"Did you have trouble sleeping?"

"Normally, I do. But once I closed my eyes, I slept like a baby."

"Good."

"I'm an early riser like my dad."

"Oh." PJ yawned again. "Did I snore?"

"Not since I've been awake. Do you usually snore?"

"I've been told that I do," PJ said, opening his eyes a bit to look at her.

"I guess I'll find out in time."

PJ kissed her lower lobe; then he gently tugged at it with his teeth. "Yes, you will."

Alexandria felt a surge of arousal as PJ began to rub his hand up and down her thigh before venturing to her left breast, cupping it as he tweaked her nipple between his thumb and index finger. She loved that he knew exactly how to touch her body in a way that gave her pure pleasure. Now, as his hard erection pushed against her backside, he was letting her know exactly how he wanted to start the morning.

"Your skin is so soft," PJ whispered into her ear. "I can't get enough of you."

Alexandria turned her head to face him as they shared a slow, deep kiss, which searched the depths of each other's mouths. The more they kissed, caressed, and fondled, the more aroused they each became. PJ reached inside his nightstand and retrieved a condom so they could journey back to where they'd gone last night.

Alexandria watched closely as he ripped open the square-shaped plastic. She examined his nakedness as if looking at him with a fresh pair of eyes. Last night, she'd only seen his bare body through the darkened lens of night, with just a little help from the streetlights outside. But this morning, the sun's bright, natural rays were giving her a new view of a much more detailed landscape.

She could see that just as she was checking out his strong, broad shoulders, muscular arms, tight abs, and the impressive size of his erection, he was checking her out, too. She'd always been confident about her looks. She knew that just like her mother, she was blessed with an exotically elegant beauty, and that her tall, shapely figure turned heads wherever she went. But unlike Victoria's physique, her thighs were thicker, her bottom was much rounder, and her extra lower-body weight had brought stretch marks and a few areas of cellulite to her otherwise-supple skin.

She felt confident when she was walking around in well-fitted clothes that highlighted her curves. But when she shed them, like last night, she welcomed the cover that darkness provided to help hide her minor flaws. Alexandria suddenly felt overexposed and self-conscious under the glare of beaming sunlight. She was lying openly exposed in front of a man who was so perfectly sculpted and flawless that he looked as if he'd been created in a lab. Her mind focused on the small dimple in the upper part of her left thigh as she pulled the sheet close to her body.

"Ali, what's wrong?"

"My body." She hesitated, feeling embarrassed.

PJ shook his head. "Baby, what are you talking about?"

"My hips and thighs."

"They're two of your best assets," he said with a smile. "I love your thickness."

"I don't feel comfortable. Can you shut the blinds a little?"

"Five senses, Ali. Remember?"

"Sometimes feeling is better than seeing." She winked.

PJ pulled the sheet away from Alexandria's body, exposing her complete nakedness. She was about to protest, but he silenced her with a quick kiss. Then he rose to his feet and held out his hand to her. "C'mon, stand with me."

Alexandria reluctantly accepted his hand as she stood and joined him at the edge of his bed.

He wrapped his arms tightly around her. He stroked her back up and down with one hand, while he held her by her waist with the other, swaying from side to side. He whispered into her ear, repeating over and over, "You're perfect, and you're beautiful."

He slowly sat down on the bed and looked up at her as she stood naked in front of him. His eyes roamed her body from top to bottom, and then from bottom to top again. She watched him as he appraised every inch of her that the sunlight revealed. His hands touched her all over, reaching up to savor the rise of her breasts, traveling down to touch the flatness of her stomach, going on to massage the fullness of her hips, and reaching back to caress the plumpness of her behind.

When his hands slid over the dimple in her thigh, Alexandria inhaled a deep breath, but not because she was self-conscious about her cellulite. She inhaled because the feel of PJ's mouth kissing her flesh and the sensation of his warm tongue on her skin made her weak.

"You're perfect, and you're beautiful," he said again, kissing her outer thighs. "You're sexy, smart, talented, kind, and you turn me on." He slid his finger between her legs and smiled when he saw that she was already wet. Alexandria no longer felt self-conscious because the handsome man in front of her confirmed what she should have already known—she was perfectly fine, in every way, exactly as she was.

PJ reached for the condom he'd put to the side and they returned to their places in bed. "You're perfect, and you're beautiful," he said as he entered her.

They made love slowly, taking their time as they looked into each other's eyes, tasted each other's skin, felt each other's body, moaned into each other's ear, and breathed in the love they were making as the sun washed over them.

Chapter 35

After waking up and making passionate love and then showering together, Alexandria and PJ hurried to get dressed so they could each start their day: PJ with midmorning rounds and Alexandria with errands around town.

"Damn, you sure do know how to fill out a pair of scrubs," PJ said as he gave Alexandria a sexy look.

He'd given her one of his Howard University T-shirts and a pair of his blue hospital scrubs to wear so she wouldn't have to put on the wrinkled clothes she'd come over in yesterday.

"Thanks. I'm glad I wore flats because scrubs and stilettos don't mix."

"Actually, that sounds hot."

Alexandria laughed when she saw the arousal in PJ's eyes. "I'll have to keep that in mind for next time."

"That's what I'm talkin' about!"

They walked out to the living room to finish gathering their things. Alexandria sat on his couch and stuffed her clothes into an empty Whole Foods bag, which PJ had given her. She looked at him as he spoke and moved around the room, admiring his navy trousers and crisply starched light blue dress shirt, wondering if it was possible for him to look any more handsome than he already did.

"I'm having an early dinner with my dad tonight," PJ said as he threaded his belt through the last loop in his pants. "And like I said before, I'm going to have a straight-up conversation with him about your mom."

"How do you think he'll react to you questioning him?"

"I'm going to let him know that I'm not trying to be up in his business. I just want to make sure things are cool, because of us. I don't like surprises, you know?"

"I'm with you on that," Alexandria agreed. "I'd love to be a fly on the wall during that conversation."

"Can't you use telepathy or something and listen to what we're saying?"

Alexandria nodded. "Honestly, I think I could if I concentrated really hard." When she thought about it, she was fairly certain of it. Her abilities were growing stronger and stronger each day.

"Wow, I was just kidding," PJ said. He came over and sat beside her on the couch. "You can really do that?"

"I haven't tried, but, yes, I think so. That's why I can't wait for my first visit from Grandma Allene."

PJ was about to slip his feet into his black loafers when he stopped in midmotion. "You mean she's actually going to appear to you, like a ghost or something?"

"Yes. I feel her energy around me all the time now, even at this very moment, and I can't wait to meet and talk with her. A week ago, I would've been suffering from anxiety knowing that a spirit was going to pay me a visit. But now, it's so different. I'm not afraid anymore, and I know Grandma Allene is going to guide me and show me how to use my gift. Because that's what it is, PJ, a gift."

"Ali, this is wild."

"I know. You sure you want to hop aboard this crazy train? The ride might get bumpy."

PJ leaned in close and gave her a delicate kiss on her lips. "I'm ready for anything, just as long as I can have you."

Alexandria wrapped her arms around his neck. "Thank you, just for being you."

They held on to each other for a few moments before Alexandria pulled way. "And just so you know, I'm not going to try to listen to whatever you and your father talk about tonight. Some things need to be left alone so they can unfold naturally."

"Yes, I agree. And we'll find out soon enough because regardless of whatever my father tells me tonight, he and your mom are going to have to interact at some point."

Alexandria's mind flashed back to the images she'd seen of their parents when they were young and in love, sitting on a couch in this very condo, in nearly the same spot that she and PJ now occupied. She blinked to clear her thoughts, willing herself not to look ahead to see what was next. "You're right," she responded. "And it'll be good to see your dad again after all these years."

"I can't wait to see your mom. She used to always give me hugs, and, man, could she make the best cookies," PJ said with a grin.

Alexandria nodded. She didn't have the heart to tell him that her mother wasn't the least bit interested in seeing him again, and that the sentiment was tenfold when it came to his father. She so hoped her mother's attitude would change, once she saw the grown-up PJ in person.

"You want to hang out later tonight after I have dinner with my dad?" PJ asked, pulling her from her thoughts.

"Sure, if you'll be up to it. I know you two will probably be hanging out late, catching up, since you haven't seen each other in a few months."

"No, that's why we're having an early dinner," PJ said, pulling on his blazer as he stood. "He has a presentation first thing tomorrow morning and then his flight leaves right after that, so we won't be out long. We should be done around nine or ten." He licked his lips and flashed a sexy smile. "I can't wait to see you model those stilettos and scrubs."

Alexandria returned his seductive smile with one of her own. "Your place or mine?"

★ ★ ★

Alexandria's day had been going so well, but now as she sat in one of the stylish leather club chairs in front of her mother's large mahogany desk, she could see that things were getting ready to take a nosedive.

She'd dropped by her mother's office while she was out running errands, because Alexandria knew they needed to continue their conversation from last weekend. Just as PJ was going to be straight up with his father, her gut told her that she needed to do the same with her mother.

Alexandria watched as her mother fiddled with a small stack of papers on her desk. She'd always admired her mother's smart head for business and strong convictions. Although she'd come from a privileged background and had married a wealthy man, Victoria Monique Small Thornton had made a substantial living in her own right, with her event planning and catering company, Divine Occasions. She'd worked tirelessly to carve out a niche for herself and had risen to the top of her profession, all while balancing her time between work and family. She'd been featured in magazines such as *Essence, Elle,* and *Southern Living.* She had even landed a spot in *Vogue,* when she helped organize a celebrity fund-raiser during the Avon Walk for Breast Cancer event three years ago in honor of breast cancer awareness.

Alexandria couldn't think of anyone she admired more than her mother. As she looked at Victoria, sitting behind her desk, exemplifying the picture of polished beauty, Alexandria wished she could spare her mother what she felt was going to be turmoil down the road.

"Alexandria," her mother said in a serious voice. "I have very strong concerns about you and PJ."

"Mom, why can't you be happy for me? He's a wonderful person."

"And you know that because you've spent months getting to know him?" Victoria said, and then paused. "No, excuse me, it hasn't even been a full week."

"You're jaded."

"I'm a mother looking out for my child."

"What do you have against him?"

Victoria shook her head and calmed her tone. "Nothing at all. I don't know him from Adam, and neither do you, and that's my point of concern. I feel like you're rushing in, and I don't want to see you get hurt."

"Like I said last weekend, Grandpa John and Nana are a prime example of how you have to trust your gut when you find the person who you know is right for you."

"Their's was a one in a million situation. You can't name another couple who rushed in and made it work."

"Mom, we've already been through this," Alexandria said, trying not to sound frustrated. "PJ and I are going to be together, and it's something you're going to have to come to terms with. I know it might be a little uncomfortable for you because of the history you have with his father. . . ."

Victoria twisted her mouth. "So I assume you've broken up with Peter?"

Alexandria shifted in her chair. Even though she didn't like that her mother had just glossed over her comment, she knew she had a very valid point. Peter had called last night while she was at PJ's. They'd been playing phone tag all week, having only spoken for a few rushed minutes two days ago before she'd been pulled away to avert a "crisis" in her office. She desperately wanted to see Peter face-to-face so she could break up with him like a mature adult. He'd texted her this morning asking if tonight would be a good time to meet, but she had to decline because PJ was coming over after dinner with his father. She knew the situation with Peter couldn't linger, and she needed to end things once and for all.

"Not yet," Alexandria finally answered. "We've been playing phone tag all week, but I think he already knows. The writing's been on the wall. We just need to make it official."

"Do it soon," her mother warned. "Although I was never a big fan of Peter's or your relationship with him, he deserves to know the decision you've made."

"I agree. But I don't want to break up over the phone, or in an e-mail, or by text. I want to look him in his eyes and tell him. One year is worth at least that."

"You've always been such a caring and considerate person, and that's what makes you so special. But, sweetie, I don't care if you have to write it down on a sticky note and leave it on his door, you need to end things with Peter right away." Victoria leaned forward and pressed her hands on her desk. "I'm speaking from experience when I tell you that having two men in your life at one time is a disaster waiting to happen. It's like looking for trouble."

"But, Mom, it's not like I'm trying to be a player juggling two men. I'm trying to do the right thing."

Victoria let out a sigh. "Do you remember the business principle I've preached for years?"

" 'Perception is reality,' " Alexandria said, reciting the words she'd often heard her mother say.

"That's right. It doesn't matter your intent. It's what things look like. And right now, it looks like you're stepping out on your boyfriend with another man."

Alexandria sighed and rolled her eyes.

"Sweetie, you're not thinking straight," Victoria said, looking at her daughter's clothes. "You even came over here wearing PJ's T-shirt and hospital scrubs after rolling out of his bed."

Alexandria was a little shocked by her mother's in-your-face comment. She knew her mother could be direct, and that she was the kind of person who said what was on her mind. But she'd always been diplomatic in her approach, until now. "Mom, I'm a grown woman and—"

"I gave birth to you. I know exactly how old you are."

"Since you want to go there, we can go there." Alexandria said boldly. "I spent the night at PJ's place and we made love until I screamed his name. And I'm not going to feel bad about it or apologize for it." This wasn't going the way Alexandria had imagined.

"Oh, sweet Jesus," Victoria put her hand to her head. "Please tell me you're being sarcastic as a way to get back at me for what I just said. I hope you didn't actually sleep with this boy, who you don't know from a man in the moon."

"Not only did I sleep with him, it was the best sex I've ever had."

"Alexandria!" Victoria shouted. She started to open her mouth, but then she closed it.

"Mom, please don't judge me."

"I'm not judging you. I'm trying to get you to use your head. You just met the boy last week. I know you have powers and abilities to see things that others can't, but you're still only human. It takes time to get to know someone, and, trust me, rushing into things can lead to a world of hurt."

"Just because his dad hurt you doesn't mean PJ's going to hurt me."

Victoria sat back against her chair, chewing the inside of her jaw. "I know what you think, but this isn't about me or Parker Brightwood. This is about you, my baby girl, and how I don't want you to jump feetfirst into a relationship that might get you hurt, especially when you're still involved with a man who obviously doesn't know that he's been replaced."

Alexandria was about to make another comment when Denise, her mother's longtime assistant, walked through the door.

"Hey, sugar," Denise said with a smile as she strutted over to where Alexandria was sitting and delivered a kiss to her cheek. "It's good to see you, baby. How're you doing?"

"I'm great, Aunt Denise. How're you?" Alexandria asked.

Denise handed a thick folder to Victoria. "I'm feeling good and looking even better." She winked and laughed. "Still trying to keep your mama straight after all these years."

"That's a job," Alexandria said, rolling her eyes slightly.

Denise stopped and trained her eyes on Alexandria. "I know I didn't hear any sass in that voice, did I?"

Alexandria remained silent.

"I love you just like you're mine," Denise said, placing her hands on her wide hips. "Your mama and me been close since before you were even a thought, and I know how much she loves you. I love you, too, so I'm gonna say what you need to hear, since you obviously won't listen to her." Denise shifted her weight to the heel of her stylish red pumps as she spoke. "Be careful and slow down. Just because something looks good, that doesn't mean it is good. You have to use your head and make sure you know the temperature of the water before you jump in."

Alexandria looked at her mother as if she'd just been accosted. "You told Aunt Denise about PJ?"

Victoria nodded. "Yes, I did."

Denise nodded and continued talking. "Take your time and make sure you know what you're doing. You're young and beautiful. There's no rush for anything."

"I told her the same thing," Victoria piped in.

"Well, I spoke my little two cents and now I'm gone. Bye, baby, and remember what I said." Denise gave Alexandria a quick hug and then walked back out the door. Alexandria was upset, and she'd had enough. "You freely told Aunt Denise about PJ and me, but have you told Dad?" she asked in a flip tone. "Have you told him that I'm involved with the son of the man with whom you almost cheated on him and nearly ruined your marriage?"

Victoria's back stiffened as straight as a board. She cleared her throat and looked directly into Alexandria's eyes as she spoke. "Yes. I told him."

"You did?"

"I learned a long time ago that keeping secrets only leads to trouble."

"Well, your mistakes won't be mine, that's for sure."

"You're being spiteful, and I don't appreciate it," Victoria said, hurt seeping into her voice. "I told Denise because she's a dear friend, and I know I can trust her and confide in her about how concerned I am for my child."

Victoria rose from behind her desk and claimed the empty club chair beside Alexandria's. "You're right, I've made some terrible mistakes in the past, and I don't want to see you go down the same road. But contrary to what you think, I'm not worried about what might happen between Parker and me. That's a journey that has no legs. My main concern is for you and your well-being. I see you rushing in and it scares me, sweetie. I don't want to see you get hurt."

Alexandria felt horrible about how disrespectfully she'd spoken to her mother. All she could attribute it to was the tangle of emotions and revelations she was experiencing all at once. She hadn't heard her Grandma Allene's voice in a few days, and she was missing her now. She looked into her mother's eyes and saw nothing but love, which comforted her. "I'm sorry for what I said and how I said it," she whispered softly. "I've been going through a lot lately, trying to sort things out. But please trust me, I know what I'm doing. PJ is the one for me."

Victoria leaned back in her seat and smoothed the crease in her linen skirt. "Okay, I see that you're very resolute in that belief." She paused for a moment. "Wait a minute. Have you had a vision or seen something in your future about you and PJ?"

"Not exactly, and only because I don't want to spoil the fun and mystery of building experiences with him. But I've gotten confirmation in another way, with my own eyes. He's the one with the diamond."

Victoria blinked twice, but she didn't say a word.

"When I was at PJ's place last night, I saw a tattoo on his arm in the shape of a diamond."

Victoria looked more uneasy than ever. "I don't get a good feeling about this."

"Did you hear what I just said? He's the one with the diamond."

"I don't understand. Why would Grandma Allene lead you straight to trouble?"

"Trouble for me, or for you?"

Victoria took a deep breath and crossed her long legs. "Okay, let's talk about what I know you really came over here to discuss."

"Do you still have feelings for PJ's dad?"

"Yes, I do."

Although Alexandria knew what her mother's answer was going to be, hearing it made the realization a little harder to swallow. She and Victoria sat in silence for a long pause; each one was consumed by different sides of the same troubling quandary. Alexandria finally spoke: "Do you still love him?"

"No, I don't," Victoria said slowly, shaking her head. "The feelings I have for Parker are complicated. As you know from what you saw, we had a whirlwind, intense love affair. He was embedded in my heart at one time, but things happened."

"He cheated on you, and you fell in love with Dad," Alexandria said.

A smile that was etched in sadness formed at Victoria's lips. "It wasn't that simple. It was a crazy, complicated time, and it seemed as though everything happened so fast," she said in a low voice. "Please believe me when I say that I have nothing against PJ. I'm sure he's a fine young man, and if Grandma Allene has led you to him, then . . . I'm sure it's for the best."

"It is, Mom. I feel more alive and free with him than I ever have in my entire life. He makes me happy."

"My mother used to say that all a parent wants is for her child to be happy. I didn't understand the full meaning of that until the day you were born. I would gladly give my life if it meant sparing you any pain." Victoria reached for Alexandria's hand and held on tightly. "If PJ makes you happy, you two have my blessing."

Alexandria rose from her chair, knelt in front of her mother, and hugged her tightly. "Thank you, Mom. This means so much to me. You'll love PJ, once you meet him . . . again. And Dad will, too."

Victoria released their hug and stared into her daughter's eyes. "Your father flew out on a business trip this morning and won't be back until Monday. When he gets in town, I'm going to tell him about the diamond and brace him for the fact that Parker will be back in our lives."

Alexandria smiled and forced herself not to flash ahead to see what was in the future. She already knew it wouldn't be good. But for now, she wanted to enjoy peace and happiness. She'd worry about trouble a little farther down the road.

"In the meantime," Victoria said, "I think you should make it your priority to end things with Peter, once and for all."

"I agree. I have to run a few more errands and then finish writing the piece I'm going to perform tomorrow night. After I do that, I'm going to take care of the situation with Peter—'once and for all.' "

"Good," Victoria said, letting out a relieved sigh. "Oh, and, sweetie, go home and change out of PJ's clothes before you do it."

Chapter 36

It was almost midnight as Alexandria and PJ sat in the middle of her queen-size bed, drinking wine and eating chocolate-covered fruit from a silver tray. She'd spent the early part of her evening preparing the delicious treats for them to share: strawberries, apples, bananas, cherries, pineapples, and raspberries, all covered in milk chocolate she'd melted from her Godiva box. Making the scrumptious desserts had taken her mind off her situation with Peter.

She'd called him that afternoon, wanting to meet so she could end things properly—once and for all. Contrary to her mother's advice, she knew the best way to handle her breakup was by having a face-to-face conversation. She and Peter had agreed to meet at the coffee shop near the mall, where she was running her last errand of the day. She'd waited for him for well over an hour, and had even called him several times. On her way home, he rang her phone and told her that he'd been held up on an important conference call. He asked if he could come over to her place, but she knew that was out of the question.

"We really need to talk, Alexandria," he said. His voice was serious and calm, and she felt he already knew what was coming. "Face-to-face, so we can settle things the right way and move forward."

"Yes, I feel the same way."

"Good. I have to go into the office tomorrow because of this big project I've been working on, but how about Sunday? We can meet for brunch."

As Alexandria looked at PJ, happily eating in her bed, she was glad she was finally going to end things with Peter—"once and for all"—clearing the path for her future with the man in front of her, who looked more appetizing than any of the fruit on the tray.

"This is good," PJ said as he munched on a piece of chocolate-covered banana. "I can't believe you made all this."

"It was really easy. My mom taught me how. You know she can burn in the kitchen."

"And I'm glad you can, too. There's nothing like a beautiful, sexy woman who knows how to cook."

Alexandria was thankful that over the years she'd paid attention to her mother's culinary lessons because the saying "the way to a man's heart was through his stomach" was true in PJ's case. He loved to eat, and he wasn't picky, as long as the food was plentiful and full of flavor. His chiseled abs defied the fried chicken, macaroni and cheese, pie, and ice cream he could devour in one meal.

Alexandria adjusted the oversize T-shirt she was wearing; then she took a small sip of her wine. "I guess it's time to talk about the heavy stuff, huh?"

PJ nodded. "You already know what my dad said, don't you?"

"Actually, I don't. I purposely put it out of my mind. So what did he say?"

PJ set the strawberry he'd started to eat back down on the tray. He paused for a moment before letting out a deep breath as he spoke. "Ali, he still has a thing for your mom."

"Shit!" She bit her bottom lip and frowned.

"I know. And after all these years, he said he's never gotten your mom out of his system."

"Never?"

PJ shook his head. "He knows she's still happily married to your dad. I told him that, and he figured as much. But that doesn't change how he feels. He was blunt and honest with me, I'll give him that."

"I can't believe he's not dating anyone." Alexandria said, wishing there was a woman in his life to serve as a buffer.

"Well, he has a friend." PJ shrugged. "They've been seeing each other for a few years, but it's nothing serious, and she's way more into him than he's into her. To be honest, I don't really care for her."

"Why not?"

"Her personality. She's the type of woman who's only interested in status and phony bullshit. She calls my dad, 'dahling,' " he said incredulously. "I think he's just with her for companionship every now and then, and because she runs in the same social circles."

"Wow."

"When I was younger, he never brought women around, because he didn't want to introduce me to anyone unless they were going to be a significant part of his life."

"I can understand and respect that."

"Me too. He made a lot of sacrifices raising me as a single parent with a demanding career. He always felt bad about the fact that my mom wasn't a real mother to me. She never spent time with me, so he worked hard to fill her void. You can never replace a mother's love, but my dad's done a hell of a job. He's made me the man I am today."

Alexandria smiled. "I'm the beneficiary of his hard work."

PJ leaned over and gave her a quick kiss on her lips. "I'll tell him you said thank you."

"My mom still has feelings for him, too," Alexandria blurted out.

"You're shittin' me."

"I wish I were."

"This isn't good, Ali."

"I know. It's going to be awkward, especially for my father."

PJ nodded. "Yeah, unfortunately, my dad told me about their adversarial history. Damn, this is like something out of a novel."

"I wish this were fiction, but it's real." Alexandria shook her head. "It's so weird. Our happiness is going to bring about their pain."

"Why do you say that?"

"Because it's true. You don't have to have the gift in order to see that."

PJ sat for a moment without saying anything, looking focused and serious. He reached over, removed the tray from the bed, set it on the floor, and then gathered Alexandria in his arms. "As long as we have each other, we can deal with anything that comes our way. Your parents and my dad will have to resolve things in their own way and time. We can't help what happened in the past. All we can do is move forward in our future together. Your parents love you, and my dad loves me, so they'll find a way to work things out for our sake and theirs."

Later that night as Alexandria drifted off to sleep, she tried to enjoy the feel of PJ's hard body next to hers and the low hum of his snoring. But try as she might, she couldn't shake the twisting feeling in the pit of her stomach that what happened in the past was sure to creep into the present.

Chapter 37

Alexandria was sitting at a table in the back of the Lazy Day, sipping from her glass of Moscato, waiting for PJ to arrive. He was late, which was unusual because he was a stickler for time. But since she wanted to rehearse her performance as many times as she could before she took the stage, she didn't mind.

Just as she was beginning to recite the verses again mentally, she looked up and nearly lost her concentration. There, in front of her, was PJ—and his very handsome and debonair-looking father.

"Surprise!" PJ said, giving her a happy smile.

"Mr. Brightwood?"

Parker smiled, flashing the same sexy Hollywood grin as his son's. "PJ was right. You are absolutely beautiful," he said.

Alexandria stood and accepted Parker's embrace, which was warm and welcoming. She immediately felt comfortable with him, and the easiness of his way shocked her. "Thank you, Mr. Brightwood. It's great to see you after all these years."

"Yes, my dear. It certainly is," Parker said in a deep, rich voice, which was reminiscent of PJ's.

As Parker and PJ joined her at the table, Alexandria marveled at their startling resemblance. She didn't have to concentrate on a vision to see what PJ would look like when he got older, because she had living proof sitting to the right of her. He was the kind of handsome that still turned heads, and he could hold a woman's interest at any age. His extraordinary good looks were complemented by a polished refinement that let you know he was of a certain pedigree.

"Dad was supposed to leave this morning after his speech at the medical conference," PJ said. "He decided to stay through the weekend, when I told him that you were going to perform tonight."

Parker smiled. "PJ raved about how talented you are, and, well, I'm a man who deeply appreciates art, in all forms, so I couldn't miss this opportunity, since I was already in town."

"I'm honored that you stayed so you could see my performance, Mr. Brightwood," she told him. She looked at PJ and thought about the piece she'd written for tonight, which he'd inspired. The content was sensual and a bit spicy. Suddenly she wasn't so sure she felt comfortable performing it, now that his father would be in the audience.

She knew how important first impressions were, and she wanted to make a good one. PJ told her last night that his father had once again voiced similar worries to her mother's about the fact that they were moving too quickly. Given that concern, she didn't want him to think his son was rushing into a relationship with a woman of questionable morals.

I want this night to go well, Alexandria thought. Just as she was about to forewarn PJ's father about the racy content she was going to perform, she realized she had a much bigger problem on her hands than a few seductive words. *This can't be happening!* she shouted inside her head. But it was, so she braced herself for fireworks when she saw her mother coming straight toward their table.

Although Alexandria had told her mother that she was working on a new piece for tonight's show, it hadn't crossed her mind that Victoria would actually come to hear it.

Victoria had seen Alexandria perform many times, and was one of her biggest supporters. However, clubs weren't necessarily her cup of tea, especially if she had to step out alone, which she did tonight, since her father was out of town on business.

Alexandria's breath quickened when she saw her mother's confident stride begin to slow as she approached the table. Even though his back was turned to Victoria, Alexandria knew her mother could sense that the tall man, with the broad shoulders, occupying the seat beside a younger version of himself, was none other than Dr. Parker Brightwood.

Alexandria cleared her throat, looked at PJ, and then toward his father. "My mother is here."

No sooner had the words tumbled from her lips, than Parker turned in his seat just as Victoria reached the table.

Alexandria could see that he was admiring her mother, and she couldn't say that she blamed him. Victoria was all beauty and grace as she strutted in a fierce pair of three-and-a-half-inch rhinestone-studded sandals. Her black Capri pants fit her slim curves, and her sleeveless silk white blouse swayed with the rhythm of her stride. Silver hoops bobbed at her ears, framing the elegance of her long, slender neck.

Victoria's ruby-colored lips formed a small smile, which grew into a wider one as Parker stood to his feet and hugged her in a long embrace. Alexandria watched them closely, waiting for them to release each other, but they didn't. They stood wrapped in one another's arms as they exchanged initial greetings and then light banter. Parker whispered something into Victoria's ear, causing her to laugh and then shake her head before she finally broke his hold around her waist.

Alexandria was dying to know what PJ's father had said. She knew she could find out if she really wanted to, but she knew that intruding into people's thoughts without their permission wasn't a good idea, unless absolutely necessary. As her mother once told her, when you look for trouble, you usually find it.

She saw PJ glance at her, and then over to their parents, and she knew he was just as concerned as she was about what was possibly brewing. His dad and her mom were still standing near the table, talking to each other in whispers, as if trading top secret codes in the back of a club. Finally the two turned toward the table.

"PJ," Victoria said with a warm smile, offering him outstretched arms, "it's so good to see you again."

"You too, Mrs. Thornton." PJ smiled back as he stood to receive her hug, and then moved to the side to let Alexandria do the same.

Once everyone was seated, Victoria planted a small air kiss on Alexandria's cheek. "You look beautiful, sweetie. That color makes your skin shine."

"Thanks mom," Alexandria said with a smile. She was wearing a sexy, crochet-knitted gold-colored halter dress, which puddled at her ankles and hugged each one of her sassy curves. Had she known that PJ's father was going to show up, and then her mother, she would have worn something a bit less seductive, but it went along with the theme of her performance—if she decided to do it.

After the server took their drink orders—Ketel One on the rocks for PJ and Parker, and a pomegranate martini for Victoria—the table fell into an awkward silence. When Alexandria saw Kyle motioning for her up front, she welcomed the opportunity for escape. She felt bad that PJ would be left in the uncomfortable spot, but she knew he'd be able to handle it because of his even temperament.

"I have to go up to the stage now, because I'll be on in a few minutes," Alexandria said, looking around the table.

"I can't wait to hear your new piece, sweetie. I know it's going to be wonderful," Victoria said, beaming with pride.

Alexandria smiled, looking from her mother to PJ's father. "I have to warn you, this piece is a little provocative. I didn't know you were coming tonight, and—"

Victoria smiled and answered, "Do your thing. You're a grown woman. . . . Isn't that what you told me yesterday?" She winked at her daughter.

"All right, hold on to your seats."

"Knock it out of the park, baby!" PJ cheered.

Alexandria sauntered to the side of the stage and waited. It would be only a minute or two before Kyle introduced her. As she took deep breaths to calm her nerves, her Grandma Allene's voice gently seeped into her ears. It had been a few days since she'd heard from her. When she recognized the whisper, she smiled.

"I'm gonna be with you from here on out, baby girl. And I'm gonna help you and teach you everything you need to know. So don't worry about a thing. You're gonna do real good tonight. Speak your heart, baby."

"Thanks, Grandma Allene," Alexandria whispered. She smiled even wider and walked onstage just as the crowd erupted in applause when they heard her name.

She stood in front of the microphone as the crowd settled and the room fell silent. The house was packed and ready as she greeted them with her usual, "How y'all feelin' tonight?"

She cleared her throat and smiled, zooming in on PJ in the very back of the room. "Let me tell you how unpredictable life is," she began. "Last week, when I stepped onto this stage, I talked about the kind of love I desired and the kind of relationship I wanted. And now, just a week later, I've got it!"

The crowd broke out into hand clapping, finger snaps, and one or two "Go 'head, girl" applause.

"My great-great-grandmother, Grandma Allene, told me these exact words. She said, 'Speak what's in your heart. Say what it is that you desire, and watch it walk into your life,' " Alexandria said with a smile. "Those words are not only profound, but they're life-changing. My journey is a testament to the power, beauty, and truth that blossoms when you speak your heart's desires, and then open yourself up to them without fear or trepidation.

"So tonight I'm going to share something with you that I wrote this week. This piece is for all of you who have that special someone in your life who ignites a fire in you. It's about that person who makes you tremble at the very thought of him, or at the sound of his voice, or the mention of his name. Simply put, it's about the desire you have for that special person, whom you don't want to be without. So that's what I've titled this piece, 'Desire.' "

Alexandria took a deep, cleansing breath and began to speak:

"Desire—sexy and bold. Bright and beautiful.

"Shining like the burning sun beaming down on my skin. Making me weak and strong all at once. Flooding my body with a new awareness. The softness of your lips and the fire in your touch make me shiver. You make me smile. You give me butterflies. I feel giddy. That's what you do to me with just one look, one simple gesture, exciting me because I like the man you are.

"Grown and sexy.

"A real man.

"Yes, I'm smiling.

"Hot—is how you make me feel when your tongue explores the depths of my mouth, then rolls across my lips, traveling down to greet my breasts. Engulfing, sucking, gently biting and nibbling, applying just the right amount of pressure. You know exactly what to do when you reach the meeting between my thighs, burying your head there, answering all my questions with each swipe of your tongue. I like returning the favor, taking you into my mouth, tasting you, swallowing you, licking and sucking you, enjoying the way your thickness feels against the back of my throat.

"You . . . are . . . delicious. A satisfying mouthful.

"Desire—sexy and bold. Bright and beautiful.

"Chocolate thighs wrapped around mocha hips—that's how we lay when you're stroking me. Hard flesh pressed against soft skin—that's what I like when you're deep inside me. You make me wet, causing me to drip sweet juice, preparing me for what's to come when I spread my legs across the sea you've parted, eager and ready to receive you.

"Hard—and oh so good—is how you feel when you enter me, filling my empty space, hitting that special spot, making it throb on command, delighting my moist middle with the promise of a sweet relief that will be met with the most pleasurable resolution.

"Sweet pain is what I feel when you're pounding me from behind, rocking me from the side, stroking me on an angle, molding me while I'm on top. The rhythm of your thrusts dances in concert with the stride of my hips. Strong hands, hungry mouths, nimble fingers, soft caresses, heated flesh, skilled tongues, insatiable lips—it's all so sweet. Exposed and naked. True and believing—that's what we are when we do what we do. This is a soul connection.

"I like it all. I want it now. I'm ready.

"Yes, you are . . . Desire—sexy and bold. Bright and beautiful.

"I'm flying high, letting your light shine through me. . . .

"Thank you," Alexandria said, bowing her head to the audience. And just as it had been last week, she received a rousing round of accolades.

She floated off the stage as if she were on a magical carpet, high on the applause, which still sizzled in the air.

"You set this crowd on bloody fiah!" Kyle said as he greeted Alexandria at the side of the stage. "We've got to talk about signing you to a contract for a regular gig."

"Are you serious?" she asked with excitement.

"Aftah that performance, you betta bet your ass I am," he said, slurring his words as the smell of bourbon oozed from his breath. "I'll give you a call this Monday."

"Thanks, Kyle. I can't wait."

After stopping to accept warm words from the Dead Poet and a few other artists, Alexandria finally made her way to the back of the club, where PJ stood and clapped as she approached. He walked up to her, opened his arms, and hugged her tightly.

"Baby, you rocked it! That was tight!"

"You liked it?"

"Hell yeah," he said, and then whispered into her ear, "You got a brothah hard as nails."

When she pressed against him, she could tell he wasn't joking. She looked into his eyes. "That was about you, you know. How you make me feel. You're sexy, bold, bright, and beautiful."

PJ held her even more tightly. "I can't wait to get you back to my place."

Alexandria wanted to leave right then, but there was the matter of her mother and his father, who were looking on at the table just a few feet away. She and PJ walked to the table, hand in hand, and took their seats. Right away, Alexandria noticed that something was wrong.

She could see that her mother and PJ's father seemed visibly uncomfortable. They were sitting as far apart from each other as space at the small table would allow.

"Is everything okay?" Alexandria asked, looking at the two.

"Yes."

"Sure."

"Everything's fine."

"You were great!"

Victoria and Parker both fumbled to say their praise at the same time, talking over each other as they stammered their praise.

It wasn't until that moment that Alexandria realized what she initially thought was discomfort between them was really sexual tension. When she stared into her mother's eyes and Victoria looked away, her mother's actions confirmed it. Alexandria didn't even want to look at PJ's father, for fear that his thoughts might be too much for her to handle.

Alexandria had never seen her mother look nervous or guilty. Right now, her face and body language were wrought with both. When she glanced over at Mr. Brightwood, Alexandria could see that he'd regained his composure and was now the perfect picture of suave, cool calm. Meanwhile, Victoria gulped down her martini and signaled for the server to come their way.

I need another drink, too! Alexandria thought.

"I told you she's fantastic!" PJ said with enthusiasm. "Wasn't that piece great?"

"Yes, it was outstanding," his father chimed in, nodding his head toward Alexandria before turning to her mother. "Victoria, you've done an amazing job raising such a beautiful and talented young woman. You should be very proud."

Victoria smiled and nodded in return. "Thank you, and, yes, her father and I are very proud," she said, throwing her husband into the conversation. "But we can't take all the credit. Alexandria's always been an extraordinary young woman in her own right."

Parker smiled a sly grin. "The fruit doesn't fall far. And from where I'm sitting, the tree is still standing tall and blooming."

What the hell? Alexandria thought. *I know he's not tryin' to get his flirt on!* She and PJ looked at each other, shocked by his father's boldness.

"See, Parker," Victoria hissed, "this is why your ass frustrated me back then and you still piss me the hell off now. You can't leave well enough alone. You always have to push and push, until you get what you want." Victoria swiftly unleashed her fury; everyone at the table was stunned.

"Oh, and what is it that you think I want?" Parker asked calmly with a smile.

Victoria ignored him, took a deep breath, and smoothed her hand over her neatly coiffed bob. "I don't think I'll be needing that drink, after all. It's time for me to go. I'll see you tomorrow, sweetie," she said to Alexandria, giving her a quick hug. She leaned forward and smiled at PJ. "It was a pleasure to see you again after all these years. You've grown into a fine young man, and you're more than welcome to come by the house tomorrow for Sunday dinner." She cut her eyes at Parker without saying a word as she pushed her chair back, ready to leave.

Alexandria had hoped the evening would go well, but she should've known that when old lovers reunited, it was a tricky thing— especially, if they still had feelings for each other, and were both attached to other people. It was a bad scene waiting to happen.

Although she wished her mother would stay, Alexandria knew it was best that she leave because at the rate PJ's father was throwing out hints, the evening could easily spiral out of control and into an even bigger mess.

"I'll walk with you out to the door," Alexandria said as she stood to her feet, joining her mother. She was relieved they were going to avoid further drama. But just as her hopes had risen, they fell again. She blinked her eyes and nearly bit her tongue when she saw Peter storming toward their table.

Chapter 38

Madeline's limbs were weary as she lay across the bed, wishing desperately for pain medication or anything that would give her relief. It had been a half hour since Slim left, and her injuries were starting to get the better of her. The large bruise on her inner thigh was hot to the touch; her jaw throbbed; her mouth ached. But that pain was lightweight in comparison to the agony pounding in her head, which felt as though it was going to roll off her shoulders.

"I hope he gets here soon." She seethed in pain, wishing John would walk through the door any minute. She knew that he'd planned to stay out well into the night and then take a drunken Maxx home after all their partying was done. But she was counting on the fact that once Slim went back to the club and tried to explain what had happened, John would rush back to the hotel and to her rescue, feeling responsible and guilty.

"Come on! Where the hell are you?" Madeline called out. She sat up and was about to go to the bathroom to replace the cold washcloth she'd been holding over the knot on her forehead, when she heard a soft knock at the door.

At first, she wondered who it could be, but then she realized that John had probably forgotten or lost his room key. The softness of the knock let her know he was standing outside, filled with remorse.

Madeline smiled; then she slowly limped over to the door. She fixed her face into a frightened, vulnerable expression before turning the knob.

"Hello, Madeline," the woman said, hands on her hip, eyes blazing as she stood in the middle of the doorway.

"Who the hell are you?" Madeline asked, straightening her back as much as her pain would allow.

"The real question is, who the hell are you?"

Madeline studied the attractive woman closely and then it came to her. She'd seen her at the club earlier that night. "How do you know my name and where I'm staying?" she asked. Madeline's hand was on the door, ready to shut it, but the woman was too quick.

She pushed past Madeline as if she were a rag doll and strutted into the room.

"If you don't get out of my room right now, I'm going to call the police!" Madeline threatened.

"Go right ahead," the woman replied. "As a matter of fact, I'll dial the number for you."

Madeline's heart quickened as she looked into the woman's eyes. If it was one thing she knew, it was that crazy knew crazy—and the woman standing in front of her was crazy like a fox. "Bitch, you don't scare me," Madeline said, leaning on her one good leg. "So if you don't get the hell out of my room right now, I promise you, you'll regret it."

The woman laughed and folded her arms across her chest. "I guess it takes a bitch to know one, so I'm not gonna get upset about you calling me out of my name, like you just did. But let me tell you right now, if you lay one hand on me, I'll beat your ass worse than you beat your own."

Madeline swallowed hard and looked around the room, as if someone else was in there with them.

"That's right. I know what you did," the woman said. "Slim told me the whole story from beginning to end."

"He's lying!" Madeline screamed. "That savage beat and raped me when I wouldn't give in to his advances."

"Oh, stop the bullshit," the woman said. "Listen, I'm gonna make this quick, because I want your crazy ass to be gone by the time John gets back here."

"Wait a minute," Madeline said. "Who the hell are you?"

"Heffa, if you ask me that one more time, I'm gonna blacken your other eye. Now sit your ass down at that desk over there and listen to what I have to say before I knock you down."

Even though Madeline wanted to resist, she could see that the woman was dead serious. Slowly she walked toward the desk and took a seat, placing her hand atop the wooden surface, where the ashtray she'd used to beat herself now sat.

"And don't even think about doing anything with that ashtray. You may have hit your fool self with it, but I promise you, if you make one move to pick it up, it'll be the last thing you do before the ambulance comes to get you."

"I'm getting tired of your damn threats. Now tell me what the hell you're doing here!"

The woman narrowed her eyes at Madeline. "Okay, I'm gonna get down to the nitty-gritty. First off, forget about crying rape on poor Slim. We both know you did this to yourself. Next, I want you to use that pen and stationery on the desk to write John a letter telling him that you've decided you two aren't right for each other, and that you're ending things. Then I want you to pack your bags, put the note in an envelope, and leave it with the clerk at the front desk. After you do that, I want you to call a cab to take you to the Greyhound station so you can get the hell out of Dodge," the woman said, smiling as if she'd just delivered good news to Madeline.

"I don't know who you are, or what the hell you're trying to pull, but you don't scare me, you country tramp. I'm not one of those slow-minded, small-town bamas that you're used to dealing with. Nothing you do is going to rattle my chain," Madeline shot back, still easing her hand toward the ashtray. "Now *I'm* gonna tell *you* what *you're* going to do."

Before Madeline could say another word, the woman rushed up to her and punched her in her one good eye, delivering on her promise. Madeline grabbed the side of her face and grimaced in pain. *"Aggghhh!"* she cried out in agony, too weak and stunned to strike back.

"I'm tired of foolin' with you! I told your crazy ass to shut up, but you don't believe fat meat's greasy, so this-here country tramp had to show you." The woman huffed and regained her footing. "If you don't do exactly what I just told you to do, I'm gonna have to tell John, as well as the police, all about you."

Madeline was in so much pain; she couldn't stop the tears welling at her eyes. "I'm going to have Slim arrested for rape and you for attempted murder," she hissed, still holding her hand to her face.

"That'll be very interesting, considering not only have you attempted murder, you've committed it at least three times."

Madeline's whimpers quieted a bit at the woman's words.

"That's right. I know all about the fire you set, which killed your parents, and about the poison you put in your aunt's tea, which slowly killed her over time. The only thing I'm fuzzy on is where you dumped your last boyfriend's body. Roger was his name, right?" the woman said as she watched Madeline gasp as she continued. "But since he's been missing for a few years, I guess the mysterious disappearance of one black man in a city of millions is a cold case that's not too high on the authorities' radar."

If Madeline's eyes hadn't been almost shut from swelling, she would have bucked them wide. She shook her head in disbelief; for the first time, she was scared.

The woman let out a satisfied laugh. "Who would've ever thought that out of all the people in this big ol' world, we'd know some of the same folks. Larry Johnson is my first cousin."

Madeline drew a blank stare through her puffy lids. She didn't know a Larry Johnson, or what in the world this woman was talking about.

"Oh, I forgot," the woman said. "You probably know him as Harold Boston. When I visited him last year, we went out to a club and you happened to be there. You didn't see me, but I certainly saw you because Larry pointed you out. He was plumb crazy about you."

Madeline nearly fell out of her chair when she heard the name pass through the woman's lips. "Harold Boston" was the wayward con artist she'd hired to meet John and pretend to be her brother. A few days after she'd paid him for his services, she'd heard he'd died of a heroin overdose, which she was thrilled to learn because it saved her the trouble of disposing of him herself. "I thought he was dead," Madeline said in disbelief.

"Everybody did, even me. The dead guy who the police found in the drug house where Larry passed out, while he was getting high, had stolen his ID, so they thought it was Larry. It scared him shitless, but it also saved his life. He's been clean, going on nine months," the woman said proudly. "Once he got himself straight, he told me about some of the terrible things he'd done and how he wanted to change his life. He even told me about you, so imagine my surprise when you showed up at Maxx's party with my dear friend, John Small. You know, I heard that respectable folks should stay out of clubs."

Madeline sat motionless as shock overtook her pain. She couldn't believe what was happening. Her mind raced to figure out what kind of scheme or angle she could concoct that would get her out of the mess she was in. Her first impulse was to kill the woman, but she knew that wouldn't do her any good. Besides, she barely had the strength to hold her head up, let alone engage in a fight.

"You're out of moves," the woman said, snapping Madeline back into the moment. "John won't be back over this way for at least another hour or so. That gives you plenty of time to be long gone when he comes walking through that door."

"Why are you doing this? What's in this for you?" Madeline asked.

The woman put her hands on her hips and smirked. "The satisfaction of knowing I helped a friend. You're a low-down woman, Madeline, and if you ever try to contact John again—so help me—I'll kill you dead with my bare hands. Do you understand me?"

Madeline squinted through her slits-for-eyes and could see that the woman meant every word she'd said. Slowly she nodded her head in defeat.

"Good," the woman said. "Now that's more like it." She turned on her heels and stopped just as she reached the door. "Oh, and don't forget to put on your sunglasses and wrap something around your head before you leave. We wouldn't want folks asking what happened to you, now would we?" And with that, she strolled out the door.

After she slammed the door behind her, the woman walked across the parking lot to where Slim was waiting and hopped into his truck.

"If you hadn't come out in another few minutes, I was gonna call the police," Slim said, his eyes bulging wide with fear. "I was scared that crazy woman had hurt you, or worse. I think she's capable of anything, even murder."

The woman smiled. "You shouldn't have worried about me, Slim. As you can see, I'm just fine."

"What happened in there?"

"Just what I said would happen. I talked to her, woman-to-woman, and I got her to see how wrong she was for what she did to you. She's packing her bags right now and she'll be on a Greyhound headed back to New York when the next bus pulls out."

"What?" Slim asked, with a puzzled look. "You mean she's gonna leave town, just like that?"

"Yep. Just like that," she said, snapping her fingers. "But to be on the safe side, let's sit here for a little while to make sure she comes out of that room with her bags in hand."

Slim nodded and then looked at the woman with a questioning stare. "I know I ain't the smartest fella around, but tonight learned me somethin'," he said as he touched one of the scratches on his face. "Things ain't always what they seem. I know that crazy bitch didn't back down as easy as you say she did. I ain't no fool. What did you do to her?"

The woman smiled sweetly. "I told you, I talked to her, woman-to-woman. I can be very persuasive when I have to be."

Slim was quiet for a moment as he thought about the situation. Finally he nodded. "Okay, I'ma let it go. I guess it don't really matter what went on between you and her. The most important thing is that this nightmare is over."

"Yes, it is. You won't ever have to worry about seeing her again."

Just then, they saw Madeline limp out of the room, wearing sunglasses, a head scarf, and a heavy jacket, which probably belonged to John. She was carrying an envelope in one hand and a suitcase in the other as she headed toward the front entrance of the hotel.

"Well, you did it," Slim said. "I don't know how, but I'm thankful and I owe you."

"No, you don't owe me a thing. Someone once told me, 'you can never go wrong doing right'. When I saw you all broken up, like you were in the hospital parking lot, and you told me what happened, I knew I had to help because it was the right thing to do."

"I'm glad you believed me. Some people might've turned me in."

"You're a good man, Slim. You wouldn't hurt a fly, so I knew you'd been set up. Just remember to be more careful when it comes to women. There are some crazy heffas out here."

"You got that right. If there was more good women like you, this world would be a better place."

"Awww, thanks, Slim. That's so nice of you to say."

"You always been a nice person, always treatin' people right."

She smiled and tilted her head. "You're a good person, too, Slim."

"Thank you, Mary-Marie," Slim said with a smile as he turned on the engine and pulled out of the parking lot.

Chapter 39

John lay in bed, exhausted, feeling as if he could sleep for another full day. He glanced over at the alarm clock on the nightstand beside the bed. "I can't believe it's already noon." He yawned and turned over on his side. It seemed as if he'd just gone to sleep only minutes ago, but it actually had been closer to 4:30 A.M. by the time his head finally hit the pillow. "I'm glad I changed my flight to leave out tomorrow afternoon," he mumbled with relief. He'd decided that after all he'd been through in the last twenty-four hours, he needed one more day to recuperate.

He yawned again and stretched, thinking about all that had happened since he'd arrived in Nedine two nights ago. His weekend visit was supposed to have been free of stress and relaxing. He'd had every intention of combining business with pleasure and enjoying himself, particularly since his life always seemed to be so hectic. But instead of a slow and easy weekend filled with fun and laughter, it had turned into the exact opposite.

John willed himself out of bed and lumbered into the bathroom. He turned on the light and took a long look at himself in the mirror. "Damn, I need more rest," he said, examining the tired look draped over his eyelids. He turned on the faucet and splashed cold water on his face before twisting the knob on the showerhead. *At least, Maxx is going to be all right, and I don't have to deal with Madeline.* He stepped under the warm stream of water and thought about the crazy chain of events that had occurred.

It was the wee hours of the morning when Maxx's doctor had come into the waiting room and announced that Maxx had made it through the surgery without complication, but he still wasn't completely out of the woods. Because of all the blood loss, he'd needed a transfusion; and because the bullet had chipped a bone in his right hip, he would also need another surgery. But the most important thing was that he was going to live and he had an excellent prognosis for a full recovery.

After hearing the good news, John embraced Elizabeth in a loving hug filled with relief. They ignored Grace's disapproving stare and enjoyed their moment, blocking out everything around them except each other. John had wanted to hold Elizabeth in his arms until the sun came up. But it had been a long, arduous night and he knew she needed rest. He also knew that he needed to head back to the hotel so he could deal with Madeline. Despite the late hour and the fact that she was probably pissed to high heaven that he'd stayed out all night, he was fairly certain she would still be awake—waiting for him— primed and ready for an argument.

He told Elizabeth he would take her home and they left the hospital, walking together, hand in hand. Even though her parents' house was only fifteen minutes away, John had relished each second and mile traveled as if they'd driven on a cross-country adventure. He felt that time spent with Elizabeth was worth its weight in gold. He'd heard people talk about how the right woman could change a man, and his own father had spoken those very words. Now he had experienced it firsthand, because Elizabeth made him want to be a better man.

He'd seen the time when the opportunity to bed Mary-Marie wouldn't have slipped by him. But when she'd approached him in the lobby, he realized that having wild sex with her was the last thing on his mind because all he could think about was Elizabeth. She'd changed him in just one night.

He explained to Elizabeth that once he returned to the hotel, he was going to check into a new room and then break the news to Madeline about ending their relationship. "I think it's best to get it out in the open," John had said. "No need in having a huge fight once we get back to New York, and knowing her, she'll probably want to book a separate flight."

Once John returned to the hotel, he headed straight to the front desk so he could get a key to a new room before facing Madeline. However, to his surprise, the pleasant night clerk handed him a quick and simple note that changed everything.

> *John,*
> *By the time you read this note, I will be on a bus headed back home. After sitting alone in the room all evening and thinking about our relationship, I now see that we are moving in different directions. I believe it is best to end things now, rather than experience the inevitable. I wish you the best in your future.*
> *Madeline*

Although John was concerned about Madeline's well-being and her safety as a woman traveling on a long bus ride all by herself, a part of him was overjoyed that he was free of her. The first thing he did was rush to his room to share the good news with Elizabeth before she went to bed. Knowing that her parents weren't there to pick up the phone made his call even sweeter. They chatted briefly before making arrangements to see each other later that afternoon.

Just as John was about to undress and crawl into bed, he heard a knock at the door. "Who could this be at this time of the morning?" He shook his head and walked to the door, prepared to tell whoever it was that they had the wrong room. But when he looked through the peephole, he knew that the person standing on the other side had not only come to the right room, they'd come with a purpose.

John's first thought was that something had happened to Maxx, and whatever the news, it was so bad that it needed to be delivered in person. But if something had happened to Maxx, Elizabeth would have known and she hadn't mentioned a thing. He quickly opened the door, ready to get to the bottom of the early morning visit.

"What are you doing here?" John asked.

Mary-Marie smiled slyly. "Well, it's good to see you again, too."

"It's late." John said, arms folded at his chest. "How did you even know what room I'm in?"

Mary-Marie pushed past John and walked straight in, sauntering over to his bed. "Where're your manners, John? It's a shame I have to invite myself into your room."

"I didn't invite you in because you shouldn't be here. Now please answer my question." He was tired and he was losing patience. "How did you know what room I'm in?"

"First things first, sugar." Mary-Marie licked her glossy lips and smiled.

"I'm not up for any games. I've tried to be polite, but you have to leave. I don't even want to know how you got my room number. Just go, please."

Mary-Marie shook her head. "You won't want me to leave after I tell you how I saved you and Slim from a world of trouble."

John sat in the chair at the desk as Mary-Marie quickly recounted the entire fiasco that happened tonight, including details about Madeline's shady and very dangerous past.

"So you see, John, if I hadn't come forward when I did, who knows what would have happened to poor Slim, and you, too. I came back here and sat in my car in the parking lot to make sure that crazy woman wouldn't come back. I saw you move your things down here to this room, so I gave you a few minutes to unwind before I knocked on your door so I could tell you what happened."

John was almost in disbelief of the story, but after witnessing Madeline's behavior, it all made sense. "I'm going to go see Slim before I leave town to make sure he's okay. Thank you for what you did," John said. "I'm very grateful."

Mary-Marie cocked her head to the side. "How grateful?"

He knew what she meant and he wasn't in the mood. He was glad Mary-Marie had literally saved two lives, but he also knew he needed to get her out of his room before something else erupted. "Like I told you tonight, I'm seeing someone."

"I just got rid of a woman for you. Who have you jumped to so quickly?"

"You need to leave." John stood to walk her to the door. "If I have to ask you again, I'll be forced to call hotel security."

Mary-Marie was outraged, but not insane, so she rose from her place on the bed and walked to the door. "This is the thanks I get after trying to help you?"

"I thanked you properly."

Mary-Marie smiled. "I can think of a whole lot of other ways you can thank me."

"Good bye," John said.

"See you around."

John closed the door and thanked God above that he'd just dodged another bullet. "Now maybe I can get some rest."

John emerged from the longest shower he'd ever taken, feeling fresh and renewed. The puffiness had disappeared from his eyes, the luster had come back to his robust skin, and energy had been restored in his spirit. He'd washed the last two days down the drain and was ready to make the most of the afternoon in front of him.

After he dressed, he called Elizabeth.

"Hello," she answered on the first ring.

"Hey, baby." John smiled into the phone; Elizabeth smiled into hers, too.

"It's good to hear your voice," she cooed.

"Yours too. How are you feeling? Did you sleep well?"

"I tossed and turned, but I feel surprisingly good, considering all that has happened."

"Me too."

"And I'll be even better, once I see you," Elizabeth said.

"You sure do know how to make a man feel good."

"I mean it, John. I can't wait to see you."

"Same here, and I can't wait to tell you about what happened after we hung up the phone this morning."

"What happened?"

"Mary-Marie came by my room and told me a crazy story about what really happened with Madeline."

"Mary-Marie?!" Elizabeth squeaked.

"Don't worry, baby," John said, sensing her concern, and for good reason. "I'll tell you all about it on our way over to the hospital to visit Maxx."

"Okay, if you say so," she said hesitantly.

"I also have a surprise for you."

"What is it?"

"If I tell you, that defeats the entire purpose of a surprise."

"I guess I'll just have to be patient."

"It's nothing big, but I think you'll like it. I'll be over to pick you up in about a half hour. Will you be ready?"

Elizabeth smiled. "I'm ready right now!"

Chapter 40

John peered into Maxx's hospital room, hoping that Grace and Milford had already left. On their drive over, he and Elizabeth had shared an open and honest discussion about her mother and the rest of her family. They both knew it was a high probability that any engagement with her parents—and, in particular, her mother—might turn hostile. John didn't want to have words with Grace in front of Maxx, especially not in his present condition. So when he didn't see them in the room, he breathed a little easier, squared his shoulders, and walked in with Elizabeth by his side.

Josie was sitting in a chair beside Maxx's bed, reading one of the many get-well cards that had already started pouring in. Flowers and balloons were beginning to fill the room as word of Maxx's shooting had spread. John had decided not to hold Elizabeth's hand, as he'd done on their way into the building, because he wanted to be respectful of his friend's condition. He knew that Maxx had no idea about his budding relationship with Elizabeth. Depending upon the shape his friend was in, he didn't want to give him another jarring shock.

Maxx's eyes lit up when he caught sight of John and Elizabeth. This was the first time the three had seen each other since the shooting last night.

Elizabeth went straight to her brother, leaned over his bed, and hugged him gently. "Maxx, I'm so glad you're going to be all right. I've been praying for you."

"I appreciate that, Lizzy. Prayer is a powerful thing."

"He ain't been up long," Josie said, looking at Elizabeth. "He opened his eyes right before your parents left, just a little while ago. They was here all night, just like me, so they finally went home to get some rest. Matter of fact, y'all just missed them."

John nodded his head, secretly thinking that was a very good thing.

Elizabeth examined her brother's pale skin, parched lips, and weakened eyes. "How are you feeling?"

Maxx reached for the plastic cup of water sitting on the tray next to his bed. "I ain't even gonna lie. I feel like shit."

"You kinda look like it, too." John laughed.

Maxx's face broke into a smile. He held out his hand, turned over his palm, and waited for John to slap him five. The two friends greeted each other with brotherly love.

"You had us worried, man," John said. "But I knew you'd be all right."

"I'm glad you did, 'cause for a moment there . . . Man, I just didn't know."

Maxx went on to tell them that his doctor had said that if he continued to improve, he could be released in a few days. He would need to undergo another surgery next month to repair a chipped bone and then reset his hip. He'd also need months of physical therapy to regain full mobility and restore his natural walking gait. But that aside, his prognosis was good.

Just then, a nurse entered the room. "Time for your pain medication, Mr. Sanders."

"That's the best news I've heard all day," Maxx joked. He gladly gobbled down the pills the nurse handed him and thanked her before she left the room.

"You're in a lot of pain, aren't you?" Elizabeth asked.

"Yes, he is," Josie spoke up. "He been tryin' to act all tough, but I know when he's hurtin'. I got a good mind to go down to that jail and beat Thelma's ass right through those bars."

John and Elizabeth looked at Josie with alarm.

"Don't talk about doin' nothin' to nobody's ass," Maxx said. "I'm sensitive about that subject right now. Hell, 'kiss my ass' has a whole new meaning now."

Josie shook her head "Since you put it like that, I guess I'll just pray for the heffa."

"I think that's best," John agreed. "After everything that happened last night, the last thing we need is for you to get arrested."

"Yeah, you right." Maxx nodded. "Things been crazy enough as it is. And speakin' of crazy, look at all these cards, flowers, and balloons. I been asleep most of the day, but Josie said people been stoppin' by to visit since early this mornin'."

"Has Slim come by to see you?" John asked.

"Funny you mention Slim. He ain't been by or even called my room."

John and Elizabeth looked at each other.

"What's wrong?" Maxx asked.

John took a deep breath. He didn't want to alarm Maxx because he had enough worries of his own, so he sketched out a story that was mostly true. "We stopped over to see him right before we came here. He's a little under the weather but I'm sure with a little rest he'll be feeling better soon."

"I'll give him a call later today if I'm up to it."

"I'm sure he'd like that."

Maxx looked around. "Where's your girl? I'm surprised she let you outta her sight," he said with a small laugh.

John shifted his weight to his right leg. "She's not my girl. Besides, she left town last night on a Greyhound headed back to New York."

Maxx took a long look at John and then glanced over at his sister. "What's goin' on with you two?"

As if on cue, Josie rose from her seat. "I'm gonna walk down to the cafeteria," she said. "John, Elizabeth, I'll see y'all later."

Maxx, John, and Elizabeth were quiet until Josie left the room.

John and Maxx stared at each other, while Elizabeth fiddled with a piece of string on her shirt.

John knew right away that Maxx was hip to what was going on between him and Elizabeth. Since they'd been small boys, they understood each other better than anyone else. They knew each other's likes and dislikes, temperaments and tastes. They shared secrets between them that they'd both carry to their graves. They were loyal to each other, brothers through thick and thin. So John had no doubt about the conversation that was coming. He had wanted to ease into things carefully, but he respected Maxx too much to beat around the bush.

John took Elizabeth's hand in his and began to speak. "I know this is going to sound strange to you, and I can understand why, but the truth is, I want to start dating Elizabeth."

There was a long pause filled with dead quiet. Maxx turned his eyes away from his best friend and toward his sister before he spoke. "Lizzy, I think you better leave the room so me and John can talk."

Elizabeth shook her head. "No, Maxx. I'm not a little girl. I'm a grown woman, and I want to be with John, too. Anything that you say to him, you can say to me."

"Lizzy, I'm gonna talk to John, man-to-man. You don't need to hear some of what I'm gonna tell him, trust me."

John could read Maxx's mind and he knew what his best friend was thinking. They were both ladies' men. Between the two of them, they'd bedded enough women to fill several harems. Throughout all their escapades, neither of them had ever known the other to be completely faithful in any of his relationships. Now that he had announced his intentions with Elizabeth, Maxx was not pleased.

He knew that Maxx would gladly take a bullet straight through his heart before he allowed Elizabeth to be hurt in any way—even at the hands of his playboy best friend. But he also knew that Maxx had no idea that his appetite for women had changed literally overnight. Elizabeth was the perfect serving size and he didn't need another helping. She made him feel like no other woman ever had, and she'd managed to make him do something he'd never experienced—want to become a one-woman man. It was more than he'd expected. Standing there holding Elizabeth's hand inside his, he wouldn't trade that feeling for his annual end-of-year bonus.

John knew that given his reputation, Maxx had every reason to be concerned. If the shoe was on the other foot, he probably would be, too. But he also knew that Maxx understood what kind of man he was, and he hoped his friend was taking this into account as he digested the situation.

Maxx looked at John. "Do you really want my sister to hear what I'm gonna say to you?"

"She might as well," John said, holding Elizabeth's hand even more tightly. "I don't have anything to hide from Elizabeth."

"Suit yourself."

John held his breath and readied himself.

"Man, you get more pussy than any cat I know, including me, and that says a lot. How you gonna walk into town and try to get my sister's? We supposed to be brothers. This is fucked up."

"I didn't plan on falling for Elizabeth, but I know what my heart is telling me."

"*Your heart?*" Maxx said. "After just one night! Negro, did you fuck my sister?"

"Maxx!" Elizabeth gasped.

"Lizzy, I told you, you needed to leave," Maxx huffed.

"You know Elizabeth's not that kind of woman," John cautioned.

"I'm not questionin' *her* morals. I'm questionin' *your* scandalous ass."

John let go of Elizabeth's hand and rubbed his chin. "I can't get offended because you know how I've behaved with women in the past. But you also know that when I say something, I mean it. I've always been that way. When I said I want to start dating your sister, I meant it. I want to be with her."

Maxx shook his head. "I can't believe this shit."

"Have I ever, in my entire life, told you that I wanted to be with a woman? Any woman?" John asked.

Maxx was silent.

"Have I?"

"No," Maxx finally answered.

"Do you think I would take advantage of Elizabeth?"

"Not knowingly."

"Not ever," John corrected. He took a deep breath and walked around Elizabeth so that he was standing close beside Maxx's bed. "Hurting her would be like hurting you, and I'd never do that, man."

"Hell is paved with the best of intentions. Sometimes people don't mean to do the shit they do, but it happens. I love you better than my own brothers," Maxx said, "but, John, we're talkin' about Lizzy."

Elizabeth stood silent like a fly on the wall as John and Maxx went back and forth about her.

"I didn't want to believe what I saw in the club last night," Maxx said as he shifted in his bed. "I tried to blame it on the liquor when I saw you grinnin' like a damn fool and lookin' at Lizzy all funny-like. I prayed like hell that I was wrong, that you wasn't interested in my sister."

John raised his brow. "You don't think I'm good enough for Elizabeth?"

"John, you one of the best cats I know. You wouldn't be my best friend on earth if you wasn't. But like I said, this is Lizzy we talkin' about." Maxx looked at his sister and shook his head. "Man, I'm havin' a hard time with this one."

"I understand, but you've got to know that what I'm telling you is solid. I'm not bullshittin' around. I can't explain how it happened, and I'm not even going to try, because it won't make sense to you. But I can assure you, man-to-man, I'm going to do right by her, Maxx."

Maxx turned his head and let out a sigh. "Lizzy, is this really what you want?"

"Yes," she answered. "I know this is hard for you, Maxx, but I've wanted to be with John for as long as I can remember."

Maxx shook his head. "I don't believe this."

Elizabeth cleared her throat and continued. "I'm not some little girl who's lost in the dark. I'm a grown woman. I know what I want, and I know my heart. I'm well aware of the fact that John's had more women than you can shake a stick at, and I know he's never made a commitment to any of them. But those women don't have a thing to do with me. What he did in the past is going to stay back there, where it belongs. What the two of us build together from today forward is going to be ours alone." Elizabeth stepped forward and reclaimed John's hand. "Maxx, you're the best big brother a girl could ever ask for. I love you and I want your approval, because it would mean the world to me. But if I don't get it, I'm still going to be with John."

John looked at Elizabeth and smiled. She'd not only stood beside him—she'd stood up for him. She'd shown what kind of mate she would be, and it made John feel like nothing was impossible with Elizabeth by his side. "Well, Maxx," he said to his friend, "do we have your support?"

"But you're gettin' ready to move back here so you can open your bank. It's been your dream. And Lizzy's gettin' ready to take a teachin' job in North Carolina in a few weeks. How y'all gonna have a relationship when you livin' in different places?"

John nodded. "She can stay here and find a teaching job, or I can take my dreams to North Carolina. We'll work it all out."

Maxx stared at John without blinking. He let a long pause linger before easing out a deep breath. "Man, if I hear about Lizzy sheddin' one tear over your ass, or I find out that you stepped out on her, I'ma find you wherever you are and beat your ass. And you know I'm sensitive about the ass!"

Maxx's comment eased the tension and the three shared a laugh. Elizabeth hugged her brother, and then Maxx and John slapped each other's palms. By the time Josie returned to the room, they had fallen into an easy conversation.

An hour later, John and Elizabeth walked down the hallway just as they had arrived, hand in hand. They were happy that they had

Maxx's blessing. John knew the rest of the Sanders family was a losing cause, but he didn't care—and neither did Elizabeth. All that mattered was that they had each other.

They were about to open the exit door when John stopped and turned to her. "We just crossed our first hurdle as a couple. This proves to me that as long as we stick together, we'll be just fine."

"Yes, we will."

John kissed Elizabeth slowly and tenderly. "C'mon, I'm going to take you to your surprise."

Chapter 41

"Where are we going?" Elizabeth asked John, filled with curiosity.

"You'll know when we get there."

"Can you give me a hint about where or what it is, pretty please?" Elizabeth cooed, batting her long, dark lashes as she smiled.

"Your feminine wiles aren't going to work this time." John laughed. "Besides, you'll see where we're headed soon enough."

True to John's words, five minutes and two right turns later, Elizabeth knew exactly where they were going. A feeling of excitement and nervousness spread through her body as John slowly eased his car around a steep curve. Once they turned off the main road, they were greeted by majestic trees and splendid greenery, which set itself apart from the rest of the town.

Elizabeth took in a deep breath. "We're going to your parents' house, aren't we?"

"That's right."

Although she had never been to the famed Small property, she'd always heard about its grandeur, especially from her brother. Maxx had practically lived under the Small family's roof during his senior year of high school. Elizabeth remembered Maxx's stories about how huge John's house was, how nicely it was decorated, and how they even had a mosaic-tiled pool in their backyard. But she hadn't just taken Maxx's word for how well the family lived, she'd heard the same thing from people in town. They'd boasted about the beautifully manicured lawn, imported Italian bricks, and sweeping windows, which all made it look like something straight out of a magazine.

The Smalls' home was one of the nicest houses in all of Nedine, black- or white-owned, and that hadn't sat well with the white establishment in their segregated town. But over time, Isaiah's wealth and reputation had grown so powerful that no one bothered him—and for good reason. The rumors that swirled around the Small property had always intrigued Elizabeth; and to this day, she didn't know what was really fact or fiction.

Legend had it that the KKK had tried to burn down the Smalls' grand estate shortly after Isaiah had erected the custom-built home. It was a known fact that the Klan in the town where the Smalls once lived had burned them out of their home when Isaiah had attempted to build a new one. But, obviously, he hadn't learned his lesson. Not only was he building a home large enough to house three families, he had the nerve to hire dozens of black men in town to work the two large tobacco farms he'd purchased, paying them a wage that was higher than most white people earned at the local factory. His audacity outraged the white community; they were determined to put him in his place and make an example of him.

However, the scheme they'd plotted was foiled, and the tale surrounding what had actually happened was a mystery that had become town folklore to this day.

It had been rumored that KKK members in Nedine and in two surrounding towns planned to burn the palatial house down to the ground, once final construction was complete. Late one Sunday evening, nearly forty white men gathered on the Small property carrying guns, torches, large rocks, Molotov cocktails, and an eight-foot cross. Some were drunk, some were sober, and all were ready to destroy the home they felt no Negro should ever own.

The angry mob was about to send a large rock sailing through the first-floor window, when a bone-chilling wind sliced through the hot night, leaving them motionless. In the blink of an eye, the temperature dropped so low that the men could see their breath clouding the air like giant plumes of smoke. It was unclear as to what happened next; but within a matter of minutes, every man who had assembled in Isaiah Small's front yard had retreated to his truck, heading for the hills.

The next day, the men never spoke a word beyond the murky details of what had happened after the sudden chill had gripped them. It was all a mystery, but one thing was certain—whatever they'd experienced in front of Isaiah Small's house had put a bone-numbing fear in each of their hearts, leaving none of them able to speak of it. And stranger still, it was said that within a few days of the event, some had moved their families to other towns, and one man even left the state altogether.

Over the more than three decades since that fateful night, rumors and speculation had shifted about what had actually happened. But there was one nugget of truth that was indisputable—no one messed with Isaiah Small, his family, or any of his business dealings.

Elizabeth had always wanted to see the Small property for herself, but she'd never had the opportunity. The Smalls lived on the opposite side of town from where she had grown up. Given the fact that she didn't have her own transportation, and that her mother held a strong dislike for the family, she might as well have been a virtual world away. Maxx had told her that the rumors and tall tales were ridiculous, and that the Smalls were just regular, down-to-earth folks who happened to live in the lap of luxury.

"So I'm finally going to visit the famed Small property. Are all those old wives' tales true?"

John sighed, and then chuckled. "You've heard some wild things, I'm sure."

"You know how people in this town talk and gossip. They say your Grandma Allene put a spell on the Klan and ran them away from your house."

"People love to make up outlandish tales. Gives them something to talk about."

Elizabeth nodded in agreement. "So . . . I get to meet your folks, huh?" She tried to control the nervousness seeping into her voice, but her jittery hands gave her away.

"You've met my parents before, haven't you?"

"Yes, I see them in passing every now and then out in town. But, well . . . this is different."

John glanced over at her. "You nervous?"

"A little."

"Why?"

"What if they don't like me?"

"You mean the way your folks—excuse me, mainly your mother—doesn't like me?"

Elizabeth's heart sank a little. She felt awful just thinking about the bitter truth that she and John had discussed at length earlier that afternoon. She was embarrassed by her mother's backward, prejudiced views, and disappointed in the fact that her father had the spine of a jellyfish, basically cosigning Grace's outrageous behavior.

"I'm sorry, John," Elizabeth said. "I've always prayed that my mother and the rest of my family would change their ways. It's hard for me to stomach their attitudes. But no matter what they think or how they feel, they can't stop me from being with you."

John reached over and put his hand on top of her trembling fingers. "What you said in Maxx's room, it made me feel like the luckiest man in the world." John cleared his throat. "When I said I want to be with you, I meant it from the bottom of my heart. This is a soul connection."

She smiled and squeezed John's hand. "That means nothing, not even our families, can stand in our way."

"My folks are going to love you. Trust me."

When they turned onto the long road leading to John's parents' house, her eyes grew wide when she saw what looked like a small mansion in the distance. As they drew closer, she read the official-looking, large white placard that announced, THE SMALL PROPERTY, written in elegant calligraphy. She'd expected a nice home, but nothing as opulent as what sat just a hundred feet away.

Elizabeth had grown up in a modest three-bedroom, two-bathroom home; its most extravagant feature was the Frigidaire her mother had upgraded to five years ago after finally getting rid of their old-fashioned icebox.

But nice homes weren't entirely foreign to her, either. She'd had a glimpse of how the well-to-do lived when she'd visited the home of her privileged Spelman roommate, who hailed from one of Atlanta's most affluent black neighborhoods.

But none of those houses came close to the jaw-dropping abode in front of her. She turned and looked at John. Her mouth was open in silence; her voice was unable to register a sound.

John stared back at her as if to say, *This is no big deal.*

"John," she finally said, "your home is absolutely beautiful, and it's *huge!*"

John smiled. "This is my parents' home, not mine. My pad in Manhattan is a matchbox."

Elizabeth swallowed hard, suddenly feeling smaller than her five-two frame. She couldn't help but think that some of her mother's dislike for the Smalls was rooted in jealousy, as much as it was in pure ignorance. Grace thought that people who looked like *them* shouldn't live in houses that looked like this—especially since she, with her nearly white skin, didn't.

John parked in the middle of the large, circular driveway in front of the house and turned off the engine. "You okay?"

"Honestly, I'm nervous. I don't come from a fancy family like yours," Elizabeth said, looking out her window at the huge wrap-around porch framing the house. She brought her hand to her mouth and sighed. "You know how backward my folks are. I just hope and pray that your parents don't think I'm anything like my people."

John gently rubbed his fingers over Elizabeth's still-trembling hands. "First of all, my parents are two of the most down-to-earth people you'll ever meet. They're wealthy, but they've never forgotten where they came from. And second, your parents are who they are, and you're who you are."

"Are you sure they won't flip their wigs when they see who you've brought home to meet them?"

"Of course, they won't."

"How can you be so sure?"

John grinned, showing his straight, pearly white teeth. "I called my mother this morning and told her I'd be bringing you by for Sunday dinner."

"Oh boy."

John brought Elizabeth's hand to his mouth for a gentle kiss. When his soft lips met her flesh, all her jitters slowly melted away. She smiled and waited for him to walk around to her side of the car and open her door. "I love you, John," she whispered as she braced herself for a meeting with her future.

Chapter 42

Henrietta was in the kitchen, putting the finishing touches on the meal she was preparing, while Isaiah and Allene relaxed a few feet away in the family room. They were watching one of their favorite Westerns on the television and talking back to the screen. Henrietta smiled to herself as she listened to the sound of their laughter. This was part of what had become their Sunday routine over the years.

The day would start with Henrietta and Isaiah rising early, saying their prayers, and then reading Scripture together from their Bibles. After that, Henrietta would cook a small breakfast—nothing fancy— scrambled eggs, freshly made buttermilk biscuits, homemade strawberry jam, a colorful fruit salad, and gourmet coffee prepared from her French press. Once they finished their meal, they would shower, dress, and drive over to Allene's house in time to pick her up for the 11:00 A.M. service at Rising Star A.M.E. Zion Church. Following an uplifting sermon from Reverend Raymond Daniels, they would head back home for a delicious family meal filled with good conversation. A few hours later, once they'd all taken a light after-dinner nap, Henrietta and Isaiah would round out their day by taking Allene home with a supply of hearty leftovers.

Henrietta stirred the slotted spoon in the simmering pot of the freshly snapped string beans she'd picked from her garden the day before. She smiled, thankful for her family and the little things that made her life full—like picking fresh vegetables from her own garden, cooking a good meal for her family, listening to her husband and mother-in-law enjoy each other's company, and having her son home, safe and sound, were the treasures that she knew were priceless.

As Henrietta thought about her many blessings, she said a quick prayer for her son's best friend, Maxx Sanders. "Jesus, please heal him and keep him safe," she whispered aloud. She shook her head and thought about the young man's circumstances. She could still hear John's voice in her ear from his phone call last night.

She and Isaiah had been asleep when their phone rang well after midnight, pulling them from their slumber. As soon as John came on the line, her stomach tensed in knots, anticipating bad news. She hadn't wanted to think that John was in danger because Mama Allene had told Isaiah he'd be all right. But even with that knowledge, her motherly instincts led her to ask, "What's wrong, son? Has something happened to you?"

"No, Mama, I'm fine," John assured her. "But Maxx is in the hospital."

John had been calm in his recount of the details surrounding Maxx's shooting, but Henrietta heard the hidden fear beneath the strong layers of her son's voice.

She'd been worried that something like this would eventually happen. Maxx's womanizing had finally caught up to him, putting his life on the line. How many times had she told him to settle down, date one girl at a time, and lay off all the partying? Henrietta loved Maxx like he was her own son, and she'd worried, mothered, and fussed over him, just as she did with John.

She still remembered the long-ago afternoon when John had come home from school with a busted lip, disheveled clothes, and a note pinned to his bloodied shirt, and that had cemented Maxx into their lives.

"Maxx helped me, Mama," John had said proudly. "And we beat those boys a lot worse than they beat us."

Henrietta shook her head as she dabbed one of the cuts on John's cheek with a peroxide-soaked cotton ball. "I read that in the note. But no matter what those other boys said or did, you shouldn't have gotten into a fight with them. You should've called for your teacher."

"But she won't on the playground."

Henrietta cut her eyes and raised her brow.

"Excuse me." John corrected himself, "She *wasn't* on the playground."

A small part of Henrietta ached because she knew this was one of the reasons why her son had been attacked. Adults weren't the only ones who could be jealous and cruel.

"Mama, they said I talk like white folks and I think I'm better than them 'cause I'm rich and we live in a big house. Are we rich, Mama?"

"Don't listen to what those boys or anyone else says about the way you speak or how we live. Sometimes people say things just to hurt you, and this is one of those times. You're a good boy, John. You just keep minding your manners and do what your father and I tell you, and you'll be just fine, okay?"

John nodded. "Maxx said I'm a good friend, and he's my best friend!" He smiled through his busted lip. "That's why he helped me fight those boys, Mama. He said he wasn't gonna let me take a beating by myself because I didn't do anything wrong."

From that moment forward, Henrietta had unofficially adopted Maxx as her own.

Henrietta rubbed her hands across the front of her apron and sighed, thinking about Maxx lying in a hospital bed. She would have rushed over to Nedine Memorial right after receiving John's call, had it not been for the fact that she knew that her presence there would only cause further harm. There were too many dynamics in play, and she didn't want to make an already tense situation worse.

"Please keep me updated," she'd told John.

Henrietta could only imagine the scene that could have played out, had she shown up at the hospital. Grace Sanders had made it clear over the years that she didn't like John, which hurt Henrietta ten times more than the fact that the woman cared even less for her and Isaiah . . . especially for her.

There wasn't an ounce of love lost between her and Grace Sanders. Henrietta looked out her kitchen window, thinking back on the past. She sighed as she turned the small black knob, lowering the flame under the pot of rice boiling on the stove's front burner. She was cooking up a storm, trying to take her mind off the dark cloud that always seemed to rage within Grace Sanders's soul.

Henrietta shook her head, thinking about how Grace had grown more bitter and spiteful as the years had passed. She thought about the cruel words she'd heard Grace speak about her shortly after she and Isaiah had moved to Nedine.

"She's as tall as a man and as black as my shoe," Grace said to another woman while standing in the small grocery store that all of Nedine's black residents frequented.

"She's pretty enough, though," the woman said.

"Not nearly as pretty as me, or even you," Grace brazenly said without shame. "It's not right that someone like her is going to be living in a house like that."

"I hear her husband is rich, too," the woman said. "And I also heard she's got a college degree from some fancy school in Atlanta, Georgia."

"It makes my blood run cold."

Henrietta refused to listen to another word. She came from the back where she was standing and walked right by Grace and her friend. Her back was straight, her head was held high, and her smile was radiant. "Excuse me ladies," she said as she breezed by. "Have a good day . . . oh, and by the way, the name of the college I graduated from is Spelman."

The woman who'd made the statement looked embarrassed and

remorseful, but Grace was so mad she looked as though she could explode. From that day forward Henrietta and Grace had little dealings.

Henrietta was drawn from her thoughts of the past when she heard her son's deep voice bounce off the walls.

"I'm home!" John called out.

"Come on back," Isaiah yelled from the family room.

Henrietta wiped her hands on the dish towel near the sink and took a deep breath.

When John had called earlier that morning with an update on Maxx's condition, he'd told her that he wanted to bring Lizzy Sanders over for Sunday dinner. At first, she thought it was simply a kind gesture to comfort his best friend's sister during a difficult time. But when he'd called her "Elizabeth," and said her name in a tone that carried a ring of the familiar, Henrietta's womanly instincts told her there was more to the invitation than offering a comfort meal to a guest.

She hadn't seen much of Lizzy Sanders since the young woman had left to attend Spelman College four years ago. Henrietta had been delighted that there would be another black woman in Nedine besides herself who could claim attendance at the prestigious all-girls college, or at any college, for that matter. And she'd been even more delighted when Lizzy graduated a few months ago, making her one of only a handful of black women in town who had earned a four-year college degree.

In many ways, Lizzy Sanders reminded Henrietta of herself. She was smart, resourceful, and had dreams beyond her small town. The two were also the first women in their families to attend college. Through scholarships and grants, Lizzy had been able to fund her education on her own, not having to rely on anyone but herself. Henrietta had done the same, but she'd also gotten some extra help along the way.

Every time she thought about the fine education she'd been blessed to receive, she thanked God for Isaiah. He'd sent her money every month like clockwork to help with her school expenses. He'd worked in the fields so she wouldn't have to work in anyone's kitchen but her own.

Henrietta stood at the edge of the kitchen and listened to the conversation going on just a few feet away. John and Elizabeth were in the family room talking with Isaiah and Allene. She could hear the happiness in her son's voice and the the delicate laugh, which belonged to Lizzy.

Henrietta let out a small, whispered request: "Lord, please let me *really* like this girl, because I have a feeling that my son already does." Then she gathered herself and walked out to greet them.

"Hey, Mama!" John smiled when he saw Henrietta enter the room. He walked over and gave her a kiss on her cheek; then he stepped to the side. "You remember Elizabeth, don't you?"

Elizabeth smiled and held out her hand. "Hi, Mrs. Small. Thank you so much for having me over for dinner."

Henrietta shook Elizabeth's hand and understood why she wasn't Lizzy anymore. The young girl whom she remembered by that name had been replaced by a stunning beauty, who commanded attention. She was still petite and soft-spoken, but she'd blossomed from having a stick figure into a curvy silhouette. The adolescent hairdo she'd once sported had been supplanted by long, wavy hair, which flowed down her back, and her teenage awkwardness had taken a backseat to the quiet confidence she now possessed. Henrietta liked her already.

"We're glad to have you, and we're overjoyed to hear that Maxx is going to be all right," Henrietta said.

"Thank you so much." Elizabeth smiled in response. "We just left the hospital. Maxx is still in a lot of pain, but he's doing so much better. Hopefully, they will be able to release him in a few days."

"Praise the Lord," Allene said, raising her hands in the air.

Henrietta nodded in agreement with her mother-in-law. "Yes, that's certainly good news."

"It really is," John said. "Things could have turned out much differently."

"I heard they arrested that gal that done it," Isaiah chimed in. "It's a real pity, I tell ya. I'm just glad she didn't hurt nobody else."

Henrietta sighed; then she looked over to John and Elizabeth. "Well, make yourselves comfortable. Dinner will be ready shortly."

Elizabeth inhaled deeply. "Mmm, it smells wonderful, Mrs. Small."

"My mama can burn," John said with a big grin.

"Thank you, son. And on that note, I better get back in the kitchen before we start smelling smoke."

Elizabeth stepped forward. "Can I help you with anything, Mrs. Small?"

"Thank you, dear, but I can manage. Like I said, you just make yourself comfortable."

"I feel comfortable in the kitchen."

Henrietta looked at Elizabeth with surprise. "You like to cook?"

"Yes, ma'am. And I'm sure I can learn a thing or two from you. I'd love to help, if you don't mind?"

Henrietta knew that most college-educated girls didn't want anything to do with kitchen work. Despite her best efforts and constant coaxing, her own daughter, Phyllis, despised cooking and barely knew how to turn on a stove.

Thank you, Lord, I really do like this girl, Henrietta thought. She smiled and turned on her heels. "Follow me. The kitchen is this way."

Chapter 43

They were all fanned out around the elegantly appointed dining-room table, eager to enjoy a delicious meal. Isaiah sat at one end, while Henrietta was settled in at the other. John and Elizabeth were seated beside each other, and Allene was happily planted across from them. They bowed their heads as Isaiah blessed the food. Once the amens had been echoed, they were ready to partake in the down-home Southern meal in front of them: smothered pork chops, buttered rice, seasoned string beans, sautéed okra, fresh-from-the-oven biscuits, and scrumptious banana pudding, all prepared with loving care.

John couldn't wait to dig into his mother's food. With the exception of the peanut butter crackers he'd eaten while filling the tank of his rental car at the HandiMart before he'd picked up Elizabeth, he hadn't had a bite since lunchtime yesterday.

He was thankful that this meal and the entire mood were decidedly different from yesterday's when he'd brought Madeline home to meet his parents. What a mistake that had been! As John looked beside him at Elizabeth, he smiled, appreciating the difference twenty-four hours had made. More important, he realized what a difference having the right person in one's life meant.

He'd exhaled with relief when he saw his mother's eyes light up the very second Elizabeth had offered to help her in the kitchen. *Thank you, God!* he'd silently shouted.

John smiled as he passed another serving platter to Elizabeth.

"Thank you," she said, smiling back. She pierced a large pork chop with the silver serving fork and plopped it onto her plate, ready for the next dish to pass her way.

Unlike Madeline, who'd skimmed over the food his mother had prepared, Elizabeth gladly filled her plate until it was covered from one side to the other.

Damn! John thought as he watched her lift her fork to her mouth with vigor. She must have caught him staring, because she smiled and said, "Despite my size, I've always had a pretty hefty appetite."

"That's good." Isaiah grinned. "Ain't nothin' wrong with a woman who likes to eat. Plus, you like to cook, too. That's always a winnin' combination in my book."

"And she cooks well," Henrietta said, nodding. "Elizabeth sautéed the okra, and it turned out absolutely delicious."

"You did?" John looked at Elizabeth with surprise. He put a spoonful of okra in his mouth and wanted to moan when he tasted the flavorful goodness, which was close to his mother's perfection. "Elizabeth, this is really good."

Elizabeth blushed. "I can't take full credit for it. Your mother instructed me and I just followed her directions. A little garlic here, a pinch of salt there, and a dash of pepper. It was easy."

John could see that Elizabeth had won over his mother, which wasn't an easy feat. Although Henrietta was kind and loving, she could be ferocious about protecting her family, especially her children. This was one of the reasons why John had been reluctant to bring women home in the past. But now, everything had changed. In his heart, John knew that Elizabeth was the last woman he'd be introducing to his family. However, little did he know, another woman was going to take it upon herself to do the honors that very afternoon.

The next hour was filled with laughter and good conversation. John was pleased that Elizabeth blended seamlessly with his folks. A small prick of disappointment gnawed at him when he thought about the fact that he couldn't experience this kind of feeling with Elizabeth's family. As he looked over the table full of food, the happy smiles, and the laughter, he hoped that one day he'd be able to break bread like this with the Sanderses. But he was a realist, and he knew that the probability was unlikely, so he decided to be grateful for the moment in front of him.

John pulled himself away from his thoughts and glanced over at his grandmother, who had been largely silent during most of the meal. He knew this wasn't like her. Allene always had something interesting to say. She was a natural storyteller and loved regaling company with tales from what he called "the olden days."

"Grandma, you all right?" he asked.

Allene raised her napkin to the corners of her mouth, brushing away a few crumbs. "I'm fine, baby. Just sittin' back, enjoyin' my family and this lovely young lady you brought home to meet us. It's real good to have you here, Elizabeth."

"Thank you, Mrs. Small." Elizabeth smiled. "I'm so happy to be here. You-all have made me feel right at home, and I appreciate it."

Allene nodded. "You mighty welcome."

"Yes, we're glad to have you, Elizabeth," Henrietta said as Isaiah smiled in agreement.

Allene tilted her head and looked at Elizabeth with a warm expression. "You got a royal name. Did you know that?"

Elizabeth nodded. "Yes, ma'am. My mother said she named me after Queen Elizabeth."

"I don't know about the queen of England," John said, "but you're my Nubian queen."

The moment he made the statement, he could feel every eye at the table firmly aimed on him. He knew his family understood that there was something going on between him and Elizabeth, just by virtue of her being there. But he wasn't sure if they knew how he really felt. When he looked back around the table he could see they were staring at him with concern. Finally, his grandmother spoke up.

"Sound like you two done already gone way beyond courtin'," Allene said, looking from John to Elizabeth.

John smiled. This was the Allene Small he was used to: straight to the point, wise, and all-knowing. He'd been waiting for his grandmother to make some sort of comment, and he was surprised it had taken her so long to speak up.

He took hold of Elizabeth's hand as he answered her. "Yes, ma'am. I know this seems sudden, and, honestly, it caught Elizabeth and me off guard, too."

John couldn't read the expression on his grandmother's face, but the intensity in his parents' eyes left no question. He knew they were wondering if he'd lost his mind.

Henrietta nearly choked on her sweet ice tea. "When did all this happen?"

"Mama, I know this seems sudden, but, trust me, this is real. I've never been so sure of anything in my entire life. I know I've made some recent mistakes, but this isn't one of them. I know what I want, and I know what I'm doing."

"What you want?" Isaiah said, with raised brow.

From one man to another, John knew the meaning behind his father's question. Isaiah wanted him to be crystal clear about what exactly it was that he "wanted" to do with Elizabeth. "Yes, Pop. I know what I want out of my career and out of my life. I'm going to open the bank, and I want Elizabeth to be a part of my future."

Allene sat back and smiled. Isaiah sighed loudly and leaned forward on the edge of his seat, while Henrietta moved her napkin from her lap to the table, signaling that she was finished with the business of eating.

The energy in the room had completely shifted in less than five minutes.

Henrietta looked at her son. "I'm sorry, but what did you just say?"

John cleared his throat. "Elizabeth and I have started seeing each other."

"Since when?" Henrietta said. "How have things changed so drastically in just one day?"

John silently cursed himself for bringing Madeline home, but he was ready to address his colossal mistake. "I know what you're thinking. And if I were you, I'd probably be concerned, too." John held Elizabeth's hand even more tightly. "Madeline was a huge mistake. I wish I'd never brought her here to Nedine, much less to this house to meet you. But that situation has been corrected. A very wise woman once told me that making mistakes is a part of life, but it's what you learn from them that counts." John had just used the words his mother had told him once.

"Yes, son. That's true." Henrietta nodded. "I'm not implying that you're making another mistake. What concerns me is that you're talking like you and Elizabeth are in a relationship. And unless I'm mistaken, you've been seeing each other for . . . um . . . how long?"

John shifted in his seat; and with complete confidence, he said, "One day."

Isaiah rubbed his temples. "Son, I know you got a good head on your shoulders, but do you realize what you just said?"

"I know how it sounds, Pop. But like I told you, this is real. I can't articulate it so that it'll make sense to you, but it makes perfect sense to Elizabeth and me."

Elizabeth nodded her head. "And now that we have this opportunity to be together, we're going to take it . . . with your blessings, we hope."

Everyone around the table was silent for a long beat. John and Elizabeth's news wasn't as easy to digest as the delicious food.

Isaiah finally broke the stillness that had blanketed the room. "I've done a lot of livin', and one thing life's taught me is that nobody knows a person's heart but them." He looked at John, giving him a thoughtful stare. "Son, you a fine young man and I'm proud of you. You doin' great things and you got a big future ahead of you. I trust that when you make a decision about somethin', especially somethin' this serious, that you know what you doin'."

Allene smiled and nodded her head. "Yes, indeed. It don't take but a minute to know certain things. Y'all got my blessin'."

Now all eyes were on Henrietta. John watched his mother as she moved her plate to the side and rested her elbows on the table. He knew she was beside herself. Breaching table etiquette told him that, so he braced himself for what she had to say.

Henrietta took a deep breath and looked from John to Elizabeth. "I'm not the kind of person to tell anyone what to do with his or her life. But, John, you're my son, so I'm going to speak my piece." She paused, and then looked at Elizabeth. "I think you're a fine young woman, Elizabeth. And I know what a good person my son is—not because I gave birth to him, but because it's the plain and simple truth." Then she turned her eyes to John. "It's going to take me a little time to sort all of this out in my mind."

"I understand, Mama," John said. "This is quite a bit of news we're springing on you, but, believe me, in time you'll see that this is real."

Henrietta nodded. She was about to respond when the doorbell rang.

"You expectin' company?" Isaiah asked his wife.

"No, and I wonder who it could be. Excuse me," Henrietta said as she rose from the table.

When she opened the door she was surprised to see the pretty young woman who was standing on her front porch, still dressed in her Sunday best from service today. "Well, good afternoon Mary-Marie. This is certainly a surprise."

Mary-Marie smiled wide. "Good afternoon Mrs. Small. I hope I'm not interrupting your afternoon."

Henrietta immediately became suspicious. She'd first met Mary-Marie several years ago after the young woman joined Rising Star. She'd heard the rumor that despite having a boyfriend, Mary-Marie was seeing John on the side, and she was willing to bet money that was one of her reasons for joining the church, which John often attended when he came home. Mary-Marie had never visited their house before, but now here she stood, and the look in her eyes told Henrietta she wasn't there for a friendly chitchat. "What can I do for you?" she asked.

"I was hoping I could speak to John." Mary-Marie looked behind her. "I see his car in the driveway, so I was just hoping—"

"I'm sorry, but we're having dinner right now."

"Oh, I'd love to join you," she said with a smile.

Henrietta shook her head. "I'm sorry Mary-Marie, but John brought a dinner guest."

Mary-Marie frowned. "Let me guess. Lizzy Sanders?"

"I'll let him know that you came by," Henrietta said in a polite but firm voice. She wasn't about to tell this woman any of her son's business.

"Mrs. Small, I know that it might seem a little strange . . . me just showing up like this. But I want you to know that I care a great deal for your son. I just saved him from making a big mistake with the wrong woman, and I don't want to see him make another one. That's why I'm here."

Henrietta was adamant. "You'll have to take that up with John at another time."

Seeing that she wasn't making any headway, Mary-Marie raised her voice. "Can you please just ask him to come to the door."

Henrietta was about to caution the young woman when she felt a hand on her back. She looked over her shoulder and she saw Allene standing close to her.

"I'll take care of this," Allene said, "you go on back to the dinner table."

"But Mama Allene—"

"Go on, now."

Henrietta was a little hesitant, but she did as her mother-in-law asked. She walked down the hallway and stopped when she got far enough out of sight that she couldn't be seen. She wanted to know what was going on, so she stood and listened. She couldn't make out everything that was said, but what she did know was that whatever

Allene told the young woman, it made an impact because the next thing she heard were the wheels of Mary-Marie's car screeching away.

Henrietta nearly jumped out of her skin when Allene appeared in front of her.

"Why didn't you go back to the dining room like I asked you to?" Allene said with a chuckle.

"I'm sorry Mama Allene, but I wanted to know what was going on. What did you say to her to make her leave?"

Allene smiled. "I talked to her, woman-to-woman, and I let her know that she needed to stay away from around here, and from John too."

"That son of mine. I love him to life, but he's going to give me high blood pressure behind all these women."

"You don't have to worry about that. He's got the one he needs to be with."

Henrietta looked closely at Allene. "I've never asked you about how you know what you know. I just accept that you do. But this is one time I have to inquire, because this concerns my child and his happiness. Are you sure about Elizabeth?"

Allene paused and then smiled. "When I looked at you and Isaiah playin' in my front yard when y'all was kids, I knew you was gonna be his wife. When we stood in front of the shack that you and my son shared, and we watched it burn to the ground, I knew the next house you lived in was gonna be fit for a queen. And as sure as we standin' in that very house, I can tell you that that gal in there is the one for John. And when they bring your granddaughter to town for visits, make sure you keep lemon drops in your candy dish cause she gonna like them."

Henrietta stood in silent awe, and finally, she smiled. She put her arm around Allene. "Let's go back to our dinner, shall we."

Chapter 44

"I think that went well," John said to Elizabeth with a smile. They were riding in his car after just having left his parents' house.

Elizabeth nodded. "Considering the situation, I think it did, too. Most people are gonna think we're crazy, John. Who falls head over heels after just one day?"

"You and me."

Elizabeth leaned over and planted a soft, warm kiss on the side of John's neck. "Yes, you're right."

"Keep that up and you're gonna have problems, young lady."

"What kind of problems?" Elizabeth purred.

"You see what you're doing to me," John said, glancing down at the seam of his pants.

Elizabeth became quiet.

"It's okay, baby. Relax." John smiled, sensing her concern. "I'm just a man who's attracted to a beautiful woman."

"You're leaving in the afternoon, right?"

"Yeah, I wish I could stay longer, but I've got to get back so I can rearrange some plans, especially since I didn't get a chance to meet with one of my potential investors, as I'd planned. But don't worry, I'll make arrangements to fly you up to New York this Friday."

"That's five days away."

"But only four nights." He winked.

"John?"

"Yes . . ."

"Let's go back to your hotel."

"Elizabeth, I was just kidding. I'm not trying to put any pressure on you. I don't expect anything like that. You know that, right?"

"Yes, I know. But that doesn't change the fact that I want to spend the rest of what little time we have together, alone . . . in your hotel room."

John respected Elizabeth as a woman and as a lady. Her gentle way was already changing his sensibility and had tamed his wandering eye. But his lust and desires were another matter altogether. Being with her in the close quarters of a hotel room—with a king-size bed—was sure to test him, and this was one time he wasn't so sure he would pass.

"Elizabeth," he said, "we can catch a movie and then dinner. Or we can go to the park, or—"

"We can make a left at the next stoplight and go to your hotel room."

"I'm trying to respect and protect your honor."

"Is that what you're going to do when I come to New York?"

"I have two bedrooms."

Elizabeth leaned in even closer, until her mouth was at his ear, her lip touching the tip of his lobe. "For what I want, only one bed is required."

John nodded and kept his hands steady as he made a left, heading in the direction of the hotel.

John and Elizabeth were silent as they stood in front of the king-size bed in his hotel room.

He took the lead, directing Elizabeth down to the soft bed as he blanketed her body with his. When they were standing up, he towered over her; but lying together in bed, they fit perfectly together. They kissed each other softly, working their tongues in a slow dance as their hands aptly searched one another's body in new exploration.

The more they kissed and fondled, the harder John's erection became. Elizabeth's excitement was equally growing, evidenced by the wetness flowing between her legs.

"John," Elizabeth said in between heated kisses, "I have to tell you something."

The serious tone in her soft voice stopped him cold. "What's wrong?"

Elizabeth blinked, then looked away. "I've never been with a man."

"What?" John wondered if he'd heard her correctly.

"I'm a virgin, John. This will be my first time."

John slowly raised his body off hers and lay next to her on his side. "Elizabeth, look at me."

Elizabeth turned her eyes back to him; her heart was beating fast. "I've wanted to be with you for so long, John. I want to make love to you, but you need to know that I'm not experienced like the women you're used to, and I'm not—"

John put his finger to her lips and silenced her. "Baby, please don't ever compare yourself to any other woman."

"But you're a man of the world, and I'm a small-town country girl, who's never been past second base with a man."

John ran his hand over his smooth chin. "We don't have to do anything, Elizabeth. I'm serious. We'll have all the time in the world to make love. I don't want you to do anything that you're not ready for." He took a deep breath and said something that surprised even himself. "As a matter of fact, we can wait until after we're married, if you want to."

"Really?"

"Of course. We're moving fast, but this is one thing we can take our time with."

Elizabeth smiled. "You make it easy to love you."

"That's my goal." He held Elizabeth in his arms and kissed her on her forehead.

"I wish you didn't have to leave tomorrow."

"Me too. But I'll make flight reservations for you and we'll see each other when you come to visit this weekend. And once I move here next month, we'll be closer to each other. Raleigh is only a few hours away. And who knows? I can open a bank there just as easily as I can here in Nedine."

"But you've always wanted to open your bank here," Elizabeth said, surprised. "If you move to Raleigh to be with me, all your plans would have to change, and you'd have to start from scratch."

John nodded. "I'd definitely have to restructure everything, and it would take some time. But if it means being with you, I'll do it. I'll be fulfilling two dreams."

They shared another long, slow kiss. In that moment, John knew that all was right with the world.

Chapter 45

Alexandria didn't have to smell the liquor on Peter's breath to know that he'd been drinking heavily. The stagger in his walk, the uncharacteristically wild look in his eyes, and the extra bravado in his body language told her all she needed to know. His usually neat appearance was disheveled. As he made his way toward her, with his pants sagging and the wrinkles in his shirt seeming to move right along with every step he took, Alexandria prayed that her encounter with him wasn't going to end with police squad cars and a trip downtown for anyone.

"This is why you've been avoiding me?" Peter said, looking at PJ as he spoke.

Alexandria was standing next to her mother, frozen in place, unable to move. She couldn't figure out why out of all the times that Peter could have come to see her perform, he'd picked tonight. She looked into his eyes and could see that the alcohol had given him courage—the kind he wouldn't have normally had—and she knew that was a dangerous thing.

"Answer me!" he said, raising his voice.

"Hold up, man," PJ said, standing to his feet with quickness as his father followed his lead. "Lower your voice and watch how you talk to her."

Alexandria looked on with panic in her eyes as she watched the two men standing within just a few feet of each other. They were virtually the same towering height, and both laid claim to athletic, muscular builds. But when it came to lean bulk, PJ had the advantage of the two, along with a more rugged stance, which contradicted his sweet nature. On the flip side, even though Peter looked more docile, Alexandria knew better. He had a harder, nastier edge than PJ ever could have. She knew his temperament, fueled with liquor, was a deadly combination.

Peter glared at PJ. "Who the fuck are you to tell me how to talk to my girlfriend?"

"Oh, Jesus!" Victoria said.

"Girlfriend?" PJ said as he turned toward Alexandria. "Ali? What's going on?"

Alexandria shook her head as all eyes zeroed in on her. All she could think about was the fact that if she had listened to her mother, Peter wouldn't be standing in front of her acting like a jackass and causing a scene at this very moment. But she hadn't taken Victoria's advice, wanting to do things in what she thought was the right way. Now she knew she was going to have to learn a lesson the hard way.

Peter looked at Alexandria. "You've been playing me for months. All that 'It's not you, it's me' bullshit you've been feeding me was a fucking lie. This explains why you've been a ghost for a week."

Alexandria could see people around them beginning to stare. She knew she had to do something to defuse the situation she had caused. "Peter, you're drunk and you're angry. Let's step outside."

"Fuck that," he said. "I've been trying to talk to your ass all week long, and now we're gonna settle this shit right here, right now."

PJ's chest puffed like a peacock's. He narrowed his eyes and shifted his body dangerously close to Peter's. "Say one more word to her out of order and I'm gonna fuck you up, right where you stand."

Alexandria's eyes widened with alarm. She knew PJ had a sexy edge, but she didn't know he could "break bad," as her mother called it. If it weren't for the fact that physical harm was looming in the air, his tough posturing would have turned her on. But this wasn't a fantasy, this was real life unfolding. She could see it was about to turn ugly.

She raised her hand and looked directly at Peter. "I asked you nicely to step outside so we could discuss this in private. But since you want to raise your voice and show your ass in public, fine. Let's do it," Alexandria said in an even tone. "Our relationship is over, Peter, and that's what I've been trying to tell you for the last week. I would've told you before now, but I wanted to do it in person so I could look you in your eyes and be straight up with you, like I'm doing now."

"Straight up, my ass. I asked you if you were seeing someone and you said no." Peter motioned his hand toward PJ without looking at him.

"I wasn't seeing anyone at the time," Alexandria said. "But as you can see, now I am. I'm sorry it had to end this way, but our relationship was over long before tonight, or even last week, and you know it."

"Fuck you!"

In the time it took to blink an eye, PJ's fist was in the air, ready to make contact with Peter's face. But Parker was quick on his feet. He grabbed his son and pulled him back just in time to avert what would have been a crushing blow and a full-on brawl.

"Use your head, son!" Parker yelled. "Calm down."

Two hulky members of the security team rushed up. "Let's break it up," one of the men said. He moved to help Parker restrain PJ, while his partner stood close to Peter, ready to subdue him if he made a sudden move.

"This is fucked up, Alexandria," Peter said, letting his alcohol talk for him. "I wanted us to work things out. I even came out here to support you. I sat up front this whole time and watched and waited so I could surprise you after you performed. But I guess I got the fucking surprise, didn't I?"

"All right, it's time for you to go," one of the security guards said to Peter.

Peter threw his hands up in the air. "I'm gone!" He turned around, stumbling slightly, and walked toward the exit.

Victoria reached over and hugged Alexandria. "Sweetie, are you okay?"

"I should've listened to you, Mom. If I had—"

"He still may have acted crazy," Victoria said. "You can't go back to what you could've done. All you can do is move forward and be thankful that it's over, and that no one got hurt tonight."

Alexandria nodded her head and looked over at PJ, who was talking in hushed tones with his father. Parker patted him on the back and the two moved over to where she and her mother were standing.

"You ladies all right?" Parker asked.

"Yes, we're fine," Victoria answered.

Alexandria looked at PJ, feeling utterly humiliated and embarrassed. "I'm so sorry. I handled the situation with Peter the wrong way, and I almost caused a disaster tonight."

PJ reached for Alexandria's hand and held it. "Let's talk about this later. Right now, I think we should just leave."

Alexandria, PJ, Victoria, and Parker stood outside the Lazy Day, breathing in the hot, sticky air, which seemed to have risen in temperature since they'd all entered the club earlier. The night had started off with awkward surprises and had ended in contentious disaster. Alexandria wished she could have a do-over so badly. She knew PJ was still tense and a little upset, her mother was full of concern and worry, and Parker looked as though he was chewing on a host of emotions.

"I'm going to head home now," Victoria said, breaking the silence as she looked at her daughter and PJ. Even though they were standing side by side, there was a visible distance between them. Victoria took a deep breath before she spoke. "Please don't let what happened in there ruin your evening. If you two truly want to be together, you'll have a lot of challenges that you'll have to hurdle over, and those might make tonight look like a walk in the park. Go and talk this out and then keep moving forward."

Alexandria's eyes widened with disbelief at her mother's words. Just yesterday, she'd cautioned her about rushing in too fast, and tonight she was giving advice about how to overcome relationship challenges. So many things had surprised her in the last week, and again, she knew that life was too unpredictable to know what would happen next, even for those with the gift. She knew that only God could determine what the future would hold.

Victoria smiled and hugged Alexandria good-bye and then embraced PJ. "I hope I'll see you for dinner tomorrow afternoon. The offer still stands."

Alexandria noticed that Parker looked as though he was going to say something, but then he decided to keep his mouth closed in favor of a more appropriate gesture. "I'll walk you to your car so these two can get going."

Victoria shook her head. "Thank you, but I'll be fine."

"Victoria, it's late, and you don't need to be walking around here by yourself."

"I walked here by myself, and that's the way I plan to leave."

"Woman, will you stop being so difficult! I told you yesterday that . . ." Parker stopped himself in midsentence, smiled, and then turned toward Alexandria and PJ. "You two kids enjoy what's left of your evening." He reached for PJ and gave him a solid hug. "Son, I'll call you before I fly out tomorrow." He smiled again and leaned in to hug Alexandria. "It was a pleasure seeing you again, Alexandria. You're a talented, beautiful young woman, and my son is a very lucky man. I hope you know that?" he said, looking at PJ.

PJ didn't respond; instead, he simply nodded.

"All right, shall we?" Parker said to Victoria, extending his hand in front of her, mimicking a chauffeur.

Victoria ignored Parker's hand and started walking in the opposite direction of the club. "See you two tomorrow."

As Alexandria stood beside PJ watching her mother and his father walk off into the distance, she wondered what would happen once they reached her car; but more than that, she wondered about Parker's slip of the tongue and what he and her mother had talked about yesterday. Alexandria now knew that tonight's meeting hadn't been their first encounter since he'd arrived in town, and she had to fight the urge to peer into time and see what the two of them were up to. But for now, she had to let that temptation go to the side because she needed to attend to her own relationship and the thoughts that she could feel swirling around in PJ's head.

Chapter 46

Fifteen minutes later, PJ and Alexandria were sitting on his couch, looking at each other in silence. Alexandria knew she needed to make the situation right, so she eased close to him and took his hand into hers. "I'm very sorry, PJ."

"I know. You said that already."

"You're very distant toward me right now," she said, holding tightly to his hand. "Please let me in and talk to me. Tell me how you're feeling."

"You already know."

"I'm not going to use my gift. I want you to tell me."

"I'm pissed, Ali. You told me that you'd ended it with the guy you were dating."

"I did. But I didn't end it the way I should have, and I truly regret that. If I could change things, I would. Like I said in the club, I wanted to tell him in person that our relationship was over, but we could never seem to meet. One day morphed into two, and before I knew it, there he was, standing in the club and causing a scene." She shook her head. "I ruined my meeting with your dad."

PJ let out a deep breath. "So many thoughts ran through my mind when the dude stepped to you."

Alexandria nodded. "Same here."

PJ turned to her and looked into her eyes. "I can't express every-thing I'm feeling right now because my words won't do it justice, so I want you to look into my eyes and read what's there."

"Are you sure?"

"Yes."

She looked deep into PJ's brown eyes and then closed her own as she ran through all his thoughts and emotions in the matter of a nanosecond. What she saw made her hand tremble and her heart pound. She looked at him again and then sat silent for a few minutes.

"You know how I feel now?" PJ asked.

Alexandria nodded her head. What she'd thought was distance and anger was really overwhelming love, which he'd never known how to place until now. His mother's absence had always left an empty space in his heart, combined with a cautious reserve never to leave himself vulnerable in the hands of a woman. But when Peter approached her tonight and he thought she might be in danger, his only thought was of protecting her. Not just tonight, but from this day forward. He wanted to protect and provide for her: physically, emotionally, mentally, spiritually, financially, and in every other way that a husband would look out for his wife. He wanted a lifetime with her, and he wanted it to start tonight, right there on his couch.

PJ wrapped his arm around Alexandria's waist and pulled her to his lap, as he'd done the other night. "This is forever," he whispered. "I love you, Ali."

Alexandria smiled so widely, her cheeks hurt. In that moment, she gave herself permission to see just a tiny bit of life. She saw her grandparents young and happy, building a life together as a young couple, moving from their small town of Nedine to the growing city of Raleigh, where her grandfather would make his fortune, just as his father had done before him. She saw her mother and father, young and happy, holding her in their arms as they posed for a picture that Nana Elizabeth took after bringing her home from the hospital after she'd been born. And then she saw PJ and her holding their own baby, smiling, and happy, and in love.

"Speak what's in your heart. Say what it is that you want, and watch it

walk into your life," she heard Grandma Allene whisper into her ear. Alexandria looked into PJ's eyes. "I love you, too. I want to be your wife, have your children, and spend a lifetime with you. I'm speaking what I want, and I can't wait to see it all come true."

Alexandria put all the challenges that had been plaguing her mind behind her. She didn't think about the turmoil that her mother and PJ's father would endure eventually. She didn't worry about the difficulties she'd have controlling and maintaining her gift, and she even blocked out the eventual deception and betrayal people close to her would cause. Right now, she decided to live in the moment, claiming the joy and the love that were both in front of her as she kissed PJ softly and ushered in a future, which was starting now.

Epilogue

Allene marveled at the modern wonders in front of her as she watched Victoria and Alexandria move about Victoria's spacious gourmet kitchen, which was half the size of her small home back in Nedine.

"Will you look at that," Allene said in amazement. Her eyes widened as she studied the gleaming stainless steel microwave which sat above a matching double oven, all nestled inside the artistry of custom made cabinets. "Can't believe she heated up them potatoes so quick. That thing sure woulda come in handy back in my day when I was raisin' my family," she chuckled as she shook her head and watched Victoria remove a casserole dish full of piping hot garlic mashed potatoes.

Allene still couldn't believe she was sitting at her great-granddaughter's kitchen table as if she were parked in front of her own. She'd traveled hundreds of miles and more than a half century in time in the blink of an eye, and she knew she had Susan Jessup to thank for it. Susan had bestowed upon her yet another precious gift— the ability to come to this new, modern time so she could continue to help guide her family.

Allene smiled as she smoothed her hand down the front of her long cotton skirt and took a deep breath, inhaling the savory aroma of the delicious food Victoria was cooking. She smiled, feeling good, the way she usually did after hearing a good sermon at church or eating a slice of Henrietta's delicious pound cake. But her smile and good feeling quickly took a back seat to the trouble that was brewing.

"So?" Alexandria said, looking at her mother as she transferred pieces of rosemary herbed chicken from a baking dish to a serving platter.

"What?" Victoria responded.

"C'mon, Mom. What happened between you and PJ's dad the other night?"

Victoria removed her jeweled studded apron and smoothed down the front of her stylish pencil skirt, just as her great-grandmother had done. "There's nothing to tell. Parker walked me to my car and then I drove back home."

"That's it?"

Victoria let out a sigh. "Yes, that's it. What? . . . are you reading my mind or something?"

"No, I'm not. Why do you ask?"

"Because you're questioning me like you don't believe me."

"Mom, it's not that I don't believe you. I just have a feeling that I can't explain. A feeling that something else is going on."

Victoria leaned against the sink, bit her bottom lip and then shook her head. "I don't believe this is happening. Not again."

"What're you talking about?" Alexandria asked.

"Let's have a seat."

Even thought Allene knew they couldn't see her, she sat perfectly still as Victoria and Alexandria sat at the table, each woman flanking her on either side.

"I caught Mr. Brightwood's slip of the tongue."

Victoria nodded.

"Did you plan to meet at the club?"

"No, I was just as surprised to see him as you probably were. But I did talk to him the day before. He called me." She chuckled. "That's the one thing about running a successful business. Your phone number never changes."

"Mom, I'm not going to press you, or try to jump up in your business. I'm just worried about you because I can't shake the feeling that there's going to be trouble ahead."

Allene wished she could intervene, but she knew she couldn't. At least not now. She was all too aware that the time would come when she needed to step in. Deep down, she hoped it wouldn't come to that. But if it was one thing she knew for sure, it was that nothing was certain and life was full of mystery.

"What kind of trouble do you sense?" Victoria asked.

"It involves you and PJ's dad."

"I figured that. What I mean is . . ." Victoria bit her bottom lip as her words trailed off.

"You want to know if you're going to have an affair with him?" Alexandria said.

Victoria rose from her chair. "Forget I asked. Let's finish getting this food ready. Your father will be walking through the door any minute."

Alexandria nodded without saying a word. She tucked away the answer to her mother's question, deciding to enjoy a meal with her family while they were all still happy.

"She's smart," Allene said to herself as she looked at Alexandria. "As I always say, there's no need to fight the devil on an empty stomach."

LOOKING FOR TROUBLE

Trice Hickman

ABOUT THIS GUIDE

The questions that follow are included to enhance your group's reading of this book.

DISCUSSION QUESTIONS

I hope these discussion questions help to enhance your book club experience, or your own personal reading enjoyment. I love meeting with book clubs, so if you'd like me to join your club's discussion, please email me at tricehickman@yahoo.com, and we'll make it happen!

1. Do you believe people can possess the gift of prophesy? If no, why not? If yes, do you know anyone or have you ever heard of anyone who possesses this unique ability?

2. This story fuses the past with the present. What similarities did you see between what was happening to the characters in Nedine in relation to the characters in present day Atlanta?

3. The issue of skin color and class were very much a part of southern culture in the black community during John's and Elizabeth's day. Do you think those stereotypes and views still exist? To what degree can you see that things have changed?

4. If you could have dinner with one character and ask them anything you'd like, who would it be and what unanswered question would you ask them?

5. Who was your favorite character and why? Who was your least favorite character and why?

6. Allene and Alexandria were both afraid of their gift and had to grow into embracing who they were. What events in the story do you think would have turned out differently for them had they used their gifts earlier in life?

7. John and Elizabeth, as well as Alexandria and PJ, experienced instant connections that resonated beyond the physical, and

blossomed into love very quickly. What is your position on "love at first sight" connections?

8. Victoria and Parker never got over each other. What type of relationship do you see them having as a result of their children's involvement?

9. Alexandria is discovering the boundaries of what her gift will allow her to do. What kinds of problems can you see that might arise from the abilities she's already demonstrating?

Don't miss

The Player & the Game

The latest novel in Shelly Ellis's

Gibbons Gold Digger series—available now at

your local bookstore!

Chapter 1

(Unwritten) Rule No. 3 of the Gibbons Family Handbook:
Never give a man your heart—and definitely never give him
your money.

Busy, busy, busy, Stephanie Gibbons thought as she hurried toward her silver BMW that was parallel parked in the reserved space near her office. Her stilettos clicked on the sidewalk as she walked. Her short, pleated skirt swayed around her hips and supple, brown legs with each stride.

She shouldn't have gone to the nail salon before lunch, but her French manicure had been badly in need of a touch-up. Unfortunately, that slight detour had thrown off the entire day's schedule and now she was running ten minutes late for the open house.

The spring day was unseasonably warm, but it was tempered by a light breeze that blew steadily, making the newly grown leaves flutter on the numerous maples lining Main Street in downtown Chesterton, her hometown. The breeze now lifted Stephanie's hair from her shoulders and raised her already dangerously short skirt even higher.

She adjusted the realtor name tag near her suit jacket lapel, casually ran her fingers through her long tresses, and reached into her purse. She pulled out her cell phone and quickly dialed her assistant's number. Thankfully, the young woman picked up on the second ring.

"Carrie, honey, I'm running late . . . Yes, I know . . . Are you already at the open house?" Stephanie asked distractedly as she dug for her keys in her purse's depths. "Are any buyers there yet? . . . OK, OK, don't freak out. . . . Yes, just take over for now. Put out a plate of cookies and set the music on low. I'll be there in fifteen minutes . . . I know . . . I have every confidence in you. See you soon."

She hung up.

With car keys finally retrieved, Stephanie pressed the remote button to open her car doors. The car beeped. The headlights flashed. She jogged to the driver's-side door and opened it. As she started to climb inside the vehicle, she had the distinct feeling of being watched.

Stephanie paused to look up, only to find a man standing twenty feet away from her. He casually leaned against the brick front of one of the many shops on Main Street. He was partially hidden by the shadows of an overhead awning.

He looked like one of many jobless men you would find wandering the streets midday, hanging out in front of stores because they had little else to do and nowhere else to go. Except this bored vagrant was a lot more attractive than the ones she was used to seeing. He also was distinct from the other vagrants in town because she had seen him several times today and earlier this week.

Stephanie had spotted him when she walked into the nail salon and again as she left, absently waving her nails as they dried. He had been sitting in the driver's seat of a tired-looking Ford Explorer in the lot across the street from the salon. Though he hadn't said anything to her or even looked up at her as she walked back to her car, she had the feeling he had been waiting for her.

She had seen him also on Wednesday, strolling along the sidewalk while she had been on her date with her new boyfriend, Isaac. The man had walked past the restaurant's storefront window where she and Isaac had been sitting and enjoying their candlelit dinner. When Stephanie looked up from her menu and glanced out the window, her eyes locked with the stroller's. The mystery man abruptly broke their mutual gaze and kept walking. He disappeared at the end of the block.

The mystery man had a face that was hard to forget—sensual,

hooded dark eyes, a full mouth, and a rock-hard chin. He stood at about six feet with a muscular build. Today, he was wearing a plain white T-shirt and wrinkled jeans. Though his short hair was neatly trimmed, he had thick beard stubble on his chin and dark-skinned cheeks.

"Are you following me?" Stephanie called to him, her open house now forgotten.

He blinked in surprise. "What?" He pointed at his chest. "You mean me?"

"Yes, I mean you!" She placed a hand on her hip. "Are you following me? Why do I keep seeing you around?"

He chuckled softly. "Why would I be following you? Lady, I'm just standing here."

He wasn't just standing there. She sensed it.

"Well, this is a small town. Loitering is illegal in Chesterton. You could get arrested!"

"It's illegal to stand in front of a building?" Laughter was in his voice. He slowly shook his head. "We're still in America, right? Last time I checked, I was well within my rights to stand here, honey. Besides, I'm not panhandling. I'm just enjoying the warm sunshine." His face broke into a charming, dimpled smile that would have made most women's knees weak. "Is that a crime?"

Stephanie narrowed her eyes at him warily.

She didn't like him or his condescending tone. He was attractive, but something emanated from him that made her . . . uncomfortable. It made her heartbeat quicken and her palms sweat. She wasn't used to reacting to men this way. Usually her emotions were firmly in control around them, but they weren't around this guy. She didn't like him one bit.

"If . . . if I catch you standing here when I get back, I'll . . . I'll call the cops," she said weakly.

At that, he raised an eyebrow. "You do that," he challenged, casually licking his lips and shoving his hands into his jean pockets. Defiantly, he slumped against the brick building again.

Stephanie took a deep breath, willing her heart to slow its rapid pace. She climbed into her car and shut the driver's-side door behind her with a slam. She shifted the car into drive and pulled off, watching him in her rearview mirror until she reached the end of the block. He was still standing in front of the building, still leaning under the shadows of the awning, still looking smug as she drove to the end of Main Street and made a right.

Finally, she lost sight of him.

"Shit," Keith Hendricks muttered through clenched teeth as he pushed himself away from the brick building once he saw the taillights of Stephanie Gibbons's BMW disappear.

"Shit," he uttered again as he strode across the street to his SUV, pausing to let a Volkswagen Beetle drive by.

Though he had played it cool in front of her, he had started to sweat the instant Stephanie's eyes had shifted toward him.

He was getting sloppy. He had decided to get out of his car and walk near her office to try to get a better vantage point, to see if her boyfriend, Isaac, was going to meet her here today. But Keith hadn't counted on her noticing him standing there. More importantly, she had noticed *and* recognized him from the other occasions that he thought he had been discreetly tailing her and Isaac. It had been a mistake, a rookie mistake that wasn't worthy of the four years he had spent as a private investigator.

"You messin' up, boy," he said to himself as he opened his car door, climbed inside, and plopped on the leather seat. He shut the door behind him and inserted his key into the ignition.

But he had to admit he was out of practice. This was his first real case in months.

He had been eager to accept this one, to sink his teeth into something meaty. He had been tired of the busy work that had filled his days for the past few months. Stokowski and Hendricks Private Investigators had been going through a bit of a dry spell lately. With the exception of this con artist case, they had been doing nothing but process serving for months, delivering summonses and subpoenas. When Keith left the ATF to start the PI business with retired cop and family friend Mike Stokowski four years ago, process serving wasn't exactly the exciting work he had had in mind. He had hoped things would pick up soon. Now they finally were, but this case had been complicated.

He had finally located Reggie Butler also known as Tony Walker *now* known as Isaac Beardan. The con artist and Casanova had left a trail of heartbreak and several empty bank accounts along the Eastern Seaboard. Each time Isaac moved on to his next con, he changed his name, his look slightly, and his story. It made him a hard guy to find.

One of the most recent victims from which Isaac had stolen thirty thousand dollars worth of jewelry had hired Stokowski and Hendricks PI to track him down. Keith had traced the smooth-talking bastard here, to the small town of Chesterton. Keith still wasn't sure though if Isaac worked alone on his cons. He didn't know what role his girlfriend, Stephanie Gibbons, played in it—if any. Hell, maybe Isaac had selected her as his next victim.

"Don't worry about her," a voice in Keith's head urged as he pulled onto the roadway. "You finished your part of the case. You found him. You've got photos . . . documentation. The police can track him down now and press charges. That's all that matters."

But was that all that mattered? Should he warn the new girlfriend about Isaac?

An image of her suddenly came to mind: her pretty cinnamon-hued face; the limber legs like a seasoned dancer that were on full display underneath her flowing, pleated skirt; and her full red glossy lips. He remembered the stubborn glare she had given him too, trying her best to intimidate him, but failing miserably.

"If you tell her the truth, she'll tell Isaac," a voice in his head warned. "It'll put him on the run again. The authorities will never be able to track him down."

Keith frowned as he started the drive back to his hotel. It was true. Isaac would know he had been found and only move on to the next place and start a new con. No, Keith couldn't tell her the truth about Isaac. He had worked too hard on the case to throw it all away now.

"Maybe she'll figure out he's full of shit by herself," Keith murmured as he gazed out the car's windshield.

But he knew that wasn't likely. Isaac was well practiced at this game. He was a champion player. Keith doubted Stephanie Gibbons would be any different than any of the other saps Isaac had swindled.